C000115614

Outside The Fuck

Mated To The Night: Book 1

Roxie Ray & Lindsey Devin

© 2022

Disclaimer

All rights reserved. No part of this publication may be reproduced, distributed, or transmitted in any form or by any means, including photocopying, recording, or other electronic or mechanical methods, without the prior written permission of the publisher, except in the case of brief quotations embodied in critical reviews and certain other noncommercial uses permitted by copyright law.

This is a work of fiction. Names, places, characters, and events are all fictitious for the reader's pleasure. Any similarities to real people, places, events, living or dead are all coincidental.

This book contains sexually explicit content that is intended for ADULTS ONLY (+18).

Contents

Prologue

Ten years ago…

I furtively began my walk home from the schoolhouse. Nine years old and with a chest full of worries, I wished I could enjoy the expanse of forest on either side of me, the smell of pine, and the sound of dead leaves crunching underfoot. Instead, I had my fingers crossed that I wouldn't encounter any of my classmates on the way home.

Maybe if I stick to the trees, they won't notice me. If I'm quick, I might get home before they see—

A pair of quick footsteps sliced across my thoughts. I should have run, but my small legs—my cursedly *human* legs—refused to move. Instead, I turned my head, though I knew in my bones what was about to happen.

The first thing I saw was his auburn hair, swishing around his head like flames. My fingers clenched around the straps of my old, beat-up bag just as his hands touched my shoulder. He shoved me down as hard as he could, and I went sprawling across the path. Dust kicked up around me and was caked into the arm of my oversized shirt.

I skidded to a stop with a yelp as Troy howled with laughter. Pain flared up in my shoulder, the older wounds

I'd received from Troy and the others opening again. Those wounds would already be healed if I were a werewolf like the others. If I were like them, I could defend myself. As it was, I lifted my head off the ground to face my tormentor.

He pointed at me. "Aw, look at the little girl. Are you going to cry?"

My lower lip wobbled, but I bit down hard to keep it still. Troy's friends had caught up to him and were lined up behind him. They were already laughing—their smiles pulled wide over small, sharp teeth. I shivered, looking at them.

"Why don't you run home, you fake?" Troy taunted.

"I'm not a fake!" I said, scrambling to my feet. "I'm me!"

"Yeah, and *you're* a worthless imposter." He started walking toward me, his hands in his pockets. "After all, you shouldn't even be here. No one will ever claim you as their own."

"S-stop." I backed away, but Troy caught up to me.

He grabbed my arm. "You're just a human in wolf's clothes." He shoved me down again.

His friends continued to laugh at me as I struggled to rise from the ground a second time. Troy, untiring of this game, moved as if to push me down again. So I did what any cornered animal would do when faced with a stronger foe—I lashed out. I flailed my limbs at him. He easily evaded my attacks at first, laughing delightedly, but he wasn't paying attention to the ground. He stumbled on a tree root, and my hand connected with his face as he regained his balance.

The echo of the slap rippled through the trees, and a hush fell over his friends. Red bloomed across his cheek, only to heal just as quickly. His head turned toward me slowly, and my blood chilled as he met my gaze. The lack of anything but cold, dark hatred in his eyes shook me to my core.

I ran from him then, tears streaming behind me. I ran as fast as my legs could carry me and felt the pounding of my bag thumping against my back with each stride.

I burst into my home, calling, "Mom!" at the top of my lungs. There was no need to yell because her keen hearing had detected my frantic steps up to the door. My adoptive mother, Glenda, was already waiting with her arms outstretched. I buried my face in her apron and sobbed.

"Oh, honey," she soothed, rubbing my back. "Was it Troy again?"

I gripped her skirt more tightly.

She sighed. "I'm so sorry, baby. You don't deserve this."

I looked up at her as large tears dripped down my cheeks. "I have to leave, Mom. I gotta run as far away from here as I can. I don't belong here."

She ran her fingers through my hair and bent to press a kiss to the top of my head. "Come here, child." She brought me into her arms easily and began to carry me toward her favorite recliner chair, tufts of white stuffing bursting from the seams and scuff marks on the arms.

I sniffled. "I thought I was too old to be carried like this."

Mom chuckled and eased into the chair. "Well, we'll make an exception today. How does that sound?"

"Good." I nuzzled into her neck, inhaling the scent of lavender and fresh soil, two scents that clung to my mom like perfume.

"I'll tell you a story." She cleared her throat. "Once, there was a young wolf who was cast out by her people. As she wandered through the forests, condemned to be a lone wolf who would surely die without the pack's aid, a man— a human man—happened upon her in her shifted wolf form. Not knowing the truth about her, he took her in. She remained in her shifted form for a while, allowing herself to love the man who cared for her. But one night, she felt the need to shift, so she walked away from the human's cottage to allow her human side to rule for a while. Unbeknownst to her, the man saw her shift.

"He was terrified at first since never before had he seen such a transformation. But when he saw that the human woman had the same kind eyes as his pet, he went to her, loved her, and claimed her as his own. They lived a beautiful life together for several years, but the man fell ill and passed without giving her any children. Still, her heart was happy and full because she had known love and acceptance. Shortly after, she stumbled upon a young wolf in the woods who was lost and confused, just as she had been years ago. She aided the young wolf, who was the daughter of a mighty Alpha. When the Alpha learned of all she had done for his daughter, he rewarded her by bringing her into his pack and giving her a home."

As the story came to a close, I pulled away from her chest, frowning. "But—Mom, the woman in your story got to have a mate and a pack because she was a wolf. I won't ever get to have a mate because I'm not a wolf."

Mom smiled and pushed a strand of my hair behind my ear. "Sweet girl, good things come to those who fight for them." She kissed the side of my head. "Never give up on fate, love."

Chapter 1 - Bryn

I arched my back off the mattress as pleasure bloomed from my core. All around me was darkness, but I had no fear. The bed beneath me cushioned my body as I pressed into it. Further south, a man was buried between my legs, his silky locks brushing across my inner thighs. His tongue lapped into me, each stroke eliciting a moan and a shiver. My heart pounded hard and fast against my ribcage, and my breaths were shallow and quick.

He held my legs in place—his calloused hands deliciously rough across my smooth skin. I couldn't move away from that wicked mouth even if I wanted to. I cursed under my breath and reached down to run my fingers through his soft hair. He growled under my touch, the reverberations of his voice sending a fresh wave of shivering ecstasy through my body.

His tongue dipped deeper, and heat flared through my body. I gripped his hair tighter and looked down, desperate to see him. The man—who devoured my pussy like it was his last meal on earth—was shrouded in darkness. And then he glanced up at me, and I saw his eyes, shining bright green. I bit my lip, transfixed by the only points of light in the pitch black.

His lips found my clit, and I jerked back onto the bed with a cry. I released his hair and ran my hands slowly over my stomach and up my chest. I gripped my breasts, pinching my nipples between my fingers. Below me, the man groaned. Those eyes were watching me, luminous with intensity.

I ran my fingers over my breasts again, more slowly this time. His hands tightened around my waist, and he pressed his face more firmly into me. One of his hands released me to slide smoothly down my leg until it reached my opening. He easily slipped a finger inside me, curling it, pressing it against that oh-so-coveted spot. I groaned, pressure mounting within me, until—

I woke with a gasp. I was no longer in that dark room. I was in my own—the familiar pinewood planks greeted me as I sat up. I sighed, pushing my hair off my damp forehead. Though my heart still beat the rhythm of desire, I was alone in the cool semi-darkness of my bedroom.

Flopping back on my bed, I let out a groan—now of frustration rather than lust. This was far from the first time I'd dreamt of that dark stranger, but I never stuck around long enough to finish or, hell, to even see the face of the man who occupied my nighttime fantasies.

These dreams weren't always sexual; sometimes, I would dream I was deep in the woods, surrounded by darkness and trees. As I walked barefoot over the warm earth, I sensed something stalking toward me, but I never felt afraid. When I turned, I would always find the purest green eyes staring back at me with desire and need. Every time I tried to walk over to him, to reach for him, I would wake up.

And now, for the umpteenth time, I was left with a fading lust and the strong desire to hose myself off. I glanced at the clock on the wall across from my bed and found that I still had an hour before dawn. If there was any silver lining to that frequent fantasy, it was that it normally woke me up ahead of schedule.

I sighed and threw my legs over the side of the bed. It was my week to help make breakfast for the pack, so I needed an early start. I took a cool shower, scrubbing away the moisture between my legs, and brushed my teeth. Then I ran a comb through my long, curly chestnut-brown hair and pulled it back into a ponytail. My room was spartan, containing only my bed, dresser, and desk—the only spot of color came from the dried wildflowers I'd set up in glass jars on the dresser. My room, Mom's garden, and the magical clearing full of wildflowers in the forest near our cabin were the only places I felt safe or at peace. The rest of the village was more like a prison.

I went to my dresser and found a pair of loose, black cotton pants and a long-sleeved teal shirt with a hole in the seam at the armpit. I'd need to repair that when I had the chance, but it wasn't noticeable, so for now, it was fine.

The final pieces of my outfit (such as it was) were a pair of mismatched socks, black boots, a slouchy hat, and thick gloves. I grabbed a jacket from the hook on the back of my door. It was nearing the beginning of summer in the Kaniksu National Forest, but the morning temperature was often around forty degrees Fahrenheit. Because I was human, I wasn't as tolerant of the cold as the wolves in the pack.

Dressed, I headed down the short staircase to the kitchen, where Mom was making herself a cup of tea— mint, from the smell of it. Mom was one of the oldest members of the Kings' pack, but due to the brightness of her eyes and the effortless grace of her movements, she didn't look it. Her long, slate-gray hair with white at the temples, the laugh lines around her mouth and faint crow's feet at the corners of her eyes, and the endlessly deep chocolate brown of her eyes—these were the only indications of her age.

"Dreaming again?" she asked.

I stopped in my tracks, my face warming. *Oh no. She didn't hear me, did she?*

"What's with that face?" She chuckled. "I ask because you look like you woke up in the middle of something intense."

"O-oh. Yeah. I had one of those dreams again."

"Ah, the man with the haunting eyes?"

I nodded. I elected to leave the sexual part out of my description, though I couldn't help the slight warmth that returned to my cheeks. Thankfully, Mom didn't seem to notice.

She moved with the grace of a dancer as she grabbed the honey jar from the counter. As we lived on the outskirts of the pack in our small house, honey was one of the few indulgences we could afford. The tea, however, was something we had in abundance thanks to our little herb garden in the kitchen window. The small garden included lemon verbena, thyme, rosemary, and basil.

As Mom let the honey drip into her mug, she said, "Have you ever tried speaking to the man in your dreams?"

I shook my head. "I don't have much of a voice in them." *If you exclude the moaning*, I added silently.

"Mm." She brought the mug to her lips, downing what must've been half of her tea in just a few swallows. "I think your dreams are a sign of things to come."

I resisted the urge to sigh. How often had my mom tried to convince me that I had a psychic connection to the green-eyed man? Too many to count. "Like a premonition?"

She inclined her head. "Of sorts."

"Mom…you already know how I feel about that mystical stuff. I understand respecting the land and giving back to the community, but dreams?" I shook my head. I would never say this out loud because it would hurt her feelings, but if magic was real—if I had any connection to it—why did it allow me to feel so empty inside? Why didn't I have any friends of my own and not just my mom in my corner?

Mom shrugged. "You should open your heart to this *mystical stuff* more often, love." She took another long drink of tea and set the mostly empty cup in the sink. "Are you headed to the dining hall to make breakfast?"

"Yeah. Are you ready to go?"

"Just let me put on my shoes."

Despite the strange start to the day, I smiled as Mom pulled on her boots. She always made things easier. We stepped outside to the cool, blue morning. The surrounding trees and cabins looked like shadowy sentinels against the dark sapphire sky. As a hot-blooded shifter, Mom wore cotton pants, a wrapped tunic, and nothing else. Cold temperatures didn't bother shifters, which only served to make me stand out even more in my multiple layers. But today, I didn't dwell on our differences too much as a thought occurred to me.

"By the way, Mom, how are the new peppers doing?"

"Really well, actually. I want you to look at them when you have the chance."

I grinned. Though Mom knew just about all there was to know about gardening, she often asked me for a second opinion because of my "natural affinity for the soil," as she liked to call it. The only parts of my life that weren't exceedingly difficult were those I shared with her. Especially gardening.

The best part about the community garden was feeling fresh, cool dirt on my hands and talking to my mom. Peppers were a new addition to the garden, and I felt exceedingly pleased that they were thriving. Gardening came so easily to me—it was the only thing I was any good at.

The dining hall was constructed entirely from wide pinewood planks. The floors, walls, ceiling, tables, and benches were all pine. The whole building already smelled savory and sweet. Mom and I stamped our feet on the rug by the door. With the morning dew off our boots, we walked toward the back of the dining hall to the kitchen.

We exchanged brief pleasantries with those already in the kitchen—familiar faces from other houses who shared the kitchen duty with us that morning. I glanced at Mom. The others might have stayed quiet around me because of my low status, but Mom's presence encouraged the others to be nice to me. Her status as one of the oldest members of the pack, and as someone who helped those who were sick without expecting anything in return, inspired respect throughout the pack and even adoration in some. Of course, that deference didn't extend to me.

Breakfast—oatmeal, bacon, scrambled eggs, and wild berry jam—had already been cooked, so Mom and I took our spots among the others where plates and bowls were stacked. We just needed to plate the breakfast. I enjoyed cooking and even liked washing dishes— something about being surrounded by food or burying my hands in warm, soapy water relaxed me—but I didn't so much enjoy being visible like this. Serving breakfast was fine but feeling the constant need to duck my head and avoid eye contact with the pack was stressful.

As everyone began working, murmured conversation started up around us. Though we didn't join in, the chatter added some intrigue to what would otherwise be a monotonous task. I caught murmurings of, "Such a shame about Gregor—" "—will other packs try to move in on us while he's sick?" "How many of us would even miss that old—" and "—at least when he finally kicks the bucket, the funeral will get me out of laundry duty." The latter two comments were met with harsh shushing. No one wanted to speak out of turn too loudly, or they would face the wrath of Troy or one of his goons.

Despite the mixed responses to the news of the Alpha's declining health, the general mood in the mess hall was somber and quiet. I zoned out as the conversation continued, losing myself in the mindless motions of filling bowls with oatmeal. Occasionally, a pup I knew would skip up to me and smile as I gave them food. It didn't matter how poorly the other wolves treated me or how exhausted I was, there was always a smile where pups were concerned.

But when there weren't children around to brighten my day a little, I allowed myself to zone out. As the dining hall faded to the background, I started thinking about the pack.

The Kings were a large, wealthy pack whose territory ran from the borders of the Kaniksu and Kootenai National Forests in Montana as low as Sandpoint and moved west across the Idaho panhandle and Kootenai River. The territory ended right along the border with Washington. The Kings had over five hundred homes and families and powered their compound with solar-powered electricity. They were one of the lucky packs with plumbing and clean running water at their disposal.

Every family rotated through shared tasks for the pack—cleaning, cooking, preparing for ceremonies, and maintenance. Some members had a specialty they contributed to regularly, like healing, teaching, or hunting. Due to this dynamic, wolves operated as a family—everyone looked out for each other. Though the women in the pack weren't allowed to take up positions that men held and were raised to prioritize their beauty so they could settle down with a mate. I hated the way the pack treated women like objects and prizes to be won and lusted after.

For me, as both a woman and a human in the pack, it was tough. It made me wonder how different my life would be if I were a human man. Would they respect me for my strength? My deeper voice? Would they let me hold a weapon or send me on dangerous missions? Maybe they would have killed me earlier. I don't know. That line of thinking never went down a good path.

As things were, at least I had Mom on my side. She loved me and did everything she could to make me feel comfortable, but there was only so much she could do. After serving the oatmeal, I picked up the empty stockpot and carried it into the kitchen.

There were bits of oatmeal stuck to the sides and the bottom, so it would need a good soak in hot water if the leftovers were going to be scrubbed off. As I approached the sink, I almost collided with a woman carrying a bundle of fabric napkins, nearly knocking me off balance. The heavy, stainless steel pot teetered in my arms as I swayed on my feet. Shifters rarely minded their strength around me.

"Watch it," she hissed. Given her glare, one might assume that she was the one who had almost fallen over from the impact, not I.

"Oh. I'm sorry," I murmured.

"Yeah. Right." She tossed her hair over her shoulder and continued.

I sighed and plunged the pot into the sink. I filled it with dish soap and water as hot as I could stand. As the pot filled with suds, I ran the back of my hand over my forehead. Most of the pack was anti-human. Though the Kings relied on some human goods, like dish soap, in their daily lives, shifters tended to be very private and avoided humans as much as they could due to conflicts the two species had endured hundreds of years ago.

That distaste for humans was largely due to the Redwolfs, the Alpha family of the pack. Troy, for one, did everything he could to make me feel unwelcome. Even when we were children, he had it out for me. I'd thought long and hard about what I had done to make him hate me so much; ultimately, I knew there was nothing I could have changed to make him leave me alone. Because I was human, because I was weak, because I wouldn't have a voice in the pack—I was an easy target. Wolves had a strong prey drive, and even I had to admit that everything about me screamed, "prey."

Troy's father, Gregor Redwolf, was marginally better. Though the Alpha hated humans, his misogyny made it difficult for him to take women seriously—thus, he largely ignored me. While Gregor was Alpha, I didn't have to look over my shoulder constantly, and I could get away with avoiding Troy like the scourge he was. If Troy became the Alpha, I wouldn't have that luxury.

I had been thinking about the Alpha more and more frequently these days because he had fallen ill. It wasn't the first time Gregor had been sick, but he was much older now, and defending the pack had undoubtedly put a lot of stress on his body. In addition to my dreams of the dark stranger, I had nightmares about Troy taking over the Kings' pack. The nightmares always ended with my death.

I shook my head and picked up a sponge, plunging it deep into the hot, sudsy water. I shouldn't think about that possibility. The Alpha was old, sure, but he was resilient. He'd pull through like he always did, and I wouldn't have to worry about Troy's harassment. *He'll continue to ignore me, and things will be the same. I won't have to do anything extra to protect myself from Troy…*

When I'd finished scrubbing the pot to a mirror-like shine, I returned to the table by my mom, who greeted me with a smile. The tables were old wood, well waxed and smooth beneath my touch. There were more wolves standing in line for their breakfast. The Kings accepted their oatmeal from me without making eye contact, which

was nothing like the way they greeted the other women—
with smiles and brief conversation. But after years of the
same treatment, it didn't bother me nearly as much as it
used to.

My thoughts drifted to last night's dream, back to
the green-eyed stranger who'd rocked my world. My
cheeks warmed when I thought about how his hands had
felt on my skin. If he were real, would he treat me the same
even though I was human? Would he open his arms to me?
The fantasy of being somewhere safe, of being accepted,
put a small smile on my face as I worked.

Suddenly, a woman burst in from outside, the same
one who had been carrying the fabric napkins. She still
smelled of cigarette smoke. Her face had gone pale, and her
mouth was a trembling line. I didn't need the elevated
senses of a wolf to see how hard she was shaking or to
clock the way her eyes darted from face to face until they
finally settled on my mom.

"What's wrong?" Mom asked as the woman
approached.

"It's the Alpha," she whispered.

I froze, staring openly at the woman.

Mom's face grew still. She placed her hands on the woman's shoulders and squeezed until the woman's wavering gaze focused. "What about him?"

"He…he passed away in his sleep last night," she said. "He's dead."

He's dead…he's dead… The words echoed in my mind. In my head, I pictured myself surrounded by wolves who jeered and spat at me the way they'd done when I was younger. I pictured myself cast out of the pack. My mom left to stand on the sidelines and watch while Troy exiled me to the wilds. My stomach roiled, and the world seemed to spin. Those two words spelled my doom.

Chapter 2 - Bryn

I gripped the table's edge and steeled myself against the onslaught of emotion. Nobody was paying attention to me anyway. As word spread, concerned murmuring filled the dining hall. It was too much too soon. Without a word to my mother, I exited out the same door the woman had come through for some cool, fresh air.

By this time, the sun had begun to crest over the horizon, filling the sky with gold and casting the clouds in amethyst and sapphire. Below the stunning sunrise, emerald leaves and dark blue tree trunks extended for miles in front of me. I normally would have taken a moment to enjoy the magnificent sight, but I couldn't focus on that now. Outside of the shade provided by the mess hall, the pack was abuzz with chatter and movement.

Wolves zipped from building to building with the Alpha's name on their lips. I pressed my back to the building, slid down to a crouch, and held my head in my hands. I took a few deep breaths, inhaling cool air and exhaling steam as I collected myself.

Gregor's dead, but this doesn't have to be the end, I counseled myself. *Troy isn't Alpha yet.* But it was cold comfort—he would be Alpha soon. After an Alpha died, the pack would enter a five-day mourning period. Every day of this period included a celebration, and a challenge ceremony would take place on the last night.

The right to be Alpha was passed down genetically from father to son, but during the challenge ceremony, any wolf who wanted to try for the position would enter a fight to the death with the Alpha's son. If the Alpha had no sons, the beta would host the challenge and claim the mantle if he was undefeated or unchallenged. Nowadays, challenges were usually hosted as a formality. They were generally treated as another opportunity for everyone to take a break from work and remember the deceased Alpha. Or at least, that was what Mom said—this would be my first time experiencing such a celebration.

I counted the days before the challenge ceremony, and my blood went cold. My twentieth birthday was the day after the ceremony.

The twentieth birthday for a shifter was a pretty big deal. Twenty was considered the age when wolves were old enough to mate and form a permanent bond with another shifter, and from what I had learned and read about in school, female shifters bonded with the male shifter who took her virginity. So, female shifters were restricted to only ever having one mate.

I've spent my whole life looking forward to my twentieth birthday, only for it to be ruined by Troy becoming Alpha. What's worse is that I know he'll do everything in his power to make me even more miserable. As this thought came to me, a void began to open in my chest.

I had always hoped that by my twentieth birthday, I would have found acceptance, friends, or happiness— anything to cut down on the pain of being the black sheep of the Kings' pack. I'd thought that my cynical side would have crushed that hope, but it had remained until now. So, there was no way I could suppress the darkness that filled my chest as I considered my upcoming birthday. After all, what shifter would want to be with a weak human?

To be honest, I had no intention of finding a mate, but I'd remained a virgin just in case my theory proved wrong. Holding on to my virginity hadn't been difficult; Troy had essentially mandated that everyone our age treat me like shit. So, I not only had no potential mates but also had no female friends. The girls my age were too focused on pleasing Troy just in case he, or one of his high-ranking friends, would choose them as a mate. I had seen girls swarm around Troy like bees to honey. Thinking about it left me shivering with disgust. Or with cold. It was possible the chill had started to seep through my outer layers.

I straightened from my crouch. Though I was far from okay, the fresh air had calmed me enough that I felt I could continue serving breakfast. I wiped my sweaty palms over my pants and returned to the dining hall. On my way to the kitchen, my shoulder bumped into another female shifter.

I took a healthy step back and looked up to find Trish's ice-blue eyes glaring down at me. I took another step back and glanced at the two women standing at Trish's side—Tara, a brunette, and Tanya, whose dirty blonde hair was cut short around her chin. The three were always together, and, like Troy, they thrived on my misery. They were often present for Troy's bullying, egging him on to do worse, to hurt me more.

Their flashy clothes clung to their lithe, muscular frames and showed off their assets to any interested male. And there were plenty of men who were interested. They wore the latest in human fashion, unlike me and Mom, whose wardrobe consisted mostly of hand-me-downs.

"Ew," Trish dusted off her shoulder as if coming into contact with me had left a residue. "A rat."

"Someone ought to call an exterminator before it becomes an infestation," Tanya added.

Tara covered her glossy, pink lips with her hand and snickered.

I'm surprised you notice anything beyond that massive ego, Trish. I kept the thought to myself and schooled my expression into a neutral mask. After years of this treatment, it took much more than this to crack through my shield. Though inside, as always, the insults pelted me raw. These were the Terrible T's, as I thought of them, and they had bullied me almost as horribly as Troy.

"It's a shame that Alpha Gregor is dead," Tanya said, crossing her arms over her chest. "Troy will be alone without his family to help him through this. But I'm sure you'll be there for Troy, right, Trish?"

Trish's laugh was the sound of an ice cube crunching between teeth. "Of course. I'll visit him as soon as he's feeling up to it."

The girls giggled, and I wished the ceiling could cave down on me or that I would spontaneously combust— anything to avoid having to entertain the possibility of Trish and Troy ruling the pack together. Dying would be preferable to enduring their torment twenty-four seven.

Trish and her friends knew that, which was why they were talking about it in front of me.

"Oh, you're still here?" Tara asked as if she'd completely forgotten about my presence. "Can't you take a hint?"

Trish's hand, lightning quick, suddenly grabbed my shoulder. I winced under her viselike grip, which caused the other girls to laugh.

"Such a fragile thing, aren't you?" Trish said, her long, flaxen hair spilling in perfect waves over her shoulders as she bent toward me. "Better scurry along now, little rat, before one of us *accidentally* crushes you."

The moment Trish released my shoulder, I accepted the dismissal and hurried the rest of the way to Mom. My shoulder throbbed. I knew I'd have an awful bruise tomorrow, but considering how badly that could have gone, it was a small price to pay for colliding with the Terrible T's. I'd learned that it was always better to stay silent and unseen when they were around. News of the Alpha's passing must have made me careless.

I took my spot beside Mom, who leaned in close to speak to me. "Are you okay?"

I nodded. "I'm fine. Let's just get this morning over with."

"Agreed. Things are about to get very busy around the pack."

I tried to focus on passing out bowls of oatmeal. I kept my eye on the door, dreading the moment when Troy or one of his friends would walk in, but to my surprise (and relief), he never showed. In fact, as I looked around the dining hall, I noticed that half the normal number of wolves were gathered around the tables. Word of Alpha Gregor's passing must've made the rounds. News like that wouldn't take long to spread. Many wolves would have rushed home to prepare for the days of mourning.

In addition to the celebrations, the older wolves would share stories of the bravery and valor of the old Alpha. Young male wolves would fight each other to impress Troy in hopes of being promoted to be his beta or at least part of his inner circle. The of-age females, including some older unmated ones, would primp and preen and flaunt their bodies in front of Troy. For these hopefuls, there was much to do around their homes.

Breakfast was over sooner than usual because of Gregor's sudden passing. After the dishes were clean, Mom and I headed home.

"Mom, what will we do for the days of mourning?" I asked.

"We'll harvest all the fruits and vegetables we'll need for the feasts." She set her gaze on me, a knowing gentleness in her eyes. "You don't have to worry about Troy. I doubt you'll come in contact with him at all because of his father's passing. He'll be far too busy with preparations."

I gave her a small smile. It was a relief to hear that I wouldn't have to worry about Troy. Most of the pack worshipped the ground the Redwolfs walked on, so the thought of having to watch Troy's already overinflated ego grow even larger left a sour taste in my mouth.

Keeping my focus on the garden would also allow me to think of an action plan for my escape. I had five days, and I needed to use that time wisely.

Mom and I went immediately to the community garden, which was visible from our house. Mom wanted me to look at the peppers and do some prep work for the time of mourning. I walked through the wooden gate that Mom had built before I was even a part of her life, and the welcome smell of fresh vegetables greeted me. Mom's green thumb was supernatural.

I had heard talk around the pack that Mom had always possessed a spiritual, magical connection that allowed her to know the land like no one else. When I was younger, I had imagined that she was a fairy or a nymph—like the creatures in the fairy tales I loved to read. I believed that Mom's fey blood allowed her to grow plants even in the winter. As I grew, I understood that whatever connection she had to the earth, it wasn't fey.

No, Mom was a shifter through and through. Still, the respect and dedication she showed to the land and the care with which she looked after not just the plants in the community garden but also the vegetation and fauna that surrounded the pack grounds—these were the things that allowed Mom to form her bond with the land.

Unfortunately, life had done more than enough to convince me that if magic was real, it didn't want anything to do with me—and honestly, the possibility of magic was beside the point. The benefits that Mom's green thumb provided for the Kings' pack were evident. I liked to think that I had some connection to the land, but it wasn't as strong as my mom's. I could only hope that I would one day accumulate a fraction of her knowledge.

As we stepped over the tilled fields, I switched out my winter gloves for the old, worn gardening ones. They were designed for hands larger than mine, but they fastened at the wrists for easy adjustability.

The garden expanded for acres. Corn, squash, and even tomatoes and cucumbers were among the plants that spread across the ground. Though we were well past the last frost of the season, it still got cold at night in the mountains, so the vegetables that required the warmest temperatures grew in a greenhouse of PVC pipes and green-tinted plastic. I had designed and constructed the greenhouse myself; it was one of the few things I was really proud of.

The pack had no clue that the small building had been my idea. I worried that the Terrible T's or Troy would quickly see to its destruction if they knew, despite how useful it was to the pack. Mom was reluctant to take credit for it, but at my insistence, she did. That was why, as safe as I felt in the garden, it was yet another reminder that I didn't fit in with the Kings' pack and needed to escape.

Mom and I entered the greenhouse, which was already warm enough that I didn't need the jacket while inside. After I took it off, I looked at the tomatoes and touched one of the ripe fruits with my fingertips.

I can't stay here anymore.

"What was that, love?"

I flinched. I hadn't meant to say that out loud. "Nothing, Mom."

I plucked the round, juicy tomato from the vine and took a bite. The savory, sweet taste spread across my tongue. The greenhouse was about twenty feet long and seven feet wide. With the abundance of greenery growing on either side, there was just enough room for Mom and I to stand shoulder to shoulder across the path.

"Look at them." She pointed to the peppers. There was a variety growing from the vine—shishito, bell, and jalapeno. "You've done a great job already. And they're thriving."

I finished off the tomato and touched one of the green bell peppers. I gently prodded the skin and found it to be nice and firm. I grinned. Mom had tried for months to convince the pack to purchase a greater variety of seeds when they bought supplies from the humans. When they finally agreed to do so, the peppers were the first plant that Mom let me grow totally on my own. Now that the peppers were here, I had no doubt they'd add a ton of flavor to the meals that we prepared for the pack.

Not that this pack deserves the hard work that we put into this garden. The thought put a cynical frown on my face.

"I'm proud of you, baby," Mom said, tugging at the corner of my mouth. She smudged a bit of dirt across my cheek. "One day, I'm sure you'll be even closer to the land than I am."

"Mom, stop," I whined, though my mom's ministrations coaxed the grin back onto my face. I hated the people who bullied me and who wronged me, but I could be proud of what I'd accomplished here. I'd worked hard to grow something new, and things had paid off.

Mom smiled and put her arm around my shoulder. "Let's get started, shall we? If we have enough peppers, I'll make some salsa and tortilla chips. Sound good?"

I perked up even further. That was a special treat, a favored snack that I'd enjoyed when I was younger. With the peppers, I could only imagine how delicious it'd be.

I grabbed one of the wicker baskets from the back of the greenhouse and began to harvest the peppers. As I worked, I put aside my excitement about the salsa to think about what I would do if I managed to get clear of the Kings' territory. Where would I go? I didn't think another werewolf pack would accept a human, and even if they did, there was no guarantee that another pack would treat me any better than the Kings. Not to mention, I could run across a member of the Wargs pack. The Wargs were an awful, borderline-feral wolf pack that occasionally plagued the Kings while out on patrol.

When the basket was full, I wiped away the sweat that had collected under my chin with my forearm. I placed the heavy basket to the side and retrieved an empty one from the back.

If the wolves won't accept me, maybe I could try living with the humans? It was the first time I'd tried to think about how I would make it among other humans. I remembered the story that Mom had told me about the lone wolf shifter who fell in love with a human man and wondered if something similar could happen to me. Not that I'd fall in love, of course—I didn't believe there was anyone (outside of my dreams) who could love someone like me. But maybe a nice human would take me under their wing and teach me how to fit in.

The truth was, the pack was all I'd ever known. I had no idea what it would be like to live among humans. The little I'd heard about their ways made me doubtful that human life was for me. Then again, maybe I would only struggle if I were a shifter. Humans might protect their own, just as wolves did. If that were true, I think I could make it work.

I entertained the idea for the duration of the pepper harvesting. As I set the basket to the side, Mom called out to me. I pulled my jacket on again as I went back out into the cold. She had already assembled a large pile of pumpkins, butternut squash, and other gourds.

"What's up, Mom?" I asked.

"Do you mind checking to make sure that the root cellar is unlocked?"

"Yeah, I'll be back soon." I pulled off my gloves and stuffed my hands in my pockets as I walked along the outskirts of the pack. There wasn't a lot of activity going on. Some who were on cleaning or landscaping duty zipped here and there, but the majority of the pack was holed up in their houses. With so few out and about, the community was uncharacteristically quiet.

If the Terrible T's or Troy were looking for me, they would find me easily. I felt exposed as I reached the shed that sat on top of the root cellar. Once I was done here, I'd need to hurry back to the safety of the garden. The shed was made of pine, and it held a few landscaping supplies. The trapdoor that led to the root cellar had a heavy-duty brass and iron lock on it, but it was kept unlocked during the day. Today, fortunately, was no exception.

I turned back to the door, but before I stepped through it, I heard voices on the other side. A pair of women, from the sound of it.

"—mate told me that the humans just get worse and worse," one of them was saying. "Did you hear about them?"

My eyes widened at the word *human*. I stepped closer to the door and pressed my ear against it.

"No, what happened?"

"Well, apparently, when he went into a nearby city, he learned there was a major sex-trafficking ring busted."

The other woman gasped. "No!"

"Yes! They've been trading young girls and boys of their own kind to the highest bidder, and so many of the poor things are runaways or sold by their families."

The second woman clicked her tongue. "That just goes to show that humans can't be trusted. They're so greedy and wasteful, even their own kind suffers."

"Makes you wonder if that sort of thing is innate. It's no wonder that girl doesn't belong. The human species just isn't as noble or as prideful as us wolves."

"What a shame."

I winced. It was obvious they were talking about me. I waited until the two women walked away before I ventured back out. I fought tears as I jogged back to the garden. *If humans treat their own young that badly, maybe there isn't a place for me among them either,* I thought, biting my lip hard. *Maybe I'm doomed no matter where I go.*

Chapter 3 - Night

I stood in my cabin in front of the fireplace. To my left, a window showed a night sky as dark as my swirling emotions. My home had obviously seen better days—the floors creaked underfoot, the walls were cracked, and the entire place would have thrived with a good waxing. But in the Wargs pack, *my* pack, there was hardly any time for those luxuries.

We were seventy-five cabins strong, making us the smallest of all the other packs in the area. The largest, of course, was the Kings' pack, with over seven times our number of homes and the largest amount of resources.

Though there were other small packs in the area, we had to make do with much less than the others. We used candles and lanterns and old, gasoline-powered generators to power the compound. Nestled in northern Montana, our soil was as rich as could be found anywhere, and we had dozens of hot springs hidden in our woods. We had very few luxuries, but before I had taken over, we had even less.

I placed my hand on the mantle and brushed my fingers over the old, rough wood. My hand almost spanned its width. All wolves were strong, but as an Alpha, I could rip the mantle off the wall with the same amount of effort it took to pluck a weed. I'd never trash my own place. But with my mood lately, I half wanted to.

The kindling inside the fireplace was little more than a smoking pile despite the cool Montana winds blowing against the wood. I didn't care about the cold. I didn't care that my cabin was little more than a large pile of kindling for a much bigger fire. I liked the old, rustic look of my place—it matched me in almost every way.

I closed my eyes and pulled my shoulders back, feeling my muscles crack and ripple. Inside, my wolf paced back and forth, his hackles raised. I had let him out only a few hours earlier to go on a run, but I might have to do it again. My wolf and I were usually in sync, but lately, we had been at odds.

As Alpha of the Wargs, a position I'd held since I was sixteen years old, I carried enough responsibility on my shoulders to make a lesser wolf crumble. That was why I kept myself and my wolf on such a tight leash. That was why I expected nothing less than perfection from both of us.

So it was always such a pain in the ass when my wolf grew restless. It made me feel on edge—less in control of myself. When I got like this, anything could set me off, and it became difficult for me to keep my goals in focus. A run through the cold night air might just get my wolf to settle the fuck down.

I cracked my knuckles and my neck just to move around. Part of the reason my wolf was so out of sorts was because I'd had the dream again—the dream about *her*, the girl with those blue-gray eyes. I saw them even now when I closed my own, like a pair of will-o'-the-wisps tempting me to come closer. Whether those wisps lured me toward my doom or my fortune, I had no idea, but it didn't matter either way.

My wolf growled low, and my teeth began to pull back from my incisors. As wonderful as those dreams felt when I was in them, when I was awake, I resented them for how much they fucked with my head. Including the night before, there'd been at least a dozen times I'd had similar dreams, but I had no fucking clue what caused them or what they meant.

More than once, I'd tried to talk to my mom about how the dreams plagued me. Violet Shepherd was one of the few wolves in the Wargs who truly understood the mystical aspects of being a wolf shifter. She was a voracious reader of the old ways—the ways of magic and myth made real. She worked closely with our Elders, who were each pillars of wisdom in their own right. She often performed spiritual rites for the wolves who requested her assistance. But when I told her about my dreams, I couldn't be sure she wasn't fucking with me.

"Rough night?" she had asked me that morning when she saw my black hair messy with sleep and the crease from my pillow imprinted on my face, just below my cheekbone. "Did you dream of the girl with the ghostly eyes?"

I'd rubbed my face with my hand. It wasn't uncommon for Mom to let herself into my cabin while I slept. It used to annoy me, but I had given up on telling her to keep away long ago. Besides, her visits didn't interfere with my duties, so there was no reason for me to fuss about it.

"It's too early for this, Mom," I'd said with a sigh.

She had grinned, and her teeth shone in the morning light. Her hair was pushed back from her face; her small hands wrapped around one of my larger mugs. "I disagree. Now is the best time to talk about your dream while it's still fresh in your mind."

Reluctantly, I had admitted that yes, I'd dreamed of the girl again, and no, I was no closer to figuring out who the hell she was. As always, it was too dark in the dream for me to make out any details of her face. That last bit was particularly frustrating for me. I had perfect vision during the night as well as the day; why would these dreams take that ability away from me? Just to keep the identity of the girl a secret? Why?

"Ah, well, these things tend to be part of figuring out your divine destiny," she'd said. "As you get closer to realizing your destiny, I'm sure your dreams will give you a little more to go on than just a beautiful girl whose face you can't see."

I'd glared into eyes that were as green as mine—but at the moment, hers were more playful. "Mom, be serious. You know I don't believe in that destiny shit."

She'd brushed past me, unbothered by my bad mood. "You'll understand better eventually I'm sure, my dear. You're on the cusp of something wonderful."

I wasn't so sure. Destiny had dealt me a shit hand a long time ago. There was no way it was making its way back around to grant me something good now.

"I don't know, Mom. Maybe the dreams are telling me I need to put my plans into action."

She'd paused, her shoulders stiff. "Maybe you're right," she'd said, the smile gone from her tone. "And if that's the case…well, know that you're not destined to be the same disaster your father was."

I didn't like to argue with her, but that was another subject that we disagreed on. Dreams, destiny, disaster…all of these things held the same negative connotations for me. Why should I let myself dwell on the "could be's" when I had a pack to take care of? I was the one who had control of my life. Any risk I took, any chance I let slip away, those were my decisions to make. A pair of long legs, smooth, warm skin, and a pussy that tasted like salted honey shouldn't have been enough to knock me flat on my ass.

Yet there I was, restless and distracted.

It was after midnight now, and I was wired with energy. I began to pace back and forth in front of the mantle. I didn't have the mind for mysticism, and I didn't have time to dwell on those dreams, but I could agree with my mom about my being on the cusp of something.

There was a different energy to the air—a tension. I felt it in my bones. Something was about to change for me and for my pack. I felt sure that whatever that change would be, it would finally put an end to the rule that the Kings had held over the land for decades.

A knock sounded at the door, and I whipped around, my wolf snarling inside me. I had very nearly shifted right then. *Easy…easy,* I soothed, and my wolf began to calm. There was a familiar scent coming from behind the door—my beta, Dominic Slate. As I got myself under control, Dom came inside.

I crossed my arms. "You haven't learned your manners, Dom."

He grinned. "Why bother learning them? It wouldn't stop me from coming in when you need me."

"Who says I need you?" I scoffed.

He chuckled. "I think we both know how lost you'd be without me, Night."

I considered the man who was my beta, my right hand, and my best friend. Dom didn't quite reach my height of six feet four inches, but he was only an inch or two behind. He had broad, muscular shoulders that made him look like a walking boulder and old scars running up and down his arms. He had those scars on display twenty-four-seven. As far as first impressions went, it would be reasonable for someone to assume that he was dangerous because of those scars. But that assumption went right out the door the moment you took in his dark brown eyes, ash-blond hair, and the damned dimples that came out when he smiled.

Dom was a walking contradiction, either pushing away those around him with his snark and his bluntness or pulling them in closer with that mischievous smile. He could befriend anyone, and unless they crossed him, he would never betray them. He was good at throwing people off their game, at figuring out what made them tick.

The worst part was, Dom knew the effect he had on people. When he wasn't being a snide-ass, I even found those traits useful. We'd grown up together in the poverty of the Wargs' territory. We fought together for scraps, and we defended each other when larger wolves ganged up on us. Dom was family, and as such, he was one of the few who were allowed to call me by my first name. Everyone else called me Alpha Night or Shepherd.

Dom walked up to me, and I uncrossed my arms. We gripped each other's forearms and went in for a quick hug before he pulled away again. The smirk on his face had completely vanished—drawn eyebrows and the hard line of his mouth replaced the joking beta I was familiar with.

"Walk with me?" he asked.

I nodded. At his expression, I pushed all thoughts of Mom, destiny, and the woman haunting my dreams aside.

The cool night air outside my cabin smelled slightly sweet; the blossoms of late spring had released their scent for everyone to enjoy. My pack was encased in darkness, but because shifters tended to keep late nights, torches and lanterns were ablaze within most cabins. It was a rather enchanting sight, but Dom and I turned away from the compound and into the thicket of trees near my cabin. We had something serious to discuss.

"I've got news," Dom said.

"Go ahead."

"We received word last night that the Kings' Alpha died."

Stillness fell over me, so total that even my wolf was silent. It wasn't the silence of dread or sadness—it was more like the calm before a terrible storm.

Dom, sensing the shift in me, took a step to the side but continued speaking. "The week of mourning and celebrations has already started. In five days, Troy Redwolf will ask for challengers before taking his spot as Alpha. Apparently, no one expects him to have to face anyone."

My growl cut across that final word. *That's just like that asshole, isn't it? Even his title will come easily to him.* My wolf howled and snapped inside me, rushing for release, and I was about ready to let him out. My desire for vengeance fed the rage boiling inside me. The Kings' pack should never belong to Troy. The Redwolfs ruled their pack through fear, control, and popularity contests. It was disgraceful.

The Kings' pack was meant to be mine, and I had every intention of storming in there and taking it for myself. Gregor Redwolf, a bastard and a coward, was finally dead after weeks of being bedridden. I ought to feel satisfaction at the news of his death, but all I felt was numbness. Gregor was more than just the Alpha of the pack that had ensured the suffering of the Wargs pack—he was my father, the man who had lain with my mom only to abandon her to a life without a mate. And me to one without a father.

"How did he die?" I asked. Even the leaves were silent and still, and Dom and I had stopped walking.

"In his sleep."

I snatched a thick, sturdy branch off a nearby tree, the wood groaning as it splintered. With a snarl, I broke the branch in half against my knee and tossed the remains away. "A peaceful death is too good for him," I snapped.

Dom didn't flinch in the wake of my rage. He was an excellent beta who did nothing but serve as my second to the best of his ability. He would go to the ends of the earth for me.

I wasn't alone in my hatred for the Kings' Alpha. There wasn't a wolf in my pack who wouldn't relish the opportunity to kill a Redwolf. But Dom was the only wolf, other than my mother, who knew why I hated Gregor so much.

I knew I confused him at times, but Dom understood my capabilities. He knew that I sought to bring an end to the oppression that our pack had endured. Once that happened, there would be no more skirmishes when Wargs and Kings happened to be in town at the same time. We would no longer be subjected to surprise ambushes while out patrolling or hunting. And we would finally be able to trade with other packs in the area, like the Camas, who had once been friendly with the Wargs.

But a good beta wasn't a mindlessly obedient one. Sometimes he and I would disagree on how to approach an issue. The ensuing discussion was a huge part of what made the Alpha/beta dynamic so important.

"I disagree," Dom said.

I speared him with a glare. "After everything the Kings' pack has done to us, you think Gregor got what he deserves?"

Again, Dom remained steady. "I would've loved to rip his throat out just as much as the next guy. That's not what I'm saying. To die in his sleep is no way for a warrior to go. He should have gone down fighting, but he didn't get to have that honor."

I paused, letting his words sink in. I'd had dreams of confronting Gregor on the Kings' territory, of ripping the Alpha mantle from the Redwolfs and taking it as my own. In light of Gregor's death, and with this new perspective that Dom had just given me, I realized I didn't have to see the way he died as an affront to my honor.

With one less obstacle in my way, I could take on Gregor's sniveling son—my sniveling half-brother—head-on. I looked at Dom with growing gratitude. I needed to remember that I had people on my side, lest I become the same shameful man that my father had been.

"Maybe you're right," I said, calming. "Maybe he got exactly what he deserved."

Dom nodded. "And it gives us an advantage."

It was true. With Gregor dead, and Troy without any real Alpha experience, the Kings were a much easier target.

"So, what's the plan, Night?"

I crossed my arms, thinking. "I'll go for what's mine on the night of the challenge ceremony."

Dom's grin showed canines that were just as sharp as mine. "They won't expect anyone to challenge him, so your presence will make Redwolf lose his shit."

"Exactly." In the dim light from the cabin, Dom's eyes glowed amber. I was sure mine shone too. "We'll storm the territory, and I'll kill him in front of his entire pack. No one will be able to dispute our rule."

"Stealth will still be key."

"Of course. And while the celebration is going on, everyone will be too drunk or too distracted to stop us."

"It's hard to believe that victory is so close. After everything the Wargs have been through…" Dom shook his head. "I can't wait to see the ground red with his blood."

Neither could I. In fact, at the thought of blood, my wolf was salivating at the mouth. This lust for blood made me think that even if I did end up having a destiny, it would be anything but "divine." I crossed my arms and began walking again. Dom followed.

"I'll want to pull our best hunters to nail down the details," I said. "It'll be five days until the challenge ceremony. That's less time than I'd like, but we need to have an airtight plan of action for this to work."

"Of course. I'll get the guys together. Once we know what we're doing, I'll put together obstacle courses and practice runs to make sure we move like a well-oiled machine."

"That's what I like to hear." My lips pulled away from my teeth as I grinned. "Earlier, I was debating whether or not I should go on another run, but I think I've made my decision now."

Dom grinned. "Do you want company?"

"No, I'm good. You get things started. We'll talk again once we have something more in place."

"Understood."

He ran back toward the compound while I removed my clothes. The moon was waxing high in the sky as I gathered my clothing into a bundle and stashed it in the branches of a tree to pick up later. It was only ten degrees that night, but I didn't feel the cold.

I let my wolf move to the forefront of my mind as I receded to the background. The shift rippled across my body, replacing skin with thick, black fur. In seconds, I dropped to all fours. In this form, I could smell the scents of spring blooms so strongly that I could almost taste them on my tongue. I stretched my forepaws out in front of me, shook out my pelt, and then took off, disappearing between the trees like a shadow winking into the darkness.

My senses, heightened in my wolf form, allowed me to scent out a small rabbit only a few yards ahead of me. It wasn't a full meal by any stretch, but it would give my wolf the chance to let loose a bit. With murder fresh on my mind, I pursued the rabbit with dogged intent. All I knew was the depth of the night, the crisp scent of the cold air, and the anticipation of hot blood on my tongue.

Chapter 4 - Bryn

Two days had passed since Gregor's death, but I was no closer to finding a solution to the Troy problem. I stood in front of the mirror in my room, smoothing down the skirt of my dress for the Alpha's funeral. In the reflection, I saw the wildflowers on my dresser casting long shadows across the room—dusk was quickly approaching. Everyone in the Kings' pack would begin gathering at the eastern portion of the compound in a few minutes. Mom and I would be among them soon.

"Mom," I called. "Are you sure I have to go to this? Won't I...attract attention?"

"It's a pack thing, sweetie," Mom called back. "It would be stranger if you didn't show up."

"Are you sure? Because I'm pretty sure no one wants me there."

"Bryn, honey, it's not about whether or not they want you there. This is pack business, and you're part of the pack. Gregor, for better or worse, was just as much your Alpha as anyone else's. You must pay your respects to his memory, even if it's brief."

I sighed. "Okay..." Though I had never felt truly part of the Kings' pack, I'd grown up on its territory.

Gregor hadn't given a damn about me, but he'd kept the territory safe from humans, Wargs, and anything else that wanted to cause harm to his pack. I knew well that he would have forced me out if not for Mom, whose agricultural skills were unmatched by anyone else in the pack, but I supposed it would be disrespectful not to say my goodbyes.

I met my stone-blue gaze in the mirror and again ran my hands down my skirt. The dress was one of my mom's nicer hand-me-downs, something she called the "little black dress" of her youth. Though I was reluctant to attend the funeral, I had to admit that the half-sleeve sheath dress showed off the curves of my bust and hips nicely. My hair, curled after a night in rollers, fell to the middle of my back in perfect, bouncy ringlets.

I'd borrowed Mom's worn-down pencil liner and had drawn a thin, black line around my eyes the way that she showed me when I was young. The slight change helped make my eyes pop against the pale, smooth skin of my face. I spent many long hours in the garden outside, but I'd never been able to keep much of a tan. In the summer, I normally darkened for a few days, but it always faded away by the time winter hit.

Pale as the snowcapped mountains, I smirked at myself. *I wonder if that mystery man in my dreams would like me much if he could see me outside of the dream.* Of course, he probably wasn't real, so I'd never know how he felt about me.

I pushed my hair over my shoulder and bent to pick up my shoes, a pair of black ballet flats that were so worn down I'd have to be careful if I wanted them to stay on my feet. I frowned at them for a while, and then inspiration struck. I removed the black laces from my work shoes and looped them under my soles. I crisscrossed them over my calves and tied them off at the back.

I studied my feet in the mirror. Heels would have been better—they would've added flattering height to my five feet four inches—but all we had access to were outdated, old-fashioned clothes. My outfits were limited to what the rest of the pack no longer wanted or had outgrown.

The Kings' pack loved to look as fashionable and as wealthy as possible. Wolves who went to human towns for supplies often brought back clothing and home goods for the pack. As the hierarchy went, the wolves who were close to the Redwolf family had first pick of the new clothes. After the Redwolfs' inner circle, the younger wolves who sought to attract mates were given preference. Then came the families of the compound, the ones who had already settled down. Finally, Mom and I were so far down the pecking order that we were never given the opportunity to pick from the new goods.

Because the Kings' pack went through apparel so quickly, there was an abundance of wasted fabric. Sometimes that fabric would be recycled into the pack as blankets or home textiles, but the bulk of the fabric was dispersed among other packs in the area, beginning with those most in the Kings' pack's good graces. The Wargs, of course, were never given any of the Kings' resources.

My solution to the issue of the worn-out flats was a little spur of the moment, but I'd make do. And maybe I was biased, but I kind of liked the way the black laces looked against the pale skin of my legs. I wondered if I'd ever be able to find someone who made me feel confident and desirable.

That question caused me to think about the green-eyed stranger again. Lately, whenever I had a quiet moment to myself, he returned to my thoughts. The only place I felt safe and warm, other than with my mom, was when I was with him, in my dreams. I wished desperately that he were real.

Mom's head popped through my open door as I pulled on my jacket. "Are you ready?"

I jumped. "Y-yeah! Are you?"

Mom grinned and stepped further inside. "What do you think?"

My eyes widened. Mom looked twenty years younger in her own black dress. It was a warmer day, so she wore nothing on her feet, as was the custom of shifters when the ground wasn't wet. Her silver hair was wrapped into a chic chignon bun at the nape of her neck, with a few tendrils hanging at the sides, brushing gently across her shoulders.

"Oh, wow, Mom! You look like a stone-cold fox."

She burst into laughter, and I joined in. It felt good to laugh so hard, to feel the happiness bubbling up from my stomach and spreading like warmth around my heart.

"A fox, huh?" she asked, carefully wiping a tear from the corner of her eye so as not to smudge her eye makeup. "Oh, my dear heart, there used to be one of those in my life, but he has been gone a long, long time."

I sobered. My mom had once had a lover, but she lost him. The reminder upset me more than I'd have thought. I watched her twirl one of the free tendrils around her finger to put more of a curl in it. I loved her fiercely, and it didn't matter that we didn't share a drop of blood. I had always admired Mom for her protectiveness and her bravery. When she had taken me in, not a soul in the pack supported her—though Gregor, who hated humans the most, didn't seem to care as long as she kept me out of his way.

That said, I was never formally accepted into the pack. This meant that I was condemned to being an outsider, and Mom, who used to exist higher up in the pack hierarchy because of her gardening skills and knowledge of the mystic, was brought down to my level.

Mom had to make do with much less now, but she insisted that she didn't care what her former friends or the larger community said. "You were mine," she had said to me, "I knew the moment I saw you."

That story always made me tear up. I wished I were the kind of woman who could stand up to those who ridiculed me. I wished I could rise above the bullying and the bullshit that Troy and his lackeys put me through. But I was weak. Female wolves had few rights and very little power in the pack already, and I had even less.

A woman like Mom deserved every good thing that life had to offer, not ostracization and second-hand goods. For all the respect and kindness that Mom showed the others in the pack and for how hard she worked to grow delicious crops for the community, shouldn't she enjoy an easier life?

Looking at her, I felt the deep bond we shared travel like a root down my spine and spread like vines through my veins. Something inside me stirred. The feeling was strange, causing me to step back from Mom and put my hand on my chest. There was something else, something like a whine in the back of my mind. Was there a wolf somewhere nearby?

Mom noticed my stiff expression in the mirror. "Are you okay?"

"Yeah, I just have some jitters, I guess." I forced a chuckle. But the tug I'd felt in my chest was nothing like the nervousness that spiked in my gut when Trish or Troy were nearby. I had never felt anything like that. What's more, Mom was the only shifter in the house. Where had that whine come from?

I tried to shake it off and looped my arm through Mom's. "Let's get going. The faster we get there, the faster we can be done with this."

She gave me a sympathetic smile and let me tow her downstairs. "That's one way to think about it, sweetie."

The entire pack had gathered on the eastern corner of the territory to say goodbye to Alpha Gregor. At our backs, the sky was ablaze with the colors of the setting sun. The compound's infirmary was nearby, and those who were recovering from injuries, ailments, or births were pressed against the windows, staring down at the proceedings.

In the middle of the crowd was a circle of people, and in the middle of that circle, a wood coffin lay without a lid. Gregor's lifeless body was inside. He'd rarely eat with the rest of the pack in the mess hall and often avoided interactions with me or Mom. From the occasional glimpse I'd caught of him around the camp, I'd only known him to be stern and unfriendly, with a permanent scowl darkening his features. It was surreal to see him look so peaceful.

His straight, auburn-brown hair was carefully styled around his face, and his large beard was combed and coifed. Though he had been dead for days already, he was handsome even in his casket; the only thing marring his face was the old scar on his right cheek. He looked like he could wake up any second, and his dark emerald eyes would survey the crowd. The coffin was made to suit his body, but his large shoulders pressed awkwardly against the walls.

Women sniffled and dabbed at their eyes while men stood statue-still, ready to show their respect. Though the atmosphere was heavy, no one was as sorrowful as Gregor's mate, Nora. Her dark eyes stared dolefully at the coffin, tears pouring silently down her face and dripping from her chin. I couldn't help but stare at the sad, beautiful woman. *It's hard to believe that even someone like Gregor could be loved so much. So much for a fair world.*

A few minutes later, the pack Elder parted from the crowd. Forsythe, an old, bald man who used a cane to walk, stood near the body and waited for a raised platform to be wheeled over. Once it had arrived, he mounted the platform, and a woman brought him a burning torch, which he held aloft over Gregor's body. The orange flame danced and crackled in the cool wind.

The ceremony was about to start, so I tried to dissolve into the crowd behind my mom and a few other women. Then something made me stop, a shiver passing between my shoulder blades—it felt as though I was being watched. My eyes darted around the crowd until they finally settled in the direction of Gregor's mate again. But I wasn't looking at the mourning woman anymore—I was looking at Troy.

Troy stood at his mother's side, dressed head to toe in an expensive-looking black tuxedo. His auburn-brown hair was tied back in a bun at the base of his skull, and his square jaw was clean-shaven. He had no scars, unlike the wolves who stood at his side, which was evidence of his high standing. The moment his gaze met mine, he snarled. I stopped breathing as a chill spread across my skin. Those eyes were like two black holes, pulling me into their path of destruction, sucking my air away, making me feel small and compressed.

It had been days since I'd last seen Troy, but he was no less intimidating even at the site of his father's funeral. That one look made it clear that he had his sights set on destroying me. I shivered and watched as he peeled away from his mother's side to stand on the platform by the Elders, keeping his eyes on me the whole time.

"We have gathered to celebrate and mourn the life of Alpha Gregor Redwolf," the Elder's powerful voice carried over the crowd, silencing the murmurs and the sniffles. "Alpha Gregor was a strong and incredibly steadfast man. He was tough, but he was fair, and he made sure that no one in his pack went cold or hungry."

Murmurs of agreement rippled through the crowd, but Mom and I remained silent. *It's so weird that none of them seem to remember how arrogant he could be,* I thought. *The fact that he refused to eat with them was certainly something people used to grumble and complain about when they thought no one was listening.*

"His absence will undoubtedly be felt and remembered by all of us, but we of the Kings' pack are fortunate that his mantle will be passed to his son, Troy Redwolf." The Elder turned to Troy and offered the torch.

Troy finally released me from his terrible stare to accept the torch. I wrapped my arms around myself and blinked back tears.

Troy held the torch over Gregor's body. "My father really was a great man, but I promise all of you that I will do everything I can to continue leading the Kings into prosperity. It will be as if my father never left us."

The Elder nodded. "Please, Troy, repeat after me— With this flame, I release my father, Alpha Gregor Redwolf, to the spirits of the forest. Please accept his soul and allow him to enjoy the afterlife that he so rightly deserves."

Troy repeated the words and then closed his eyes for a few moments. When he opened them, he dropped the torch onto his father. The flames licked across Gregor's body and ignited the coffin. Sparks and embers drifted up toward the darkening sky. It was almost beautiful, but I couldn't enjoy it. My eyes were riveted on Troy. The flames cast terrible shadows across the sharp lines of his face, making him look like an avenging demon from my worst nightmares.

As if he sensed my gaze on him, he looked at me again. Even the pyre didn't cast enough light to reflect in his black eyes. There was a dark promise in those eyes that shook me to my core. He was out for blood.

When the fire stopped burning, people began to move around and talk amongst themselves. I wanted nothing more than to go home, a desire that Mom seemed to share, though she wasn't aware of the expression on Troy's face.

"I thought it would never end. All that talk about Gregor and his valor…" She shook her head. "It's not wrong to remember a man for the good qualities he showed his friends, but it's shameful to lie to the spirits. Most of us only know him for his hatefulness."

I opened my mouth to reply, but a voice called out, "Glenda!" There were a few older women standing to the side, gesturing for Mom to come over. She cursed under her breath.

"I'm sorry, baby, but they probably want to plan their dishes around what's growing in the garden. Do you mind if I speak with them?"

I shook my head. "Not at all. You go ahead. I'll be fine on my own."

"You sure? You could come if you wanted—"

"No, no. I'm okay. I just want to get home to eat the rest of your salsa."

Mom smirked. "Okay. I'll see you at home, sweetie."

I put a smile on my face, but it fell the moment she turned away. I needed to get home as soon as possible. The last thing I wanted was for Troy to find me and make good on his silent threat.

I tried to keep my head down as I walked through the crowd. My pace was quick, but I hoped that the uniform crowd of black outfits would allow me to blend in. As I passed between a few trees, a figure stepped into my path, and I almost collided face-first with Tanya's chest. Dread was like ice filling my bloodstream as I took a step backward. *Damn, damn, damn!*

"She's going nowhere fast, don't you think, Trish?" Tanya asked.

"I'm surprised she can move at all in those clothes." Trish snaked around a tree trunk, her red lips lifting in a mocking smirk. "You're drowning in that jacket, girl."

Tara snickered from behind me. She bumped my shoulder roughly as she walked past me to stand with the other Terrible T's. This was exactly what I'd wanted to avoid. They had stopped me just out of Mom's sight. There was no telling what the group had planned for me, but I'd be lucky if they let me go with a few insults.

"It's a shame no one ever cared enough to tell you how to dress properly," Trish said. "Poor baby. Maybe I could help you." Trish bent to grab a stick that was partially buried in a particularly muddy area of the ground. She flicked the stick toward me, flinging mud and leaves across my chest.

I winced, staggering a few steps back as it hit me.

"Oops, so sorry," Trish said as her friends cackled. "That was supposed to make you look better, but all I've done is make you look like a wet rat." She tutted and feigned a look of pity. "You poor thing. To be so lost and alone, to be hated by the Alpha and everyone else, to have no one but a crazy old woman to love you."

I bristled. The Terrible T's could do and say whatever they wanted about me, but the moment they started talking about my mom—well, they'd gone too far. I wasn't sure what possessed me to step forward. All I knew was that the stress of the last couple of days and the knowledge that Troy was going to try to destroy me had become too much. I couldn't have stopped what was about to happen even if I wanted to.

"I'd rather be hated by everyone in the pack than throw myself at a man who didn't care about me," I snapped back.

At my words, the three women's smiles dropped. Trish's sharp, white teeth showed as she grimaced. "Watch your mouth, little rat. Your days around here are numbered."

"You think I don't know that, Trish? After all that you guys have done to me?" I crossed my arms over my chest. "If you were as confident as you try to appear, you wouldn't be wasting your time with a girl like me. Makes me think you're not as secure as you try to make everyone believe you are."

Trish's upper lip twitched. Her pretty face sharpened with anger, and she raised her hand to strike me. When she brought her hand down, I wasn't there, but not because I'd dodged.

If my first mistake had been to allow myself to be cornered by the Terrible T's, then my second was not paying attention to anything going on behind me. If I had noticed the quick pair of footsteps headed my way, I might have been able to do something to prevent the shock of the large, strong hand gripping my shoulder.

The hand shoved me to the side and pressed me roughly against the trunk of a tree. I yelped from a combination of surprise and pain. A second hand slammed against the tree above my head, nails digging into the hard pine. Troy's sharp, angular face loomed above—my nightmare made manifest.

"Did you forget your place, bitch?" His voice was the slithery hiss of a snake about to strike. "Did you forget what you *are*?"

His hand shifted from my shoulder to my neck. It was large enough to wrap around my throat—his fingertips almost met at the back of my neck. Fear quaked through my body as he held me still against the tree. My body felt as cold as ice, as if every drop of blood had congealed in my veins. I stared up into those endlessly black eyes and saw my own death reflected back at me.

The tip of his tongue ran slowly along the inside of his lip, a hungry predator licking his jowls in anticipation of his prey. "You better watch that filthy mouth, girl," he said. "Don't forget who has the power here."

He pressed closer to me, and, against my will, a whimper slipped past my lips. Troy's hands tightened around my neck. It wasn't enough to cut off my air supply, but it established how easily he could snap my bones if he wanted to. I was completely at his mercy, and he wanted to make sure I knew it. From the corner of my eye, I saw the surprise on Trish's face morph into a satisfied smirk. She crossed her arms and enjoyed the show that the object of her affection was putting on.

He tilted his head, grinning from ear to ear. "Now that I'm in charge, not even Glenda will be able to save you from what's about to happen." Without warning, he tossed me to the ground. I scrambled to catch myself, skinning my palms against the rough roots of the trees.

He threw his head back and laughed. "That's exactly where you belong."

The Terrible T's laughed with him. Their combined laughter grated on my ears, and tears stung at the backs of my eyes. I sat there for a while, even after the group finally left me alone. I clenched my hands tightly despite the way my palms ached and throbbed. There was nowhere in the territory that was safe for me. Whatever Troy intended to do with me, I couldn't stay here beyond the fifth day of mourning. I needed to come up with something, and fast.

Chapter 5 - Bryn

Thankfully, the third day of mourning was uneventful for me. All of my time was spent in the garden, the kitchen, or the root cellar. I was constantly washing, cutting, and sorting fruits and vegetables for the grand banquet meals. After the way I had come home—with bloody palms and a ruined dress, Mom no longer made me attend any of the events. Instead, when she got home from the third night's festivities, she caught me up on everything that was going on. Mom told me about the dance held in the dining hall. All the pack families brought offerings of support and comfort to the Redwolf family, and afterward, the men got together to participate in a fight ring.

Some part of me was curious about how these sorts of proceedings went because I was so rarely allowed to be part of them, but a much greater part of me was relieved that I could stay out of the line of sight of Troy and the Terrible T's. On the third night, I'd gotten little sleep because the wolves were so loud as they fought each other for dominance. It was the last place I wanted to be; all those horny, angry shifter men amped up with testosterone made it far too dangerous for female wolves to attend, never mind a weak human.

If one of those men wanted to attack me, there would be nothing I could do to defend myself. So, instead of sleeping, I buried myself in the books I had first read when I was younger. These novels always featured beautiful damsels in distress and handsome princes who whisked them away to their kingdom. The princes always married the women to make them queens and showered them with jewels and gifts, and in the end, they always lived happily ever after.

Real life was nothing like these fairy tales, but I couldn't help but get lost in the stories. I again found myself thinking of the green-eyed stranger. I hadn't dreamt of him in a while, and I missed him. It was pathetic of me to miss a figment of my imagination, but at least those dreams had been comforting when the harsh realities of my life were too much.

The best thing for me to do now was focus on the tasks that had been assigned to me and on creating a plan to escape. If I didn't get far away from Kings' territory quickly, my life would soon become much worse. There was no future for the only human in a wolf pack that didn't want me.

On the fourth day of mourning, I had a full schedule planned. The next day would hold the ceremony in which anyone who wished to challenge Troy could fight to the death for the right to the Alpha spot. There was even more food cutting and prepping for me to do—fortunately, Mom had treated my raw palms with bandages that kept my pain to a minimum.

I wasn't familiar with the forest surrounding the Kings' compound beyond the few miles I had explored with Mom when I was young. I knew it was easy for humans to catch hypothermia if we didn't bundle up carefully—and that could happen even when the weather was warmer. Sneakily, so as not to call attention to myself, I gathered more jackets and long-sleeved shirts to wear while I traversed the forest.

I would need some way to navigate, but wolves didn't need maps to travel. They could direct themselves with their senses alone. The closest I had to a map was a depiction of the area that I had received when I was a kid in school. The drawing was of an oblong shape with marks indicating the location of the river and other pack territories. It didn't mention where human cities started. I understood generally that the humans lived north of the Kings, but I had no other details beyond that.

The schoolhouse taught all the children of the pack how to survive in the forest (how to build a fire, how to construct a shelter out of rocks, tree branches, and mud, and how to hunt) just in case a wolf was injured and unable to shift. I knew exactly how to take care of myself in the woods; the real trick would be figuring out how to survive while navigating the forest with wolf packs on all sides.

Wolves were generally mistrustful of humans in their area. They would likely try to chase me out if I didn't stick to the trees or try and mask my scent. But I had heard talk around the Kings' compound that human hikers occasionally ventured out into wolf territory with no issues, so I might be okay as long as I was careful and identified myself as visiting from "Las Vegas" or "Los Angeles" or another human city that I had heard about.

I had no idea what I would do once I reached the human cities.

I tied my hair back and put on an oversized hoodie and cotton pants. Outside, Mom was getting started on the harvest. When I noticed that her basket was already full of corn, I fetched another basket for me. When I returned, Mom gave me a grateful smile. I began at a new line of stalks and ripped the ears free in deft, quick twists.

"Hey, Mom, could you tell me more about how the challenge works?"

"Oh, tomorrow?" She took a drink from her water bottle and gathered her thoughts. "The challenge is open to any wolf willing to die for the chance to be Alpha of the pack. If Troy wins, or if no one challenges him, he's the new Alpha by default because it's his birthright."

I nodded. That part I understood well enough.

"Of course, there will be a huge feast either way to welcome the new Alpha," Mom explained, "but the talk around the pack is that no one will challenge Troy."

I frowned. The thought of Troy taking up the mantle without a struggle made my stomach feel tight. "Do *you* think anyone will come forward to challenge him?"

She stopped picking corn and turned to me. "No, honey, I don't believe so."

"But what about outside packs? There's the Camas that border Colville forest, or the Wargs…" I trailed off, noticing Mom's stiff expression.

"The Camas are far too quiet and peaceful to want to move up the ranks, Bryn. And as for the Wargs, you already know that they are vicious, no better than feral wolves. It would be best for them if they stayed on their own territory because a challenge from them could mean all-out war."

I suppressed a shiver. Mom's words, combined with such a somber warning…it sounded like an omen. Ferals were wolves without a real pack, sticking together in small groups. Creatures of opportunity, they were wild and territorial over the few scant miles of land they could claim between the pack territories. It was a harsh criticism for Mom to levy against the Wargs.

I tried to remember what I knew of the wild Wargs pack and its Alpha, Night Shepherd. He was known as the crazed Alpha, a man who had some sick vendetta against the Kings' pack because the Kings were on top. Every few months, Night's hunters staged attacks against Kings' wolves when they left the compound. It sounded terrifying, but the Wargs couldn't be all that powerful because the Kings always won in those skirmishes.

I had heard so much about the Wargs and their history because the rivalry between the packs was so well known. The Wargs and the Kings had been in a struggle for dominance ever since the packs formed hundreds of years ago.

In the schoolhouse, the history of the Kings, the Wargs, and the Camas packs was well documented. There was information recorded about every Alpha and their years of rule. I had even seen a picture of Night

Shepherd—the faded, black-and-white photo had to be out of date now, but it showed a boy a little younger than I was. Night had challenged the previous Alpha of the Wargs when he was just a teenager and had made the pack his own.

In the photo, his dark black hair gleamed in the light and fell gently over his forehead. The soft, boyish hairstyle was contrasted by the sharp glare he directed at someone unseen, his face a hard, humorless mask. Broad-shouldered and lanky, with sunken cheeks and a sharp-toothed grimace, he looked like he'd had to fight for every scrap of food he'd ever eaten.

The shirt he wore in the picture looked a lot like the hand-me-downs I wore to garden or work. It was dotted with small, moth-bitten holes. The traces of a tattoo peeked out from under the worn collar. I knew that he was my enemy, but I couldn't stop myself from relating to the poor boy in the image. I didn't know what it was like for a teenager to fight for his spot as Alpha, but I *did* know what it meant to struggle. Even in the richest pack in the Kaniksu National Forest, Mom and I were not treated equally. The Redwolfs could afford so many luxuries, but out of spite, they left us with scraps and leftovers.

I wondered what Night looked like now. Would he have grown into a lanky adult full of sharp angles, his ribs jutting out in emaciated directions? No, that image didn't quite suit the savage, feral man who had instilled such fear in the younger me. Would he be built like a boulder? With muscles so large, he could hardly flex? I smiled to myself. No, that was just silly. I sifted through a slew of potential images in my mind, but nothing felt right. I supposed I'd never know.

"Honey," Mom's voice pulled me from my thoughts. I turned and found her standing with her fingers knotted in front of her, in an uncharacteristically awkward stance. "I know you're frightened. With the way Troy has treated you, you have every right to be concerned about what your future is going to look like. But, I…I want you to know that with a bit more time, I think you'll be able to find a place for yourself here. When I found you alone beneath that tree, I just knew that fate had big plans for you. I wish I could help you see that for yourself too. If we keep trying, you'll find belonging."

"Do you really think that, Mom?"

"I know it, honey. I believe it in every cell of my body."

I searched her gaze for any indication of doubt, but when I found nothing, I let my gaze trail downward. I knew she wasn't oblivious to the bullying. The number of bruises and scratches that I had come home with over the years provided more than enough evidence. The problem was that neither Mom nor I had the power to do anything about it. Neither of us was high on the pack's priority list. What hope did either of us have of taking on Troy or Trish—two wolves whose social standing was leagues and bounds ahead of ours?

Mom tried hard to help me fit in. Even teaching me how to garden had been an attempt to make me an asset to the pack, but none of her efforts had panned out. We were fighting a losing battle, and though Mom held onto the hope that the Kings could one day accept a human, I had long since given up. *That's why I can't give up on my plan to escape. I have to get out of here, whether Mom approves it or not.*

"It's okay, Mom," I said. "Thanks for explaining the challenge to me."

She lifted an arm as if to lay a comforting hand on my hair but pulled back with a sigh. "I love you, sweetie."

"I know. I love you too, Mom."

Hours later, I was in slightly better spirits. The land was empty of vegetables, and I had just finished tilling the area in preparation for reseeding it. It was a job I had enjoyed even when I was younger because it allowed me to think about the fresh bounty of plants that we'd be able to harvest in a few weeks. The supposed magic in the land was what allowed the plants to grow so quickly and so robustly.

Mom had left me to take the fruit to the root cellar, so I was alone to take care of pressing the new bulbs and seeds into the cool, moist earth. I was so engrossed in the task, immersed in the peaceful quiet of my thoughts, that I didn't hear the faint sound of shifting soil as someone approached me from behind.

Finished, I straightened, dusting my hands off on my work jeans. I could already imagine the vibrant colors that this next harvest would bring to the lot. It was brown and boring now, but in a few more weeks, that would change—

I froze as I felt heat against my back. I knew it was Troy even before I turned to face him. My shoulder brushed his chest as I moved, and he shoved me away from him. I staggered but stopped short of losing my balance.

"You're not clean enough to touch me, human bitch," he snapped.

I stared at him, my blood rushing through my veins. "Why are you here?" I asked.

"What do you mean? This is my territory now. All of this," he gestured to the field that he had never put even a minute's work into, "belongs to me. That includes the land, its resources, and everyone living on it."

I clenched my hands so hard that my palms began to sting again. I wanted to tell him that I didn't belong to him or anyone, but of course, that would result only in his anger. Troy had been raised by a sexist, domineering Alpha. I understood that as a woman and a human, I would never be viewed as anything more than a plaything to Troy.

"Th-that doesn't answer my question."

He sneered at me. "I just wanted to inform you. Think of it as a common courtesy for someone as useless as you. Without anyone to challenge me, it's a sure thing that I'll be made Alpha tomorrow night."

My eye twitched. My body wanted to tremble with fear, but rage filled my chest with fire. *Did he go out of his way to tell me that?*

"Good for you, Troy," I said, voice dripping with sarcasm. "If that's all you wanted to say, then consider your message received." I tried to walk past him, but he crowded me.

"I remembered something," he said. "Your birthday is the day after the challenge ceremony, isn't it?"

I stiffened.

Troy gripped my arm and pulled me close to him, his grin full of sharp teeth. "You'll be twenty and of age."

"It doesn't matter what age I'll be," I retorted. I tried to pull my hand away, but his grip was a vise around my wrist. "It doesn't affect you because I'm obviously not going to be on *your* list of future mates."

He tightened his grip on my arm and snarled, his eyes bright with sudden, wild energy. "You aren't going to be on *anyone's* list, Bryn. Your weak human blood will never be allowed to mix with a wolf's. I'll see to that myself."

What little bravado I'd summoned completely disappeared when he started speaking in that growling voice. In the wake of what he'd just said, I couldn't hide my terror.

Troy's tongue snaked out to lick his lips as though he could taste my fear in the air. I felt a bulge in his pants pressing against my thigh. I nearly gagged. I couldn't escape. I couldn't pull away. Night Shepherd was supposedly the savage Alpha, but Troy was ready to force himself on me in broad daylight. I clenched my teeth against the overwhelming urge to vomit, my eyes watering from the effort.

Taking my tears as more evidence of my weakness, Troy laughed and shoved me onto the ground. "Make sure you're ready to ring in your birthday in a way that you won't forget because it'll be the last one you see as a free woman. By the way," he looked me over, "you're at your most attractive when you're on the ground and covered in dirt."

When he walked away, I rushed off the field. I barely made it to the tree line before bile burned up my throat. I fell to my hands and knees and threw up in the grass, hot tears streaming down my cheeks. After I'd emptied my stomach, I sat back. My throat was raw, and my arm was bruised where he'd gripped it, my humiliation complete. And Mom wanted me to find a place for myself under these conditions? There was no chance.

Though pained, though defeated, I closed my eyes and made a wish ahead of my birthday. I didn't wish for a way to escape. I wished for Troy's death. *I don't want another wolf to challenge him at the ceremony,* I sent to the heavens. *I wish that I could be strong enough to challenge him, just to feel the bones in his neck snap between my teeth.*

Chapter 6 - Night

Dom and I walked through one of the village boroughs, and I took in the activity of my pack. Before I had taken over, there were much fewer cabins, and interactions between pack members were tense and unfriendly because their Alpha wasn't doing his job. After I took control, I set the pack on a course to a new order. I galvanized the community and rebuilt the cabins that had fallen into disrepair...and the cabins that had been razed to the ground during the Kings' violent raid a decade ago—a raid that had resulted in the deaths of many Wargs, including Dom's siblings.

I had poured so much blood, sweat, and tears into the land and the community, and I was proud of what we had built together. But there were still so many things we needed to do—and resources that we didn't have access to because of the Kings. The pack was growing, and we needed more.

I had planned to bring just a handful of my men along for this mission. Our goal wasn't to attack the entire pack, so I didn't think I would need more than my beta and a couple of other hunters to back me up. But when the rest of my pack heard of my intention to challenge Troy, they refused to let me go without a small army. After hearing the news that there were dozens of fighters—men and women—who wanted to join me on the mission to take over the Kings' pack, I turned to my beta.

"Do they think I can't win?" I asked in a low voice.

"Actually, they just care about you," Dom replied. "Even if you do win, they're worried that the Kings will attack and kill you if you don't have enough people with you."

I scoffed. "The Kings would be welcome to try."

Dom rolled his eyes. "I'm not surprised to hear you say that, Night, but that's probably just your ego and your restless wolf talking."

I sighed, knowing he was probably right. I was eager to reclaim my birthright to help my pack. "I'm still not sure if having a big team with us is best," I said. "If stealth is key, the smaller the group, the better."

"We trained this group ourselves, so you know they can be discreet."

That was also true. I knew I could trust my hunters to do their jobs well, but there was another downside to bringing along such a large number; there was a greater risk for injury if things went south. I wasn't willing to put the lives of my pack at risk without reason.

We stopped walking as we reached the training grounds next to the Elders' cabin. Training had ended hours ago, and now there were pups rolling around and wrestling in the circle instead. Some of their parents were hunters who might accompany me on this attack. If the worst happened, I would have to look into the eyes of a crying child and tell them that their father or mother wouldn't be coming home.

As if to emphasize that point, the ball that the pups were playing with rolled into my path. One of the children, a little girl who must have been five or six, rushed over to grab it.

"Sorry, Alpha, sir," she said in a small, gentle voice.

I smiled. I remembered being her age and growing up under Peter's rule. Back then, children were to be seen and not heard, and if we were ever in Peter's way, we were shamed for it.

"No worries, little one." I kicked the ball gently back to her. "Have fun."

She gave me a wide grin, revealing small—yet sharp—teeth, and then returned to her game.

"Night," Dom pulled my attention away from the playing children, "I get you're worried, but I don't think they'll let you do this without all the protection you can get.

You've done a lot for the Wargs since you took over, so let them pay you back."

I sighed again. I saw Dom's point, and I knew my hunters would jump at any chance to make the Wargs pack stronger while also taking down the Kings and ending their reign of the Kaniksu National Forest area.

Two days after that conversation, I found myself with my shoulder pressed against the thick trunk of a Douglas fir tree. The needles rustled in the breeze above my head as if nature itself was as anxious to be through with all of this as I was. My thoughts pulsed and thrummed along with the beat of my heart as I waited for the sun to set. Only a few yards away lay the border of the Kings' territory.

I took a deep breath, filling my lungs with the scent of the land. The Kings' territory smelled much sweeter than the Wargs'—no doubt because the Kootenai River made the ground so rich and lush. The abundance of resources that the Kings' pack had was enough to make any Alpha jealous. But it wasn't jealousy that had me clenching my teeth—I hardly cared about any of that—it was the way the Redwolfs ran their pack, the way they flaunted the land that was rightfully mine. It was the fact that Gregor Redwolf was my father, and yet he'd abandoned me to take control over a more successful pack rather than fix the mistakes he made with the Wargs.

The Kings' pack wolves enjoyed the fourth day of celebration with feasts and dances. Unmated women in flashy, skintight costumes and makeup flitted around the males. They gorged themselves on alcohol and a variety of meat, some of which was obviously purchased from humans. They laughed and clapped and gyrated, a display of hedonism that only the very wealthy and very fortunate could afford. Their compound was lit not with torches but with electric light generated by the solar panels installed on the southeast side. The luxuries were endless, flashy, and grotesque. Bottles, cans, and food wrappers littered the ground like toxic confetti.

Adding to my distaste, I had seen the way that women were treated at these gatherings. They were made to stand at the side, to be less rowdy, to be all dressed up. These sorts of celebrations were much too intense to have children in attendance, and there were no older wolves mingling with the younger ones. This was purely a celebration of masculinity, of testosterone, before the males would pick out their lover for the night.

My hands clenched tight. Sexism, hedonism, and their clear lack of respect for the land they partied on—they squandered what was rightfully mine. My anger burned in my chest, but I had to acknowledge that even the Wargs had once been similar. Before I took over as Alpha, the women of the pack were treated almost like prisoners, unable to go off on their own without a chaperone or mate. Unmated women were coveted, competed for, and won as prizes. Rarely could they choose their own mate, and there were no protections for them if their mate ever chose to abandon them. That was why Gregor had been able to abandon Mom and me without any repercussions.

Gregor hadn't been a good pack leader of the Wargs. Under Craig, Gregor's father, the Wargs were thriving. We weren't the ruling pack, but we were well on our way to becoming so. Unfortunately, that progress stagnated and even regressed after Craig died and Gregor became Alpha. Gregor's short temper, arrogance, and outdated views on women made him a poor leader. The Wargs didn't respect him, and instead of trying to repair that relationship with his pack, he abandoned everyone.

He left the Wargs weakened, and when the next Alpha took over, a scummy wolf named Peter who had no idea how to lead, things became even worse for everyone. I challenged Peter as soon as I was strong enough and then performed a massive overhaul of the social hierarchy of the pack. I made things equal between the sexes, and if ever there were cases of domestic violence, the perpetrator was swiftly and severely dealt with. Though the Kings' pack weren't quite as ass-backward as the Wargs once were, it was clear they still hadn't figured out how to put female wolves on equal footing as the males.

And they dare to call us *primitive.*

I spotted Troy walking with a blonde woman across the courtyard. They laughed and chatted with each other, totally unaware that they were being watched. My knuckles popped when I clenched my hand. *Good. He should enjoy himself while he can. My victory will be even sweeter when I step out to challenge him. I can't wait to beat that smirk right off his face.*

We had all arrived earlier that day. I had sent a few scouts to case out the area and to find out if anyone had stepped up to challenge Troy. Apparently, no one had, which suited my plans perfectly.

Branches crunched softly under Dom's feet as he walked to the other side of the fir's trunk. Dom could have moved silently, but to avoid startling me, he purposefully made a bit of noise to announce his presence. I gave him a grateful nod and continued to survey the Kings' pack.

Because of the celebration, Troy didn't have any hunters keeping an eye on their borders, so it was absurdly easy for us to surround the compound. That sort of laziness and arrogance was exactly what I expected from a Redwolf. Though I was away from my territory, I knew that my pack continued to run smoothly. I had hunters and sentries guarding the perimeter of our compound without even having to tell them to do it. Clearly Gregor, and likely Troy too, had become complacent in their luxury—in their dominance. They no longer considered any of the other packs in the area a threat.

And that arrogance would work perfectly into our plans.

Around me, the air was thick with anticipation. My hunters were almost as eager as I was to get things started, but we still had twenty-four hours before the challenge ceremony was to start. I had three-dozen wolves stationed at strategic points along the perimeter of the territory, and I could only pick out five of them from where I stood. Among those, I could see Kai and Redford, who had both been with me for years, and Jasper, a young wolf who, despite still being wet behind the ears, was a damned good fighter. I could have staged an attack that same night with this assemblage, and my chest swelled with pride. I was glad that my pack was so determined to stay by my side through this.

Looking over the wolves of the Kings' pack, I couldn't help but bristle. Far too many times, the Kings had attacked my hunters when they ventured out of the Wargs' territory. Troy often led these attacks himself; the only purpose for them seemed to be to intimidate the Wargs and to piss me off.

We had lost too many lives because of Troy's bullshit, so I made it a rule that none of my hunters went out without a partner. That adjustment leveled the playing field quite a bit, and I no longer lost wolves when they went out for a hunt. So, the Kings stepped up the frequency of their attacks. Once, Troy had attempted to ambush me and Dom while we were out hunting together. When faced with the wrath of the Wargs' Alpha, Troy had attempted to give an order to his men, but instead of listening, they turned tail and ran. Literally. It was the most disgraceful thing I had ever seen, and it solidified to me which pack had the better wolves and the better leadership.

I would gladly give my life to ensure the prosperity of my pack. That was something I doubted Troy, or Gregor, could ever understand. Trust and loyalty were the keys to forming an unbreakable bond with your pack, but the Redwolfs didn't have that.

"Night?" Dom's voice was just above a whisper, but I easily heard him. "We still have time before the challenge night. Are you sure this is how you want things to go down?"

I whirled on him, the sense of calm I felt from thinking about my men and my goals dissipating in an instant. A low, barely-audible growl built in my chest as I glared at my beta.

"I have more than earned this, Dom." *Even when I never should have had to.*

Dom leveled me with a serious stare. "You can lash out at me for asking a question all you want, Night," he said, "but you need to get your head in order before you make a mistake.

Those words were enough to snap me out of it. I stopped short of hanging my head, but shame burned in the pit of my stomach. I reined in my wolf and took a few deep breaths.

"You're right. I'm sorry. I need to get control of myself." I ran my hands through my hair and looked at the Kings' pack. "Troy is an awful, awful man. Every bit as terrible as Gregor was, if not worse."

"Hey." Dom laid a gentle but firm hand on my shoulder. "I get it. We want the bastard dead. That's more than enough justification for me."

I stopped talking. It was starting to sound less like I was trying to justify my plan to my beta and more like I wanted to convince myself that my reasons to attack the Kings were not selfish ones. Trying to articulate my scattered thoughts in front of my friend caused me to slip up. I cleared my throat, trying to smother the doubt that briefly flared to life deep within me. *This was for pride*, I assured myself, *and for justice.* My wolf growled in accordance. He, too, wanted his birthright—the land, the resources. At least my wolf understood me, even if I sometimes stumbled.

I turned to Dom again. "Let's go over our plan again, and I want this communicated to each of our fighters."

Dom nodded. "Of course."

"Tomorrow, during the challenge ceremony, we'll go in from the back and sides of the compound, but we'll stay hidden. When no challengers appear, I'll show up at the last second. I just need you and the rest to get me inside without issue."

"At the last second, huh? Look at you. I never thought you'd be one for theatrics, Night."

I chuckled. "I just want to make a good impression."

Dom grinned. "I'll let them know." He slipped into the darkness, as quiet as a shadow. Moments later, I felt a tug in my mind.

Dom was contacting me through our telepathic link. When an Alpha took over the pack, this connection was normally one way so that Alphas could contact or command anyone at a moment's notice. In wolf form, an Alpha could use telepathy like second nature, and it had a wider reach. But in human form, it was reserved for special circumstances or stealth missions because it took effort to maintain, and its reach was much shorter. Though Alphas were the only ones with this power, betas were able to use the connection to contact their Alpha.

I preferred to keep the line open in high-stress situations because it was the only way the rest of my wolves could reach me if they needed help. Dom and I, however, were able to speak privately without tapping into that main line.

"Are they allowed to use lethal force?" Dom asked.

I made eye contact with Dom. He crouched beside Jasper a few yards west of me. I shook my head. *"Only as a last resort. Otherwise, we want this to be as bloodless as possible."*

"Understood."

The goal was for me to kill Troy. There was no reason to kill those who would soon be part of my pack if I could avoid it.

"One more thing, Dom," I sent, *"tell everyone to fall back. We need to rest up for tonight and tomorrow morning, so we're in fighting shape."*

"Got it."

I stretched my arms and drew away from the tree and the Kings' pack. My wolf whined, yearning for his future territory. I quieted him. *It won't be much longer now. Come tomorrow night, we'll become one large, united front. I'll have my birthright. I'll be able to throw Troy's severed head at the feet of the Elders, and the rivalry between the packs will end. The Kings' pack's hierarchy is stupid; those who have been mistreated under the Redwolfs will finally be able to live comfortably. Then everyone will see who the true Alpha really is.*

Only twenty-four hours before I would be able to claim what was rightfully mine. I knew my hunters were ready. I just needed to make sure I did my part. But that shouldn't be a problem for me. On the eve of the challenge ceremony, there was nothing and no one who could come between me and my goal. I couldn't wait to watch Troy bleed.

Chapter 7 - Bryn

The last day of mourning had finally arrived, and I was ready with my plan. I would use the challenge ceremony as my opportunity to escape. I had overheard that the sentries and hunters would all be off duty to enjoy the party. It was my one chance to get away without anyone noticing or caring.

But before I could put my escape plan into action, I had to get through the challenge ceremony. I knew it was childish, but a big part of me wanted to enjoy the event, even if the joy was momentary. I wanted to dress up like the wolves did. It was my last night on the compound. I might as well enjoy myself.

I pulled my hair back into one long braid so I wouldn't have to worry about it. I wore a pair of jeans, my usual black boots, and a soft, blush-pink blouse with bell sleeves. It was another inherited piece from my mom's closet, and it was my favorite. I liked the way the pink looked against my skin. The only downside to wearing it was that it would likely get dirty when I escaped, and I would have to keep it hidden under a jacket for the most part.

I met my own gaze in the mirror. I was surprised to see the sadness in my downturned eyebrows and the slight frown on my lips. Troy's warning was fresh on my brain. I remembered the way he'd loomed over me like the devil incarnate. He tormented me even while I slept—I found myself waking in a cold sweat with the memory of his hot breath blowing over my face.

After I finished my braid, I tied it off with a hair tie and tossed it over my shoulder. The end bounced against my lower back. I turned away from the mirror and rubbed my upper arms. *"Make sure you're ready to ring in your birthday in a way that you won't forget because it'll be the last one you see as a free woman."* That was what he'd told me.

I didn't want to think about him making good on his threat or about the bulge he'd pressed against my thigh. After I'd thrown my guts up in the grass, I'd scrubbed myself raw to get the memory of him off my skin. For all my effort, I hadn't succeeded. I would see Troy at the ceremony tonight, and the thought of being anywhere near him made me sick to my stomach all over again. He was the reason I needed to get the hell out of here—I couldn't let him control my life.

I wanted to forget about Troy entirely and try to enjoy one last night before I ventured out on my own. At around midnight, the challenge ceremony would begin, and then those closest to Troy would have full run of the compound; but for now, everyone—the elderly, the mothers, the children—could sit down and enjoy each other's company.

I was looking forward to watching the young wolf pups enjoy the music and celebration. Other than Mom, the children were the best part about living in the pack. The little girls and boys were all so cute and so clumsy, and they weren't nearly as put off by my humanity as their parents.

Mom and I would get to dance carefree in the moonlight with the other women of the pack and eat delicious meals that neither of us had to prepare. The idea of being surrounded by such jovial, happy energy caused tears to push at the backs of my eyes. I tried to push them away, but a few wayward droplets escaped down my cheeks. I was going to run away from the only home I had ever known. Hopefully, I would find a new place that suited me, with people who liked me, with friends and community. I wanted to belong somewhere so badly my heart ached—somewhere that wouldn't force the women and children to hide while the men ran wild. But I was afraid to hope.

I winced at the knock on my door. I quickly wiped away the tears. "Yeah?"

Mom opened the door. She tilted her head when she saw me. "Are you okay?"

"Yeah, I'm fine. I just got something in my eye."

"Mmhm." It was obvious I wasn't telling the truth, but she wasn't going to push it. Instead, she gave me an encouraging smile. "You look beautiful in that top, hon. It reminds me of the good old days when I was rocking bell-bottom jeans and dancing at human concerts."

I laughed. "I can't believe you were so wild when you were my age."

"You can't? Why? Is it because I'm too old and boring now?"

"Hardly! It's because you're all about gardening and drinking tea." I smiled, allowing myself to fall into the rhythm of the banter. "It's not about being old, but...I mean, you can hardly stay up past midnight, Mom."

She cackled. "Wow. Well, now I see what my daughter really thinks of me! I'll show you tonight that I can keep up just as well as you young folks."

"I'm looking forward to it."

"Let me put on my earrings, and then we'll head out, okay?"

"Sure." In better spirits, I looked around at my room—the old, faded blue sheet and the duvet that Mom had crocheted for my sixteenth birthday, the dried flowers, the white walls…As I implanted the view of my bedroom in my memory, I was struck by the sudden realization that this would be the last time I would see my bedroom.

I immediately shook off the feeling. *Stop letting Troy get in your head! Ignore his stupid threat, and let yourself enjoy one night! After all, you really are leaving tonight.* I nodded to myself and stepped out, closing the door behind me.

In another few minutes, Mom and I headed outside arm in arm. It was dusk now, and the sky was a beautiful gradient of bright marigold and fuchsia to violet and royal blue. Stars glinted throughout and left me feeling breathless and spellbound. I tightened my hold on Mom's arm slightly, and she squeezed me back.

If I had to leave right now and grab the pack I'd stashed in the branches of a tree near the dining hall, I would forever feel nostalgic for this moment with my mom and nature. But it wasn't time to go. Not yet. I hadn't experienced the party yet, and I wanted to spend more time with Mom before I left.

We walked toward the dining hall to eat an early dinner. In a few hours, the challenge ceremony would begin, but the arena had already been set up—there was a large dirt circle within view of the dining hall. In acknowledgment of the rite, men walked around shirtless, showing off the battle scars they'd earned when they were hunting.

Once the ceremony began, the competitors would shift into their wolf forms. The challengers would step up one by one to fight to the death against either the Alpha or the man in line to become Alpha. The men who weren't competing would gather around the circumference to make sure no one tried to escape the circle. The wolf left standing would become the Alpha, and afterward, an even larger celebration would occur. The pack would gather to drink and party and vie for the attention of their new Alpha to get in his good graces.

I took a cursory look at the shirtless, muscular wolves and then decided I'd keep my eyes to myself. I didn't want to risk spotting Troy. I didn't know if I could stand to be anywhere near him without dissolving into a puddle of tears. Instead, I looked at the women. Less of them wore flashy outfits, and there was quite a bit of skin showing. The women who were mated or claimed wore more muted colors to indicate that they were no longer on the market, and they kept their distance from the ruckus.

A mated pair might stick together at first and then drift apart, while a claimed pair were bound together forever. It was the single most important bond within a pack, just as strong as the one the Alpha shared with his people. From what Mom had explained, claiming happened during sex. The man would bite the woman, which would mark her as his and bond them together as true mates. As serious as being mated was, it was an even bigger deal for wolves to claim or be claimed because it could only happen once.

I thought the concept of being claimed was a really romantic one, but it was just one more difference between myself and my peers. The closest thing humans had to claiming was something called marriage, but they could separate after marriage. Wolves couldn't do that.

Mom and I headed inside the dining hall. Tonight's food would be the most plentiful and the most succulent because it was the final day of mourning. I took a deep breath, and my eyes began to slip closed at the savory scents that filled the air. I didn't need to have a shifter's sense of smell to tell that there was deliciousness in my future.

I loaded my plate high with vegetables that had been either simmered with salted meats or roasted over low flame. Main courses included braised beef, roasted poultry, and steamed fish. Mashed potatoes and rich, buttery gravy rounded out the meal. I intended to eat myself into a food coma. After Mom and I finished assembling our dinners, we looked around the packed dining hall for a place to sit.

Fortunately, there were a couple of empty spots at the table where mothers ate with their children. Mom and I shared an excited look. We were quite familiar with the younger generations of the pack. Mom knew them from the agricultural classes that she taught at the schoolhouse, and I often looked after the children in the summer when school wasn't in session.

We sat down at the end of the table, and the kids squealed happily at getting to sit near their two favorite people. Their mothers looked up at the ruckus and smiled at us.

"It's a beautiful night, isn't it?" one of the mothers said…to me!

I perked up. "Yes, I think so. I don't think the final day of this ceremony could have happened on a better night." After I said it, I winced inwardly and sent a glance at the tree that hid my bag. *Will they think that was stupid? Did I come off as trying too hard?*

But when nods and murmured agreements went around the table, I realized my fears were unfounded. The conversation continued without my input, but I didn't mind. I felt warmth in my chest at being included at all. Mom bumped me with her shoulder, and when I looked at her, I found a proud smile on her lips. I ducked my head, my cheeks flushing with pride. This, too, would be a memory that I would cherish once I had left.

I outright avoided the wolves my age because they were all under Troy's control, and the older wolves rarely acknowledged me. So I never really got the chance to speak to anyone other than Mom. That said, the newer mothers of the pack were more tolerant of my presence because I had such a good relationship with their children. Chatting with them was such a rare treat.

I focused for a while on the delicious foods. The flavors melted on my tongue, at once spicy and sweet and tangy and savory. The fruit and vegetables tasted so fresh and tender, thanks in no small part to Mom's skills in the garden. The richness of the food lulled me into a kind of non-thinking state where all that mattered was my plate and shoveling as much food inside me as I could. I occasionally snapped out of the fugue to speak to my mom or to drink some water, but for the most part, I kept my head down and enjoyed my meal.

When I finished, I raised my arms over my head and stretched out like a cat. *That was so tasty, but I shouldn't have eaten so much. It might come to bite me in the ass once I get going.* I felt a tug on my sleeve and looked down to see one of the children peering up at me. His name was Taren, and he was ten years old. He had his mother's light-brown hair and his father's blue eyes. When he smiled up at me, he revealed the adorable gap between his two front teeth.

"Look, look, Bryn," he said, pointing toward the entrance.

I looked and saw that while I'd been inhaling my food, most of the dining tables and buffet tables had been moved outside so everyone could eat under the stars. Because the Alpha challenge was still a few hours out, couples were out there dancing to the beat of pop music that played through portable speakers. Because so much had moved without my paying attention, I looked again at the tree where my bag was stashed. *Phew. It's still there.*

Out loud, I said, "Wow. Are you gonna go out there and dance, Taren?"

He nodded. "Uh-huh, I want to, but I don't want to go by myself. Would you dance with me?"

My heart swelled with affection for the boy, and I nodded. "Of course, as long as that's okay with your mommy?" I sent a questioning look to Taren's mother, who laughed and nodded.

"You'll be doing me a favor," she said. "He's been bugging me about going out there since they started moving the tables around."

I grinned. I looked at Mom, who winked back. "I hope the next dance is reserved for me."

"Of course," I laughed. "I'll come and get you after the next song."

"Come on, Bryn, come onnn!" Taren tugged me to my feet and towed me along to the dance floor. He was only ten, but his grip on my hand proved that he had incredible strength already. I decided not to think about how I was weaker than even a shifter child. That would only make me feel more out of place.

The air was cool enough to make our breath fog, but as Taren and I started moving, I hardly noticed the cold. We held hands and did funny dances together. To my delight, those closest to us would occasionally glance our way and smile at how silly we were. My heart beat quickly in my chest, and my face warmed with pleasure. Those glances were the closest thing to pack acceptance I'd ever experienced in my life. They left me feeling lighter than air and like I could do anything.

When Taren got tired and went to sit down, I made eye contact with Mom and gestured for her to come outside. When she arrived, she immediately fell into the rhythm of the song, moving gracefully to the pulse-pounding beat. As I shifted from silly dances to the way my body naturally wanted to move, Mom's dark eyes glimmered with amusement.

"It's so good to see you smile like this, honey," she said, raising her voice to be heard over the music. "And you dance so well! We should do this more often!"

I laughed. "Maybe, but nothing tops working in the garden with you!"

Mom beamed at the compliment and broke rhythm so she could pull me in for a hug. "I love you, sweetheart."

I hugged her back. I took in her lovely, earthy scent and felt tears in the back of my eyes. I would miss my mom so much, but hopefully, we would meet again someday.

Before the tears could flow, I pulled away so I could take her hand and twirl her around. "Love you too, Mom."

I danced for hours, but I kept a close eye on my bag, trying to figure out the best opportunity for my escape. As midnight drew near, the music shifted from pop to more traditional wolf music, which involved a lot of brass and pounding drums. The pack started to perform the traditional dances that accompanied the music, so we peeled away from the crowd. Mom gave me a kiss on my forehead and turned in for the night. I told her I would stay a little longer to watch the dancing.

Thus far, my night had been perfect—no, better than perfect. I had danced and eaten and had even shared a few smiles and laughs with the wolves. I wondered if I would feel this way more often if I were truly part of the pack. If I could shift, I wouldn't have to hide behind my boots and jackets in the cold—I could be as free as the others. I would know the sharp, graceful moves to the traditional dances. I had never been allowed to learn them because, according to my instructors and classmates, to teach a human would violate the tradition that established these dances.

If I were pack, I might have already caught the eye of a strong young wolf eager to prove his worth to the

Alpha before claiming me as his own on my birthday. For the first time in hours, the old sadness crept back in. I yearned to feel part of something larger than myself, to belong. But that would never—could never—happen to a human like me. Not here.

I've stayed long enough. No one's paying me any attention, so this is the perfect time to make my escape. I pushed myself to my feet.

"Bryn?"

The tiny voice made me stop. I looked down to see another young pup at my side. I couldn't remember this one's name, but I recognized him.

I smiled and crouched to be eye-level with him. "What is it, sweetie?"

"I got you some punch." He held up the cup. "Want some?"

"How did you know I was thirsty?" I gently pinched his cheek. "Yes, I'd love some."

He blushed when I accepted the drink and then ran away. I chuckled as I straightened from my crouch. The boy acted like he was handing me a bouquet rather than a drink.

I downed the punch in a few long gulps and wiped my mouth with my sleeve. There was a slightly bitter aftertaste in the punch, but I figured someone hadn't mixed it properly. I headed toward the tree, but as I walked, the tree began to shift and distort before my eyes. I stumbled forward and placed a hand to my head as if doing so could hold back the onslaught of dizziness.

What's happening to me? Why am I suddenly so...sleepy...? I heard a whine, brief and distant. My pulse spiked, but not from excitement. A wave of anxiety prickled across my skin. Something was very, very wrong. I tried to walk back to the cabin, toward my mom, who would help me. I made it a few more yards, stumbling over the ground that shifted beneath my feet, but before long, I was overcome with exhaustion.

I groaned as I slowly pulled myself out of a void of unconsciousness. I opened my eyes, but my vision was still unstable. All I could make out was that I was in a dark room. I sat up, my body stiff and sore. I lifted a hand to push my hair out of my face and noticed something chafing my wrist. *What...the hell?* I turned my head, and my stomach dropped. My wrists and ankles were bound to the wall with thick rope. I realized with a second surge of horror that I was naked but for my bra and panties.

Oh, no! No! My vision was still blurry, but the last of my grogginess quickly disappeared. I tugged as hard as I could at my bindings, but the ropes were too secure.

"Help!" I shrieked. "Somebody help me, please!"

Silence answered me. I tried again to yank at the ropes but only succeeded in exhausting myself. I sank against the wall, tears of frustration and panic welling in my eyes. I quickly rubbed them away. I needed to be able to see where I was. Maybe I could get a handle on how to escape.

My vision had cleared enough that I could see there was a window in the left-hand wall. Light from the moon entered the room, but it illuminated only four, maybe five feet in front of me. It wasn't enough for me to see where I was or how I was tied up. I cast desperate eyes around the room. I could dimly make out the dark shapes of a bed and a couple of nightstands through the darkness, but little else.

Movement on the armchair caused my breath to catch in my throat. One of the inky black shadows of the room was *moving,* gathering itself up and stepping toward me. I shrieked even before my brain processed that the person stepping into the moonlight was Troy.

He laughed at me and reached for his crotch to adjust himself. I immediately stopped screaming and pressed my back against the wall. I knew my fear turned him on, but I couldn't stop the tears that slipped down my cheeks. Troy's expression was full of malice, but his gaze was that of a famished man. I couldn't tell if he was after my blood or my body. Either way, it couldn't be good for me.

"What's happening?" I asked, my voice the trembling squeak of a frightened mouse. "How did I get here?"

"How do you think?"

I tried to search my memory, and for a second, it was frightfully blank. But then flashes of the night's festivities returned to me. I remembered the little boy and the drink, and…

"D-did you slip me something?"

He slammed his hand against the wall beside my head, and I flinched in spite of myself. "That's right. I told that pup to bring you a drink. I knew you'd never drink it if I gave it to you."

I shuddered. I could hardly wrap my mind around the sickness that allowed Troy to take advantage of my soft spot for children.

"I had my men follow you so when you passed out, they could carry you back here. To my bedroom." As he spoke, he flicked on a light—briefly illuminating the clean white walls, gold bed sheets, two nightstands, an armchair, and the rope and pulley system that kept me bound—and then flicked it off again. "Oh, and they noticed that you kept glancing at one of the trees near the dining hall. One of them climbed up and found your bag."

I couldn't hold in a gasp and immediately hated myself for making another noise, for giving him the satisfaction. Troy walked toward his bed at the back of the room, and I heard him open a drawer. He walked back into the light and held up the worn bag that I'd stashed in the tree. A bit of sap had rubbed off on the strap.

"Look at this. Look at this. Aren't you a clever one?" He opened the bag and began to toss around the map, the clothes, the rations, all the things that I would need to help me escape. "I bet you were thinking you could slip away during the challenge ceremony." He grinned. "Lucky for me, I had already planned a few steps ahead."

He tossed the bag to the side, kicking and stomping on my things as I looked on in horror. He giggled, watching the color drain from my face.

"Truth be told," he went on, "I was hoping you'd wake up before the challenge ceremony so I could see the look on your face when you realized how fucked you are."

I stared at him, my heart pounding against my rib cage.

He laughed and again shifted the bulge in his pants. "Yeah, that's the one."

I looked away from him, my lower lip trembling. "What are you going to do with me?" I had to know, even though I knew the answer was likely that he planned to kill or torture me.

"Oh, I've got something *wonderful* planned for the little human who could never be pack no matter how hard she tries."

He moved across the room to where the pulley system was hooked up to the right-hand wall. As he cranked, the ropes on my limbs began to drag me against the wall and up into a standing position. I screamed and fought, but no matter how hard I struggled, I couldn't stop the ropes from pulling me flush with the wall. My limbs were spread out, leaving me exposed to him.

He licked his lips as he walked toward me. "I set up the ropes myself," he said. "You should be grateful because it's for your birthday."

"What are you talking about?"

"You'll be twenty in just a few hours, when the moon reaches its apex in the sky. After I claim my position as Alpha, I'm going to come back here and take your virginity from you."

I gasped sharply. "N-no. You c-can't!"

"But I can, Bryn. As Alpha, no one can stop me, and you'll be bound to me for the rest of your pathetic little life." He pressed his hand against the wall next to my head and leaned in close, overwhelming me with the miasma of his presence. "Then you will never find another mate. No one would have you once your purity is mine. And you, poor thing, will live as my slave for the rest of your days."

He stepped back. Tears continued to drip from my chin as the awful enormity of what he'd just said slammed into me.

"What a sad face. I'll tell you what, Bryn—if you're a good little girl, I'll let you suck my cock every night before bed. After all, it's the best treatment you can hope for."

I felt myself beginning to get sick again, but I didn't understand. I *couldn't* understand what Troy could mean. "But *why?* Why would you want to claim me when you hate me so much?"

Something in him snapped. He spat at me. The glob, cooling en route, landed on my cheek and slid down my chin. I almost vomited right then, but somehow I kept it together. It was probably the fear of what he'd do to me if I dirtied his floor.

He came at me again, growling in anger. "How stupid can you be? I would never want to be with filth like you. I would never taint my line with your weak blood. No, you are mated to me, and you'll never be with another man. But make no fucking mistake, Bryn—I'll tear your body apart with this cock, but I will never claim you."

My head swam. *I-it doesn't matter! I'm human, so he can't bind me to him forever. It doesn't work like that!* I wanted to introduce some hope to the situation, but even that bit of comfort couldn't compete with the bleak future Troy proposed. *Doesn't matter whether you're wolf or human. He's still going to rape you tonight, and he's going to force you to be his slave. And no one will save you. Not even Mom.*

As if he knew the dark path my thoughts had taken, he laughed at me again and reached between my legs. He gripped my sex in his hand and squeezed hard enough for me to cry out. And then, just when I thought the pain would be too much, he pulled back and slapped me across the face. Pain sparked across my cheek as I blinked stars out of my vision.

"Don't worry, Bryn, there will be plenty more where that came from." He started to walk toward the door. "I've got a challenge ceremony to prepare for, but I'll see you tonight." He sent one more awful smile at me before walking through the door.

My head fell, and tears poured and poured out of me. I knew it was over. Troy had won. If only a dashing knight would appear to whisk me away to safety. But no, that was just a desperate attempt to escape into fantasy and away from the awful reality that I faced now.

Chapter 8 - Night

I bounced on the balls of my feet and flexed my muscles in anticipation of what was to come. The winter air was crisp and clear, the silver, full moon hung high and pregnant in the dark sky, and all I could think was that it was a perfect night for staging a takeover. My wolf whined and panted within me, practically turning in circles, eager to get things started. I couldn't blame my wolf for being so hyped up. The smell of the excitement in the Kings' compound, combined with the knowledge of what I was about to accomplish, would make any wolf lose its shit.

Tonight, I would end the reign of the Redwolf Alphas. My mother could go on and on about destiny all she wanted, but tonight? I would take my fate into my *own* hands, take back what belonged to me, and I would lift the Wargs up to our rightful place at the top.

I knew there would be fallout once I killed Troy. I knew that the Kings would be worried about what I was going to do to them, but I had thought this through. I wasn't a tyrant—those who wanted to leave could leave if they wanted, and those who wanted to challenge me for the position could try. It was within their right. All I wanted to do was restore some balance to the Idaho panhandle. And all I had to do was get rid of the cruel little boy who stood in my way.

I was ready and rearing to go, but I kept my focus turned outward, not in. I heard Dom's footsteps approaching from behind, even though he was trying to keep quiet. I felt more in tune with the area around me and my senses than ever before. I felt *alive.*

"What's up?" I asked, turning to Dom.

"The squads are in position. They're ready for your command."

I grinned slowly. My wolves and I were closer to the compound than we'd been last night, but not so close that we weren't able to mask our scent. The extra precaution wasn't necessary. As I suspected, all of the Kings' pack was in attendance for the Alpha ceremony, including their hunters and sentries. We scouted around the compound once an hour just to make sure that their borders remained unprotected and, of course, nothing had changed.

I chuckled to myself and shook my head. *What a shame, the new Kings' Alpha is too cocky for his own good. He would leave his pack unprotected just to make sure that everyone is present to see his coronation.*

"Listen, Dom." I turned to my beta. "There are still a few hours before the ceremony, so I want to use that time to our advantage."

Dom raised a brow. "I'm almost afraid to ask, but how are you planning on using that time?"

"I want to enter from their own compound when I announce that I'm here to challenge him as Alpha. I want to see the look on his face when he realizes how easy it was for me to get in." If Troy's men tried to apprehend me, my hunters would emerge from the forest and surround them, thus leveling the playing field.

"Wow. That's…not exactly what I was expecting to hear from you. What are you going to do while you're over there?"

"I'll probably do some snooping in his cabin." Why not? It would be mine after tonight anyway.

Dom let out a long-suffering sigh and shook his head. "You're just full of good ideas tonight, aren't you? Well, when it's time, I'll let our team know you're doing recon and to wait for your signal."

I reached over to ruffle Dom's hair, just as I knew my beta and oldest friend hated. "That's what I keep you around for, Dom." I was in a rare mood tonight. But then, on the eve of my ascension, I figured I was allowed to let loose a little.

"Really?" Dom moved out of my reach, his hair mussed into an unfortunate mop on his head. He patted it back into place, glaring at me. "You just make sure you get out of there at the first sign of trouble, got it?"

"Sure, sure. I've got it." I smirked at Dom as he tried to tame his hair back into a more respectable style.

I looked up at the moon's spot in the sky. The challenge ceremony would be happening soon. I needed to get moving.

"It's time, Dom," I said. "Let the others know to be ready."

Dom nodded and sprinted off to carry out my orders. The night before, I'd had my men verify which cabin belonged to Troy. Now that it was finally time, I did my name justice by slipping into the shadows to infiltrate the compound.

I slipped from building to building, but I didn't have to—everyone was too drunk, too sleepy, or too distracted to notice that I had snuck through their borders. I was sure I could have waltzed in through the opening without alerting any suspicion. But it was better to remain cautious during these sorts of missions—even if the opponent threw caution to the wind.

It wasn't hard to find Troy's home. He lived in the Alpha's cabin, a property that was much larger than not only my own cabin but also the other cabins of the Kings' pack. It had likely started out more humbly, and as the territory passed hands, each Alpha added more to it. Given the lumber that was piled near the western side of the cabin, Troy was probably in the process of expanding it even further now that our father was dead.

On the second story, there was a window large enough for me to fit through. With one leap, I grabbed hold of the sill and tested the window. It was unlocked, so I pushed it the rest of the way open and slipped quietly inside.

I landed in a crouch and surveyed the room. It was dark here, but my wolf senses allowed me to see what was around me. I seemed to be in a den filled with shelves and shelves of books. I scoffed at the idea that any of the Redwolfs would ever crack open a book or that they were even capable of reading. If they cared at all about books, they wouldn't be such a disgrace.

Now that I was sure I was the only one in the den, I went to touch one of the spines of the books. My fingers came away dusty. As I'd thought, none of these had been used in years, maybe even decades. They were likely just for display, meant to impress visiting Alphas, or they had belonged to previous Kings' Alphas.

I froze. I thought I'd heard something. It was just for a second, nothing more than a squeak or a sigh or something like that. I tilted my head, listening for any sign that there was another soul in the cabin. But the sound didn't come again. *Must be a rat.* I told myself to keep moving.

The den opened to a large hallway. As I reached it, the smell of dusty books and old rugs gave way to Troy's scent. My wolf sneezed repeatedly, and I tried to soothe him. The odor was terrible and pungent, and it made both me and my wolf want to gag. It was the stink of someone who had nothing to offer other than the corroded sludge they were made from. It left me wishing for an open window or something that I could use to get the scent out of my head.

Because it was so overwhelming, it didn't take long for me to acclimate to the smell. I continued down the hall. The cabin was furnished with antique furniture, and the flooring was freshly polished. It didn't so much as creak as I stepped across it. On the walls were pictures of Troy,

Gregor, and Troy's mother. I scowled at them. The sooner I could burn this place down, the better.

As I neared the far corner of the cabin, another scent hit me. Hard.

I inhaled deeply and marveled at the way the aroma clung to the air like perfume. I took another deep breath, and the scent wrapped around me like a warm blanket. It was like nothing I had ever smelled before. It was like the smell of spring grass first thing in the morning when dew still clung to each blade. It was sweet magnolias mixed with the scent of fresh earth, and something about it made my wolf howl.

I had to investigate where it was coming from. I couldn't complete this mission without finding its source. So I followed it, allowing it to take me out of that hallway and toward a closed, red door. I leaned forward and took a few tentative sniffs at the door. Oh, yes. Whatever was behind this would reveal what was causing that divine smell.

Now that I was so close to it, I realized the scent was laced with the spicy scent of fear. That thought disturbed me more than a random smell ought to, but I couldn't shake it off. I took another whiff, and my shoulders relaxed somewhat. I thanked the powers that be that I couldn't detect any indication of sex behind the door. The last thing I wanted to do was walk in on Troy balls-deep in one of his mistresses. Though, if nothing else, it would make a great story for me to bring back to the Wargs.

I placed my hand on the knob. I was prepared to head inside, but right before I opened the door, the faintest sob reached my ears. Despite the enticingly potent aroma, I stepped back—my wolf whined at the delay, but I ignored its protests. That sob—it didn't belong to Troy. It had come from either a woman or a child, but none of the intel I had on Troy revealed that he had a family or a mate.

I frowned, considering what to do next. I didn't relish the idea of hurting—or worse, killing—another wolf, especially if they were a woman or a child. At the same time, I couldn't risk being caught. I'd put too much work into this moment for it to fail just because I'd startled someone.

A scream from whoever was behind the door would either result in one of two things. Either I would be carted away before I could challenge the piece of shit, a humiliation from which I would never recover. Or I'd have to run, an awful defeat. Neither of those outcomes was appealing to me after I had worked so hard to steal back my birthright. I took another sniff and was confused when I didn't detect the bit of spice that told me there was another wolf nearby.

If I fucked up here, the Kings would undoubtedly step up their patrols and their guarding. I might not get another chance to end Troy.

I ought to walk away and continue my mission before this person found me out, but my curiosity won. I had to know what was going on in this room. So, I slowly twisted the knob and took a tentative step inside. I was prepared to be ambushed by a shifter, regardless of what my nose was telling me. But there were still no wolves nearby. The first thing I noticed was an empty bed so big it would take up over half of my living space back home.

I scowled. *Really? Troy sleeps on gold sheets? I cannot wait to knock this fuck down a peg and then quickly torch this place to the ground.*

My gaze roamed to the back wall, and my heart just about stopped. There was a woman stripped down to her underwear and tied to the wall. Ropes had left her skin raw and red, and she was silently crying tears that dripped onto the wood floors. I stared at her, a slew of questions forming in my brain before I finally settled on one. *What kinky bullshit is this?*

I should have known that a man like Troy would leave a woman so vulnerable while he partied it up with the other Kings. I could judge him, but for all I knew, this might have been consensual. The woman's head was down, and she was whimpering quietly to herself. She hadn't heard me, which meant I could still salvage this.

If I was quick and quiet, I might be able to leave the room without her noticing me. I took a careful step back. I never once made any sort of noise, but just then, the woman looked up. My reflexes kicked in, and I crossed the room in a blink. Worried she'd scream, I went to cover her mouth, but I stopped when I saw her eyes. They were steel blue and almost glowed in the darkness. I knew those eyes—they'd plagued my dreams for weeks, maybe even months now.

What did this mean? Was the girl in my fantasies real? I didn't know what to think. Those dreams fucked with me, and it seemed they continued to do so even as I stood awake.

I sniffed the air again, smelling nothing but the earthy sweet scent of her natural aroma. She was every bit as beautiful as I'd thought she'd be—thick auburn hair bound back in a braid and a sweet, heart-shaped face with features so delicate they were almost elven. As for her body, she wore only a bra and panties. She was petite and lithe, but there were curves to her hips, to her thighs, to her chest—I quickly looked away. It was wrong to ogle her when she was in such a compromising position.

This woman was the source of the fear I'd smelled outside the door, and she was clearly a prisoner. I'd never known a human—hell, I'd never known a *wolf* to smell this wonderful. How was any of this possible?

Though my thoughts spiraled out of control, my wolf wasn't anywhere near as alarmed or perplexed. He wagged his tail and howled again, pining to be closer to this woman. The urge was so powerful, it actually made me take a step closer before I got control of myself. *Stop that.*

"Who are you?" I asked the woman.

She didn't immediately respond. She continued to stare at me, those will-o'-the-wisp eyes spearing right through my soul. My hands clenched and unclenched as I waited for some kind of response. Did this woman see something familiar in me too? If so, did that mean that we'd shared all of those intimate dreams? I didn't know how I felt about that.

The woman's tears continued to fall, dripping from her chin to the ground, but her gaze never wavered from mine. The longer we looked at each other, the more I realized that I saw something darker and older than just fear in her expression. It was something I recognized in myself, something I'd felt more than once when I was just a teenager, before I took over the Wargs pack.

Back then, every day had been a struggle. The previous Alpha was lazy and preferred to let my pack waste away rather than trying to fight for resources. He would hog the better things for himself and leave my people with nothing. I was sick of watching my friends and my mom waste away to nothing just trying to get food on the table, and I'd finally felt strong enough to do something about it. Unlike me, this girl seemed to be at the mercy of an actual monster. She couldn't fight back, not as she was. Whoever this girl was, she'd seen some shit, and it had left her scarred. Like I was scarred.

"Who are you?" I asked again, and my voice came more softly this time.

Hearing my voice again seemed to get her to snap out of it. Some of the shine returned to her eyes, but she remained silent. I watched her war with herself over how she ought to respond. Her only options were to scream for help or ask me to save her.

I ran my hand through my hair as she debated. I wanted to ask her more questions, but we hadn't gotten past the first one. I wanted to know what the hell she was doing in the Alpha's room, naked and all tied…up. I stopped. My eyes moved from the ropes to the red welt on her cheek. Realization hit me at a hundred miles per hour. Rage surged up within me, and my wolf snarled.

Troy, the sick fuck, was planning on taking advantage of this girl tonight. He probably wanted to use her to celebrate after he became Alpha. Whatever else he wanted to do to her could only get worse from there. I'd known that the women of the Kings' pack were treated poorly, but *this?* This was foul.

Something yanked at my chest, and the need to save the woman overruled everything else—the challenge ceremony, my mission, and even the opportunity for victory. I couldn't afford to think about any of those things while this woman was in such obvious danger. I needed to get her as far away from Troy as possible.

I glanced at the door. Troy could come in at any moment. I could take his life without thinking twice about it, but could I do it without risking harm to this woman? Could I get her out safely? Or should I leave her here and save her after the challenge ceremony had ended? When I became Alpha, I could make sure that anyone involved in her capture suffered dearly. But the idea of leaving her like this made my blood boil. I needed to come up with something better.

Fuck me. Why do I care about this random woman? The question echoed in my mind with no answer. I knew there was no logic behind it. Even stranger, I found that I didn't need logic. She needed me, and that was all that mattered. Now, if I could just come up with my next move, I could stop acting like a sitting duck.

"Hey." Though her voice was soft and hoarse from all the crying and yelling she must have done, it stopped everything for me. I turned my attention to her, ready and willing to do whatever she needed me to do. But her next words left me speechless.

"Who the hell are *you*?"

Chapter 9 - Bryn

I knew that this stranger had asked who I was, but given my current situation and the fact that this man had clearly broken in, I figured I was owed an answer first. As he considered how to answer, I tried to figure out what to do next.

I had never seen this man on the compound before, but those eyes were the same emerald green of the man who haunted my dreams. More than that, I knew exactly who he was from the photo that hung in the schoolhouse. There was no mistaking that hard jawline, those sharp cheekbones, or that thick hair as dark as the midnight sky, even in the dimness of the moonlight shining in through the window.

He didn't look exactly like the photo. His shoulders had become much broader, his hair had been buzzed down on the sides while the top was left long, and he was much taller than I had imagined—he had at least a foot on me. But of course, there were the tattoos that peeked under the collar of his black, long-sleeved shirt. I had a better view of them than offered by the blurry picture in school; they appeared to be tribal tattoos intersecting with each other at his neck and shoulder and spreading down his right arm.

He was Night Shepherd, Alpha of the Wargs pack.

What the hell is he doing here? My mind raced to come up with some sort of explanation. It couldn't have anything to do with me—no one knew I was there. And more than that, why was he looking at me like he knew me?

I opened my mouth to ask him these questions, but my voice died in my throat when he stepped closer to me. He was only a few inches away, and I could smell the scent of him. It was like pine and crushed wildflowers. He evoked memories of the forest in summertime—warmth and freshness and life. I wanted to lean closer to him, to get a better sniff, but my brain revolted against that impulse. *This guy is from the Wargs! What the hell am I thinking?*

I pulled at my restraints, my eyes widening as he leaned a few inches closer. Those *eyes*—how was it possible that they could be so green, so vibrant, and so full of danger? How could someone so gorgeous carry such a wild, terrifying energy about him?

"Who *are* you?" I demanded again, surprised when my voice didn't waver.

He tilted his head at my question, the way an animal would when listening to a new sound. He grunted in reply and moved even closer. The ropes strained as I recoiled.

Practically naked, I was in such a compromised position—at the mercy of yet another Alpha male.

"No, who are you?" Night's voice was gruff and yet so smooth—the timbre of thunder. "And what are you doing here?"

I swallowed hard, but I didn't look away; I couldn't even if I wanted to—the jewel green of his eyes wouldn't let mine go. "Because of Troy," I replied. "He put me here."

"That much is obvious," he said. "His scent is all over this place. I'm asking why?"

I clenched my hands against a deep shudder. "He said he—" I stopped as tears spilled onto my cheeks. My hands clenched tighter, so tight I felt my nails digging into my palms. "He said he plans to rape me and keep me as his slave."

Memories of Troy and that awful smirk flashed through my mind, and my blood rushed hard and fast in my veins. I hated him, hated that he'd put me in this position. He didn't view me as a person, just as an object that he could use for his own pleasure, and it was infuriating that I was so powerless to stop him.

Night's nostrils flared, and a deep growl emanated from his chest. He flashed his canines, slightly sharper than the average wolf's in human form, and I felt something spark deep within me. That spark spread across my skin, making me feel warm and tingly all over. I'd felt this way before, but only in the warm darkness of the dreams I'd had of the stranger with the green eyes. *Were those dreams about him? Night Shepherd?*

No. No. I couldn't get distracted. Now wasn't the time for me to be thinking about the tension in his jaw, or the way his dark hair had fallen over his forehead, or those vibrantly green eyes...

Stop it! I gave myself a mental shake. *Troy could be coming back at any moment! This guy is probably dangerous, but if it's either staying here or asking him to help me, I think my choice is obvious.*

The challenge ceremony would begin just before the moon reached the center of the sky. The idea was that starting it at that moment would allow the new Alpha to fight his way into the new day and claim his position of power. I knew Troy had left to prepare for the ceremony, but that didn't mean he wouldn't come back.

The last thing I ought to be doing was thinking about a stranger as anything other than a jumping-off point. Escape was all that mattered.

"Listen, that doesn't matter now," I said. "We need to get out of here."

His lips slowly covered his teeth, and one of his eyebrows rose as if to say, *we?*

Panic began to prickle up and down my spine. There was a possibility that this guy would abandon me here. The thought reawakened the hopelessness I had felt when I was alone in the room with Troy.

"Please," I whispered. "I need your help. At least— at least let me out of these restraints. I-I'm sure I can handle things on my own from there."

But I wasn't sure of that at all. My legs had started to go numb before Night showed up, and now I could hardly feel them. My arms weren't much better; I could move them and clench my hands, but even my upper body had started to lose feeling from lack of blood flow. However, Night didn't need to know that right now. I could figure it out once I wasn't in restraints any longer.

Night's gaze shifted to the door. *No, no, no, no!*

"Please," I said again, more forcefully. Tears stung in my eyes, but I was beyond caring about the warmth slipping down my cheeks and dripping from my chin. "You—you can't leave me here like this. I don't want to be here when Troy gets back because if I am, he'll stop at nothing to kill me. He'll even go through you."

Again, Night raised an eyebrow. Skepticism. I realized then that the reason Night was here was most likely to take advantage of the challenge ceremony. Whether he planned to challenge Troy or steal something from him while he was away was unclear, but I knew he thought he could take Troy down. With those muscles and that height, well, maybe he could. But I doubted Troy would fight fairly.

"Alright, alright, don't cry," Night said. "I'll get you out."

Relief crashed over me, a balm to the itch of anxiety that coursed through my body. Night stepped close to me and reached for the restraints. Our chests were almost touching, and I could feel the heat of his body radiating from him.

"I'm Night, by the way," he said. "Night Shepherd."

I nodded. "I figured as much."

His gaze flashed to mine briefly before returning to the restraints. "How did you *figure* out who I was?"

"We, um…we learned about you in school, of course."

"Right, of course—a human learning about me—in a school taught by wolves." His large hands worked at the knot around my wrist. "Just hold still while I get you out."

I was surprised when a chuckle escaped my lips and was even more surprised when I joked, "Not like I'm going anywhere right now."

Night's lip twitched. It wasn't quite a smirk, but it was very close. I knew that being tied up for so long must have done something to my head because I felt some amount of pride that I'd made the Alpha of the Wargs almost smirk.

He tried to loosen the knots around my wrists but finding he couldn't, claws extended from his nails in a partial shift. I had seen wolves shift plenty of times before, but they always glared at me when they noticed me nearby. When I asked Mom about it, she said that it was because wolves always got paranoid about shifting around a human, given the way humans tended to treat them.

But Night didn't hesitate to shift in front of me. Later, I'd wonder if it was because the situation didn't call for that sort of paranoia or if he genuinely didn't care.

He sliced through each of the ropes, and I dropped to the ground. I gasped at the pain that shot through my body from my knees and shoulder. I tried to push myself up to my feet, but my legs buckled. My worst fears were realized; after hours of being suspended, I could no longer support my own weight.

Night's hand shifted back into a human one as he reached out to me. "Easy, easy."

At his touch, another spark ignited within me. I jerked out of his grasp and stumbled back against the wall, losing my balance and sliding to the floor.

He released a tight, frustrated breath. "Just stop moving for a minute, and you'll—" Then he stopped speaking, and his body went stiff.

I wasn't sure why until I heard the creaking hinges of the front door. My entire body shuddered, goosebumps itching across my skin. *Oh no, oh no, he's back!* My thoughts crashed into each other, no longer words, just images of Troy bursting into the room and catching Night and me—free but weakened—together.

I tried again to get to my feet. I managed to stand but had to press my hand to the wall to support myself. There was no way I could run in this state. I was as good as dead, and I knew it.

Night, his eyes glowing an intense green, glanced from me to the door and back again. He knew just as well as I did that Troy had to be on his way up here—with his enhanced senses, he probably knew exactly where Troy was in relation to us—but he didn't seem afraid or even nervous. His widened pupils, twitching fingers, and slightly elevated breathing all indicated to me that he was practically salivating at the prospect of Troy finding us.

That was when the realization hit me. *He's here to kill Troy, not to steal anything from him!*

"Oh, Bryn," Troy's voice had raised several octaves in a sick, singsong tone. He was on the stairs. "Bryn, are you awake?"

I shivered and pushed away from the wall. My heart was thumping at a galloping pace, threatening to beat its way right out of my chest. What could I do? I looked at the window, and inspiration flared inside me. The only way out, my only hope, was the window. I wouldn't have the strength to escape, but maybe Mom would see me.

Or maybe the fall would kill me.

"Bryn," Troy said again, "I hope you're excited about tonight. I've come up with even more *activities* for us to do after I've claimed my throne."

I bit back a whimper as I forced myself to move closer to the window. My body denied my urging to go faster. My knees threatened to buckle again. But Troy was even closer now, likely right down the hall, and what's worse—his words were slurred. I needed to *move*. Who knew what he was capable of when he was drunk?

"I just had to see you squirm again, Bryn," Troy said. He sounded hungry. "I want to imagine your fear when I become Alpha—"

Suddenly Night let out a growl. It was louder than the one he'd made when he and I were alone, and it was full of warning. I looked back at him so fast that I nearly lost my balance again. Was he angry on my behalf?

Troy's singsong voice stopped immediately. I froze, my body tense. The silence that followed was icy and filled with apprehension.

And then Troy let out a vicious snarl. He knew there was a stranger in here with me. It had probably only taken him so long to notice because he was intoxicated. Troy sprinted to the door, kicking it in so hard that the wood ripped from the hinges and flipped end over end into the opposite wall. The door shattered, chunks of wood flying across the room.

I would have screamed, but the sight of Troy's face—red with rage, his lips pulling away from glistening fangs—caused my voice to die in my throat. I began to slowly move toward the window again, never taking my eyes off Troy.

Recognition flashed across those dark, terrible eyes as he saw Night. The rivalry between them was legendary—deep, bloody, and stretching back for years.

"Get the fuck away from her, Shepherd," Troy spat, his voice deeper and slightly muffled for having to speak around those sharp teeth. "She's *my* toy. No one else's!"

I could no longer see Night's face because I was behind him, but his expression caused Troy's fingertips to slowly shift into claws, fur coating the backs of his hands. In response, Night's claws shifted too.

"I'll kill you where you stand for daring to cross into my territory, Shepherd," Troy growled.

Night remained still, watchful. Compared to Troy, who was about ready to shift completely into a wolf, he appeared calm, collected, and controlled.

I didn't want to wait to see what would happen between the two. My hand found the windowpane. I'd made it. Finally. I flattened my palm against the cold glass and pushed it upward. I tried to be discrete, but the window squeaked. Troy's gaze flashed to me, and again, I froze, a rabbit in the path of a hungry, crazed wolf.

Troy let out a loud howl. His muscles tensed, straining beneath his clothes, and then he charged toward me. My hands clenched into fists. I was going to die. I was—

Night's hand flashed out, lightning fast, and gripped the back of Troy's collar. The fabric of Troy's shirt tore like paper, no match for the strength of two Alphas, but Troy stumbled, his momentum interrupted by Night. As he began to lose his balance, Night's claws clamped down on Troy's wrist. He yanked him back and slammed his other fist into Troy's gut.

The air whooshed out of Troy's mouth, along with spittle and blood. He flew back onto his bed, clutching his midsection. Blood coated his lips from where his fangs had bitten into his tongue.

Night stalked toward the bed with a bloodthirsty purpose. Troy looked up at him, his eyes wide with an emotion I had never seen on him before—fear.

But then answering howls from outside brought Night up short. Reinforcements were on the way. We were out of time.

Night spun on his heel and sprinted toward me. The front door of the cabin slammed open again as Night reached me. I gasped as he wrapped his arm around my waist. He yanked the window the rest of the way open and shoved me outside. I screamed as I fell...into a bush just below the window. The branches scratched at my arms, but I hardly noticed over the chill of the night air. I was still practically nude and immediately began to shiver from both cold and adrenaline.

A brisk breeze caused goosebumps to rise across my skin. I grunted, struggling to break free from the bush as Night slipped gracefully through the window after me. Footsteps reached Troy's room, confused yells echoing down from the window as Troy's entourage checked on their almost-Alpha.

"Let's go," Night said, scooping me into his arms. I felt the heat of his skin beneath his shirt, a warm comfort compared to the cold and confusion around us.

Chapter 10 - Bryn

Night threw me over his shoulder, wrapping his strong arms around my lower legs, and he started running. The Kings' compound became a blur around me as he sprinted for the tree line. His steps fell almost soundlessly across the ground. Everything was happening so fast that my brain was slow to catch up.

"I need all of my men to me now!" Troy's voice boomed from the cabin. It seemed he'd recovered enough to holler at the top of his lungs. "Bring her back here!"

I looked up and saw Troy's face, red with anger and humiliation, standing at the window, pointing down at us. And that was when the gravity of the situation caught up with me. I was being kidnapped by the Alpha of the pack that my mom, my schoolteachers, and every wolf in the Kings' pack claimed was aggressive, feral, and unhinged.

I can't just sit back and allow this to happen to me! I balled my cold hands into fists and beat at his back, pretending that Night's tight, muscular ass wasn't flexing just a few inches from my face as he ran. I tried to wiggle my legs, but his grip on me was as tight as steel, and my feeble attempts at fighting were no match for him.

I felt another burst of heat and anger flash through me, and I screamed, cursing both Night and Troy as loudly as I could.

"Put me down!" I called. "Put me down, you asshole!"

Night ignored me, so I continued.

"I'm so sick and tired of werewolves doing whatever they like to me! Why can't any of you listen to me for even one second?" I punctuated my questions with another volley of ineffective blows to his back.

"Probably because you're so fucking annoying," he growled. "Shut up already."

"No! I hope I scream until all you hear for the rest of your life is *my voice!*"

I had spent my entire life with my head down. And now I was mad enough to leave any wolf who crossed me bloody and blue—if only my strength could match those desires. All I had going for me was my voice, but it was unlikely that any of the Kings would hear me; the ceremony was still in full swing, and everyone would be focused on getting drunk or getting lucky. Few would pay the screaming any mind.

Angry tears filled my eyes and were stolen by the wind. Once again, I was powerless to do anything as another Alpha stole me away to do whatever he wanted to me. Why couldn't I be in charge of my own life?

I wiped the tears on my arm and lifted my head to look back toward the Redwolf cabin. I saw Troy's men burst out from the door, eyes glowing brightly in the darkness. Because they weren't encumbered with a screaming, fighting girl, they closed the distance much faster than Night could run. They were within thirty feet, now twenty, and the tree line was still a few yards away.

But before they reached me, men I'd never seen before exploded from between the trees, intercepting Troy's men before they could reach us. Howls split the night as the men engaged each other, some transforming into wolves, others remaining bipedal. I knew those noises would alert the rest of the pack that something was going on.

Night ignored it all. His pace never slowed or faltered, and he never looked back—not even when the sounds of fighting grew louder.

Soon we reached the woods, and my vision of the fighting wolves, the cabins, and the only home I'd ever known was swallowed by trees and darkness.

Night was still running even after we had left the Kings' compound behind for what felt like several miles. The parts of my body that were directly in contact with Night were fine, but my back and my arms were lit with goosebumps, and my fingers were starting to feel numb. *I need to get out of this somehow.* I knew I needed to escape, but actually freeing myself from Night was another story entirely.

Of course, Night was extremely strong. Yelling and fighting had done nothing to deter him—his grip on me hadn't let up once, and he seemed to have enough energy to keep running at this pace forever. I thought about the wolves I'd seen emerging from the forest to defend Night. Then again, I liked my prospects with one werewolf rather than a small pack of them.

He'll have to set me down at some point, right? Even wolves need to sleep or eat or go to the bathroom. I knew he would easily catch up with me if I wasn't smart about my escape. Unfortunately, there was nothing I could do to level the playing field between us in terms of strength, agility, or speed. If he wanted to find me, he would probably be able to track me by scent.

Troy had discovered my bag with the supplies I needed to escape, so even if I did get away, I would have no clothes, no food, and no real way of navigating through the surrounding werewolf packs' territories.

My prospects were bleak, but I still needed to try, didn't I? I squeezed my eyes shut against the stinging tears. *Maybe dying of exposure or hypothermia is better than whatever this Alpha has planned for me.* I'd known Troy all my life, but I'd had no idea he was capable of something as sick as confining me to his room to be his own personal sex toy. Who knew what depraved plans this wild Alpha could have in mind for me?

In my dreams, those green eyes had been filled with nothing but tenderness and lust, but I couldn't trust that, could I?

I stiffened when Night's pace suddenly began to slow. He let out a sigh as he came to a stop. *Here's my chance! I need to—*

"Ouch!" I cried out as Night dumped me onto the cold, hard ground. I was sure I'd bruised my tailbone. "Damn it," I snapped, pulling myself into a sitting position onto a nearby stump. "Can't you be a little more gentle? Don't you know that I'm human, and I'm freezing my butt off right now? Or have you never met one before?"

Night grunted in response, sounding like an animal. Which, I supposed, he was.

I continued grumbling to myself, pulling my knees up to my chest. My plans were dashed now that I was free of his grasp. I realized that I was in much worse condition than I'd thought. Away from the comfort of Night's body heat and the firm strength of his grip around my legs, my whole body was now shaking with shock and adrenaline. I tried to control my breathing and buried my face in my knees in an effort to calm myself. *This stupid wolf is just standing there watching me have a panic attack...*

And then something warm draped softly over my head and shoulders. I gasped, lifting my head to see that Night was offering me his black cotton shirt. I was inundated with his woodsy and slightly floral scent, and I eagerly shoved my arms through the sleeves, pulled the shirt down over my knees, and popped my head through the collar.

I froze as I laid eyes on the shirtless Alpha. I had seen countless shirtless men on the Kings' compound, but none of those men held a candle to Night. His body was all hard muscle, defined and tight. I now had a much better view of his tattoo and the way that the heavy, black lines sliced across each other. The tattoo spilled across his shoulder onto his chest and down his arm, where it ended in a thick, black band around his wrist. Old scars slashed across his chest, stomach, and shoulders.

My gaze slowly followed the trail of dark hair that ran between his washboard abs down to the hard "v" that I'd read about in the books I'd borrowed from Mom's personal library. In those books, the woman always went crazy for the body of her man—looking at Night, I thought I finally understood exactly why. My gaze lingered around the waistband of his black sweats, and my face went hot. This man was a god.

Night made a low sound, something between a scoff and a growl, and my eyes snapped back up to his face. His eyes were almost too bright to look at, but my gaze didn't waver. This burly Adonis had just kidnapped me, and no amount of hotness or intensely green eyes could change that I was by myself with an unknown, likely dangerous man. I couldn't allow myself to forget that.

"Thank you for the shirt," I said. "But I'll need to go back for the rest of my things. You have to take me back."

His mouth smoothed from a slight frown into a straight line, and he turned away from me to look back in the direction we'd come. Unbelievable. Was he ignoring me?

"Hey," I snapped, rising unsteadily to my feet. His shirt fell down to my knees, and I limped over to him. My legs hadn't totally recovered from hours hanging in Troy's room or the shock of our escape, but at least I could sort of walk. "Are you listening to me?"

He remained quiet, staring into the darkness. I clenched my fist. At home, I was always afraid to speak out of turn around a wolf even after they disrespected me. With Troy especially, I tried to keep my head down and hold my tongue. It should have been the same with Night, but it wasn't.

Around him, my tongue became sharper, and I didn't hesitate to let him know how I felt. Maybe it was the adrenaline that still vibrated in my body or the fact that, in kidnapping me, Night had rescued me from Troy, but there was more to my bravery than that. Of course I was afraid of what he could do to me, but deep inside, I knew that Night was someone I could speak my mind to without worrying about violent retaliation. After all, if he'd wanted to kill me, he would have done it already.

I nudged his shoulder, and when I didn't get a response, I punched his perfect, sun-kissed bicep. I winced at the sharp pain that ignited from my knuckles and spread across my hand. All the while, Night remained statue-still, his attention never wavering from the trees.

I pulled my hair in frustration and moved in front of him. From this angle, his larger, broader body shielded me from the cool spring breeze. He seemed especially large with the moonlight at his back; his dark body cut an impressive figure. But I wasn't thinking about that. I was thinking about how angry I was and how anxious I was to get home.

"Listen," I said, jabbing his chest with my finger. "Take. Me. Back. Now." Each word was another jab to hard muscle.

Finally, Night's bright green gaze fell onto me, and the rest of my words caught in my throat. The moment his eyes met mine, I remembered the dream I'd had just a few nights before. In it, my back had been pressed against the trunk of a tree, my arms and legs wrapped around the green-eyed stranger's hard body as he thrust into me over and over again, forcing me to feel pleasure the likes of which I'd never known—

Night's eyes narrowed, and a low rumble emanated from his chest. I took a couple of steps back, a jolt of fear raising goosebumps on my skin. I knew a warning when I heard one.

"Why don't you sit back down and shut up," he said. "I need to listen for my wolves, not some dumb girl who doesn't know how to be grateful."

"Grateful?" The fear began to subside, and anger surged in its wake. "I thanked you for the shirt, didn't I?"

"Not just about the shirt," he said. "I saved your ass from Troy and whatever fucked up shit he had planned for you tonight." He crossed his arms over his chest. "You owe me, girl, but you're lucky that all I'm asking for is your silence."

My hands balled into fists. "*I'm* lucky? The girl who was kidnapped from my home only minutes ago, who's standing here practically naked? You're saying *I'm* lucky? When the person who kidnapped me can't offer even an ounce of sympathy or—or understanding. I owe *you*?" I shook my head hard enough that my hair freed itself from the collar of Night's shirt and fell around my shoulders. "Forget this. I ought to just walk myself home."

He scoffed. "If you're stupid enough to walk yourself back into the lion's den, then go on already. Save me the trouble of listening to you nag at me."

"Fine. I will." I turned from him in a flurry of indignation and marched into the forest, heading back the way we'd come. From the position of the North Star in the sky, I knew that if I kept heading straight, I ought to find my way back to the Kings' compound.

But as I pushed my way through the trees, I found the forest much more unforgiving than it'd been when I was draped over Night's shoulder. The floor, covered in layers of sharp sticks and pine needles and jagged rocks, sliced at my exposed feet. I couldn't see very well, and I found myself almost running into the thick trunk of a tall tree every few steps. All the while, branches snatched at Night's shirt, my legs, and my face. All this combined with the fact that my body hadn't recovered from Troy's harsh treatment, made the experience ten times worse.

I was exhausted after only ten minutes of trudging through the forest, but my pride and determination didn't allow me to turn back to Night. Though it was miserable, though I knew I was doomed to miles and miles of this torture, I kept going. I hoped that the activity would keep me from succumbing to my exhaustion.

I tried to think of Mom and of the garden to keep my spirits up. *When I get back, I'll talk to her about leaving with me. After I tell her about what happened with Troy, she'll understand exactly how unsafe it is with him as Alpha of the Kings.* Mom knew everything about the forest, and she knew more about what human cities were like.

She'd be able to guide me to safety if only I could get back home in one piece.

I stumbled when a tree root snatched at my feet. I fell into the hard, cool trunk of a tree. As I tried to right myself, howls pierced the night air. A deep fear shook through my bones as I heard the sound of dozens of light footsteps headed my way. Soon, shining eyes emerged from the darkness, followed by large, dark shapes—the hulking forms of the wolves that had burst from the treeline earlier.

My arms wrapped tightly around the tree's trunk as if I could blend into it simply by holding on as tightly as possible. When the wolves reached me, would they hurt me? Would they kill me? They were closing in fast, and there was nothing I could do to defend myself.

All the rumors said that the Wargs were bloodthirsty, vicious beasts even when they weren't in their wolf form. Was I about to see that firsthand?

I squeezed my eyes shut as they drew nearer, giving up any hope of making it out of the forest alive.

Chapter 11 - Bryn

Suddenly, a pair of warm arms wrapped around me and lifted me to my feet. I knew it was Night without having to turn around. He held me against his body, his arm firm across my chest. I was sure he could feel the hummingbird beat of my heart against his skin.

The wolves' steps stopped at the sight of their Alpha. I shivered, my eyes still shut tight as I waited for Night to feed me to his pack. Seconds passed, during which nothing and no one made a sound.

Eventually, I slowly opened my eyes. In front of me, large wolves of various colors had gathered around us. Some had their tongues lolling from their mouths, huffing warm puffs of air in front of them as they caught their breaths. Others had tufts of missing fur and bloody wounds. They had clearly dealt with the worst of the Kings' pack.

I noticed movement out of the corner of my eye. I yelped at the sight of another large man dressed in a long-sleeved black shirt and pants. He walked to Night's side, chuckling at my reaction before turning to his Alpha. I tried to pretend I wasn't paying close attention to them as he leaned over to speak into Night's ear.

From the way he stood, just to the right of and behind his Alpha, I knew that this newcomer had to be Night's beta. Growing up in a wolf pack, I had picked up on these displays of pack hierarchy. Though I wasn't allowed to participate in their rituals and activities, I knew how subordinate wolves acted around their Alpha.

As I watched the two men, I realized that the new man was watching me too. He was subtle about his observation, considering me from his periphery. He was handsome, though in a different way from Night. He was almost as tall as his Alpha, but Night had a few inches on him. His face had a boyish charm to it, and his light blond hair and striking brown eyes gave him a kind, mischievous air. The look was heightened when he smiled at me, revealing the dimple in his cheek.

He'd caught me checking him out, but I wasn't embarrassed. I was instead more distracted by the scars that marred his tan, olive-toned skin. Old wounds were visible at the collar of his shirt and over his hands. He was built for killing and fighting, just like any wolf.

Whatever he whispered into Night's ear caused my captor to tighten his grip around me, making it more difficult to breathe. I tried to wiggle in his arms to give myself more room, but it didn't help. The wolves began to shift into their human forms, completely naked.

There were women as part of his team, which surprised me. In the Kings' pack, women were discouraged from joining patrols or from being put in any position that could get them hurt. All children were taught that women were too valuable to be put at risk, but I had observed female wolves hefting crates of vegetables or dried goods just as easily as any man could. Even Mom could lift or maneuver bookshelves and dressers without needing my help.

I found it oddly refreshing that Night didn't subscribe to that same prejudice. I wondered how things would be in the Kings' pack if the women were on a more equal footing.

Though I was, of course, no stranger to nudity, I averted my gaze as best I could to give them some respect. There wasn't much I could do, however, with the Alpha's arms locking me in place.

"Alright," Night's beta sighed, drawing my gaze again, "now that's out of the way, Night, I think you're strangling the prisoner."

At his words, Night immediately loosened his grip on me, allowing me to suck in a much-needed breath of air.

Thank goodness he said something. As I began to relax again, the beta slid in front of me, blocking the naked wolves from my view, another blessing.

He smirked at me. The expression was cute despite the fact that he was another wild Warg wolf. "I'm Dom," he said, "I can't say we get too many humans in these parts…?"

It took me a couple of seconds to realize that he was leaving room for me to tell him my name. I considered whether I ought to reveal that information before ultimately deciding it wouldn't matter either way. "My name's Bryn Hunter."

"Bryn? That's a cute name." He gave me a brief once-over, not bothering to pretend he wasn't. "So why would the Kings' Alpha keep a human toy around?"

The word "toy" struck me like a blow, and my lips pulled away from my teeth. "Back off," I snarled at him, once again surprising myself with my boldness. "I'm no one's toy."

Fortunately, Dom didn't seem to take offense to my response—in fact, it made him laugh. "You're pretty feisty for a human, aren't you? But that doesn't really answer my question, does it?"

I took a few moments to calm down. The exhaustion was getting to me. "I've lived with the Kings' pack my entire life. That's all I'm going to say about it."

"That's fine, that's fine. I'm sure you'll have plenty of time to tell me all about it later." He smirked at me again. I felt myself begin to bristle, but I didn't snap at him again.

"That's enough, Dom. I need you to make sure we've got everyone here. If there are stragglers or badly wounded, you need to round them up."

Dom nodded once and jogged off to do as his Alpha ordered. I yelped as Night lifted me from the ground, holding me bridal style in his arms.

"Put me down!" I wiggled in his arms, trying to kick myself free. But his grip remained viselike. "I can walk just fine, damn you!"

He ignored me.

I continued to fight, but I was much weaker now than I had been when he first kidnapped me. I gritted my teeth, thinking about how stubborn Night was. How was my luck so terrible that I could plan my escape from one terrible wolf only to wind up the prisoner of this jughead Alpha? Didn't he have parents? Or a mother? Did he ever stop to think of how upset she'd be if she saw him treating another woman this way? But no, he was just a typical Alpha male from what I'd seen.

"Why do you never listen?" I demanded. "I said, put me down!"

Night stopped walking and pressed his lips to my ear, his breath hot on the side of my face. I immediately froze at his closeness. "Listen, girl, my wolves have just come from a fight, and they're a little hostile right now."

His words made me shiver.

"I can't put you down and risk you trying to run again. If you want to live, you need to stay close to me until I've explained the situation to them, or I won't be able to guarantee your safety."

My mouth clamped shut. That was more than enough reason for me to stop fighting him so much. Given the fact that I felt unsafe even in my own home whenever the Kings' wolves got a little too excited at night, I wasn't too keen on seeing how rowdy wolves could get when I was within yards of them.

Night moved a little farther away from his team as they calmed themselves down and got dressed. Meanwhile, I tried to regain control of the thunderous pace of my heart. I was too close to the Alpha, and it was so hard to keep my mind from straying to the times when the man from my dreams and I had been…intimate. Especially when I could feel the beat of Night's own heart through my shoulder, which was pressed against his naked chest.

Fortunately, I was only alone with Night for a few more seconds before Dom returned, holding something in his arms. I couldn't tell what it was in the darkness. He glanced from Night to me and back again. His smile was more relaxed than it'd been a few minutes ago.

"Good news, Night," Dom said. "All of our team are accounted for and relatively healthy."

Night nodded and let out a breath. He gently let me stand on the ground, still close enough that he could grab me at a moment's notice. I winced as my raw, tender feet felt the sharp sticks and rocks beneath me. "I'm glad to hear that we didn't suffer any casualties."

"You and me both. It's a relief that everyone got out in one piece despite the sudden shift in the plan. But we can discuss that later. For now…" he turned his attention to me and offered me the bundle, "here."

I stepped away from Night to accept the bundle—pants and boots from the looks of it. I stepped into the pants, which were so big that the ankles pooled at my feet on the ground. The boots would also be big, but they would be better than traversing the forest barefoot. I didn't care. I was just grateful for the comfort of wearing clothes again.

Night, snarling, grabbed hold of the waistband of the pants. Before I could react, he had ripped them off me and tossed them aside. For the second time, I stood shivering in the cold, my second pair of clothing in hours taken away from me in only the blink of an eye. I could have cried.

I whirled on Night, my body trembling from the anger flowing through my veins. But I found that Night had Dom backed up to a tree, growling at him for some reason. Dom had his hands up in supplication, confusion evident in the furrowing of his bushy, honey-blond eyebrows. Chilled at the sight of an Alpha manhandling his beta like that, I took a few healthy steps back. Why would he allow Dom to offer me the clothing, only to rip it away seconds later? If he didn't want me to have clothes, why had he given me his shirt?

Yet again, it hit me that I was in the middle of the woods surrounded by a pack of psychotic wolves whose own Alpha could snap at his beta for no apparent reason. I shivered and held my arms tightly around myself. How could I have ever felt secure in Night's presence when he was capable of acting so unhinged? What could be waiting for me at the Wargs compound? Would I even make it there with Night acting like this?

After a few more tense moments, Night slowly stepped away from his beta, but his shoulders were still taut with rage. Dom, keeping an eye on his Alpha, slowly walked toward the spot where the ripped pants had landed. He gathered them up along with the shoes and reached up into the branches of a nearby pine tree. He pulled down a black bag and stuffed the clothes inside it.

Now that the clothes were gone, Night's shoulders finally began to relax. He kept a close eye on his beta, watching him move to one of the nearby trees. Dom pulled down another bag from the branches and removed a pair of pants and shoes from them. He slowly approached Night and showed him the clothes.

Night relaxed a bit more and nodded. I frowned, confused. Was I watching a Warg ritual? But no, once Dom had Night's approval, he walked back to me and gave me the new clothes. I pulled on the new pants, boots, and a second long-sleeved shirt over my head. I was finally warm, and I realized that these clothes smelled familiar. They were Night's.

A shiver ran through my body as I crossed my arms. *Great. Either Night is a control freak, or he's claimed me as his own personal human plaything.* I seethed even as dread penetrated down to my bones. This marked the second time that I was stuck with an Alpha who seemed hell-bent on ruining my life.

"There, now that you're comfortable," Night said, walking toward me, "take a seat over there and stay quiet. Don't even think about running off, or I can't guarantee that I'll be able to keep you safe."

I huffed a sigh, but I didn't have the energy to argue. I rolled my eyes and found a spot to sit down against a tree. I was planning on escaping, but I could take this opportunity to both rest up and hear what Night had planned for me.

Now that the rest of the pack was dressed, Dom instructed them to establish a camp. Those who were injured were seen to by Dom, Night, and a few other wolves, while the able-bodied went off to collect wood.

They worked as a unit, everyone knowing exactly what they were doing without having to be told. This was a sharp contrast to the few training exercises I'd observed in the Kings' pack. The Kings were a fearsome force who were known for their strength, but I had seen the men use their exercises to show off for the women. I couldn't say how the men behaved outside of the compound, but it was clear that they didn't take their training seriously.

I watched the Wargs put together a fire and make pallets from tree branches. They even set up a pallet for me. I knew it was for me because it was the only one that Night paid close attention to. He was particular about its positioning in relation to his own pallet, as well as in relation to other male wolves. I tried not to roll my eyes when he snapped at one of his men for placing my pallet too close to the tree line.

When the preparations were done, and the fire was crackling away, I moved closer to the fire, eager for its warmth. The wolves had gathered in a circle around Night to hear what he had to say.

"I'm sure you all must be confused by this turn of events. We go in to challenge Redwolf, and we leave with a human girl. Unfortunately, the plan changed when I infiltrated the Redwolf cabin. I found her," he nodded toward where I sat huddled by the fire, "tied up in Troy's room."

Murmuring began among the wolves as they looked at each other and snuck glances at me. I tried to ignore their curious stares, but my face heated at their attention.

"Troy returned to the cabin unexpectedly, and I realized we could use her to our advantage."

Shivers coursed down my spine. *I don't like where this is going. At all.* I lifted my head, turning my attention from the fire to meet Night's blazing emerald gaze.

"We lost out on the opportunity to challenge Troy tonight, but she'll give us another opportunity." He smirked at me, and the shadows cast over his face in the firelight gave his handsome face a sinister edge. "Troy clearly values her, so she'll be a perfect bargaining chip for our next move."

Chapter 12 - Night

I was already awake by the time the sun began to rise. I took the last watch of the night, so I had the treat of watching the golden sun spread across *her* face. She slept curled in a ball on top of her pallet, her hands resting beneath her ear. Her chestnut brown hair fell gently across her cheek. My fingers itched with the urge to brush the hair off her face, a desire that confused the hell out of me.

She—*Bryn*—was my prisoner, my pawn in a war that had officially started last night. I ought to know better than to allow myself to feel anything for her—especially when I fully intended to let her go once I'd carried out my plans.

The rest of the pack arose shortly after me. Bryn was the last to wake. When she did, her eyes parted slowly as if she were waking from a long dream. I was the first person to meet those light blue-gray eyes, and my wolf was practically purring inside me.

I ignored the wolf and got brusquely to my feet. "Today we cross the river," I announced as Bryn sat up, rubbing her eyes. "Redwolf is going to be pursuing the girl, so we should try to keep moving."

After we'd put out the fire, taken down the pallets, and eliminated any other evidence of our camp, we began to trek down to the Kootenai river. We needed to cross it to return to Warg territory. When we reached the river, my pack removed their clothing and shifted into their wolf forms because it was easier to traverse the water. I opted to stay in my human form. I threw Bryn over my shoulder, ignoring her flailing arms and stammering protests, and trudged through the cold water.

She called me any name she could think of, including "kidnapper" and "overgrown asshole," but none of them fazed me.

"If you keep talking to me like that," I said when she stopped yelling long enough to let me get a word in, "I'll drop you in. I don't think I'd mind watching you turn into a sopping wet rabbit."

"Go to hell, Night," she snapped, panting from all the unnecessary movements she was making.

She was weaker than she'd been yesterday. I knew this because there wasn't as much power behind the blows she delivered to my back or her attempts to kick free of my arm, which held her legs.

When we reached the clearing on the other side, I set Bryn down on the ground. Despite my efforts, she had been splashed with water. She stood in her oversized clothes, trembling in the cool breeze of the spring morning. I stood near her and called for my pack to take a break.

Dom, still in the light brown fur coat of his wolf form, tilted his head. *"We could keep going,"* his voice entered my mind.

"Not with her like this, we can't," I replied. *"We should let her get warm and dry before we go on."*

"Understood."

The wolves shifted back into their human forms and dressed in the clothes they'd tied in bundles to keep with them. They stretched and talked amongst themselves while I found another stash of my clothes for her to wear. I handed them to her, and she accepted with a brief nod. I turned my back to allow her to change, and I stood in front of her so that none of the men nearby could sneak a peek at her body.

After she'd changed, I found a felled tree to sit on. I patted the spot next to me for Bryn to sit.

She wore my dry clothes, practically drowning in them because they were so big. Her body swayed a little with fatigue, and I could hear her heartbeat racing. Though she was clearly unwell, she raised a haughty brow as if to say, *What? I'm fine.*

I sighed. "You're obviously still in shock and exhausted, unsurprising given last night's events. Let me help you."

She frowned, shifting from foot to foot.

I thought she would resist me further,r but to my surprise, after a sigh, she came willingly. She sat next to me, and I wrapped an arm around her waist, pulling her flush to my chest. She fit nicely against me as if she was meant to be there.

"I don't know why I'm doing this," she muttered under her breath.

"Because you need to rest."

That seemed to be enough of a reason for her. She leaned against me, and with another sigh, she nuzzled into me.

Concern twisted in my gut, and I felt an answering whine from my wolf. *She's yelling at me one minute, practically cuddling with me the next. The trauma of Redwolf's treatment of her...She's clearly confused. We need to get home as soon as possible so she can be somewhere warm. Safe.*

Of course, I needed her to be healthy if I was going to use her to get to Troy, but more than that, the idea of her being so upset made my chest ache. But I didn't have time to look into those sorts of worries. I needed to keep my mind on my goals, namely, to end the Kings' reign and take over the pack that should have been mine all along.

It was so hard to keep my mind focused on anything beyond Bryn. I put on a show of not caring what she did or said or responding to her when she spoke, but in truth, she was impossible to ignore. Every move she made, every sound that slipped past those plump, pink lips had me riveted. And her smell…she was so sweet, so intoxicating. It took everything in me not to press my nose into her hair and inhale deeply.

I couldn't do this. The urge to be intimate with her, to hold her with both arms and to taste her lips the way I had in so many dreams was maddening. When the urges became too strong, I pulled away from her despite my wolf's protesting whine.

"You feel better now?" I asked.

She looked up at me, blinking slowly as if she were coming out of a dream. Her hair had fallen into her face again, and she brushed it behind her ear.

"Y-yeah, I think so." She nodded.

"Great." I sat up too quickly, almost knocking her off the trunk. *"Dom, I'm going to scout ahead for a few miles."*

Dom met my gaze across the clearing. *"Got it. Let me know if you need anything."*

I nodded. I would have shifted right there, but given the way Bryn looked away from my pack when they were nude, I decided to do it behind tree cover. I jogged away from the clearing. When I was a few yards away, surrounded by trees, I stripped off my clothes and shifted.

In my wolf form, I shook out my thick, black fur and stretched. My senses were heightened now, and my reflexes were sharper. The air was a vector for smells and sounds and tastes. I pawed at the ground, scenting the soil to orient myself, and then I began to run. I wove between the trees like a shadow and ran a few miles ahead to check out the path home.

The run allowed me to relax. By the time I returned, I felt I had finally gotten rid of the pent-up emotions and impulses after twenty miles (ten toward the camp and ten back) of running. But after I'd shifted into my human form and gotten dressed, I emerged from between the trees to find Bryn talking to Dom. They weren't standing close to each other, there were still a couple of feet between them, but he'd managed to put a slight smile on her face—the first one I had seen from her since I saved her from Troy.

My heart began to pound at the sight of her face—the way her cheeks lifted, the slight spark in those beautiful, gemlike eyes—but my wolf growled at Dom's proximity to her. In that moment, my wolf almost saw Dom as an enemy, someone who could *never* be near her like that. Fortunately, the run had tired my wolf enough for me to take control. Instead of going over and pulling Bryn to my side, I made a brief, sharp whistle, calling my team to attention. Dom immediately jogged from Bryn's side to mine.

Good, I thought, my wolf calming. It was a much more diplomatic solution to the issue than snapping at my beta in front of my pack. "The path ahead is clear," I announced. "Let's get moving."

The group trudged onward. After a few hours, we decided to set up camp a few miles from the river. I could still hear the sound of the river rushing. I directed my team to begin setting up camp and instructed Jasper to kill a rabbit and set it up to cook by the fire. My team could go longer without food while remaining strong, but I'd heard Bryn's stomach growling as we walked.

I heard it growling again as my team got to work on the camp, but she was further away from them—already almost a mile north, following the flow of the river rather than trying to cross it. She was trying to escape. Again.

I sighed as Dom came to stand near me. "I'll give her this," I said, listening to the crunch of branches underfoot and smelling her sweet scent on the wind, "she's resilient." *And stubborn.*

Dom chuckled. "She's a spitfire, for sure. Should we send someone for her?"

"Not yet. Let's let her run for a little while longer just to tire herself out."

"Understood."

I continued to feign disinterest around Dom and my people, but I never stopped listening to her footsteps. I heard when she stumbled and when she coughed. She'd made it a decent distance away despite the rough terrain and her oversized clothes—almost two miles from the sound of it—but when her pace began to slow, I had Dom bring her back.

I knew that Troy would send his men to get Bryn back. They would likely try to intercept us before we reached Warg territory. We needed to pick up the pace, but there wasn't much we could do about Bryn. She was much slower, and carrying her was out of the question given the way she fought—just as she was fighting Dom as he dragged her back to camp.

"Damn you!" she seethed, turning her glare from Dom to me. "Why can't you just let me go, you asshole?"

I rolled my eyes. I wished I could duct tape her mouth shut. "You already know why."

Dom set her down, glancing at me over her head. I didn't need to telepathy to know what he was thinking. It was a look that said, "Don't be too hard on her." I almost rolled my eyes a second time. As Dom walked away to oversee Jasper as he prepared the rabbit, Bryn marched up to me—her arms wrapped tightly around herself. There were small sticks and pine needles attached to her sleeves. She was panting as she stormed toward me, but her eyes blazed at me, almost gray in the shaded light of the forest. She was so upset that I doubted she even realized how disheveled and exhausted she looked.

"Why don't you go and warm yourself by the fire instead of trying to get yourself killed?" I asked. "There's a rabbit roasting there with your name on it."

She scoffed at me. "You think food will get me in your good graces? Hell no. I have zero interest in participating in your game with Troy," she raged. "I don't want to be used for your or his benefit. You don't own me. No one does."

I scoffed at her. "And what do you think will happen when you go home? Do you think you'll be able to return to whatever shitty life you had with the Kings?"

"I—"

I didn't let her speak. "Troy will tie you up again. He'll drag you back to his bedroom, and then he'll *own* you, whether you want him to or not. *That's* what you're trying to get back to?"

I expected more of a fight. I expected her to continue to rage. But instead, her lower lip wobbled. To my horror, her eyes again filled with tears, spilling over onto cheeks reddened with emotion. It seemed her fear was finally catching up to her.

I took her wrist and pulled her against my chest without thinking, eager to calm her down, to stop her from crying. Immediately, I sensed my annoyance lessening the longer I held her to me. Her tears were wet against my chest, and I slightly tightened my hold as if I could force some comfort into her traumatized body. I felt her heart beating quickly and felt an answering quickness in my own chest. I could have held her forever.

But as soon as her small sobs subsided and her body calmed, she pushed at my chest. I let her go immediately, startled by her desire to get away. She teetered for a moment on her feet, her head lowered toward the ground, her hair covering her face. She turned away from me quickly, but not before I caught a glimpse of her face in the firelight. Her cheeks were bright red.

I watched her walk over to the fire and sit down next to it, hugging her knees to her chest. She reached for the rabbit, fully cooked by then, and took a few nibbles. I let out a long breath and turned away from her. I put a hand on my chest, where my heart still beat almost as quickly as it had when I'd gone on my run earlier. I was grateful for the distance from her; I needed to get a handle on my emotions and impulses concerning this woman. But there was a tiny, sweet thrill in my chest accompanying my thunderous heartbeat. I refused to read into it, forcing myself to focus on the path ahead. Deep down, I understood that I was far too pleased to see her calm, eating, and warming herself by the fire—I was happy that she was safe.

Chapter 13 - Night

Finally, after two additional days of walking through the forest, the end of our journey was near. We had set up camp in a little clearing with a canopy of trees that almost covered the sky. As I helped take down the camp, I drew in a deep breath. Over the scent of pine and moist earth, I could smell the familiar warmth of my pack lands on the air. We were on track to reach home before midnight on our final day of travel. Without Bryn, we would have been home in only a day's travel, but after shifting to cross the river, we all remained in our human forms to keep her safe.

I couldn't fucking wait to be home. My emotions, my thoughts, my wolf—everything had been in flux since I decided to take Bryn with me. I tried not to dwell much on why I had become so possessive of her, but I felt as if I'd known her for years despite our having met only three days ago. Those eyes, the blue of robin eggs, stayed in my mind every night long after I closed my eyes and went to sleep.

I couldn't shake my emotions. Maddeningly, I wanted to get as far away from her as possible, yet I became restless when she wasn't within arm's length of me. I found my attention drifting toward her even when in conversation with one of my hunters. My wolf yearned for her. To be near her. Knowing where she was at all times wasn't enough for him—he needed to be close enough to hear her heartbeat and to feel her body heat. I wanted that too.

It was like I was being pulled in two different directions—on one end was my responsibility to my pack and to make sure that I took over the Kings' pack, and on the other was Bryn.

As the days passed, her pull became even stronger.

Every time I thought back to finding her in Troy's bedroom, my wolf still bristled. When Troy had returned and said those awful things to her as he crept up the staircase, I could have killed him in cold blood right then. Now, I'd completely abandoned my original plan and dragged some human girl along with me.

I had to believe that in kidnapping her, I had delivered a blow to Troy. That having Bryn in my possession meant that Troy couldn't have her, which would put him off his game. Without Bryn, he would get restless, and then I would have another chance to end the bastard. That was what I told my team, what I told Dom, and what I planned to tell the rest of the pack once we returned. But the truth was that I had no idea why I had taken her.

And more than that, having her around made me feel off. That was clear just from the fact that I'd almost ripped Dom's head off when he first offered clothes to her. He must have seen that she needed shoes to protect her feet from the rough ground. He was probably trying to make sure she didn't suffer, but that hadn't mattered to me or to my wolf.

I looked back on that moment with enough embarrassment to make me squirm. My head was a confused mess of thoughts and emotions; I hadn't felt this strange in my life. Even my first shift made more sense than this. That interaction with Dom wasn't one of my prouder moments. In fact, there was a lot that had happened over the past couple of days that I wasn't proud of—namely, abandoning my original plan and kidnapping Bryn. And yet, I couldn't bring myself to truly regret the decision, even as I could admit that it was a bizarre move, to put it lightly.

With all of that on my mind, I felt a twinge of annoyance right at the base of my skull as I listened to Bryn and Dom chat behind me. We were finishing up the last leg of our journey. I should have been focusing on how I was going to make sure that kidnapping Bryn was worth it, but my attention was on her voice and her laugh.

Dom had managed to cultivate a friendly relationship with Bryn, which made my skin itch. The two were chatting about Bryn's favorite books—a lot of fairy tales and romances from the sound of it—and her passion for gardening. There was so much I didn't know about my captive that Dom had easily gotten Bryn to share, and that irked me more than I wanted to admit. Still, I hung on to her every word as she answered Dom's questions.

"You seem to care a lot about cultivating plants," Dom said. "How did you get interested in that?"

"My mom takes care of the pack gardens," she replied. "She taught me everything I know, but I still have a lot to learn."

"I don't know, Bryn," Dom's voice took on a teasing tone. The way you talk about gardening, you sound like you could be an expert."

She snorted in response.

"So, you mentioned your mom—what's the rest of your family like?"

"Oh…" she paused. "Well, it's actually just me and my mom. I don't have any siblings, and my mom has never had a mate or even a lover since I've known her."

The word "mate" stood out for me and not just because of the dreams that I'd had about Bryn. Dom seemed to have picked up on it too.

"You said 'mate,' but your mom is human, isn't she?" he asked

"No. My mother found me as a baby alone in the woods by the Kings' pack, and she adopted me on the spot. I don't have any idea what happened to my original family."

So she was literally raised by wolves. No wonder she's got so much courage. It also explained a bit about why she was so eager to get back home. She probably missed the woman who raised her.

"What about your family?" Bryn asked. "Do you have siblings?"

I turned my head to look at Dom. This was a touchy subject for most of the wolves in the Wargs pack. Considering the fact that Bryn had been raised with the Kings' wolves, if Dom told her the truth about what happened to his family, it could introduce some animosity into their almost-friendship.

"No. Not anymore. But that's a *long* story meant for another kidnapping," Dom said, effectively evaporating any potential tension that another answer—the *true* answer— could have caused.

Bryn laughed, and the sound of it ate at me. Over the past couple of days, she had been able to relax and even joke with Dom. With him, she almost seemed accepting of her kidnapping. But with me, she was snappy and angry and tried to run. Jealousy burned in my chest. I could admit that the circumstances under which we had met weren't exactly ideal—but Dom was part of my pack—shouldn't Bryn be just as upset with him as she was with me?

These emotions were made much worse by the fact that I was obsessed with being near her. Her scent alone was enough to take over my senses, but often when we stopped for a rest, Bryn would go off by herself to cry. She probably thought that she was quiet enough that none of us could hear her, but I heard every gasp, every sob. When she came back, I could smell the salt of her tears. Something tugged at my chest every time.

Outside of those quiet, somber moments, and when she wasn't being friendly with Dom, she was arguing with me. And though her angry face, balled fists, and stiff posture told me that she hated me, I tasted the spice of her arousal on the air. It washed over me whenever we were near each other or fighting with each other. She was turned on by me, and I felt an answering ache in my own body. The aroma of her arousal was so potent, it kept me up while everyone else slept.

I had never in my life experienced something like this, and the fact that a human woman was the one who drove me mad was even more ridiculous.

When our pack lands finally came into view, I let out a sigh of relief. I had been more concerned about retribution from Troy than I had fully acknowledged to Dom or even to myself. But now that we had reached home, I knew that as much as Troy obsessed over Bryn, the new Alpha wouldn't send his men miles away from the Kings' compound to cross the Kootenai to retrieve Bryn— at least, not while he was still getting used to his new role.

As we continued moving, the cabins came into view, and I heard Bryn gasp beside me. I hadn't heard her come up, the sight of my home had been enough to briefly distract me from her, but I was actually grateful for her closeness.

We had taken things slower to accommodate her, but she had kept up with us remarkably well. One of the female members of the pack had let Bryn exchange her large boots for a smaller pair, and she was wearing almost all of the clothing that I had stashed around the woods. (I'd need to make a note to build up my stash again when I found the time.)

The shock and exhaustion that Bryn had suffered at the beginning of our trek hadn't slowed her down. I had made sure we stopped to have breaks and to catch a few hours of sleep, but we had never taken a full night's rest, and there were always wolves on guard.

After days of travel, my pack lands, neatly tucked into the side of Gypsy Peak, were such a welcome sight. I think that was true even for her.

As she looked over my pack lands in awe, pride filled my chest. The Wargs had so little compared to the other packs in the area, but we were a family, a unit that raised our pups together and shared resources. We Wargs had worked for years to fix up the lands after the mess that first Gregor and then Peter had left them in.

There were still things that needed to be done, but we now looked and felt like a tight-knit pack. And for reasons I didn't really understand, Bryn's approval of the land pleased me a great deal. My wolf, too, purred in satisfaction.

On the final mile of the trip, most of the men and women sprinted ahead to meet their mates and children who had heard us approach. I was relieved that we'd suffered no casualties, that the wounds we had collected were minor enough that the injured were already back to full health or close to it. But the weight of guilt settled on my back when I thought about how badly things could have gone. Changing the plan to kidnap Bryn was one thing, but my lust for vengeance was another. I couldn't let myself become blinded again, not by revenge and not by whatever was going on between me and Bryn either.

I spotted my mom squeezing through the small crowd at the gate. The moment I saw her smile, I left Bryn's side and jogged to meet her. Her arms were open, ready to pull me into a tight hug. She patted my back and hummed a sweet, happy note. I let her hug me for as long as she wanted. I'd missed her more than I'd expected, and I felt nothing but joy at her attention and love.

After a few moments, she pulled back. "Glad to see you safe and sound," she said, her hand warm on my cheek.

"You and me both," I said.

She smiled and glanced around me to look at Bryn. I turned to look too. She stood a few yards away, looking incredibly out of place in her bulky, borrowed clothing. And yet, as I stared at her, the sun emerged from behind the clouds to brighten her hair and cheeks. Her dark hair lifted in the breeze, and her blue-gray eyes were captivating. Bryn looked like an angel confined to mortal clothing.

"And who is she?" Mom asked, slightly breathless herself. "A new *friend* perhaps?"

I rolled my eyes. I wanted to chastise her for the ridiculous question, but I caught the rest of my pack staring at Bryn. They weren't just stares of confusion or curiosity; they were also lingering stares of appreciation from many of the single wolves in the pack. Not even four days of traveling through the wild and being covered in my scent protected Bryn from the attention. Part of me couldn't blame them. My wolf, however, was less forgiving.

Though my pack didn't discriminate against humans, we hardly interacted with them, so the males didn't see Bryn as anything but a fresh female. We didn't have a large supply of single females, a problem that would only be worsened by Bryn's presence. I hadn't considered that this would be a problem.

This presented a dilemma for me. I couldn't let her go unattended, but I sure as hell couldn't watch her twenty-four seven either. Besides, she was my prisoner, and letting her go off on her own would give her the opportunity to try and find a way back to the Kings. The only solution I saw was to show everyone that she was not a new addition to the pack.

"It's just such an interesting twist of events," Mom said when I didn't reply. "You leave to kill an Alpha and return with a woman. A *human* at that."

I ignored her joke and marched over to Bryn. She looked up at me with those gorgeous eyes and that lovely hue of red coloring her cheeks. She opened her mouth to say something, but I didn't want to hear it. I grabbed her wrist and began towing her after me.

"What the hell?" she demanded. She tried to yank herself free, but her efforts did nothing.

I ignored her protests as I pulled her behind me, a clear display to those gathered around that she was not an equal. I felt Mom and Dom's concerned gazes on my back.

"Enjoy the rest of the night with your families," I said to my team as I passed. "You've all earned a good rest."

Bryn continued to struggle to no avail. *At least she's got her strength back*, I thought as I brought her to my cabin. My home was located just outside of the main village, close to the forest, and near my mom's cabin. I needed to work through what I wanted to do with Bryn long-term, but the only thing that came to mind at that moment was to keep her out of my hair and away from the rest of the pack by keeping her in my own cabin.

"Night, let me go!" Bryn said. "I don't understand what you're doing or why or—"

"I'm putting you someplace safe," I said, my voice rougher than I'd meant for it to be. Seeing the way the males coveted her was too much for my frazzled brain to take. "Someplace no one will be able to hurt you, and where *you* won't be able to escape."

"You mean another prison?" she demanded.

Her comment was like a slap to the face. Guilt panged through my chest. Had I saved her from one prison only to put her in another one? But I gave himself a shake. *There are no other solutions,* I told myself. *This is the only way to make sure she stays put.*

"I mean my home," I growled back.

Without another word, I pulled her into my cabin and up the stairs to the spare bedroom. I tossed her in. She stumbled onto the bed and whipped around to face me. Her tearful, fiery gaze blazed at me as I closed the door and locked it tight.

Chapter 14 - Bryn

In the books I loved, the girl was always rescued by a handsome prince with whom she lived happily ever after. I had been rescued, but I'd left one monster just to be captured by another, and there didn't seem to be a happily ever after at the end of my story.

Night shoved me inside the room, and I turned toward him, watching as he dispassionately slammed the door closed. I was such an idiot to feel anything stir in my heart as he and I had looked over the Wargs pack lands at the quaint, beautiful cabins that were scattered around the clearing. How could I have allowed myself to feel anything other than rage for the Alpha? The moment the lock turned, I scrambled to my feet and ran to the window. If I was quick—if I was careful, maybe I had a chance to escape.

But alas, no matter how hard I pulled at the window, it was jammed shut. I grunted with effort and yelped when I broke my pointer nail. I pushed through the pain and beat my fists against the window. My hands bounced off the glass. The window wobbled in its frame as though it were laughing at me. I realized with a chill that I must have been more exhausted than I thought—all I'd done to the glass was smudge it a bit. I yanked open the drawers of the dresser, shoving my hands into each drawer. All I found were a few unlit white candles and a matchbox. The rest of the drawers were empty.

I ran back to the door. I pounded my fists against it over and over again. I screamed Night's name, I screamed for help, I screamed anything I could think of to get someone's attention. But no one came. Of course they didn't. I had never known a wolf who was capable of defying their Alpha. I was no longer hanging from the wall tied up in ropes, but I was still imprisoned in another man's room.

I took a few deep breaths and examined my finger. It throbbed, but it wasn't bleeding. After all that activity, I felt too hot in so many clothes. I removed first my boots and then the outer layers of my clothes until I was standing in a pair of loose pants and a large t-shirt. I sat on the bed and looked around.

The bedroom was simple and clean. I figured that this wasn't actually Night's room but was in fact a spare bedroom because of the lack of personalization. The walls were made of old, brown wood, and there were no posters. The bed was covered in clean, beige linen and a faded blue quilt folded at the footboard. The only furniture was the oak wood dresser and bed. It looked nicer than the rest of the cabin, of which I'd only caught a glimpse. The rest of the place could use some TLC, including a good waxing.

Across from the door was the entrance to a half bath. There was a toilet and a sink and another, much smaller window. It was about the same size as my old bedroom, but I doubted I would ever feel comfortable here. *Will this room be where I die? Will I ever see home again?* My eyes stung with tears. Outside the window I'd tried to break, the sky had turned a rich, dark blue. I was exhausted, but how could I get even a wink of sleep in an unfamiliar room surrounded by strangers who might want to hurt me?

I knew that I had planned to escape the Kings' pack on my own, but after all that had happened to me—first Troy holding me captive, and now Night—I missed the creature comforts I'd gotten used to back at home. I longed for anything familiar—the plants, the dried flowers, the snacks Mom would make me.

Oh, Mom! My body ached when I thought about her. Would she ever know what happened to me? What lies had Troy told her to cover for his crimes? I could almost hear his awful voice recounting a long tale about him bursting into his room to find me naked and being taken advantage of by the Wargs Alpha. He probably talked about his loss to portray Night as the coward, throwing sand in his eye, that kind of thing.

Whatever he had said, I knew he'd make sure that he sounded like the hero, not one of the villains, and the pack wouldn't be able to contradict him because he was the Kings' Alpha now. What did it matter anyway? There wasn't much I could do to change my current situation.

I shook my head and sat up. I needed to be smart about this. *What do I know about the Wargs. Anything that can help me here?* Everything I knew about them came from Mom and the schoolhouse. According to the stories I'd heard, the Wargs used to have a mighty Alpha. But once he died, his son was tasked to take on the mantle of leadership. Unfortunately for the Wargs, the son was incredibly cruel—especially to outsiders and to the women of the pack. The son was abusive, selfish, and so much like Troy, it made me shiver.

The son ruled the Wargs for a few years, but the pack suffered for it. And then he abandoned them, leaving the pack in the control of a wolf, who, while physically strong, had no mind for leadership. Many wolves left the pack, while those who remained attempted to make things work. Things changed for the Wargs when Night Shepherd challenged the incompetent Alpha, who was twenty years his senior. That was twelve years ago, which meant Night had to be fifteen or sixteen at the time, which is incredibly young.

The stories went on to say that the Wargs had always wanted to take the Kings' pack lands specifically because of the Kootenai River. The river allowed the Kings' pack to have access to fresh water, to send things to and from surrounding villages and packs, and it sustained an abundance of wildlife. It provided tons of resources for the pack that controlled it but, most importantly, the river was a symbol. When I was in school, one of the focal points in pack history was the exchange of the river back and forth between the most powerful packs over the last thousand years. In school, I had learned that the Kings had control of the river for hundreds of years, but Mom had told me that some believed the Wargs pack used to have control over it not too long ago, and the Kings stole it from them. Both packs had their versions of the story.

But the most terrifying thing I could recall from those stories was that the Wargs had very few women in their pack. To make up for that, the males would kidnap, rape, and force mating with wolves from other packs. Some stories told that the Wargs were known for coming in the dead of night and removing females from their beds, dragging them away against their will, and forcing them to bear children to grow the pack. That was how the Wargs had gained back their power after living so pitifully when their Alpha abandoned them decades ago.

When I thought back to our arrival at the Wargs' compound, however, I didn't recall a bloodthirsty pack full of rapists and thieves. In fact, I'd watched families reuniting with each other. Children and mates ran from their cabins to meet with those who had been part of Night's team. Tears fell, and laughter bubbled on the wind as everyone embraced.

I had been touched by the display of love, and before Night had grabbed my wrist and dragged me through the compound, I had been about to tell him so. Why I would share that with him, I had no idea, but his treatment of me afterward had soured any desire I had to try and connect with him again. If the women were all stolen from other packs, there was no indication of it here. They were all smiling and seemed genuinely happy to be here. Then again, maybe they were putting on a front to appease the returning Alpha.

An idea struck me. *Could I use that to my advantage?* Perhaps I could slip one of the women a note to see if they'd help me escape. If they were here against their will, they would understand my predicament even if I had been paraded through the village like a prisoner. Surely they'd be kind and want to help me avoid the same fate. And, even if they really were content to be members of this pack, maybe they'd be willing to help me out of the kindness of their hearts. If they couldn't outright smuggle me out, perhaps they'd give me a clue or a tip that would be helpful.

Either way, I needed to find a way out of the cabin, away from the pack and its awful, uncaring Alpha.

Movement outside caught my attention. I sat up quickly and moved to the window. Two wolves stood just a few yards from the house. They were laughing and chatting with one another the way friends would. I couldn't make out what they were saying, but I could faintly hear the sound of their voices through the window. I couldn't tell if they were there to watch over me or if they were just local pack members out for a stroll.

Seizing the opportunity to find some help, I rushed to the bathroom and turned on the sink. I lathered up my hands with soap and rushed back. Returning to the window, I wrote H-E-L-P in blocky, easily read letters. I did this over and over again, hoping the soapy residue would leave enough of an imprint that it would stand out against the clear glass. I didn't know what would become of this attempt, but I had to try, didn't I? Maybe someone would see the message and help me out.

After tracing the same letters over and over again until my arm started to go numb, I stepped away from the window with a sigh. Another idea struck me as I turned toward the pile of clothes on the floor. I could jam them under the door. It wouldn't stop a wolf from entering, but it might slow them down long enough for me to at least ready myself. I gathered the clothes together and shoved them under the door, making sure to pack them in. By the time I was done, my already exhausted muscles throbbed, and my heart was pounding hard. I felt wired and unsettled.

I wasn't a wolf, but that didn't mean that a male wolf wouldn't sneak in and force himself on me the same way Troy had planned to. Not knowing what they planned to do to me here sent a fresh wave of fear down my spine, and I returned to the door, pounding against it and screaming out horrible threats that I knew I couldn't back up. I returned to the window too, but the wolves below had already wandered away.

Tears filled my eyes and poured down my cheeks as the gravity of my situation hit me again. I was stuck here for the night. As much as I hated Troy and the way that most of my pack treated me, I was desperate to be home, to sleep in my own bed, and to know that Mom was watching over me. It seemed so ridiculous that I had ever tried to leave everything I knew when the unfamiliar was this terrifying. Who's to say that humans would treat me any better than this?

I wrapped my arms tight around myself and sank down to the floor. Life on the Kings' compound was awful, nigh unbearable. But I thought it was far, far better to deal with the enemy you knew than the strangers who kept you locked in a bedroom after kidnapping you from the only home you'd ever known.

Chapter 15 - Bryn

I woke up the next morning to a knock on the door. I groaned and rolled on my side away from the noise. For a few precious moments, I believed I was safe and sound in my own bed, but the smell of the detergent used on the sheets caused me to quickly open my eyes. The first thing I laid eyes on was the message I'd left in the glass. H-E-L-P.

I slowly sat up. Now that I was moving around, I could feel how sore my muscles were. I didn't even remember getting into bed last night, but the clothes I'd packed under the door were still there, so I must have crawled into bed on my own.

The knock sounded again, and my head snapped toward it. It occurred to me then how strange it was for the visitor to knock before entering the room of a prisoner. If they were courteous enough to do that, would they leave if I didn't say anything? My hands tightened around the comforter as I waited.

Eventually, the lock turned, and the visitor pushed on the door. My gaze dropped to the clothes I'd jammed beneath the door. Would it make a difference? To my surprise, the clothes did halt the visitor. With a slight grunt, they pushed harder on the door and slowly slid it open. As the visitor came into view, I relaxed slightly. It wasn't a man—it was the woman who Night had embraced the day before.

The woman looked down at the clothes with a raised brow. "That's pretty resourceful, girlie. If you packed them in more tightly, I think even my son would have a bit of trouble getting it open."

I pulled my legs into my chest and said nothing. My guard was up. If Night trusted this woman, it was unlikely that she would be any help to me.

I watched the woman step inside and close the door behind her. The roll of clothes was no longer packed beneath the door, so it slid shut more easily. She was beautiful and looked to be in her early fifties. Her thick, snow-white hair was collected into one long braid down her back. She was slender and graceful, and she had eyes that were just as green and vibrant as Night's.

At the scent of something savory, my gaze lowered to the woman's hands. She'd brought a glass of water and a bowl of rice, and what looked like some kind of thick sauce or curry. The smell was divine, especially after four days straight of eating small rabbits and berries. My mouth began to water.

"I'm Violet Shepherd," the woman said. From the way she smiled, she didn't seem offended by my silence. "I guess you could say that I'm responsible for the man who brought you here."

Oh. She's his mother. My eyes narrowed wearily. Violet had a calming presence, one that reminded me a bit of Mom, but I wouldn't let her sway me. It was becoming increasingly likely that this woman might turn out to be my enemy, just like Night.

"Your name is Bryn, right?" Violet asked, stepping a few inches closer to the bed. "Are you hungry? Thirsty?"

I scooted away from her. "Is it poisoned? I don't see you eating any of it."

"Poison?" Violet chuckled. "No, sweetie. There isn't a person in the village who wants to see you dead."

I hesitated. I needed to be smarter, but the smell of the hot dish was getting to me. And within seconds, my growling stomach gave away how badly I wanted that food. When Violet offered it to me, I pulled it close and spooned the dish into my mouth. My initial suspicions were correct; it was a rabbit curry with white rice. The dish was full of flavor and spice that spread across my tongue like a warm hug. It was exactly the kind of food I wanted after such a long trek through the wilderness.

As I ate, Violet walked around the room, tutting about the sparse furnishings. She was mumbling under her breath, and all I caught was, "…such a shame…keeping a girl against her will."

I glanced from Violet to the door. If Violet was in here, the door must have been unlocked. I wondered if the woman had come alone, and if so, was I willing to attempt to tackle the older woman to try and escape?

"I understand why you might think my son is a monster," Violet's voice took my attention away from the door. "But he isn't. He's just…had a tough life, and there's a great deal of responsibility on his shoulders."

Annoyance was a sharp spike at the back of my head. "I mean no offense, ma'am, but I don't think I want to hear about the man who kidnapped me."

Violet didn't seem offended, but she did give me a curious stare. "Didn't he save you from a man who was about to take your innocence and your future away from you?"

I winced inwardly. "He did, but then he refused to let me go back home."

Violet still held the water. When she caught me looking at it, she approached the bed and sat at the foot of it, reaching over to hand me the glass. I set down the empty bowl and drank. Water had never tasted cooler or more refreshing than it did then.

When I finished, Violet was still watching me, but her eyes had softened. "Why don't you tell me a little bit about what happened?"

I sighed. "It happened on my twentieth birthday," I said. "Troy drugged me and tied me up in his room so he could—" I cut myself off, not wanting to relive the horrible things he'd said to me. "Anyway, Night showed up and untied the ropes around my wrists and ankles, and then he rushed out of there with me. He's forced me to stay by his side ever since."

Violet reached out to touch my knee. "I can't imagine how scared you must have been through all that, Bryn. I'm so sorry."

It was the first time since it had happened that anyone had empathized with me. Moisture filled my eyes, and suddenly I didn't feel like keeping my life secret from Violet. I went on to explain the way I'd been treated, not just by Troy, but by all of the wolves in the Kings' pack. I detailed some of my worst memories and even shed a few tears. Through it all, Violet listened to me, at times shaking her head or cursing under her breath at what I had to say. It felt good, so good, for Violet to validate all of the pent-up negative feelings I'd harbored for the home I'd been taken from.

As I stopped talking, even Violet was wiping tears from the corners of her eyes. "Honey, if it was all so awful back at home, why are you so desperate to get back?"

"My mom," the reply came without hesitation. "She'll be wondering where I am and if I'm safe. And I can't even imagine what kind of lies Troy must be spinning to explain my absence."

"I understand all of that, but you said you were planning on leaving that night anyway. I'm getting the feeling that there's more to it."

I bit my lip. There was more, but it brought more shame and more sadness. I thought about what I'd just shared with Violet, every wrong thing that had ever been done to me or said to me. There was nothing else about the Kings' pack that warranted my returning. I had, after all, been planning to leave on my own anyway. I just hadn't planned on being kidnapped. Still, I felt compelled to give some sort of answer to Violet.

"I wasn't ready to leave," I admitted. "I thought I was ready to find my own pack—er, place to belong, but I never wanted to leave like this." I had been scolded for using wolf terms in relation to myself when I was a child. I wasn't a wolf, so I didn't get to try and pretend to be. "Now that I'm so far from home, I just want to go back."

Violet nodded. "Ah, now that makes perfect sense. Night being who he is, I've gotten desensitized to wondering what sorts of dangerous things he must get into when he leaves the compound, but if I had a daughter…" She shook her head. "I know your mother must be terrified for you."

I nodded. Tears again stung at the backs of my eyes, but I held them back.

Violet patted my knee. "But I think you're not giving yourself enough credit. You were ready that night. You were prepared to go off on your own and to find your place to belong, your pack." She smiled, and I felt a small burst of warmth in my chest. Violet wasn't making me feel bad for my slip-up. "I know that things didn't happen the way you planned, but you can think of this as an alternate path to your goal."

"Alternate path?"

"Yes, girlie. This is a new adventure for you. And as a reader yourself, you should know that new adventures offer new opportunities."

Something about that response irked me. "I'm not interested in opportunities that end in kidnapping."

The older woman laughed. "I like your energy, girlie. I see he has his work cut out for him."

I paused, tilting my head. "What do you mean by that?"

Violet waved the question away with another chuckle. "Never mind. Let me get out of your hair for now." She stood up and grabbed the empty glass of water and bowl. She approached the door and raised her hand. She proceeded to knock against the wood in a brief pattern that alternated between her knuckles and the heel of her hand.

I tried to memorize the pattern before the door opened. Violet gave me another smile, and a wink, and then left. *If she visits me often, I might be able to use her to escape after all,* I thought, hope bubbling through me.

But that hope deflated when Night walked inside. I gasped at his presence—I hadn't thought I'd see him again so suddenly. *So Violet wasn't alone. That will be something I need to keep in mind next time she visits.*

He had his arms crossed over his chest and a frown on his face as he looked down at me. "You can take a shower if you want."

I blinked at him. Then, as his words began to sink in, my eyes widened. "I can?" I didn't think prisoners were allowed such luxuries.

"Don't make me say it again," he said, looking away. "Let's go."

His response made me roll my eyes, but I did get out of bed. I hadn't felt so filthy in all my life, and I was eager to get the grime and sweat off my body.

But, as I followed him out of the bedroom and into the hallway, I couldn't help but make a retort. "Maybe after I take a shower, you'll let me head on home, huh? I think I might have left something on the stove."

I watched him as I spoke, hoping to get some sort of rise out of him. For some reason, though I knew my life was at the mercy of this Alpha, I enjoyed getting on his nerves. His reddening face, the downturn of those thick, dark eyebrows, and the way his mouth quirked as if he was trying to hold back his reaction always made my stomach fill with a tingling warmth.

But this time Night gave me no such reaction. "No," he said, his voice even, almost casual. "I guess your house will just have to burn down."

I frowned at him but decided to keep quiet as he led me to the bathroom down the hall.

Inside, the floors and walls were tiled with small white and blue squares. To the right was a shower with some bar soap and generic shampoo, to the left there were fresh towels folded neatly on top of the toilet as well as a change of clothes, and across from the door was the sink with a new toothbrush and tube of toothpaste.

"You get twenty minutes," he said. "I'll be standing outside the door, so don't even think about trying to leave."

I whirled on him. "You know, if you weren't such an ass, I might not even mind being stuck in this cabin with you people."

He scoffed. "You say that like I want you to enjoy yourself here. This isn't a vacation, Bryn. You're here as my pawn. Nothing more, nothing less."

"I *know*. You've done nothing but tell me as much since you kidnapped me."

"I'm just making sure you don't forget."

"It'd be impossible for me to forget. I know that you just want to use me, like every Alpha I've ever had the misfortune of knowing."

"Don't compare me to that coward," Night snapped. There was an underlying growl to his already deep voice. "I would never behave the way he does."

"No, you're two very different men," I conceded. "But I have only known three Alphas in my time on this earth, and every single one of them has been determined to make my life hell."

He rolled his eyes before giving me a tiny nudge to my shoulder, just to get me out of the doorway, and then closed it behind me.

I balled my fists, glaring at the spot where his eyes would have been before turning back to face the mirror. I decided to brush my teeth first. I started at an aggressive pace, ripping open the package and squeezing a larger glob of toothpaste onto the bristles than was necessary.

"You still there, Night?" I asked, wetting the brush under the tap.

Instead of responding verbally, he knocked on the door hard enough to make me wince.

"Asshole," I grumbled under my breath.

"I heard that."

"Good!"

He bumped the door again. "Eighteen minutes."

I huffed out a sigh and brushed my teeth furiously before spitting in the sink. With that done, I turned to the shower and got the water as hot as I could stand. I was pent up with energy, wired from the exchange I'd had with

Night. Now I had to take off my clothing and get into the water, with the man who made my blood rush in my veins standing right outside my door.

I stared at the dark wood as though I could see through it to him. There was an extra layer of complication to my emotions because I was wearing *his* clothes. I took off his shirt, then his pants, and finally my bra and panties. It was a bit surreal to stand there naked with him less than five feet away. He could walk in here at any time and see me wearing nothing at all.

Just to be safe, I crept to the door and turned the lock on the knob. It wouldn't be enough to stop him if he really wanted to come in, but it made me a bit more comfortable.

With that done, I got into the shower and stood in the hot water, letting it seep into my aching muscles. I grabbed the bar of soap sitting on the side of the tub. It had rosemary and wildflowers floating in a cream-white bar. It was likely homemade, unlike the bars that the Kings brought back from human cities.

I took a sniff and found it had a lovely smell— neither a masculine or feminine scent—it was pleasant and clean. It reminded me of Night. I washed my hair until it no longer felt dirty and greasy, and then I moved on to the rest of my body. I had never enjoyed a shower more. Hot water and soap had never felt more like a luxury.

I hadn't forgotten that I was there as a prisoner, but things might not be so bad as long as I had a shower, food, and nice company. Violet would stop me from escaping, I knew that for sure, but she was a kind woman who made me think of Mom. I would keep looking for an opportunity to escape, but I figured it was important to enjoy the little things I had access to rather than focus on all the negatives.

Outside the door, I heard Night cough. The reminder of his presence sent goosebumps over my skin. I moved my hands down from my shoulders and upper back to my stomach, my arms brushing across my nipples. I bit my lip, my mind flashing back to the dreams I'd shared with the green-eyed man. Night? I shifted even lower, remembering what the beast behind those green eyes had done to me in those dreams. My heartbeat quickened as my fingers found my core. They brushed over that sensitive nub, and I accidentally let out a small moan.

Night began to pound on the door, startling me out of the erotic moment.

"Hurry the fuck up," he growled. "I have better things to do than wait outside for you."

I showered more quickly after that, my face on fire. When I finished the shower and dressed in the clothes, another pair of pants and a t-shirt, I unlocked the door and slipped out. I ducked my head as I walked past Night, hoping he attributed my red face to the heat of the shower and not embarrassment.

Chapter 16 - Night

I woke to the sound of a door closing shut. I knew it was Bryn's door when I heard Mom's footsteps walking down the hallway, the sound of silverware jingling in time with her gait. She'd taken to having breakfast with Bryn every morning. I wondered what they talked about or if they talked at all.

When my mind went to Bryn, I thought *again* about what had happened a few days ago, after her shower. She'd stood there, her hair wet, my shirt hanging from her shoulders, her face red from the tiny moan she'd made as she showered…I guess it's no wonder those steely-blue eyes continued to follow me into my dreams.

Alluring woman that she was, Bryn had quickly become the bane of my existence.

I sat up with a growl and tossed my legs over the side of the bed. I heaved a sigh, resting my elbows on my knees and letting my hair fall forward. I wasn't sure what I should do now that I was awake. That dream made me want to go for a run.

I took a deep breath and was immediately inundated with Bryn's sweet scent. It brought me back to my dream, to the memory of the soft woman in my arms and the way she felt bouncing on my cock—

I stood up quickly when my wolf began to pace with energy. I needed to go for a run alright, but not in my wolf form. I couldn't trust him to behave himself, not when Bryn smelled so good and was so close.

Something needed to change about this arrangement. When I'd first brought her onto my territory, having her stay in my cabin had seemed like the only option. But if just the scent of her could drive me wild, this setup was unsustainable. And it wasn't just her smell or her closeness that disturbed me and set me on edge—it was also the way she sobbed at night when she thought I was asleep. Her cries agitated my wolf, and it was impossible for me to get any rest.

Bryn was going to drive me into an early grave if I let things go on like this. I needed to find a solution, and maybe going for a run would help.

I got dressed and washed up. When I was ready, I stopped by Bryn's door just to make sure Mom had locked it. The bolt held tight, and I let out a quiet, relieved breath. Honestly, I didn't feel like I could fully trust Mom when it came to Bryn. She had taken an immediate interest in Bryn, and I didn't understand why. I had tried once to talk Mom out of visiting with Bryn, declaring that making nice with Bryn wouldn't matter in the end because she wasn't staying once she'd served her purpose. But of course, Mom had ignored me.

I guess she must get something out of these morning meetings with Bryn if she kept coming. I knew better than to continue debating the issue with her, so I allowed the morning chats and meal drop-offs to continue, even though I knew it was pointless.

Outside, the air was crisp and cool, and the sky was pale blue with splotches of gray clouds spread out along the horizon. Ideal weather for a morning run. I began at a jog, heading into the forest, my breath puffing out as white steam in front of me as I fell into a rhythm. The forest seemed to open up for me as I moved deeper along the path that I, and so many other wolves before me, had worn into the ground.

I upped my pace as I went deeper into the forest. I could almost close my eyes—I knew the path so well. When I went on runs, I felt connected to the ground beneath my feet, the trees on either side, and the tree leaves and sky above. My mind would become a blank slate, filled with nothing but the satisfaction and joy of being in my own skin. But today, my thoughts refused to shut up. Like the incessant buzzing of a wasp, they were all concerned with the huge, Bryn-sized thorn in my side.

I put my head down and pushed myself into a sprint. The woods began to blur around me as I ran faster, hoping I could force her from my mind. It didn't work.

As I came up to the hot springs, I slid to a stop. The springs were one of the few luxuries that the Wargs enjoyed. There were about a dozen pools ranging in size to accommodate two to twenty wolves at one time. The pools were built by generations of Wargs lining up large, flat river stones to delineate each one. The water was crystal clear and deliciously warm. I was tempted to get inside one of the smaller pools, but I decided to take a seat at the foot of a tall pine tree instead.

I wiped sweat from my forehead with my sleeve and leaned against the trunk. I couldn't keep ignoring the issue—I needed to figure out what I wanted to do with Bryn. I knew my wolves were curious about what exactly I was going to do with her, and keeping them in the dark for so long would be bad for morale. I needed to give them an answer soon.

So, I thought back to the night we met. Why had I taken her?

At the time, seeing her strapped up against the wall, I'd known immediately what Troy, the son of a bitch, wanted to do with her. Before I'd known her name, before I'd even heard her voice, the knowledge of what was soon to be her fate had almost sent me into a rage. Just thinking about the paleness of her face, the quick, frightened beating of her heart, and the dull, hopeless look in her eyes had me jumping back up to my feet. I started to pace back and forth in front of the pools.

When Troy had returned to his cabin, speaking in that disgusting singsong tone, the possessiveness and need to control had wafted off the new Alpha like a bad stench. At the time, I had sensed so much hatred in Troy—paired with a strange obsession for Bryn—that I hadn't even questioned my decision to leave with her. If I hadn't left with her, I knew I'd be abandoning her to whatever torture he had planned for her before the challenge ceremony.

At that moment, I had only wanted to get her as far away from Troy as possible. It was only after the fact that I started to believe I could use her as a bargaining chip. Now I had something that Troy wanted, just like Troy had something that I deserved.

Though I didn't understand it, I could admit to myself that I wasn't a neutral party when it came to Bryn.

Whatever conclusion I came to now would be tainted by this illogical interest I had in her. What I needed to do was present our options to my most trusted wolves and then have someone else make the decisions about Bryn until I could figure out how to get my head on straight.

With my mind made up about my next steps, I started the jog home. As I neared the compound, I tapped into the telepathic link I shared with my pack. I sent out a call to Dom and the others I was closest with. *"We need to have a meeting. Head to the conference room."*

I didn't need to follow up to make sure they would follow through with my command—I knew they would. So I headed to the mess hall. When I walked inside, I found several families enjoying their breakfasts. I put on an easy smile as they watched me pass.

"Good morning, Alpha," Janet, an older female wolf, greeted. "I'm glad I caught you."

"Good morning, Janet," I nodded. Though I needed to head to the conference room at the back of the mess hall, it wasn't so dire that I couldn't give her a few minutes of my time.

"I wanted to thank you for the work you did on our roof last week." She reached into her hand-stitched bag made from worn denim jeans and removed a small, green jar. "I made you some mint jelly."

I accepted the small jar with a wider smile. As was the case with my mom and so many of the other female wolves of my pack, I knew better than to argue about receiving these gifts.

"Thank you so much, Janet. I appreciate it."

She beamed at me. "Let me know if you need any recipes for it, but as you already know, it is absolutely divine on lamb."

"I'll keep that in mind." I nodded goodbye to her and then continued toward my destination.

The conference room was small, with a table in the center of it—a table that I'd built myself after I became Alpha. My wolves stood around the table at attention, all ready to carry out whatever order I had for them. As I approached the table, Dom caught my eye. A question glinted in his gaze. I usually told him beforehand about meetings. I nodded back at him; Dom would find out the purpose of this meeting soon enough.

"Let's get this meeting underway," I said, taking a seat at the head of the table. Everyone followed suit. "First, what news do we have?"

"Not much from me, Alpha," Redford said. "My mate's just happy to have me back home."

"Same here," Anthony said. A scar cut across the middle of his face. "Mine told me expressly to let you know she appreciated you making sure that we all arrived in one piece."

I smiled, though guilt again gnawed at me. Things could have gone a hell of a lot worse, thanks to my impromptu decision. To distract myself, I turned to William. He was a fantastic tracker, and he had been one of the wolves who were injured in the altercation with the Kings.

"How's your leg?" I asked. I knew William had recovered, but I could see that he had something on his mind from the way he shifted in his seat.

"Completely healed, thank you, Alpha," William nodded. He was an excellent man for me to have on my team, but he was a bit shy. "I did want to announce that my mate let me know that she's expecting."

"Hot damn!" Dom exclaimed, pounding his fist against the table. "What is this, pup number three for you?"

William nodded again, the apples of his cheeks turning slightly pink with pride.

The table erupted with congratulations and well wishes for William and his family. The men spoke about how much their mates would appreciate another opportunity to dote on a new pup. As the conversation went on, William's face became more and more red, but it was obvious that he appreciated the well-wishes. I would have liked to allow the talk and congratulations to continue for the rest of the meeting, but we had business to attend to.

I cleared my throat, and the room quieted. "Congratulations, William," I said, "this is fantastic news."

William inclined his head in thanks.

"What else is there to report?" I asked.

"We caught the scent of three feral wolves at the edge of our borders," Iggy said. "But they were probably just testing to see where our borders began and ended."

"Keep an eye on that, Iggy." The last thing I needed was a group of ferals venturing too far on my land. But it was a small concern compared to everything else on my mind. "What do we know of the Kings' movements?" I asked.

Kai spoke up. "Scouts have reported a group of Kings' hunters sniffing around our borders. They hadn't done anything until this morning when they attacked two of our junior hunters who had ventured outside our territory."

"I see." I bristled a bit at the knowledge that the Kings were already making moves. "Did they survive?"

"Barely. They managed to drag themselves back into our borders before it was too late. Last I checked with our healers, they're in stable condition."

"Good." I leaned forward and set my elbows on the table. As I digested that information, the door opened quietly. My mom, the only person who was allowed to enter the conference room when it was in use, had brought buttered rolls, dried fruits, and meats for us to enjoy while we spoke.

"That's troubling but not unexpected," I said. "As you all know, I've acquired something—some*one*—that the Kings' new Alpha desires. I believe that having her here will destabilize Redwolf enough that he'll be even more reckless than he usually is."

"We could use her as a bargaining chip," Dom said, "as long as Redwolf is as obsessed as you believe he is."

"Oh, he is," I replied. "I saw the look in his eyes. If he's got his hunters ready to pounce on our people the minute they step outside our borders, then he's desperate to have her back."

"If true," Kai said, "we can move forward with our original plan."

I nodded, pleased that my people were coming to that conclusion without too much prompting. "I want to challenge Troy on the night of the next full moon," I said.

"That's…" Anthony paused to count in his head. "That's twenty-three days away! We need to let Redwolf know."

"I'll draft the message," I said. "If Troy refuses the challenge, we keep the human. And if he agrees, I'll return her to him on the night of the challenge." As I sat back in my chair, I felt a telepathic nudge from Dom, who wore an uncharacteristic frown on his face.

"You sure Troy will go for this, Night?"

"I'm positive. His pride won't let him lose something he's desperate to possess. He'll take the challenge."

Dom nodded and turned to the rest of the table. "Prepare our most experienced hunters," he said. "We need them ready to deliver the message Night will write."

Iggy, a female wolf, spoke up. "Alpha, in the meantime, are you sure you want to keep the human in your cabin? On the chance that Troy had a hunter sneak into our borders, that would be an obvious place for her to be."

My heart thudded with relief so strong I could have kissed her. Because of Iggy, I wouldn't have to bring that issue up myself. But I kept my expression thoughtful. Neutral. "Good point. Would you be willing to take her, Iggy?"

"Ah, I'm not so sure," she said, shaking her head. "My cabin's one of the loudest in the village. I think my family would drive her crazy."

"True enough." *And I don't need to give her any more reason to try and escape.* "Any other suggestions?"

"I could keep her at my place," Dom suggested.

I sent a sharp glare his way, which only made him smirk.

"I don't think we should have her stay with anyone who has pups," Kai said. "That would put them and their families at risk."

I agreed.

Mom cleared her throat from where she stood near the sink. I had been so focused on the discussion that I'd forgotten she was there.

"Bryn can stay with me," she said. "I'll be able to keep an eye on her."

I stared at her. It was one thing to speak with Bryn and have breakfast with her every morning, but it was another thing for my mom to keep Bryn in her home.

"What are you planning, Mom?" I sent to her.

She crossed her arms and stared at me, refusing to answer. I sighed. It was obvious that she wasn't going to budge on the issue, and I didn't feel like trying to convince her otherwise.

"Alright, she can stay with you. *But* she isn't allowed to leave your home. She is our prisoner and a necessary part of our plan. She can't have free reign of the village."

Mom frowned. She looked very much like she wanted to scold me for the way I talked about Bryn, but she wouldn't contradict me in front of my team. Instead, I'd get an earful later.

"I agree to those terms. I assume she can move in as soon as I have a room prepared for her?"

"That's fine. When you're ready, let one of us know. We'll escort her to your cabin."

Mom nodded with a sigh before walking out of the room. I looked at Dom, who gave a slight shrug. Once Mom had closed the door behind her, we began to work out the details of getting the letter drafted and having it sent to Troy by nightfall.

I knew my mom was frustrated with me, although I had the impression that there was more to her frustration than just the rules I'd set. But for now, that didn't matter.

My most trusted wolves and I were on the same page, and best of all, Bryn would soon be out of my home. With her gone, my wolf would settle down, and I'd finally be able to enjoy some rest. I could hardly wait.

Chapter 17 - Bryn

I bit my lip as I crouched by the window. I had been busy since I woke this morning. Violet was later than normal, and that made me uneasy. With a burst of inspiration, I had leapt out of bed to try yet again to pry open the window.

I had managed to form one of the wax candles into a wedge that just fit under the slight gap between the window and the sill. It had taken a while to get the wax hot enough for me to mold the candle into the right shape, and I'd really believed that it might work. But as I forced the wax into the small space, the candle chipped apart. Some of the wax was too soft to take the abuse, and the part that had hardened simply wasn't strong enough to force the window open. I stepped back with a frustrated sigh. Was there anything else in the room that I could try?

Suddenly, the door opened. I jumped and tried to stand in front of the remains of my most recent escape attempt.

"Oh! I'm glad to see you awake," Violet greeted. She looked from the window to me and then gave a knowing smile. "And I see you're pretty active this morning."

I decided not to acknowledge her comment. After all, anything I said might further incriminate me. Instead, I looked at Violet's empty hands. "No breakfast this morning?"

Violet's expression brightened. "That's the good news," she said, clapping her hands. "Starting today, you'll be living with me!"

I paused, blinking. "Wait, really?"

"Yes! Night and his men decided it would be best for you to live somewhere more comfortable."

I resisted the urge to smirk. I doubted that Night would ever make a decision for me that would make me "more comfortable," but I wouldn't argue with her.

Violet is a nice enough woman, but this is a problem. Now, I'll have to get used to a whole new environment. I had a few other escape plans in development, but if I was leaving this room, I'd have to rethink everything.

"Is there anything you want to bring with you?" Violet asked.

I had literally nothing to pack, but the pillow I'd been sleeping on was the nicest one I'd ever had, so I plucked it off the bed and held it against my chest like a shield. It had absorbed many of my tears, and if I pushed my face into it, I could almost smell Night. It wouldn't have been comforting for Night to be there himself, but his scent was another story. Something about it soothed my nerves. I told myself it was because it was the only consistent and therefore familiar aspect of my abduction, but in truth, I couldn't explain it.

"Just this," I replied. "If I can bring it?"

"Of course you can! If that's all you want, let's head to my cabin."

I walked behind Violet and looked around at the cabin as we left. Now that I was seeing it in the daytime, I noted that despite how modestly Night lived, the place was homey. He didn't have any decorations in the cabin, so it lacked personality, but it seemed comfortable enough. The more I looked around, the more I felt that the space suited a man who was as hard to read as Night.

I let out a long sigh. "Violet, how could a nice woman like you ever give birth to the asshole who likes to keep me locked away?"

Violet laughed so hard, we had to pause in front of the front door for her to catch her breath. "I understand why you'd ask me something like that, but he's more like me than you know, girlie."

"Sure, okay." I accepted the answer, though I'd yet to see any evidence of that.

"Alright, before we head out that door, I need to lay down some ground rules from the 'asshole' himself. You can't try anything like what you were doing in that room. Do you understand?"

I nodded. I understood alright, but that didn't mean I'd obey.

Violet gave me another knowing glance. She opened the door to reveal Dom standing on the other side. He wore a wide smile on his face.

"Hey there," he said. "Long time no see."

My eyes widened at the unexpected visit. It had been days since I'd last seen the large, friendly wolf. I couldn't keep myself from returning his smile. He'd been so kind to me on the hike to the Wargs' territory, so seeing him now was like a breath of fresh air. I knew I couldn't trust him, of course, but he wasn't as much of a jerk as Night was.

"You're not here to take me back to that room, are you?" I asked.

"Not at all," Violet said. "He's our guide."

Dom nodded, pointing over his shoulder with his thumb. "I'm here to escort you lovely ladies up to Violet's cabin."

I raised a brow. "Uh-huh, I doubt that. I bet you're really here to make sure I don't run away."

Dom's snort turned into a laugh. "Aren't you perceptive? Got any other observations for me?"

As we began walking, I looked him over, taking in the tired hue of purple beneath his eyes and the slight slope in his shoulders. "I bet you're not much of an early riser. Either that or you had a late night."

He blew out a low whistle. "My own mother never noticed those things about me. Are you a professional witness? A spy, maybe?"

"If I were a spy, this would be a really convoluted way for me to infiltrate your village, don't you think?"

"I suppose I can't argue that. But maybe that's just what you want me to think."

I chuckled. "I guess you'll just have to wait and see, huh? A good spy never reveals her secrets."

"Oh, to be young and full of wit," Violet sighed. "Those were the days, eh?"

"Please, Violet, you look younger than me," Dom said, slipping his arm around her shoulders. "And without your intelligence and wit, the pack would be much worse off, I'm sure."

"Don't let Night hear you say that," she chuckled. "He'd never forgive you.

"He's probably already upset at me for something unrelated," Dom said. "You know that man has a short fuse."

"We have that in common then," I said, surprising myself with my ability to keep up. It had seemed impossible to participate in conversations on the Kings' compound, but here it was much easier to join in. "Seems we're both in the line of fire for your Alpha's anger."

Dom threw back his head and gave a deep, loud laugh. Violet and I couldn't help but join in.

"When you put it like that," he said, wiping away a tear, "I guess we're in similar boats."

Violet's cabin was just a few yards up from Night's, and both were on the far corner of the living area. A few trees separated their homes from the rest of the pack. The wood was painted canary yellow, and the windows were trimmed with white.

The front door was a deep ocean blue, and there were empty flower boxes in the windows on the ground floor. Below the windows was a beautiful pinewood deck that wrapped around the front of the cabin—one that I couldn't help but admire. On either side of the front door, there were two large clay planters that both held rose bushes. The branches were just beginning to bud as the weather warmed, and I had a feeling that soon they would boast gorgeous blooms.

Violet opened the door and held it for us to walk inside. "Alright, let's give you the tour," she said.

The cabin was smaller than Night's—two bedrooms, one bathroom, a small sitting area, a kitchen, and…that was it. It was quaint, with dozens of homemade pottery pieces and art from either Violet herself or another wolf. The furniture was brightly painted in eclectic colors, and yet somehow, it all fitted together.

I smiled as I took everything in. *Mom would love this!* With that thought echoing in my mind, my smile immediately disappeared. Sadness and the painful reality of my situation yet again fell over my shoulders. Violet and Dom chatted and joked around behind me, but I couldn't join them. It didn't matter how nicely the two of them treated me—I was still a prisoner, and they'd essentially told me as much. I was alone, without my mom or anything familiar, and I couldn't let myself get pulled in by the banter or the beautiful deck or the supposed kindness of these wolves.

I needed to keep my eyes and ears open for a way to escape.

Dom stayed around for another hour while the three of us drank tea and ate bread with delicious fruit preserves. I kept my pillow in my lap and tried to stay engaged with the conversation. By the time Dom left, I believed I'd managed to hide my sadness well.

"Bryn," Violet began, turning to me. "I didn't want to say this in front of Dom, but I don't want you to think of this place as a prison, no matter what my son or his team says."

"Do you know how long they plan to keep me as a prisoner?"

"I really can't say."

I stared at her. Violet seemed like such an open, soft person, but she could be as unreadable as her son when she wanted to be. And right then, I couldn't tell if Violet knew the answer to my question. Then again, the fact that Violet was being obtuse at all meant that she was hiding something from me, didn't it?

"I want you to feel as at home as possible while you're here," Violet said. "So, you are free to use all of my home. There will be no locked rooms unless you decide to lock them yourself. Of course, the front and back doors and all of the windows will be locked, and you won't ever be alone, but you'll at least be able to use the restroom or cook or get a drink of water when the need arises without having to ask first."

That actually sounded pretty nice—at least compared to how I was living in Night's cabin. It was a bit of freedom, and it would surely make my escape so much easier.

"One other thing." Violet pushed away from the table. "You sit tight for a moment. I'll be right back."

I thought I'd have a bit of time to myself to explore on my own, but Violet really was gone and back within just a few seconds. The older woman was much sprier than I had thought.

"I found you some clothes." She held out a pair of jeans and a blue plaid blouse. "There are a few more clothes for you in the dressers and closet in your room."

I left the pillow at the dining table to eagerly accept the clothes, and Violet let me use the restroom to change. It was amazing what having clothes that actually fit did for my mental state. I'd been on a rotation of Night's baggy shirts and pants for days and had begun to think of myself as more of a clothes hanger than a woman.

Violet explained the finer details of the house, such as where the cleaning equipment, spices, and books were kept, before she led me through the back door. My eyes lit up as I saw the garden out back. It wasn't as large as the one that Mom and I worked on, but it was around an acre of land with plenty of crops to work on and love.

But the excitement I felt was tinged with more pain. What would Mom have thought of the space, of the house? What would she have said?

"Bryn?" Violet came around to look into my face. "I'd hoped the garden would make you happy, but you seem so sad."

"It reminds me of my mom," I muttered, my eyes beginning to fill with tears. "It reminds me of the garden we tended. It was the only thing I really, truly enjoyed about living in the Kings' pack. But now it's…it's hundreds of miles away."

"Oh, honey." Violet teared up a bit herself, which surprised me. She took my shoulders and gave me a smile. "I wanted to let you know that you're free to work in the garden whenever you like. We really could use an extra pair of hands tending to the crops. Would you like that?"

I nodded. I would like that a lot. Working in the garden would not only be a wonderful way to pass the time, but it might also make it easier for me to escape.

Just as I had that thought, Violet said, "But there's something else you should know." She pointed to the tree line.

At first, I didn't see anything. But as I continued to stare, I realized with a chill that there were two wolves hidden among the trees. They looked familiar, somehow.

"Those sentries will be around twenty-four-seven," Violet explained. "They'll let Night know when you've tried to escape, and Night will be able to catch you and bring you back within minutes."

As Violet spoke, I remembered where I'd seen the wolves before. They were the ones I'd seen standing outside my window when I was first locked in Night's cabin. No wonder they hadn't helped me when they saw my window message.

"Anyway," Violet went on, "it's far, far better to let fate play its hand than to waste your energy trying to fight it."

I had no idea what the hell that was supposed to mean, but there was something comforting about it. The words themselves were not reassuring, but Mom had often used vague, cryptic messages when she talked to me too. I tried to keep the tears at bay, but everything about Violet, the garden, and the cabin made me miss Mom so much it hurt to breathe.

"Let's get you back inside, girlie," Violet suggested, seeing my discomfort.

I went back into the house without a fight. I suddenly felt drained, both emotionally and physically—I had no energy left to think of a possible escape plan.

After I set my pillow on the bed, I helped Violet take care of the dishes from breakfast. We ate lunch together, and dinner, and finally, as the sky turned the rich, dark blue of night, we sat next to the fireplace. After the garden, the rest of the day had passed by without my having to pay much attention. I was still thinking of my mom.

Eventually, I felt something warm drape across my shoulders. I looked around in the firelight and found that Violet had covered me with a pink and blue knitted throw. Violet settled down at my side and offered a cup of hot lavender and chamomile tea. I accepted it and took a deep sip. To my surprise, Violet had sweetened it with honey. That bit of kindness was all it took to push me over the edge.

As I lowered the cup, tears filled my eyes and slipped down my cheeks. I hated being Night's prisoner because it meant I wasn't free, but had I ever known true freedom? In the Kings' pack, I had been ignored, belittled, and underappreciated. I hadn't known a day of peace living under the thumbs of the Terrible T's and Troy. My home was never my home, but at least my mom had been there to take care of me when I was hurt or lonely or scared.

I had been so confident that I'd be able to escape and live on my own with the humans, but now that I was forced to be away from Mom, that no longer seemed true. How could I have ever thought that I'd survive?

Violet's constant presence while I cried was nice, but it didn't quiet my sadness. In fact, I felt even more out of place sitting in the middle of Violet's floor, sobbing my eyes dry than I had ever felt with the Kings.

After another hour, Violet lit a candle and led me to my bedroom. The candle was more for my benefit than Violet's, as she could see easily in the dark. It was more thoughtfulness than I was used to from anyone other than my mom.

Inside the room, I flopped onto the bed and pulled the pillow close.

"I'll be right down the hall if you need anything," Violet said gently. "And I mean anything, even if it's just to talk, okay?"

I didn't respond.

Violet gave me a smile. "Get some sleep, girlie. Tomorrow, you'll be able to spend the sunrise in the garden. Maybe the world will look different for you in a new light."

Again, I remained quiet.

"Alright, honey, I'll see you in the morning." She left the lit candle on the nightstand and walked out of the room, closing the door softly behind her.

I turned on my side toward the window and held the pillow tight against my chest. I had no idea how much longer I would be a prisoner here. For all I knew, I would die in this house. Violet had said she wanted me to feel at home here, but how could I when I was surrounded by enemies and strangers? How could I see the world in a new light when my future looked so bleak?

I bit my lip as more tears poured down my cheeks. Clutching the pillow more tightly, I buried my face into it. Alone in the room, with a hint of Night's scent in the pillow, I could admit to myself that the tears I shed now were different from any I'd shed before. This time, I wasn't crying because I missed my mom or because I was a prisoner. These tears were from loneliness.

I knew now that I would never truly belong anywhere—I would never have a home.

Chapter 18 - Bryn

I woke to the smell of coffee and breakfast. It had been three days since I had started living with Violet, and so far, it had been really nice. Violet brought food from the mess hall, and we ate together for every meal. Despite my circumstances, I had really enjoyed getting to know Violet and all of her little quirks.

Today, breakfast was biscuits and mushroom gravy. The biscuits were perfectly cooked and fluffy. They felt like a slightly sweetened cloud on my tongue. The gravy itself was creamy and buttery, and I savored the taste while listening to Violet talk about the people of the village.

It was lovely and entertaining to hear some gossip, but it wasn't enough. I wasn't allowed to leave the premises of Violet's home, and I missed interactions with other people. I missed listening to the sound of conversation going on around me and the way that the pups would joke around and play with me without any prejudice against me for being human. I missed the few young mothers who would chat with me.

After breakfast, I went upstairs to dress in a pair of tight-fitting blue jeans and a pink hoodie. I slipped on a pair of black boots Violet had found that fit me perfectly.

Ready to work, I headed outside to the garden, squinting against the brightness. The sun was barely coming over the mountain, and the sky was filled with hues of pink and purple. I stood in the modest garden and tried for the third time to follow Violet's advice to see it as a new day with new opportunities. What I saw was a beautiful sunrise, but it didn't make me feel better about my captivity.

With a sigh, I turned away from the sunrise. I pulled on a pair of gardening gloves and grabbed a small trowel and shovel from the crate by the back door. I crouched low to the ground and set to work, muscle memory allowing me to space out as I tended the soil.

I checked the new growth of the lettuce, cabbages, and broccoli. I could tell from the way the soil was disturbed that they had been planted relatively recently, but they were quite far along. Here, like in the Kings' pack, Violet must have known something about the land to allow her to grow gorgeous crops even in the off-seasons. I could tell that Violet's garden didn't get the kind of yields that we got at home—Mom's garden was rarely burdened with even a single weed. But with a bit more TLC, I believed I could make some improvements here.

The irony of assisting the pack that was currently holding me hostage wasn't lost on me, but it didn't stop me from plucking dead leaves and weeds from the ground. Every garden deserved to be taken care of and loved. If I could be the one to help a garden thrive, well, it was too tremendous an opportunity to pass up.

As I continued to work, I heard a noise that caused me to look up. For an awful second, I was back in the garden with Troy. *"Make sure you're ready to ring in your birthday in a way that you won't forget because it'll be the last one you see as a free woman..."*

But I snapped out of that memory when I realized there was a young woman about my age staring at me from the back door. It seemed that the sound I had heard was the woman accidentally kicking the tool crate. I slowly stood from my crouch, watching the newcomer with slightly narrowed eyes.

She was tall, likely around five foot nine, with long, jet-black hair that fell in waves down her back. It reminded me a bit of Night's. She was beautiful, but it was understated in her soft cheekbones, round jawline, and deep, brown eyes. The woman and I continued to stare at each other until she finally leapt down the steps toward me.

I flinched as she came to a stop in front of me and the squash plants I was pruning. I half-expected a confrontation of some sort, but instead, I got a hug.

"Hello, hello," the woman said, stepping back to look me in the eye. "You must be Bryn! I'm Octavia Black, and you can consider me your new best friend."

I blinked, my brain slow to catch up with that whirlwind of a description. "I—I'm Bryn Hunter—"

"I know, I know! I don't know if I said already, but I've been dying to meet you since you showed up! You're kind of the only thing the pack's been talking about. But I haven't been able to find time to stop by for a visit until today. It's good that I bumped into Violet at the mess hall. She let me know that it was okay as long as I didn't overwhelm you." She paused. "Wait. I'm not overwhelming you, am I?"

I stared at her. I wasn't sure what I thought of the new woman. Other than Dom, Octavia was the only person I had spoken to since moving into Violet's house. I was cautious, but at the same time, I felt I didn't need to be. Octavia didn't seem to be an immediate threat, and she was obviously a very interesting personality. I supposed I could see where things went with the conversation.

"You talk a little fast," I said with a cautious smile, "but I'm not overwhelmed."

"Yeah, I get that a lot. But I'm glad I'm not bombarding you." She gave me a perfect, wide smile. "Actually, I was worried when I came over that you were still going to be asleep, but it's good to see you're an early riser like the rest of us."

"Oh, well, I actually grew up in a wolf pack, so I have a pretty similar sleep schedule."

"No way!" Octavia's eyes widened. "I've never heard of a human living so closely with us! I'm dying to know everything about you."

I took a step back, uncomfortable. I didn't know Octavia, yet the girl was asking to know all of my personal business? "There's not much to know, really."

Octavia paused, and then her smile turned into a thoughtful frown. "I think I'm getting ahead of myself. I'll give you some more info about myself." She touched her chest. "I'm Tavi, as you know, and I'm twenty years old. The big, stupid brute who brought you here is like a brother to me, but we're not related by blood. How's that for a start?"

"That's not bad." I smiled, tickled by how casually Octavia insulted Night. "I'm also twenty years old, but I don't have any blood relatives. My mom adopted me."

"That wasn't so hard, was it?"

And though I still hesitated with most of the other Wargs, I started to relax around Octavia. This new person was someone I thought I might enjoy getting to know.

Two more days had passed since I moved in with Violet, but I hardly noticed the passage of time. Tavi (Octavia insisted I call her by her nickname) had come over every day, and we had spent countless hours together. Most of the time, I spent gardening or doing chores while Tavi supplied me with endless amounts of stories and gossip.

We grew closer as the days went by, and I realized with growing warmth that Tavi was my first real friend. Never had I felt I could spend so much time with another person who wasn't my mom, but Tavi was such an easygoing and open person that I couldn't help but grow to care for her.

And I was finding that I really enjoyed Violet's company as well. Violet always made sure to let me know that she appreciated having me around to help around the house or in the garden. She also enjoyed making very tasty, very spicy foods with the ingredients she had, and I enjoyed the way the dishes put such sizzling comfort on my tongue. Violet also showed great reverence for the land and the soil, just like Mom always did, and that helped me feel more comfortable around her.

Though I had stopped crying myself to sleep every night, dreading what the next day would bring, I was still unable to leave Violet's home. The wolves in the forest had their eyes on me all the time, and I could never fully relax.

On the sixth day after I moved in with Violet, Tavi burst into the cabin, announcing herself at the top of her lungs. I very nearly dropped the cup I was washing, covered in suds, but fortunately, I got hold of it before disaster could strike.

"Octavia," Violet called, "what did I tell you about knocking, honey?"

"I'm sorry, Violet," Tavi spun into the kitchen, her hair lifting around her shoulders as she did. "I'm in a tremendous mood." She wore a pair of black jeans that were ripped at the knees and a short-sleeve red shirt that tied in a knot at her waist. She looked great.

"What's the occasion?" I asked, quickly finishing with the cup so I could set it down. Now that the dishes were done, Violet went upstairs to let Tavi and I talk.

"My birthday!" Tavi took my hand and spun me around the table. "I'm officially twenty-one!"

I hadn't expected that Tavi would be one year older than me—the girl had just as much energy as the pups back home. "Happy birthday, Tavi. I'm sorry I don't have anything to give you."

"Silly," Tavi poked my nose. "Your company is all I want from you, sweet Bryn. In fact, I'd like to invite you to have lunch with me in the mess hall."

"Oh…Tavi, I'm sorry, but I'm not allowed to leave the house."

"No, no. I got special permission because it's my birthday."

I blinked. "Really?"

"Yeah! We just have to be escorted by Dom, but that's okay, right?"

"Oh…" I wasn't sure what to say. The idea of stepping off Violet's property was so tempting, especially when I'd have Tavi by my side, but it was also terrifying. For one, I had no idea how the Wargs would feel about me. Dom, Violet, and Tavi had been nice, but what if the rest of the Wargs displayed more of the savagery that I'd grown up hearing? Not to mention that disobeying Night might lead to him getting pissed off enough that he decided to throw me in a dungeon somewhere.

Then again, it had been six days since I saw him last. The closest I'd been to him was last night, when I'd heard his deep voice in Violet's kitchen. I was surprised to find that I missed him so much I was willing to get on the floor and press my ear to the floorboards just to be that much closer to him. But he had kidnapped me, hadn't he? Yet he was avoiding me for reasons I didn't understand. Against my better judgment, I wanted to see him.

"Come onnn," Tavi begged, her voice bringing me back into the present. "They're serving meatloaf in the mess hall today. It's so good."

It was true. Violet usually brought food from the mess hall, and the meatloaf with mashed potatoes was my favorite because of how creamy the cooks made the potatoes, but could I really do this?

"Don't worry, Bryn. You're good to go," Violet's voice came from the staircase. She walked down the steps with a few pieces of clothing folded across her arms. "I thought it might be good to get you some cute clothes."

My jaw dropped. "But you already let me have the ones in the dressers. You didn't have to—"

Violet waved that away. "Yes, yes, but a lot of those pieces were still too big on you, Bryn. It's time you have something cute, something you can meet people in."

Tavi grinned. "You knew I was going to ask her, Violet?"

"Of course, dear. I know everything," She winked. "Now come here, Bryn. We have to see which of these are good enough for you to officially meet the pack in."

About half an hour later, I stood in the sitting room in the outfit Violet and Tavi had chosen for me—tight blue jeans, a baby-blue top that hugged my chest before puffing out, and a thin black jacket. The boots completed the outfit.

"You look *amazing*," Tavi gushed.

"Th-thank you." I pushed my hair behind my ears, my face warm. Tavi had also brought over some makeup and hair supplies and had given me a full makeover. My wild brown hair fell around my shoulders in soft, voluminous waves. My lips were coated in a thin layer of pink gloss, my cheeks had a bit of blush, and my eyelids shimmered with silvery-blue powder. It was the first time I'd ever worn makeup or had my hair done like this, and I felt like a princess.

"And it looks like your escort is here," Violet said. "I'll go and get him."

"Um, Tavi?" I said gently. "Why would you go through all of this trouble when it's your birthday?"

Tavi smiled, looking into my eyes. "Because you're my friend, Bryn. And after I heard what happened to you on your birthday, well…" she shook her head. "Everyone deserves to feel beautiful on their special day, don't you think?"

I was too emotional to speak, so I settled on a nod.

"Besides, girl," she looped her arm through mine, "first impressions are everything, and we have to make sure that you make waves today."

"Y-yeah!" I quickly dabbed away my tears with my fingertips before they could ruin my makeup. "Let's go!"

At the front door, Dom and Violet laughed about something he'd said before Tavi and I arrived. He looked up as we approached, and his eyes widened slightly before settling into his usual easy smile. It was brief, but I noticed that his gaze lingered on Tavi.

"I can't believe you two lovely ladies got all dressed up for me," Dom said. "If I'd known, I would have worn better pants." His were covered in old splotches of paint. No doubt they were the ones he wore when he repaired things around the compound.

"Oh, Dom, please," Tavi said, lightly hitting his arm. "You say that to all the girls who're just trying to enjoy their birthday with their friends."

"But when I say it around you, I mean it, Tav."

She snorted at that and walked past him, still holding me close. "Sure you do."

I looked up at my friend and found Tavi's cheeks slightly red. I felt as though I'd just witnessed something private between the wolves, but I couldn't be sure. Female and male wolves paired off so quickly in the Kings' pack that I wasn't sure what the courting process was like for them. *Is there something there, or am I just reading into things?*

"Either way, happy birthday, Tav," Dom said, jogging to catch up with us.

"Why, thank you." She turned to smile at him, and the blush I had caught had already disappeared. "I intend to ring it in with unreasonable amounts of meatloaf."

"Really?" Dom looked at me. "Don't you think she should do something more elaborate, Bryn?"

I laughed and looped my arm around Tavi's waist. "Nope! I can't think of a better way to celebrate."

Tavi giggled. "Right? Good food is all that matters."

Dom released a long, belabored sigh. "The two of you are peas in a pod, huh?"

"Of course! We were destined to find each other."

My chest warmed at Tavi's words. The three of us continued to chat as we walked, and I was surprised at how normal and right I felt. It was so fulfilling to laugh and joke like this. If having friends was this sweet, I never wanted to be alone again.

Though I was in high spirits on the walk leading up to the mess hall, my mood changed as we stood at the entrance. The moment we arrived, Dom left us to speak to another wolf. As we stepped inside, every head turned to take in the new human. My gaze immediately dropped to the ground. I didn't want to risk reading disgust in their eyes.

"It's okay," Tavi whispered. "You're okay."

I wanted to trust her, but I couldn't be sure that she was right. As we walked toward the buffet, I fought with myself about whether to keep my eyes on the ground or attempt to read the Wargs' expressions. I decided to avoid looking directly at individual wolves in favor of taking in the overall room. The Wargs' mess hall was smaller than the Kings', but that gave it a warmer, more intimate feel than what I was used to. Families were practically piled on top of each other, but no one seemed to mind. Aside from the glances thrown my way, laughter and lively conversation filled the space.

At the buffet, I felt a shiver down my spine. I risked another glance at the dining hall until I found a table with far fewer wolves sitting at it. Two individuals stood out to me—one was Dom, and the other…was Night Shepherd. He was looking right at me, but I couldn't read the emotion in his eyes.

I licked my lips, taking in his handsome face, those broad shoulders, and the way his biceps strained in his short-sleeved shirt. I started feeling things I knew I shouldn't, and I tried to subtly rub my thighs together to quell the tingling in my core. His nostrils flared, and his hands curled into fists on the table. I licked my lips again, more slowly this time. I wasn't sure what I was doing, but I knew it felt right.

Movement just over Night's shoulder drew my attention. Dom had lifted his hand to wave at me, beaming at me from across the room. Night turned to him, shoving his shoulder. Dom laughed even as he regained his balance on the bench.

I tore my eyes away from the intense, broody Alpha and his goofy beta to take in the room again. Other than a few mutterings, no one attacked me or bullied me, and I started to relax a bit. The Wargs were nothing like the terrifying beasts I'd grown up hearing about. All I saw were happy faces, families, young pups, and community. How could my instructors and my own mother have gotten these wolves so wrong?

At our table, Tavi and I enjoyed the food and chatted amongst ourselves. Toward the end of the meal, a few other wolves joined us. Tavi introduced her friends as Jasper, Mark, Preston, Brent, Hallie, Lora, and Vanessa. I recognized Jasper—he had been with Night the day that I was kidnapped.

"It's um, nice to meet all of you," I said gently, glancing at Jasper. I wished I didn't feel so awkward, but it was the first time I'd been surrounded by wolves my own age who didn't immediately want to hurt me. In my experience, the wolves my age were the cruelest in the pack, and I was preemptively on guard.

"It's nice to meet you too," Lora said. She was blonde with chin-length hair. "We've all been so curious about you since you arrived."

"Oh really?" I tried not to squirm.

"Yeah. We heard you were part of the Kings' pack. What was that like?"

"Oh, um..." My heartbeat spiked, and for a few moments, I wasn't sure how to respond to the question.

"Lora, it's like I was telling you," Tavi said, swooping in to save me, "she was adopted by them, but she's not pack really. She hates them just as much as we do."

I stuffed my mouth full of mashed potatoes to collect my thoughts. On the one hand, my mom was part of the Kings' pack, and I could never abandon her, but on the other…it wouldn't feel right to defend the entirety of the Kings' pack—especially when the Wargs loathed them as much as they did.

After I swallowed, I nodded. "I never fit in with the Kings, and I don't consider them family."

"That's a relief," said Hallie, a wolf with curly, auburn hair tied up into a bun. She leaned forward on her elbows, her dark brown eyes full of genuine concern. "We'd heard a rumor that the Kings either kill any human they came across or keep them as slaves."

"O-oh. Really?" I tried not to let the words affect me, but I was immediately reminded of Troy and what he'd planned to do to me.

"We're just glad that that's not your situation," Lora nodded. "That would be awful.

As the wolves talked around me, I couldn't help but let my mind be dragged back into the darkness of those moments. I'd thought for sure that I would live the rest of my life as Troy's sex slave.

I felt a gentle hand on the back of mine and fought my way out of those memories. The hand was Tavi's.

"By the way, guys," her voice rose over the conversation and pulled the attention of the group, "I was hoping to get more details about the trip you're taking into the city."

I gazed at my friend, my heart full. I squeezed Tavi's hand, trying to convey how much I appreciated her changing the subject to safer territory. She squeezed back and bumped me lightly with her shoulder.

"Oh, yeah!" Preston said. His head was shaved but for a Mohawk of black hair. "Was there anything you wanted us to bring you back for your birthday?"

"I'd love a new scarf," she said. "Maybe something red this time?"

"Sure. What about you, Bryn?"

I jumped as the attention of the table returned to me. "M-me?" I stammered. "Oh, I couldn't ask you to bring me anything. I don't have a way to pay you back, and—"

Preston shook his head. "Don't worry about that. Think of it like a gift."

"Okay…" I blushed, racking my brain for something I would like. "A book."

"Yeah? What kind?"

"I'd love a romance, or maybe a fantasy. Anything new and with an exciting cover."

"Sure." Preston grinned at me. "We'll add it to the list."

The conversation resumed, and I breathed out the tension that collected between my shoulder blades. I tried to relax and allow myself to enjoy the company of these wolves, memories of Troy fading away from my mind. As we talked, I began to feel eyes on the back of my head. But these weren't unwelcome eyes—they were Night's. I was tempted to look over my shoulder and catch him, but it was safer to simply let myself be in the moment.

As lunch ended, the Wargs began to leave the mess hall, leaving behind their cups and plates. Tavi gave a little gasp.

"Damn! I forgot I'm on cleaning duty today."

"On your birthday?" Mark asked with a laugh. "That's rough, Tavi."

She kicked him under the table. "Yeah, yeah, laugh it up. Get out of here, you guys. We'll catch up later."

Her friends gave their goodbyes and left with the other wolves that weren't on cleanup duty.

Tavi looked at me. "I'm sure Dom will take you back to Violet's."

I frowned. I wasn't ready to go back yet, and I didn't like the idea of leaving her to clean on her birthday. "Could I take the shift for you?"

Her jaw dropped. "Bryn, no, I couldn't ask you to do that!"

"It's the least I could do. You can think of it as a birthday gift."

She hesitated, drumming her fingers on the table, thinking. "Well, it's tempting, but I think you'll need Night's permission unfortunately." She rolled her eyes. "But we can clean up together."

I smiled. "I'd like that." As we fell into the motion of cleaning and chatting together, I realized that I felt good—so much better than I'd felt on the Kings' compound without my mom around. It felt right for me to step in and help here, if for no other reason than to show that I had earned the right to eat at the table with everyone else. And there were so few people who were spared for cleanup duty. I imagined it was difficult work for only a handful of wolves to get done.

"Tavi," I said as we finished wiping down the last table, "who do I talk to about getting on the cleaning roster?"

"Oh, you should probably talk to Night—"

"I'm sure he needs to clear it, but I think it'll be a headache getting him to listen."

Tavi laughed. "You're probably right. Well, then you should talk to Mabel. She's over there."

I looked where Tavi indicated and found an older woman clearing off one of the vacated tables. I wasn't sure if I was still living on the high of such an eventful day or if I'd grown a bit more of a backbone from my ordeals the past couple of weeks, but I felt no fear as I approached Mabel.

"Hello," I said.

Mabel looked up and smiled. "Yes? Did you need something from me?"

Wait. What am I doing? My newfound confidence suddenly wanted to leave my body now that I was speaking out loud. I tried to hold onto the bold feelings from earlier and set the dishes I'd collected on the table. *No. I got this.*

"My name is Bryn, and I was wondering if you would mind if I gave you a hand."

"Oh, my." Her eyes widened. "I've never heard of anyone volunteering to help clean. Are you sure you want to? You don't have to feel obligated."

I nodded. "I'm positive that this is something I want to do. I'd like my name to be added to the roster."

"Hm…" Mabel's steel-gray eyes took in my physique. "I see you're willing to clean. Are you sure you can keep up?"

"Yes. I've cleaned up after meals for a larger crowd." I knew I didn't need to specify what crowd I was talking about. Mabel would already be aware. "I can wash dishes, sweep, and mop floors."

"What about cooking? Are you any good with that?"

"Yes, I'm good at memorizing recipes, and I've been told that I chop vegetables very quickly."

"My, my, you seem like a jack of all trades kind of girl."

I smiled. "I'm used to being put to work. I've been living with Violet all this time, and there's only so much that she needs doing around her cabin."

"Ah, well, I can certainly respect that! In my old age, I'm still picking up after these wolves because I can't stand being at home all day." She gave a girlish giggle, one that made me smile as well. "Alright, Bryn, we have plenty of hands cleaning up tonight, but tomorrow is a different story. All I need you to do is talk to Violet, and we'll get you on the schedule as soon as possible. How's that sound?"

I took both of Mabel's hands and beamed at her. "That sounds wonderful, Mabel. Thank you."

Chapter 19 - Night

According to Mom, Bryn had not only stopped trying to escape, but she'd also requested to work in the kitchens. I didn't like it, but we would benefit from the extra pair of hands, so I couldn't find a good reason to refuse her request. I had no choice but to allow it.

I'd wondered if this wasn't all a ruse orchestrated by Bryn. If she could get me to drop my guard, she would have more opportunities to escape. That was the excuse I used as I watched her all through dinner. Though I finished two helpings of food, I couldn't remember the taste or the texture of the meal—hell, I could hardly recall eating at all. I had hoped the time away from Bryn would give me the opportunity to regain control of myself, but the moment she was nearby, she was all I could focus on.

After lunch ended, I stormed back into my cabin, throwing open the door and slamming it shut behind me. I dropped down on my sofa, head in my hands, and when I closed my eyes, it was Bryn's soft face, tight body, and those damnable steel-blue eyes that I saw in my mind.

She was everywhere. Ever since she left my cabin, I swore I could smell her at the most random times of the day, in places of the house she had never been to. I could hear her voice echoing in the halls, a ghost tormenting me with her closeness. I tried to stay far away from Mom's cabin (and my own damn cabin with her aroma permeating every corner of it) during the day, but occasionally, I caught glimpses of her working in the gardens. Apparently, she was really talented; Mom couldn't stop talking about how overjoyed she was to see the new growths and the quality of the vegetables.

I could make the rules even stricter and forbid her from leaving the cabin at all, but even I couldn't be so cruel as deny her the small glimpses of freedom she had. And, if I'd confined Bryn to the cabin, she wouldn't have appeared with Octavia for lunch, and I wouldn't have seen the smile on Tavi's face.

Thinking of Tavi made me lean against the backrest of my couch and stare up at the ceiling. Tavi had been through a lot, to put it lightly. Though she was young, she was one of the wolves who had suffered the most at the hands of the Kings not that long ago. Because of her hardships, I made sure to teach her how to fight, though I never expected her to be a hunter or a scout or a sentinel. Though Tavi had friends, it wasn't uncommon to see her wandering the grounds by herself, her melancholy expression nothing like the light smile she normally wore.

But I hadn't seen Tavi going off by herself at all these last few days. In fact, she had seemed even more lively than usual. She was so much like a little sister to me that it made me happy to see her smile—even if it meant she had befriended the girl I had taken prisoner.

Every time Bryn and I had spoken, it ended in an argument or a snark-off. How had she managed to make friends in the short time she'd been here? When all she had for me was sarcasm and callousness, how had she made such huge impressions not only on Dom and Mom but on Tavi, too?

And it wasn't just those three—it seemed she was well on her way to charming the entire pack. The only interactions I'd witnessed between Bryn and my pack were born from curiosity, friendliness, or interest. The latter point always sent my stress level as high as it would be on an intense mission. I had fought to keep the jealousy off my face, but whenever I watched Bryn receiving attention from a male wolf during the meal, I couldn't keep from breaking plates and bending utensils in my hands.

I told myself I was reacting so intensely because I wanted to make sure the interactions were safe ones, but the truth was that I could hardly stomach the sight of them drooling over her. It made my wolf growl and snap his fangs.

Dom, who never failed to capitalize on moments when I was off my game, had talked nonstop about Bryn through lunch. He went on and on about how much he liked her, how quickly the younger wolves had accepted her, and how interesting she was. It got to the point that I chastised him for caring so much about a human woman—though I couldn't admit to feeling the same fascination about her.

As if thinking of my beta had summoned him, I heard a knock on the door. I knew it was Dom.

"Come in," I said.

Dom entered, closing the door behind him. As he looked at me, he gave a low whistle. "Wow, you look as tired as you sound." He plopped down on the sofa next to me. "I bet I have some news that'll wake you up."

I sighed and rubbed the bridge of my nose. I was in no mood to rise to Dom's teasing. "What is it?"

"We received a reply."

Those four words had me sitting up again. I turned my full attention his way. "And?"

"He agreed to your terms, but he said that this can only go down on Kings' territory."

"Yes." They would all be my lands anyway; it made sense that the battle should happen there.

"We need to prep the team—who should we bring with us?"

I had already considered this question. "The same group. Minus Jasper and the other juniors we brought with us before."

Dom nodded. "Of course."

This was good. Troy had agreed to the terms easily, and before long, word that I had challenged Troy would spread across the Idaho panhandle.

"Did Redwolf say anything else?" I asked.

"Yes. He talked about Bryn." Dom's eyes grew dark, and his placid expression turned into a grimace. "You were right—the fucker wants her back. Badly."

My lips pulled away from my teeth as my wolf growled. "What did he say?"

"He said that if he found out anyone had touched her or mated her, he would kill her in front of her mother and place her body parts along the Kings' compound lines. He wants her, but he wants her pure, otherwise the deal is off."

I gripped the armrest of the couch unconsciously. My hand had shifted, and my claws drew lines through the upholstery as I clenched it into a fist. Bryn was human, so it shouldn't matter to a wolf whether she was a virgin. He was probably saying that just to remind me of the way I'd found Bryn. It was a tactic to get inside my head—to intimidate, to make himself sound like the big, bad Alpha he wanted everyone to believe he was.

But all the idiot had done was piss me off.

"That sick fuck doesn't deserve an honorable death," I said quietly. "He deserves to die as slowly and painfully as possible."

Dom leapt to his feet. "Then let's go and murder the fucker. Why even do all of this?"

"As much as I want to watch him bleed out at my feet, it isn't right to just assassinate him, the deal—"

"Screw the fucking deal! Let's forget all about giving Bryn back, and let's go rip him apart. Tonight."

I glared at Dom. "Then what was any of this for, Dom? Why go through the trouble of kidnapping Bryn and setting the terms of the deal? We have the eyes of other packs on us now. The deal is done."

"Night." Dom met my glare. "I have never questioned you about anything. I would lay down my life just to carry out your will, but I can't condone this."

"You're letting your affection for her cloud your senses, Dom."

"The hell I am. I wouldn't force anyone back into the hands of someone who wants to do any of the batshit awful things that Troy said he wanted to do to Bryn. It's *wrong*, Night."

Dom and I held each other's stare until we both looked away. I heaved a sigh.

"I hear what you're saying, Dom. I really, really don't like the idea of Bryn being anywhere near Redwolf, but I won't let him hurt her."

Dom scoffed. It was an extremely disrespectful thing to do to an Alpha, but I knew emotions were high. "How do you plan to follow through on that, Night?"

"He won't have time to do anything to her. We take her back, and the challenge starts. I'll have sentries keeping an eye on her the entire time. Nothing will happen."

"Any time that she has to spend on the Kings' grounds is too fucking long. What if one of our sentries loses sight of her? What if they kill her the moment Troy has eyes on her? Anything could happen, Night. Anything."

Dom was right. Even though I had no intention of letting Troy spend any time alone with Bryn, there was a lot of risk to this plan. I hated leaving anything up to chance, but the terms were set. We had just over two weeks to come up with a solution to make sure Bryn was safe.

"Dom, do you think I don't hate this? You know just as well as I do that our pack is renowned for being uncivilized. Violent. How would it look if we went back on the deal? How would anyone respect us if we proved the worst things they think about us are true?"

"We'll be strong enough to keep anyone who doubts us quiet."

I shook my head. "Then we're no fucking better than the Redwolfs. You're getting too wound up, Dom. Don't forget that we have the Kings' pack lands within our grasp. We just need to see the rest of this through."

Dom wasn't impressed by my words. But then, he wouldn't be. He'd heard this explanation before, and he understood why we had to do things this way, but that didn't take away the sour taste from the back of my mouth.

"Whatever, Night," he said, walking toward the door. "You just better hope you win."

"I *know* I'll win."

Minutes after Dom left the cabin, I shifted into my wolf form. After that intense argument and after hearing what Troy had said about Bryn, it was time for me to check in with my sentries. It was good timing because I had to shift to reach the border of my territory quickly, and I longed to get rid of some of my pent-up aggression. As the change took over me, forcing me onto all fours as fur sprouted along my body, my thoughts became less structured. Instead of thinking of Bryn or Dom or worrying about the future, I could focus on the moment—on the simple task of running.

I sprinted into the forest, and the trees seemed to part around me as I zipped by. I stopped to check in with my sentries to make sure the borders were safe. In my wolf form, communicating telepathically with my team was as easy as communicating verbally. According to them, the Kings hadn't had the chance to injure any more of my pack, though they continued to sniff around the borders.

After I'd checked in with everyone, I yawned and stretched. It seemed I could allow myself to relax a bit and release the rest of my frustration. I could hear the quick steps of rabbits and foxes around me—time for a bit of a snack. My wolf whined for control, and I didn't fight him, letting him take over for a bit to give myself a few minutes of rest.

When I came to, I skidded to a halt. I was back in the village, the taste of rabbit still warm on my tongue, and

I was standing—shit. I was standing below Bryn's bedroom window.

My mom's cabin was a dark, comforting silhouette against the night sky except for the light coming from Bryn's room. She had a candle lit, and her arms were stretched over her head. She was naked, and her smooth back and perfect ass were on display in the warm, flickering light. As I watched, she turned a bit to the side, revealing her profile as she reached for the candle. Seconds before she blew out the light, I watched her hands move down from her hair to her breasts.

I had to bite my tongue to keep from howling.

Immediately, I shifted into my human form. I shivered and crouched on the ground. Seeing Bryn like this…it was too much. My wolf wanted nothing more than to run to her and claim her right then. I wasn't sure I would have been able to stop it.

I stuck to the shadows and ran quickly to my cabin. The stealth wasn't necessary—I sensed no wolf nearby enough to see me—but I didn't want to risk the embarrassment of someone catching me all alone, naked, and fully erect.

Once inside, I rushed into the bathroom and closed the door. I pressed my back to the wood and then slowly sank down to the floor. What the hell was wrong with me? I was a grown man who was no stranger to nudity. Nakedness was part of the werewolf experience; I had long grown out of the teenage stage when every sight of a breast got me aroused. So why was it that Bryn affected me like this? Why did even a glimpse of her naked form send me fucking wild?

I sighed and stood. I needed to shower and then get to bed and sleep this off. I turned on the shower and stepped into the hot water. As I lathered up, Bryn again flashed through my mind. I couldn't resist it anymore, so I took my cock in my hand, stroking it as I recalled the image of her—the way the firelight had glowed across her skin, how soft and supple every curve of hers looked. If she had turned to look at me the way that she had in the mess hall, her pink tongue licking over those full, pouty lips…I would have come undone.

I could picture her lying across my bed, her gorgeous hair spread out around her, her hands on my chest, her thighs pressing into my sides as I buried myself as deep inside her as possible. I imagined nuzzling into her neck as she pressed her nails into my back, begging me for more and more. I wondered if her lips would taste as sweet as they did in my dreams—if her keening cries would drive me as wild.

I pressed my free hand flat to the shower wall, growling low as my climax rumbled through me. I stood there for so long, shuddering in the wake of my orgasm, that the water temperature began to cool. I shivered, quickly finished up my shower, and then turned off the water.

I knew I had gotten too attached to Bryn, which didn't bode well for my plan. In seventeen days, she would be going back to the Kings. Though her stay would be brief—no more than a few hours—my wolf snarled at the thought of her being anywhere near that abusive fucker. But what choice did I have? The terms had been set, and now the future of my pack was at stake.

Still, I felt sick to my stomach at the thought of sending Bryn back into that hell. It would be better for me if I could send Bryn somewhere far, far away. That way, she wouldn't be in danger from Redwolf, and I wouldn't feel tempted to visit her or find some excuse to see her. She was going to ruin me if I wasn't careful.

Chapter 20 - Bryn

"You know, there's a bonfire tonight," Tavi began. She and I were outside in the garden. Tavi was helping me get rid of the last of the stubborn weeds that had continued to grow along the perimeter of the garden.

I paused my weeding to run the back of my forearm across my sweaty forehead. "So?"

Though the Kings' pack lived for any opportunity to celebrate, get drunk, and light large piles of sticks on fire, I had never been invited to attend. It was the same with other wolf ceremonies. I wasn't pack, so I'd never known what it was like. If I was being honest, I would love to go for the first time, but Tavi and I both knew that the Wargs' brooding Alpha would have something to say about it.

"I know you're kind of bound to Violet's cabin and the mess hall, but I did us both a favor."

I raised a brow. "Tavi, you're speaking in riddles."

Tavi laughed. "Okay, I'm sorry for keeping you in suspense. I went to Night, and I asked him if you could go with me, and you know what he said?" She didn't wait for me to guess. "He said yes!"

My jaw dropped. *Are we talking about the same Night?* "No, he didn't."

"He did! You're coming with me and my friends, and you're having some fun."

I was happy, of course, but at the same time, so confused. "But why did he say yes?"

"I don't know, and I don't care. I think if I pressed him on it, he would've changed his mind."

"Oh." I still had questions, but I wouldn't find any answers without going to the source, and I doubted Night would tell me what he was thinking. Besides, I was excited about the bonfire. "We should tell Violet."

"Agreed!"

We placed the weeding tools back in the tool crate and went inside. Violet, who was drinking a spiced chai in the kitchen, didn't look up from the journal she was writing in. "You want to talk to me about the bonfire, right?" she asked.

Tavi put her hands on her hips. "Violet, are you psychic or something?"

Violet tapped her ear with the end of her pen. "My hearing might not be what it used to be, but you don't exactly whisper, Tavi."

Tavi covered her mouth with her hands. "Oops."

Violet chuckled. She finished writing her sentence and tucked the pen behind her ear, looking up at me. "I'm glad you're getting out, girlie. It's about time you did something fun."

"Yeah, and I'll give you some of my clothes to wear," Tavi said. "I think we're about the same size."

I nodded, and the excitement that I hadn't allowed myself to feel when Tavi first brought up the bonfire began to bubble within me. "Okay." I shared my smile with Violet and Tavi. "I'm starting to get really excited."

"Me too!" Tavi gently hip-checked me. "I'll be right back. I've gotta go look through my things for an outfit for you."

I saw Tavi off, and then I went to the garden to finish up the weeding, growing more excited with each beat of my heart. Technically, I was still under strict instructions not to leave Violet's cabin, but those restrictions had eased off quite a bit. In fact, Tavi, myself, and a few of the wolves I'd met in the mess hall often met up at Violet's cabin since I wasn't allowed to leave. Night had, to my surprise, been okay with me working in the kitchens with Mabel and other wolves. And now, to my even greater surprise, he was letting me go to my first bonfire.

The last couple of days had been nice—I was able to live my life, work, and not have to hide who I really was.

I hadn't even thought about an escape plan, though that was in large part due to Tavi's company.

It felt so good to have friends and to be in a place where I could relax just a little bit. True, I was still a prisoner, but having friends like Tavi around lessened the strain. Actually, I was happier than I could remember ever being, and it was starting to mess with my mind. Objectively, I knew I ought to try to use tonight to get back to my mom, but the thought of attempting such a thing saddened me. I was so excited about experiencing something new that I couldn't find the will to ruin the evening with any escape plans.

I let my hair out of its bun and washed up for the bonfire. Tavi returned with the clothes, and I pulled them on without question. The outfit turned out to be a pair of thigh-high black stockings and a long, heather-gray sweater dress. Other than my hands and face, several inches of my thighs were on display. Tavi wore something similar, only her stockings stopped above her knees, and her sweater was a pale peach color.

"Are you sure it's warm enough for this, Tavi?" I asked.

"Of course I'm sure! Now get your boots on,. The bonfire might have already started!"

We set out into the chilly spring night. I held Tavi's hand tightly to make sure that I didn't get lost in the darkness. Without a moon to guide me, it was hard to tell where I was going. Eventually, our pace slowed, and I began to smell lighter fluid.

"Let's get the fire going as soon as we can," Tavi announced to the group of shadowy silhouettes we were approaching. "We got a cold human with us tonight. But keep that a secret."

"Right. Jasper, you got the matches?" asked one of the silhouettes.

Moments later, the fire flickered to life in the center of a pile of logs. I watched the fire lick across the wood until the entire setup was alight. Beginning to relax, I held my fingers out toward the flames, looking around at the group that had collected around the fire.

It was the same group from Tavi's birthday lunch, plus a handful of other young wolves that I hadn't yet met. There were large logs assembled in a circle around the fire that some people were already sitting and chatting on. Hallie had brought beer and soda, and Preston had a Styrofoam cooler full of meat. Lora had brought a large cast-iron pot, which she carried under her arm as if it weighed nothing. She started to set it up as another wolf with dark brown hair started playing pop music.

Tavi whooped and began to twirl and dance around the fire in time with the music. Hallie laughed and set down the drinks so she could join her. The wolves that weren't busy with setting up the grill or prepping the meat clapped or danced with them. I laughed. The night air was cool and invigorating against my exposed skin. I started to clap along with everyone else.

"Hey, Bryn," a voice came from behind me. "It's nice to see you could make it."

I turned and found Jasper walking up to me. He had dark blue eyes and tight, curly hair the color of copper. He was tall, lithely muscled, and had a bright, easy smile.

"It is nice, isn't it?" I smiled.

His grin widened. "I'm glad that you remember me. I was actually among the group that brought you back to our compound." He had a couple of cans of soda in hand, and he offered one to me. "Thirsty?"

I hesitated for half a second while I confirmed that the can was unopened. I might not have a plan for escape that night, but I didn't want to risk another scenario like the one with Troy on the night of the challenge ceremony.

"Thanks, Jasper," I said, accepting the soda and popping it open.

"I'm sorry if you wanted something stronger." He walked closer to the fire so he could stand next to me. "I'm on call tonight, so I'm not allowed to drink."

"Oh yeah?" My eyebrows rose. I remembered how lackadaisical the wolves in the Kings' pack could be about their duties. There was so rarely a cause for alarm that even those actively on duty, not just on call, could be seen getting drunk with others. "You seem really responsible," I said.

"Ahh, I don't know about that," he said, rubbing the back of his head. "I just take my position seriously."

I sipped the drink. Though the drink was cold, the fizzy, sweet, vaguely citrusy soda was really refreshing. "What is your position?"

"I'm a hunter—well," he amended with a slight blush, "I'm a junior hunter."

"That's a really important role in the pack. You must be trustworthy if you're training to become one of them."

"Gosh, Bryn, if you keep on like this, you'll make me blush," he chuckled. "Wanna sit down while we wait for the food? I feel like I have so many things I'd like to ask you."

"You do?" I followed him to one of the logs and sat beside him. "You seemed quiet at Tavi's birthday lunch, Jasper."

He rubbed the back of his head, a slight color touching his cheeks. "Yeah, I was a little intimidated."

"Intimidated? By what?"

"Well, by you."

"Me?" I had never in my life been told that I was intimidating. If anything, I'd believed my entire life that wolves would never see me as anything other than prey. "Did I do something that offended you?"

"No, no! Nothing like that. It's just that you just kinda give off this reliable, kind vibe, you know? And the way you jumped up that day to help Mabel clean up just confirmed that for me. You're just sorta…different from anyone else I've met."

"Well, what's so intimidating about that?"

He chuckled again, though his cheeks were bright pink. "You know, now that I'm saying it out loud, I don't know what I'm talking about either. You can ignore me."

"I don't think I want to do that." I smiled. "You're too nice."

His blush deepened. "Ah—well, I think I'm going to check on Hallie and Vince to make sure they don't need help with setting up the grill. I'll be back with some food, okay?"

"Sure." I watched him hop to his feet and jog over to where Hallie and a male wolf with short blond hair were setting up the pot.

I smiled to myself, tilting my head. From the way Jasper's body had turned toward me during our conversation, I knew it had been going quite well. Given the way his eyes focused on mine, my mouth, and my neck, I could tell that he was interested in me. It was flattering to know that I had so easily charmed a wolf with such a cute personality and a handsome face, but he didn't light me on fire the way Night did when he looked at me.

The moment Night entered my brain, I looked away from the wolves and down at the ground. What was wrong with me? It was wrong, *so* wrong, for me to feel this way toward the Alpha of the Wargs. For one, he was my kidnapper, and for another, he was completely unattainable. What's more, he didn't seem to like me all that much. On the few occasions where we'd spoken, it had ended in a fight. Granted, my goal had been to annoy him or get him riled up, but I couldn't even say why I'd tried so hard to get under his skin.

Even if things were different and Night and I were free to date, the way I'd behaved around him had surely made him fed up with me. Why else would he avoid speaking or interacting with me even though I lived a short walk away from him?

It didn't help that my dreams had picked up since arriving at the Wargs' territory. I had woken far too many times with images of Night beneath me as I rode him hard beneath the silvery light of the moon. Those bright green eyes were all too familiar as they watched me moan and bounce on top of him. My face turned bright red, and I tried to down more of my drink to keep the heat of my body down.

A few minutes later, Jasper returned with a couple of beef and chicken skewers for me. I accepted them eagerly. The food was cooked to juicy perfection, and it had been dressed in a tangy, mustardy sauce that awakened my appetite. I ate a few more and chatted and laughed with Jasper, Tavi, and Preston.

"If I could have everyone's attention," Vince—the one with brown hair who had set up the music—called, a beer in his hand. "I can tell that this night is already going smoothly, but tradition is tradition, and it's time to tell a story."

Tavi scooted in closer to me. I had a bottle of beer in hand by now too, and I took a sip as I leaned forward to hear what Vince would say next.

"As everyone knows, the conflict between the Wargs and the Kings runs deep. What started out as hundreds of years of mutual respect born from competition became strife and conflict. The fighting deepened the rift we see now between our packs."

I began to stiffen. I hadn't expected the story to be about this, but Tavi bumped me with my shoulder and leaned close to whisper in my ear.

"Don't worry. No one blames you for this. It's just tradition."

"R-right." I tried to smile, but I still felt a bit uneasy. I began to chew on the end of my skewer and stared at the ground in front of the fire, watching the orange glow across the dead leaves and flat rock.

"Both sides had suffered tragedies," Vince went on, "but things reached a fever pitch a few decades ago when the Kings killed a pack mother who lived among the Wargs out of pure spite."

Pack mothers were ancient, magical women who bore the first wolf shifter pups. They lived for centuries, watching over the growth of the packs. I had known, of course, that the conflicts between the packs went back for decades, but I had never heard that the Kings killed the Wargs' pack mother. If I had just recently been kidnapped, I might have pushed back against the idea that the Kings would do something so horrible, but now that I'd had some distance from the Kings, now that I'd gotten to know the Wargs and lived among them, I had little reason not to believe them.

I had believed the rivalry between the packs had started with jealousy on the part of the Wargs, but if the Kings had really killed the Wargs' pack mother, that would easily have caused a blood feud that could last until the end of time.

"But the Kings' cruelty didn't stop there," Vince said. "Only ten years ago, the Wargs suffered another great tragedy."

I heard Tavi sniffle. I turned to look at my friend and found her eyes closed and her eyebrows knitted together in pain. My eyes widened as I realized that Vince was about to talk about Tavi's past.

"The Kings sent a group of hunters to attack the villagers. In the chaos, they murdered many innocent families, leaving far too many of us childless or orphaned. The pain that attack caused could have ruined the Wargs for good. But our Alpha, Night Shepherd, has stepped up to lead us out of poverty and suffering. Since then, we have been recovering. We have been growing in strength as a pack each year until the day we can finally make the Kings pay for what they have done to us." Vince raised his bottle. "Tonight, on the night of the new moon, we honor their memory, and we celebrate the good tidings soon to come."

Vince swallowed what remained in the bottle, and everyone around the circle did the same, including me and Tavi. After a few moments of reverent silence for their dead, the conversation slowly started up again. Tavi, with tears on her face, stood and walked a few yards away from the fire. I followed her.

My heart ached, knowing what the Kings had done over the years to maintain their dominance, and I mourned for the packs who had suffered because of them. Though I was never part of the Kings' pack, I felt disgusted with myself for believing that place could ever be my home.

"Tavi, wait," I said, catching up to her. "I had no idea—"

"I know, it's okay." Tavi turned to me, tears glimmering on her cheeks, her arms wrapped tight around herself. "It's not something I like to talk about."

"I don't blame you." It was startling to see someone who was normally a ball of sunshine be so distraught. I wrapped my arms around Tavi and held her close. "I'm so sorry."

Tavi shook her head and hugged me back tightly. "You have *nothing* to apologize to me for. You have suffered a lot because of the same man who took everything from me." She held me at arm's length and looked at me with rage burning in her dark eyes. "Troy Redwolf was the one who led the attack on us."

I gasped, but I shouldn't have been so surprised. I remembered then that on Troy's sixteenth birthday, he'd gone on a joy run with his friends and some hunters to ring in his birthday. From what I'd heard, the celebration "got crazy", but I'd never known the specifics of what had happened. If this happened ten years ago, then the timeline would match up.

"They set many of our cabins on fire and slaughtered dozens of wolves. Among our dead were my mother, father, and my younger twin brothers." Tavi's voice was shockingly monotonous as she described the carnage. "The only reason I'm alive today is because I had snuck out to play in the caves near our house. When I came home, our cabin had been razed to the ground, and their bodies were…" She closed her eyes and shook her head. "They were gone."

"Oh, Tavi," I hugged my friend as tightly as I could and rubbed her back. "How *awful*."

Tavi sobbed once and held me back. "I've sat through so many of these bonfires, and Vince always tells this story. I'm not usually this emotional because I know that I'm not the only one who's suffered at the hands of the Kings, but tonight, I don't know. It hits harder, I guess."

I squeezed her. "You don't have to feel bad for getting emotional about something as intense as this, Tavi. You can cry as much as you want to. I won't let you go until you're ready for me to."

Tavi buried her face in my shoulder and sobbed gently. All the while, I held her, rubbed her back, and shed a few tears myself on Tavi's behalf.

When the sobs subsided, Tavi pulled back and wiped her eyes with the sleeves of her sweater. "That was exhausting," she said with a sniffly chuckle. "I think I've kept you away from the fire too long. You're shivering."

I laughed. "I didn't even notice." Tavi's body heat had been enough to keep me warm, but now that we'd separated, the cool night air was starting to seep in again. "That's what friends are for, right?"

"Right. Let's head back."

Tavi was uncharacteristically quiet on the walk back. I guessed that she might be embarrassed by her tears. Maybe a change of subject would make her feel better.

"Hey, I never told you this, but I met a little boy the day after your birthday."

"You did? You mean when you were working in the mess hall?"

I nodded. "Yeah! He's the cutest pup I've ever seen. His name is Pax, and he brought his plates and cups to me."

Tavi brightened. "Oh, I know Pax! He seems like such a shy boy."

"He wasn't shy with me at all!" Tavi and I had returned to a different log by the bonfire because our original spot had been taken. "He seemed a little sad, so I asked him what was wrong. He told me that he was upset about being a late shifter and asked me for some advice."

"Oh, no! Poor little guy. I was a late shifter too."

"Really?"

"*Oh,* yeah. Night gave me so much shit about it."

I giggled, imagining a little Tavi, all bent out of shape about not being able to shift while Night, who would have been in his young teens, teased her like a real big brother. It made my chest feel warm. *I wish I could see him...*

"Don't stop the story there," Tavi said. "I'm dying to know what kind of advice a human could give to a young shifter."

"Oh! I mean, we had late shifters in the Kings' pack too, obviously, so I just told him what I'd told them. I said he needed to be a brave little boy and remember to be strong and confident while his body caught up with him." I laughed. "I mean, it's a little funny because I don't feel that way about myself, but I guess you can give advice you don't relate to."

Tavi tilted her head, her smile dimming a bit.

"What's wrong?"

"Never mind," Tavi shook her head. "Go on."

"Well, ever since I gave him that advice, I've gotten a big hug from Pax every time he's seen me. He even asked me to sit with his family at breakfast."

"Wait, wait, wait." Tavi held up her hands. "Nuh-uh. It sounds like you've gotten a new best friend, Bryn, which I won't stand for. *I* have best friend dibs. I'm not afraid to challenge him to a thumb war to prove it."

Bryn threw her head back and laughed hard. "I think you'll have some stiff competition, Tavi, but you're welcome to try."

"I can't believe you would leave me behind for the first adorable pup who gives you a hug." She shook her head and gave a long sigh. "Well, I guess since you've replaced me already, I don't have to get you another drink when I get another one for myself."

I gasped. "You wouldn't dare!"

"I would!" Tavi hopped up and went to grab a drink. "But if I change my mind, you just have to wait until this next song is over." She winked at me and sashayed toward the group dancing by the grill.

I smiled after her, marveling at how quickly Tavi had bounced back after her sorrow. *Pax should've asked Tavi for advice instead. I wish I could be as strong and wonderful as she is.*

Shortly after she got up to dance, Jasper slid in next to me, taking her spot. "Hey, stranger," he said with a grin. "It looks like Tavi's feeling better."

"I think she is." I turned to him and grinned. "You know, Jasper, life here is so different than I'd been led to believe. I wish my mom was here to see how you guys live."

He nodded. "I lost my mom when I was just a pup."

"I'm sorry. Did you lose her in the attack?"

"Thankfully, no. She just got sick, and we didn't have the resources we needed to save her life." He removed the soda tab from the can as he thought about his family. "I wish she could see how far we've come as a pack."

Sensing that he might need a bit of comforting too, I leaned my head against him. He wrapped an arm around my shoulders. His body heat blocked the cool breeze that passed by, and I closed my eyes, appreciating the warmth of Jasper's body. So many members of the Wargs had suffered losses, and I felt myself softening even more for these wolves.

Suddenly, a quiet spread among the group. The volume of the music lowered, and I heard someone mention the word "Alpha." Rather than feel fearful about Night finding me away from Violet's cabin, I lifted my head, looking for the green eyes I had dreamt of. I found them peering from the darkness on the other side of the fire. As he stepped into the firelight, he looked at me with a strange mix of anger and…longing?

Night growled something I didn't understand, and the male wolves, Jasper included, all bowed their heads and moved to start tearing everything down. The female wolves were quick to help them. Tavi had her hands on her hips and said something to Night, but I couldn't understand her either. Whatever she said must not have sunk in because the powerful Alpha stalked around the fire, making a beeline for me.

He grabbed my wrist and pulled me to my feet, dragging me away from the bonfire and toward Violet's cabin.

"Haven't I been fucking lenient?" he asked. "I thought letting you hang out with Octavia and working in the mess hall was harmless, but clearly, I was just falling into one of your plans to escape, huh?"

I tried to snatch my hand back even though it was useless. How could I have ever thought I would want to see this asshole again? "What plans are you talking about? Violet and Tavi had to beg for those privileges on my behalf. You didn't let me do those things out of the goodness of your heart. And *you* were the one who said I could go to the bonfire! What were *you* planning when you gave the okay?"

He laughed, but it was a harsh sound without even a hint of mirth. "This is ridiculous. This conversation, the situation—all of it is ridiculous. I keep making mistake after mistake with you, don't I? Maybe I ought to put you under lock and key again, but this time I'll put you somewhere so far away, no one will be able to find you."

I kicked the back of his leg, but he didn't slow his pace. "Fine! Do it! Lock me up and hide me away where you won't have to be burdened with my presence. Oh, wait—the whole reason I'm here is because *you kidnapped me,* you stupid asshole!"

"You think I won't do it? Anything would be better than watching you sit in another man's lap."

"Oh, fuck off, Night. Like you give a damn about what I do or who I do it with! It's not like I ever see you. You avoid me like I'm some disease."

"A disease? More like a plague."

"Oh, that's real nice, Night. Real nice."

We stood on the deck in front of Violet's cabin now and Night, to my surprise, finally let me go. I got as close to his face as I could get and glared up into those gorgeous, emerald eyes.

"I don't want you leaving the grounds after tonight. You're confined here until further notice."

"Like hell I'm staying here."

"You. Are. A. Prisoner."

"I. Know!" I wished I could get him to understand, to see things from my point of view.

"Then maybe you should start acting like it."

I ran a frustrated hand through my hair. "Up until I met Tavi, I did nothing but plan my escape from this place, and you know what I fucking realized? I can't. Either your sentries will hunt me down, or I'll die in the woods trying to make my way back. Why do you insist on being an asshole and not let me at least pretend to be an actual person?"

"If you know you can't escape, why are you being so combative?"

"Maybe I'm not being clear enough, Night, so I want you to watch me as I say this to you—I never wanted to come here. All I wanted was to be free of my situation back home. I just wanted to feel…safe…" I trailed off. The moment I'd said, "watch me" and pointed to my mouth, his eyes had dropped to my lips. The furious, hot energy between us began to shift and morph into something more tender.

Night's own lips began to part as he looked at my mouth, and his eyes shifted from an intense emerald to a softer chartreuse shade of green. My stomach filled with flutters as he shifted toward me, bending slightly. *Is...is he going to kiss me?*

Before I could find out, a howl pierced the night air. Night stiffened, his head cocking toward the sound of the howl. His expression darkened, and he pushed me toward the door.

"Get inside, and don't leave my mother's side."

I stumbled against the door, looking at him with wide eyes. "Wait, what's happening? What's wrong?"

He glanced back at me, and for a moment, I saw something like regret flash in his eyes before he returned his attention to the forest. "I have to go. There's been a breach on the border."

I gasped.

"The Kings are attacking *my pack*." That last word became an angry growl, and he jumped off the deck, shifting in mid-air. The moment his paws touched the ground, he sprinted for the trees, leaving torn fragments of clothes to flutter in the wind behind him.

I stood alone on the porch, staring after him. Part of me longed to follow him, but I couldn't decide if it was because I saw an opportunity to escape or because I wanted to make sure he was okay.

Chapter 21 - Night

I woke the morning after the bonfire to a pounding headache. Sitting up slowly and pressing the heels of my hands to my temples, I reached into my nightstand for some ibuprofen and took three dry. As I waited for them to kick in, I heard movement in my cabin. I stilled, listening, and then relaxed. I recognized the pattern of footsteps, the humming, and the smell of coffee. Mom was downstairs.

I got up and changed from last night's clothes. My hair was still a bit damp from the long shower I'd taken after I got back from the border. The strands fell over my forehead as I entered the kitchen. Mom was indeed buzzing from cabinet to cabinet, rearranging things as she saw fit. I used to hate her habit of reorganizing my things, but I'd gotten used to it. I'd change the spices around or move the plates back into the cabinet I used most often some other time, but I didn't mind letting her do what she liked.

She looked at me as I walked in, her eyes wide and a careful smile on her lips. *I know that look*, I thought with a sigh. *She's about to give me her mystical "fate" talk.* I glanced behind me at the kitchen table. *At least there's coffee.*

"Night," she said, setting the silverware she had been holding back into the drawer, "you know it's going to rain in the next few days."

"Yeah?" I sipped my coffee. We both knew she hadn't come to me to talk about the weather.

"You look tired, Night." She slid into the chair across from me, where her own cup of coffee sat. "Could I have an update on what happened last night?"

I sighed. "The Kings sent a group of five to the north side of the border to start shit. We had two wolves patrolling the area at the time, so they were immediately outnumbered." I closed my eyes, letting the grief wash over me as I gripped the handle of my mug tightly. "We lost one of them."

"Oh, no…" she breathed.

"Of course, the Kings didn't stick around for a fair fight." Here, my grief mixed with rage. "They'd accomplished what they set out to do the minute Iggy's heart stopped beating. By the time my team and I showed up, they were running off. I sent a few after them, but they'd made it over the river before we could catch them."

She reached across the table, setting her hand on top of mine. "You did the best you could, baby," she soothed. "You acted quickly, just the way a true Alpha would."

She said that, but she wasn't the one who'd had to sit down with Iggy's family and tell them that she wouldn't be coming home that night. Mom didn't have to see the sorrow and rage in the eyes of Iggy's family. It ate me up remembering the way her pups had wailed for her.

"...Colville?"

I looked up. Mom had been speaking, but I'd been too in my head to pay attention.

Seeing the confusion on my face, she patted my hand and smiled gently. "I asked when the next group is going into Colville."

Colville was the closest human town, and we often stopped there for clothing and materials. I hadn't been expecting her to ask when we were going for our next supply run. Mom was usually self-sufficient, preferring to make or repair the things she already had rather than get something new.

"Why?" I asked. "Did you need something?"

She shook her head. "I don't, but Bryn could use a few things."

At the mention of her name, I briefly remembered last night's dream, but I pushed it away before I could lose myself in the memory. "Mom, I don't understand why you give a damn about a human girl," I said, not bothering to hide my annoyance. "You have never cared about humans—you've never gone into Colville or interacted with them when they come through the area. So why are you so focused on this one?"

She pulled her hand back so she could hold her cup with both hands and stared at me with eyes that were every bit as green and intent as my own. "Night, you're only seeing what your eyes can take in."

Whatever the hell that means, I thought, taking a deep sip of my coffee.

"Night, are you really planning on turning Bryn over to the Kings' monster?"

I hesitated, glancing up at her over the rim of my cup. There was disappointment in the furrow of her brow and the frown on her lips. It hurt to see that I was letting her down, so I quickly changed the subject.

"You mentioned rain earlier," I said. "We're going to want to get a new roof on the schoolhouse before the real heat of the summer starts. And we'll need to rethink the way we ration our food once it gets colder and food becomes more scarce."

She sighed and nodded, allowing me to shift gears. "You know, it's funny you mention food. Thanks to Bryn, I've expanded the garden to nearly double what it was before. So you can expect an increase in fresh fruits and veggies shortly."

"Wait, really?" I knew Bryn was helping Mom out with her garden, but I'd had no idea she was so efficient. "She's only been here a couple of weeks."

"I know. Isn't she amazing? That girl might know more than I do about how to cater to the land and give it what it deserves. I think she works so hard because she doesn't want to think about her home. She's probably grateful for any opportunity not to think about the life she was forced to leave behind or what her poor mother must think about her sudden absence."

I winced. Obviously, she was trying to get me to ease off Bryn. "Alright, you don't have to guilt-trip me, Mom. I get the point."

"Good." She finished the rest of her coffee. "I'll do the dishes. Why don't you get some breakfast at the mess hall? They should still be serving some."

The moment she mentioned breakfast, my stomach began to rumble. She chuckled at me as she collected our cups from the table.

I smelled Bryn the moment I stepped into the mess hall, her sweet, earthy scent overpowering me. For the second time that morning, I remembered flashes of my dream, the way her gray-blue eyes looked up at me, wide and wanting, and the way I made her scream my name in ecstasy as she gripped the bed sheets in her hands. I had to physically shake away those thoughts.

As I scanned the room, I watched her bring the last of the food out from the kitchen and to the buffet tables. Against my better judgment, I started to approach her.

I wasn't sure what I'd say to her. Last night, I had demanded that she not leave Mom's house, but she'd obviously disregarded my order. Though her disobedience ought to annoy me, I couldn't hold on to that negativity as I watched her talk and laugh with the wolves who were getting breakfast.

Our fight last night had amounted to nothing; Bryn's fiery temper had made me zone out and say ridiculous things, things I couldn't quite recall after I learned of Iggy's death. All I could remember of our argument was the sight of her full, pink lips and the way her chest rose and fell with her heavy breathing. And that outfit. Why did thinking of her legs in those stockings and the few inches of skin that weren't hidden under her dress make my heartbeat race?

I think I would have kissed her last night if not for the timing of the attack.

I drew nearer to her, my mind still blank about what I planned to say, when Mabel and Frankie, two older female wolves, entered the mess hall carrying a large tub. Bryn stopped what she was doing and rushed to help them carry it. They smiled at her with adoration glimmering in their eyes. Immediately, my chest began to ache in that way that made me want to draw close to her, to hold her.

No longer hungry and no longer brave enough to go and talk to her, I found a place to sit and watched Bryn throughout the remainder of breakfast. She only sat down to her own food after she was sure that everyone else had plenty to eat. And once she was done, she was the first to get up and start cleaning.

The other families on cleaning duty tried to convince her not to help, but she laughed them off, and soon they were smiling at her and working together. I was amazed. Somehow, a human woman had my entire pack eating out of her hands after just over a week of interacting with them. They seemed enraptured by her.

I rested my elbows on the table and really looked at her and tried to see what they saw. Her warm chestnut hair was pulled into a messy bun at the top of her head, held in place with only a few clips. Tendrils stuck out around her face, fluttering in the wind of her graceful movements. She stopped wiping down a table and removed her gray sweatshirt, exposing an inch of her stomach as she did. She wrapped it around her waist and returned to work, the t-shirt she wore underneath clinging to her chest. My eyes moved a bit lower to where the jeans she loved to wear were practically painted to the curves of her ass and thighs.

Though Bryn was drop-dead sexy, she didn't seem to be aware of it. She had no idea that nearly every single wolf in my pack was drooling after her. I'd even heard them talk about her during training. I had silenced that talk the moment I was aware of it, but looking at her now, I couldn't blame them for obsessing over her.

"Hey, Night." Tavi's voice surprised me. She stood just behind me, her hands on her hips and a smirk on her face. "I've got a bone to pick with you."

"You and everyone else." I turned my full attention to her. "What's up?"

"Don't you think it's time that Bryn became less a prisoner and more a live-in human?"

I raised a brow. I should have expected that this would be about Bryn.

"I mean, it's just that she's so intelligent and attentive to everyone's needs. Mom tells me she's doing a kick-ass job in the garden, and, I mean, everyone loves her, so by this point, keeping her on house arrest is a little unnecessary, don't you think?"

"In *your* opinion, sure."

"Aw, Night, come on." Her voice dropped into a whine. "I've never asked you for a favor or anything, but Bryn is so depressed and trapped inside all the time. Couldn't she have free rein of the compound so she can breathe a little? Please? I'll take full responsibility for her."

I snorted. "You can barely take care of a houseplant."

"Night—"

I raised my hands, and she quieted. "Alright. I suppose I can ease up on her restrictions a little more."

Tavi's eyes brightened. "That's great! Night, I promise you won't regret this!"

I nodded along. I'd agreed begrudgingly since I couldn't think of a good reason to keep tight reins on Bryn anymore. What she'd said last night about being unable to escape the camp was true; I would drop everything to track her down myself if I found out she had escaped into the forest. Keeping her bound to Mom's cabin had been more to make sure Bryn stayed in line than anything, but now that she'd stopped trying to escape, those restrictions weren't really necessary.

As Tavi started to ramble beside me about something or other, I caught movement out of the corner of my eye. A young pup—I thought his name might be Pax—ran in through the door. He paused near the entrance, frantically looking from left to right, and then his face lit up when he spotted what he was looking for. I watched him maneuver easily through the crowd of wolves and make a beeline for…Bryn?

The moment the boy reached her, he hugged her from behind. His little arms were just long enough to wrap around one of her thighs. At first, I wasn't sure what to think. Could the little boy have somehow mistaken Bryn for his mother? But no, Bryn laughed as she crouched to hug him back. He cupped his hand to his mouth and whispered something in her ear. I tilted my head. If I focused on Pax, I might just get a read on what the boy was saying…

I paused. Something Tavi had said stole my focus, but I hadn't quite heard it. Returning my full attention to her, I stopped her as she got up to leave.

"I missed that last bit," I said. "What were you saying?

"Oh! I was talking about Jasper," Tavi said, not missing a beat. "He's been asking me about Bryn nonstop, and I think it's because he has a gigantic crush on her." She giggled.

Those words caused my wolf to growl, but Tavi, who was unaware of the bomb she'd set off, went on talking.

"Anyway, he's a really good guy, and I think he's maybe the only person who could treat her the way she deserves. Plus, I think they'd look really cute together—"

"Tav," I started talking before I could think better of it. "Bryn can have free rein of the grounds, but she can't leave the territory."

"For real?" Tavi gasped. She jumped up and down and then hugged me tightly. "You won't regret this! I promise you!" She zipped away to tell Bryn the good news, leaving me to stew on my own.

I sat on the bench, seething. Jasper was the only one who could treat Bryn well? Those words made me want to break the table in half. I was so eager to get Tavi to stop talking about Bryn and Jasper together that I'd ended up giving Bryn more freedom than I'd intended.

I tried to let go of the rage pumping through my blood, but my wolf was holding on to it with his fangs. I knew I had no right to the anger that burned inside me, but my wolf disagreed. I didn't have any claim on Bryn, but I was acting like a jealous boyfriend. What was wrong with me?

I turned away from Bryn and Tavi and pressed a hand to my chest, rubbing at the spot where a new ache had started to form.

Chapter 22 - Bryn

Tavi burst into the kitchen while I was washing dishes. "Bryn," she called. "I've got great news!"

"Quiet down, young lady," Mabel called from the other room. "Some of us are trying to focus."

"Oops—sorry!" Tavi jogged up to me and took my soapy hands in hers. "You won't believe what I just convinced Night to do for you."

I tried to take in her words, but they didn't make sense to me. During breakfast service, I'd heard that Night and Dom had arrived too late to save one of the wolves that were attacked last night. I couldn't imagine that Night was taking the loss very well. The last time we'd spoken had been a fight. How could Tavi have convinced him to do anything for me?

"What is it?" I asked, hesitation evident in my tone.

"He says you're not confined to Violet's cabin anymore!" she shrieked, jumping up and down. "You can't leave the grounds, but you can do what you want now!"

I felt like I'd just had a shock. "He said that?"

"Yes!" Tavi pulled me in for a tight hug, still laughing.

I hugged her back. I could hardly believe the day I was having. Pax had come in to tell me that he had finally shifted, and he wanted me to go and watch him. I'd had to tell him no because I wasn't allowed to go anywhere but the dining hall and home. Now I couldn't wait to tell him that had changed.

I thought back to when I had found the young boy crying in the corner at the back of the kitchen after dinner. He had been hesitant at first to tell me what had him so broken up, but with a bit of bread, some strawberry jam, and a glass of warm milk, I convinced him to share what weighed so heavily on his shoulders.

Most wolves shift before their sixth birthday, but his birthday was right around the corner, and he still hadn't managed to do it. He'd run away from his cabin when one of his siblings had teased him about it.

My heart had broken for those teary, doe-brown eyes and the clenching of his little fists around his glass of milk. I sat next to him and wrapped an arm around him. While I had no experience being a wolf, I knew plenty about feeling left behind by my peers, so I could relate to Pax's troubles in that way.

"You need to be brave, little guy," I'd told him. "Don't you know that the best things take time?"

He'd shaken his head, wiping at his tears with the sleeves of his shirt.

I'd ruffled his golden blond hair and given him a smile. "I'm sure you'll shift any day now. I can feel it in my bones."

"Really?"

"Of course, Pax! You just have to wait a little while longer."

I was relieved that my words seemed to help, and he had finally been ready to return home. That night, he'd given me a big hug.

"Is it okay if I call you my friend?" he'd asked.

My heart had just about burst at the sweet, soft question. I'd agreed right away and sent him home with a strip of bacon that was left over from dinner service.

For the past two days, he'd come in to see me with a glum look on his face. When he told me that it still hadn't happened yet, we shared a tight hug, and I sent him back home with another extra piece of bacon and a message not to give up hope.

With Tavi's news that Night had eased my restrictions even further, my heart swelled with joy. Pax, with pride glowing in his eyes, had been so excited to tell me, of all people, the good news. But he had been so crestfallen when I told him that I wouldn't be able to watch him shift. Now that I was free, things could be different.

Despite everything that had led me to the Wargs pack, I was charmed by the people and the strong sense of community that they shared. With each day that went by, I felt more and more comfortable with these wolves, and I felt more like I belonged.

"So, where do you want to go first?" Tavi asked. "There are tons of places you haven't had the chance to see!"

I was so overjoyed I found it difficult to speak. "I—oh wow…" I pressed a hand to my forehead. "I need to finish cleaning here, and then I can—"

"Don't you worry about that, Bryn," Mabel said, wiping her hands on a towel. "You go on and have some fun with your friends."

I turned to the older woman, my eyes widening. "But Mabel, there's still so much to do, and I don't want to leave you hanging."

"Nonsense. The rest of us will get by just fine. Isn't that right, everyone?"

Frankie and the others working in the kitchen responded with a chorus of assurances.

Mabel put the towel over her shoulder and set her hands on her hips. "You go on now. Don't make me shoo you out of the mess hall."

My smile threatened to split my face right down the middle. I hugged Mabel tightly and thanked everyone else who was working before allowing Tavi to drag me out of the mess hall.

"Tavi, I think I know where I want to go first," I said. "I have to let Pax know that I can watch him shift."

"Wow. I can't believe the first thing you want to do with your freedom is talk to your new best friend." Tavi crossed her arms and pretended to look hurt. "How could you?"

"Oh no," I laughed. "How can I ever make it up to you?"

Tavi's grin broke through her faux frown. "By letting me give you a tour of our village."

"Hmm…Well, you drive a hard bargain, but I think I can agree to those terms."

Tavi laughed. "Let's give little Pax the good news, and then I'll show you all of my favorite spots."

"Deal."

We caught Pax as he slowly trudged home. As I had expected, his sadness disappeared the moment he learned that I would be able to watch him, and he jumped into my arms. I lifted the boy easily and gave him a kiss on the top of his head as he hugged me around my neck.

"I'm excited too, little guy," I whispered to him. "You're going to do amazingly."

After we saw Pax off, Jasper jogged up to us, a grin on his face. "I thought I saw you walking around," he said, his gaze on me. "You making a jailbreak?"

"Ha! Hardly," I replied.

"Night's let Bryn off her leash," Tavi said. She looked from Jasper to Bryn, a knowing smirk on her face. "Now we're going on a tour. You're welcome to tag along if you're not busy."

"I'm not on duty for a few more hours. I think I can spare some time for you two…as long as I can escort the lovely Bryn around the compound." He offered his elbow.

I giggled, accepting his offer. He fell into step with us as Tavi began her tour, walking on the other side of me so that I was sandwiched between the two wolves. I smiled to myself, amazed at how quickly my life had changed. I loved that I had made friends here. It made me feel like I actually fit in—even though I knew that as a human, I never really could. Tavi was a gift from heaven with her kindness, and Jasper—well, he was kind and funny, and I liked his company, but I knew I didn't want our relationship to go any further than friends.

We walked through the villages, Tavi pointing out community buildings like the food storage cabin and the small market that was kept stocked with goods from Colville. The Wargs compound was a vibrant, beautiful place. The wood cabins were built strong and painted in a variety of colors. It seemed so cozy, so friendly, and so welcoming.

"How often do you all go into the city?" I asked

"It depends," Jasper said. "Whenever we have time or if we badly need something that only the humans can provide. Colville takes a while to get to, so we rarely have wolves to spare for the trip. I think we go once every couple of months."

That was another difference between the Kings and the Wargs. The Kings had plenty of cities nearby that they frequented as often as they liked. Only male wolves were allowed to go, and from what I'd heard, the usual purpose of the trip was to fool around with human women, not bring back supplies. The Kings had so much excess material and clothes from the humans that the most fortunate families in the pack had to have small storage sheds just to have some place to store it all. Mom and I, of course, rarely benefitted from those sorts of goods.

"Oh! There's the schoolhouse," Tavi said, pointing to a quaint brick building. "There's a stubborn section of the roof that always leaks when it rains. Someone always repairs it, but it doesn't help." She turned to grin at Jasper. "I remember once that I poured the bucket that we used to collect rainwater on Jasp as a prank."

"Some prank," Jasper scoffed. "I was so wet, I kept slipping in the grass on the way home."

"Yeah, but that's how we became friends, right?"

He rolled his eyes. "I guess."

Tavi and I giggled.

"Oh, over there is the Elders' home."

Tavi pointed to a cabin whose door was painted white. It was larger than the other cabins, but not by much. It seemed that, like the Kings' pack Elders, the Wargs Elders lived communally in one cabin. When I was younger, it used to confuse me that they would want to live apart from their families, but Mom explained that the Elders were "elder" for a reason—their families were full-grown adults with little ones of their own. If they wanted to see their grandchildren, they could leave their home to do so at any time, but tradition dictated that the Elders lived together.

"I don't think you've met them yet. They tend to keep to themselves unless they have something important to say."

"And over there's the fighting ring and training grounds," Jasper said, pointing. Next to the Elders' cabin was a clearing where the ground had been packed tight and smooth.

"Is that where Night trains the squads?" I asked.

"Yep, Dom too," Tavi said.

I stared at the grounds and imagined Night there, with his shirt off, his body hard and glistening with sweat as he beat his opponents to the ground. I closed my eyes and shivered.

"You cold?" Jasper asked, pulling me close to him. "I can lend you some heat."

My face warmed because I'd been caught, but I kept my head down. "Oh. Thanks, Jasper."

"Anytime. And you know," he leaned close to whisper near my ear, "I'm going to make the core hunting team soon."

Before I could congratulate him, I spotted a small wooden sign embedded in the ground, with the word

"Library" carefully painted on it in black letters. Without thinking, I slipped out from under Jasper's arm so I could run into the single-story, wooden building. It wasn't extravagant, but books lined the wooden shelves that were built into the walls. In the back was a reading nook—a few handmade chairs with worn cushions sat beneath a window.

I clasped my hands together and held them against my chest as I took in the space. The building smelled like the pages of a well-loved book, and it gave me an immediate feeling of comfort.

Tavi and Jasper walked in after me, and I turned to them with wide, shining eyes. "This place is *amazing!*" I exclaimed. "There are so many books here that I've never even heard of."

"I was hoping you'd see the library," Tavi said. "I've been wanting to bring you here ever since you asked Preston for a book from Colville."

I grinned. "Can we stay here for a little while?" I asked. "I know you've got more places to show me on the tour, but—"

"Of course we can! This was the real point of the tour anyway, so spend as much time here as you like."

I whooped with joy and grabbed the first book that caught my eye. The next few hours went by quickly as I took my time browsing and skimming the books. Jasper and Tavi talked quietly to each other as they watched me with smiles on their faces. I wanted to take all of the books home, but knew that I wouldn't be able to take the entire library with me!

At the Kings' pack, the library wasn't well stocked or interesting. Most of the texts there were historical in nature or were just storage of extra books that the schoolhouse didn't need. What few novels it had, I'd read multiple times over already.

Finally, I narrowed the books down to around ten that I wanted to read now, each of a different genre. "Could I check these out?" I asked, a bit embarrassed by my obsession now.

Tavi nodded. "There's a book here where you write down what you've got."

The book in question was large, and the pages were blank. Tavi explained that I needed to write down my name and the titles that I was borrowing. I set the stack down on the table and carefully wrote out the information. I grew more and more excited to read each book as I jotted down their titles. When I was finished, Tavi took the pen.

"Try to remember your page number," Tavi said, tapping the bottom right corner of the book. "When you return the book, just put a little checkmark or cross next to it."

"Gotcha." I watched as Tavi wrote down the page number on the back of my hand.

"I need to start working soon," Jasper said, glancing out of the window at the darkening sky.

"Oh, I'm sorry," I said. "Did I take up too much of your time?"

"Not at all." He gave me a shy grin. "I'm glad I spent the day with you."

I smiled back. His words were so sweet, but I wished I were hearing them from a different man.

"I have plenty of time to walk you back to Violet's," he said. "I'll even carry your books for you." He easily lifted them with one arm.

"What a gentleman." I giggled. "Thanks, Jasper."

The sky went from azure to a deep cobalt as we reached Violet's cabin. As the three of us walked up the steps, the door opened. To our surprise, Night stood in the doorway looking down at us.

His gaze landed on me first, almost in greeting, before shifting to Jasper. Jasper was holding my books in one arm, and the other was draped over my shoulders. Night's nostrils flared, a low rumble leaving his chest.

Jasper stiffened and quickly removed his arm from me. I tried to suppress another shiver. That deep growl should *not* have been such a turn-on.

"Night, it's good to see you," Tavi said. If she noticed the exchange between Night and Jasper, she didn't seem bothered by it. "We showed Bryn like half of the compound so she knows which areas are safe for her to go. We even went to the library, which I guess explains why Jasper's got so many books."

As she went on, Jasper shifted from foot to foot, his gaze glued to the deck. All the while, Night continued to stare him down.

Finally, Jasper burst out, "I should get ready for work!" He handed the books to Tavi, who fumbled with them. "Bye, Bryn." He leaned in, as if to kiss my cheek, but Night's eyes flashed green, and Jasper immediately backed away from the deck with a small whimper. He gave a quick, awkward bow and sprinted back the way we'd come.

"Oh, weird," Tavi said. The confusion on her face mirrored mine. "I guess he had somewhere to be?"

"Guess so," Night said, walking past us. "I've got a meeting to go to."

I whirled on him as he stepped off the porch. "Do you always have to be such an ass?" I demanded.

I had expected him to keep walking and either ignore me or give me some sort of snarky retort over his shoulder. But to my surprise, he paused with a sigh and turned around.

Tavi and I watched as he walked up to me. I didn't back down or look away. I stood still even when he stopped a couple of feet in front of me.

"You know, I'm not really an ass," he said, his voice calm and perhaps a bit tired. "I'm actually a pretty decent guy."

"Oh really?" I crossed my arms. "I've never seen that guy."

He gazed into my eyes, his expression unreadable. "That's right," he said. "You haven't." He backed away from me and turned, walking in the same direction as Jasper.

I stood on the porch with my arms still crossed, the indignation quickly evaporating from my body. I felt like I'd somehow lost in that exchange, but rather than feel bested by Night, all I wanted to do was learn more about him.

Later that same evening, I was cleaning up the table after Violet and I had shared a few sandwiches for dinner.

"Bryn, are you alright?" she asked. "You were quiet at dinner."

"Oh, yeah, my head is just…full, I guess."

She frowned. "Do you want to talk about it?"

I smiled and shook my head. "Not right now, thanks."

"You sure?"

"Yeah, I think I just need to sort out my thoughts."

"Alright, well, I'll be in my room if you need me." She passed by and rested a hand on my shoulder before continuing up the steps.

Now that I was alone, I began to wash the dishes. As I plunged my hands into the warm, soapy water, I tried to deal with all the fullness in my brain. Part of the issue, I knew, was that I was still reeling from the afternoon. Spending time with both Jasper and Tavi had been lovely, but it was good timing that I'd seen the library when I had.

I had always wanted friends, but having to be "on" while working in the mess hall and then around Tavi and Jasper had started to exhaust me after an hour or so. I needed that library time to recharge and think. After that confusing interaction with Night, I wasn't sure how I felt about the way my life had gone.

Just a week earlier, I had been spitting fire and ready to run barefoot through the trees and underbrush while being chased by Wargs if it meant a chance at freedom. But now, I didn't feel the same pull to escape. I felt closer to the Wargs than I ever had to the Kings—to the point that when I'd heard about the wolf who had lost her life the night before, I felt some of that loss too. I didn't really know the wolf who'd died, but I understood that she was one more addition to the growing tally of bodies that the Kings were assembling.

I hated how senseless and cruel the killing was.

Violet had shown me nothing but kindness and love, Tavi had become my best friend, and I even felt close to Jasper in the short time that I'd known him. Dom, too, was someone I had stopped looking at as a jailer and more like a friend.

As I finished up the dishes, I started to wipe down the table. The Wargs pack had, without hesitation, accepted me for who I was, even though I was human. I felt that the bond I shared with them was something special and precious, something that couldn't be put into words. I was happy that I had known these people—that I had made friends. Though I missed my mom, it was impossible for me to imagine life without the Wargs I'd grown to care for.

And then there was a knock on the door.

"Come in!" I called, finishing up the table. I suspected that I was about to see Dom. He came around often to have tea with me and Violet (though I knew he was there to check in on me), but when I turned to the door, it was Night who stepped inside.

"Oh." I straightened in surprise. Butterflies filled my stomach at seeing him again so unexpectedly, but I tried to calm them down. He was probably still mad at me for the way I'd snapped at him earlier.

"Violet's already gone to bed," I said carefully. "Do you want me to see if she's awake?"

"No. I came to speak to you."

"Oh," I said again, feeling dumb. "I…do you want to sit down at the table?"

He nodded, silently taking a seat. I sat across from him, my hands in my lap.

"Sorry that the table's wet," I said. "I just wiped it down."

"That's fine."

I pressed my lips together and wiped my hands over my jeans. *Why isn't he saying anything?* I squirmed, desperately looking anywhere but directly at his handsome, stoic face. The seconds dripped by in silence, and I was too frazzled to take it anymore.

"Do you want something to drink?" I asked, popping out of my seat. "I can get you some tea or coffee or—or water?"

"No, I don't need anything," he said. "Please, sit."

I sat and tried to pretend the awkward silence wasn't so awkward.

"Tell me about your pack," he said finally. "And about Redwolf."

I looked up at him then, my eyes slightly narrowed. Though I hated what the Kings had done to the Wargs, I couldn't help but think of my mom and the pups. Would Night hurt someone innocent just to get back at the Kings for the loss of one of his wolves?

I don't know what Night saw on my face, but he quickly held up his hands. "Don't worry, I'm not going to hurt anyone you care about," he said, "I just want information. I'm planning to face Troy soon, and I want to learn everything I can to prepare."

I relaxed a bit. "Why would you come to me?"

"Because I know you hate Troy about as much as I do, and you grew up with him, so you would have the best intel."

"Aren't you worried that I'll lie to you?"

"Yes," he said. "I know you don't trust me. I can see you lying to protect your mother even after I've told you that I won't hurt her. But," he sighed, "I'm running out of options."

I paused, considering his words. His logic made sense, but he was wrong about one thing. Though he was technically still my captor, I didn't distrust him nearly as much as I had when I first arrived on the Wargs' compound. If anything, I was wary of him, but I didn't feel like I needed to watch my back whenever I was nearby.

"Okay, I'll tell you about them. Where should I start?"

"Redwolf first."

I nodded. "Troy has always been awful, even when he was a kid. He bullied me severely, but he bullied anyone who got in his way. He knew that because he was the Alpha's son, he didn't need to answer to anyone, so he exerted his influence wherever he could." I played with my hands, losing myself in those memories. "His need for violence goes deep, and he's hotheaded too. He can't stand to be the butt of anyone's joke, even as a tease."

"What about his inner circle?"

"He's got about two dozen men around him most of the time. They're all just as bad-tempered and mean as he is, but most of them are idiots. They all treat the women of the pack terribly and live for nothing but food, sex, and whatever high they can find around the territory." I paused, considering what I'd seen of the pack and the things I'd overheard. "I don't think most of the Kings really like Troy's posse, but it's much easier to go along with them than it is to face their wrath."

Night cursed under his breath. "How did you survive in an environment like that?"

"My mother is the only reason I'm alive today," I said. "I think you know that she saved me as a baby. But more than that, she maintained some clout in the pack because she manned the gardens. Alpha Gregor knew that if he banished me or killed me, he would lose out on my mom's skills. Troy was forced to play along while his father was alive, but now…well, you saw what he did to me the moment he had the chance."

Night listened, and I read sadness in his eyes when I talked about what I'd been through. I glanced away, my cheeks warming. I hadn't expected this level of intimacy.

"Do you want to see Troy taken down?"

I didn't have to think about it. "Yes. Without a doubt. I would have killed him myself if I had an opening."

The corner of his mouth lifted slightly. It wasn't quite a smile, but it wasn't a frown either. "I believe you."

My heart pounded against my ribcage. How could he make me so weak by saying only a few words?

I went on to describe a bit more about the men in Troy's inner circle, and when I was finished, Night stood.

"Thanks for the information," he said. "It's been helpful."

"You're welcome." Suddenly, I wanted to thank him for rescuing me from Troy, but the words stuck in my throat. The urge was like a tug in my chest, one I couldn't make go away. But I kept my mouth shut. I didn't know how he would take a thank you after so many days of arguments. I didn't want to ruin the first real conversation we'd had that didn't end with a fight.

I walked him to the door and waved as he walked away. My heart was still beating erratically in my chest. Troy was the only thing that we had talked about, but something about our evening left me feeling more confused about my emotions—especially regarding my captor, who now seemed less like a captor and more, perhaps, like a friend?

Chapter 23 - Bryn

Over the next two days, I took full advantage of every moment of my newfound freedom. When I wasn't in the kitchens or working in the garden, I was in the library reading.

In the afternoon of my second day of freedom, Pax came by to visit me with his mother, Lillian. Lillian informed me that there was a stash of board games hidden in a compartment of one of the chairs, so Pax and I had a fun time searching for them. Then we played checkers while Lillian relaxed with a book.

"Tomorrow, I'm going to shift in front of the whole pack," he said. "You're still coming, right?"

"Of course! I wouldn't miss it for anything in the world." I saw an easy strategy to win the game, but I chose to move my piece elsewhere to give Pax the win.

"Yay!" Pax threw up his arms and beamed at me. "I can't wait to show you my wolf!"

"And I can't wait to see him." When I noticed he was debating where to place the next piece, I said, "Oh, no! You better not move to that spot there, or I'll be in trouble."

His eyes widened. He glanced up at me, grinning deviously, and put the piece on the spot I'd indicated.

I gasped. "But from that position, you'll have control of the board!"

He gave a devilish giggle and went on to win that game and the next two after that. When he got bored of playing checkers, he asked me to read to him, which I was happy to do. He sat in my lap while I opened a book about a princess and a big strong knight who protected her. I'd chosen it out of nostalgia; I'd read the book too many times to count when I was Pax's age.

I made Pax shriek with laughter every time I lowered my voice to speak for the knight, and he teased me for not sounding at all like a man.

"Oh yeah? Can you do better, Pax?"

"Yeah! Watch." He concentrated, staring hard at the page, and said, "This is my *deep* voice."

It was several octaves above where it needed to be, and I laughed so hard I snorted, which made both me and Pax laugh even harder. Even Lillian joined in. When I finally, finally reached the end of the story, Pax looked up at me.

"Bryn, where's your big strong knight?"

For a moment, Night flashed through my mind, but I quickly pushed the thought away. "I guess I don't have one yet."

"Good!" He hopped from my lap and pointed at his chest. "Then *I'll* be your knight. I'll protect you from all the bad things!"

I chuckled and pulled him in for a big hug. "I'd be honored, little guy."

Later, when I arrived back from the mess hall after dinner, Violet surprised me with new clothes. These were a bit more modern, a bit tighter, and were all vibrant shades of blue, orange, pink, and red.

"I think this is more the style that young wolves like," Violet said. "They should all fit you, but let me know if anything doesn't."

I accepted the clothes reverently and looked at her with tears in my eyes. "Violet, you've been so wonderful to me. I wish I knew how to repay you."

"I'm sure fate will find a way," she replied with a wink.

I smiled. I couldn't pretend to understand what Violet meant, but the statement reminded me of the things Mom used to say. "You're sure there's nothing I can do?"

"Don't worry about me, girlie," Violet laughed. "I'll be just fine."

The next day was Pax's big day. I was so excited for him that I couldn't sit still even to read. It wasn't my day for kitchen duty, but I went anyway to help wash the dishes after breakfast just to have an outlet for all my energy.

The families on duty teased me for coming in on my day off, but they seemed grateful for an extra pair of hands. I loved working alongside them, especially when the older women started to talk about their childhoods and old romances. It reminded me of when Mom would reminisce about her younger years.

"You know, I dated a human a few years back," a wolf named Erika spoke up. She was a few years older than me.

"Really?" My eyes widened. It was the first time I'd heard of a wolf and a human being together.

"Yeah. He was brilliant and kind, and he told me he loved me. I thought we were going to get married, but before I could tell him that I was a wolf, he broke up with me."

I gasped gently. "I'm so sorry, Erika." I looked into the sudsy water in the sink, saddened. "To be honest, whenever I think about love, I get a little sad. I'm pretty sure I'll never have the chance to find the right guy for me. Romance is something I love reading about, but I can't imagine it for myself."

"Nonsense!" Mabel said from across the kitchen. She might have been old, but her hearing was as sharp as any young wolf. "You're too young to give up on love now. The man of your dreams will find you one day."

"Mine did," Erika said. I turned to her with surprise. "A year after I was abandoned, my Stanley scooped me up. I've never loved anyone more than him, and I couldn't be happier." She patted my shoulder. "Don't give up."

My face warmed. They seemed so confident. The only man on my mind was the one who frequented my dreams, whose eyes could set me ablaze within moments. But I knew I couldn't have him.

As we put the clean dishes away, Pax burst in through the door, a frantic smile on his face. "It's time, Bryn! It's time. It's time!"

I must have lost track of time. I left the women to finish up and grabbed my jacket from the hook. Pax took my hand, and we ran out of the mess hall together. We gathered near the Elders' cabin on the flat ground because there was plenty of space for the kids to wolf out.

Pax let go of my hand and ran to the center with the other pups. I stood with the crowd of adults, my hands at my side. The first few shifts were always rough on young pups. But once they got the hang of it, they were so excited they tended to destroy tons of clothes while they practiced and showed off.

Pax was one of the last to reveal his shift. It wasn't because he was nervous—on the contrary, he was waiting to have most of the crowd's attention so he could hop and dance around, working everyone up into an excited cheer. I laughed along, wondering when the shy, self-conscious boy I'd met had become such a ham.

A deep, rumbling laugh sounded from behind me. I turned my head, but I knew Night was standing there. He was so close that if I turned my body to face him, I would only need to step forward a bit to be flush with his chest. Heat wafted from his body, and when he caught me looking at him, he actually smiled.

My breath caught. I had thought that growly, moody Night was sexy, but this smiling, easygoing version of him nearly left me undone. I snapped my attention back to the pups and tried to keep from hyperventilating.

As Pax finished his dance, he spun and faced me. "Bryn Hunter!" he called, startling me. I hadn't known that he knew my last name. He met my gaze, bowed, and then gave a little warrior cry with his fists at his side before he shifted. Within seconds, his body became that of a small, blond wolf, and I cried out with delight and wonder at how well he'd done. I had seen pups struggle through shifts, and I knew it took a great deal of focus. For being a late bloomer, Pax was a natural, and I glowed with pride for my tiny friend.

Behind me, Night stepped closer, and my heart skipped a beat. His woodsy scent filled my lungs with each shaky inhale. The heat of him was intense, and my jacket suddenly felt too warm.

"Pax just dedicated his first public shift to you." His breath was warm across my neck. "Do you know what that means?" His question was asked quietly, a secret spoken between the two of us.

I shook my head, not trusting my voice with him standing so close and speaking so intimately with me. I had seen young wolves call their parent's name or the name of Alpha Gregor before they shifted, but I'd assumed it was just a formality that some pups participated in.

"It's an old, binding pact passed down from the old ways," Night explained, his voice growing even deeper. "When a young pup shifts in public for the first time, they can choose someone to dedicate the shift to. Usually, it's a family member or someone they respect in the pack. When they bow, it's a show of deference and a sign of commitment. It represents the young wolf promising their protection and loyalty to the recipient for the rest of their life."

"I didn't know," I breathed, so quietly the wind could have easily stolen my words.

"That's not a surprise. Most of our pups choose not to dedicate their shift to anyone because the idea of binding themselves to another is too frightening when the future is so uncertain." As he finished talking, his words became strained, like it was hard for him to get them out. "It is the most precious dedication that someone can receive. I have never seen a pup dedicate a shift to someone outside of their family."

"W-well, maybe he meant to dedicate it to you," I said. "You're standing right behind me." It was hardly a protest, more an expression of astonishment. Even after our conversation about knights and princesses yesterday, I was amazed that Pax would give me such an important gift.

"Not a chance," he said with a smile. "It was your name that Pax called."

I bit my lip. Suddenly, I felt nervous. Would Pax's family be upset with him? Would they be angry with me? Hadn't I—a human girl—just stolen an honor from them, even if it wasn't on purpose? But my doubts disappeared when I felt something soft press against my hand. I gasped quietly. When I looked down, I found Pax's wolf rubbing at my fingers, eager for attention. I had only been allowed to touch Mom in her wolf form when I was around Pax's age. I'd never felt another wolf's fur beneath my fingers.

I gave a light, wondering giggle as I petted his head, and Pax gave an answering purr when I rubbed behind his ears. His long tongue lolled from his mouth, and he jumped up to lick my face, which made me laugh even harder.

"Paxton, don't jump on people," Lillian said, walking toward us.

I hesitated, nervous that I was about to face her wrath, but to my surprise, there was nothing but kindness and joy in the tears that glimmered in her eyes.

"Thank you so much for what you did to help Pax," she gushed. "We're so grateful for what you've done for him."

"I—I…" I wasn't sure what to say. Behind me was Night—silent, steady, and warm—and in front of me stood a woman who was near tears and a happy pup who pushed at my hand for more petting. It was difficult to focus. "Pax did the hard work," I said finally. "I just fed him bacon and jam."

Lillian laughed and dabbed at a tear in the corner of her eye. "Would it be alright if I hugged you, Bryn?"

"O-of course." I awkwardly held out my arms, and Lillian hugged me tightly. Though I hadn't been expecting this bit of intimacy, I had to admit that it was a wonderful, joyful hug.

All my life, the only physical affection I had ever received had come from my mom, who hugged and loved on me as often as I let her, and the pups I babysat who didn't know any better. The Kings' wolves, however, avoided touching me like I was dirty.

But that had changed when I arrived here. Tavi practically threw herself at me at every opportunity, jumping at the possibility of holding my hand or hugging me. Jasper reached for me every once in a while too, and even Night seemed to touch my arm or my wrist when we were close. I used to watch how affectionate the Kings' wolves were with each other and crave even a taste of the same treatment.

But here, with the Wargs, I finally knew what it was like to touch and be touched by someone I cared about, someone who wasn't my mom, and it felt like a door opening for me.

When Lillian let go, she smiled at me once more before turning to her son. "Pax, it's time to go home."

Pax whined, stomping his feet.

"Pax, honey, don't make me say it a second time."

He whined again, but he couldn't argue with his mother. He licked my hand as a way to say goodbye and then followed Lillian when she started walking toward the village. Night and I stood quietly together while the rest of the crowd dispersed. I felt like I ought to say something, but nothing I could think of matched the significance of what had just happened. Also, the silence between us was laced with some tension. Some sort of energy bound the two of us where we stood, like static electricity, but I couldn't figure out what it meant.

"I should go," Night said gently.

"Right," I replied, though I was disappointed that he was leaving so suddenly.

Before he left, he leaned close to my ear again. His breath slightly jostled the strands of hair by my ear as he said, "Your laugh is beautiful, Bryn. You should do that more often."

I shivered. "You c-can't even see my face from behind me," I stuttered. The ache in my chest pulled tight. I felt like I couldn't breathe but in the most delightful way.

He gave that deep chuckle again, and goosebumps spread from my neck and down my back. When cool air replaced the heat of his body, I knew he'd stepped back. "You did well with the pup," he said.

His voice, again, had that strained sound to it. But when I turned to face him, to see the expression that came with such a tense tone, he was already gone. Like he'd never been there at all.

Chapter 24 - Night

I sat at the dinner table across from Dom, both of us nursing a bottle of beer while we enjoyed chips with salsa made from the vegetables that Bryn had helped grow. The salsa was spicy and fresh, the beers were cold, and the night air blowing in through the windows was cool and smelled vaguely sweet. It was a rare, quiet night following the public shifts of the pups, and Dom and I were relaxing and catching up.

"Oh, I have an update from the sentries," he said.

I nodded for him to continue.

"Things are quiet, but we have one wolf unaccounted for. Vince."

My expression darkened. Vince had only recently become an elite tracker. He had a bright, successful future ahead of him, so losing him would be another huge loss after Iggy.

"Hey, hey, don't worry," he assured me. "There's no indication that the Kings have anything to do with it. And besides, we've got our best trackers on it. We'll find him soon. After all, he's probably just chasing a female shifter in heat. It wouldn't be the first time that a young man broke form to get lucky."

I nodded, but after Iggy, I doubted I would ever be able to relax when one of my wolves went missing. "You say there's no sign of the Kings' involvement?"

He nodded. "That's right. So far, there've been no indications that the Kings' pack is even planning to attack us any time soon."

"Mm. Still, I think we should beef up our patrols."

"Already on it. We've got small packs of three wolves on patrol just in case. But to be honest, Night, I really don't see that Redwolf coward showing his ugly mug to get Bryn himself. Even he wouldn't be that bold."

I took a swig of my beer. *Dom always calls her by her first name. They must be close.* The thought struck me with its suddenness, but their friendship didn't bother me much anymore.

Dom cleared his throat. "Speaking of Bryn, and I know you don't want to talk about this again, but I have to bring this up."

I closed my eyes for a few seconds and opened them again. I knew what he was going to say, but I wouldn't stop him from speaking his mind.

"I think we should pull Bryn out of the deal entirely. I know we talked about how important it is that we do this right, but dammit, Night, it doesn't sit right with me." He ran a hand through his hair. "We need a new plan, one that keeps her as far away from that fucker as we can get her. I really like her, Tavi and Violet like her—shit, the whole pack is practically in love with her, and it wouldn't be right to use her like this."

He was right, but I couldn't give him an answer. I didn't like the idea of handing Bryn over at all, but I hadn't come up with a good alternative for the plan. Telling Redwolf outright that we were breaking off the deal like that might make things even more dangerous for the pack and for Bryn. Who knew how the fucker would respond if we changed plans so suddenly?

"I hear you," I said, "but for now, we should focus on how we plan on retaliating against the Kings for Iggy."

We'd buried Iggy in a plot of land in her favorite section of the forest. It was a small ceremony—just her family, me, Dom, and Iggy's close friends. It was the first time I had seen Iggy's family since I broke the news of her death, and the first thing they'd asked me was what I was going to do about her death. They rightfully wanted some retribution for their loss.

Dom sighed. "Alright, what do you propose?"

"We could do the same thing they did—send a special team to attack them while they're unawares."

"I don't know. I don't think that's direct enough."

"That's fair." I would never attack children, expectant mothers, or their infirmaries directly, but it was hard to know exactly how to respond when Iggy had meant so much to the community, and to me, as a member of my inner circle. "We could target someone who Troy keeps close to him."

"An assassination," Dom said with a nod. "We'll send a few sentries to do some recon. It'll be easier to know who to target once we know their names."

"Actually, I already know a few of their names."

Dom blinked. "Wait, really? How did you get that kind of intel?"

"I went through a good source."

Dom faced me, crossing his arms. "And who was that good source?"

I coughed and glanced away. "Bryn."

Dom paused, and then he grinned. "If I didn't know any better, I'd say you were trying to make peace with her."

"Shut up."

Dom *tsked* at me. "So testy. What did you think of my training schedule proposal? There are dozens of young wolves that are eager to show that they have what it takes to be part of the elite squads. Preston, Mark, Vince, Jasper—"

The moment I heard that young wolf's name, I growled. My wolf moved close to the surface—his teeth elongating, his claws sharpening. I nearly ripped through my chair as I gripped it, trying to breathe through the unexpected reaction. My beer rolled off the table and shattered against the ground with my movements.

Dom stared at me. *"What the hell?"* he demanded, his voice echoing in my mind.

I didn't reply, though it would be easier to do telepathically than to attempt to form words through all my sharp teeth. It took me several uncomfortable moments to get my wolf under control. As my breathing calmed from growling rasps to human panting, Dom left the table to grab me a fresh beer.

"So," Dom began as I pulled the beer close to me, "you wanna talk about what the fuck that was?"

"No." My response was clipped, brooking no argument, but Dom wouldn't leave it at that.

"Tough shit. Night, I'm your beta and your best friend. If something is eating at you, I want to help you. That's what I'm here for. Also," he added, "you're reminding me of when we were preteens just surviving puberty. If you can't control your shifts or your emotions, it'll be a problem for what we're setting out to do."

I sighed. I knew Dom was right, but it wasn't exactly easy for me to come out and say what had been bothering me. Then again, there wasn't anyone else in the world who I trusted more than Dom and my mother, so I might as well come clean.

"It's that damned woman," I admitted.

Dom blinked. "Wait, Bryn?"

"From the moment I caught her scent, my wolf has been almost impossible to control around her. He loses it whenever she's nearby."

That was part of the reason I was so choked up when I talked to Bryn during the shifting ceremony. My wolf wasn't jealous of Pax. In fact, he was incredibly proud of the display and had wanted to come out to congratulate her too. It had taken everything to keep myself in check. But damn, it had been a beautiful moment.

"I've been having dreams for months now, but they've increased to almost every night since I brought her here," I explained. "Usually, they're of me in bed with a woman whose eyes are the same color as Bryn's. I've started to think of the woman *as* Bryn, and every time I have one of the dreams, it's even more difficult to keep my wolf in check." I shook my head. "Bryn also…she gets under my skin, and I can't shake her off no matter what I do. It's been so hard that I was considering moving her to the other side of our territory just to make sure that I could avoid her.

"Obviously, I never followed through. I think some part of me knew it wouldn't help anyway because somehow, I always end up near her. And now she's got free rein of the compound. It's impossible for me not to see her or smell her or hear her voice. She's *everywhere*. And it's too late to put her back on restrictions. She's already won over everyone who's met her, which confuses the shit out of me." I rubbed my eyes. "It's fucking with me."

Dom sat listening as I let all my anger and frustration out. I felt raw and vulnerable. I waited for some sort of encouragement or advice from my beta, but the first sound out of Dom's mouth wasn't a vote of optimism or a solution—it was a snicker.

My head snapped up, unsure if my ears were deceiving me. I found Dom trying to hold back his laughter as best he could, but the amusement in his dark eyes gave him away.

"What the fuck is wrong with you?" I demanded. "You think this shit is funny?"

Apparently, that was too much because Dom let it out, laughing his ass off while I sat there, in equal parts, angry and stupefied.

Eventually, Dom gained control of himself enough to bring the laughter down to a minimum. "You must be the most jacked up fucker there is," he said. "The universe must have it out for you, Night."

"What the fuck are you talking about?"

"You kidnap a girl and try to make her life miserable, only for her to turn out to be *your mate!*" Dom dissolved into laughter again.

Mate? The word was like a silent explosion in my head. My wolf began to pant and hop around like the word had summoned him.

"No," I said. "What? No, that's ridiculous. Bryn is a human woman, Dom. There's never been a real mate pair between a wolf and a human. Ever."

"Uh huh." Dom smirked.

"It's more likely that it's just stress about blowing the mission to kill Troy when I had the chance. Now I've got the stress of this human and of trying to figure out how to keep our pack safe. That's all."

"Oh, yeah, I'm sure that's it."

"Don't fuck with me, Dom. I'm telling you, it isn't like that."

"Yeah? Then why were you about ready to shift when I mentioned a particular young wolf's name?"

I clenched my hand so tight that the beer bottle shattered in my hand, spraying blood and beer over the table. Fortunately, it was mostly empty. Dom pursed his lips to keep from laughing.

"Forget I said anything, and mind your damn business. I never want to speak to you about this again."

"That's what I thought." Dom grinned. "There's no possible way Bryn could be your mate. You're just under the kind of stress that has you in a constant jealous rage. How stupid of me to think it could be anything else."

I kicked him the hell out shortly after that.

Chapter 25 - Bryn

The next day, Violet and I worked side by side in the garden, picking the ripe fruits and vegetables so we could take them to the mess hall and prepare for the pack's next meal. The sun was high in the bright, cerulean sky, and I wiped my forehead with the back of my hand as I worked.

"So, it sounds like things are going well," Violet said. I had just finished telling her about the library and all the books I wanted to read.

"Absolutely! Pax's mom Lillian told me that she wanted to start a book club with me sometime soon. I've never been in one of those before, and—oh!" I cut myself off with a gasp. "I didn't tell you about the shifting ceremony! Pax dedicated his shift to me." My heart swelled with joy every time I thought about it. "I think it's because I helped him when he confided in me that he was a late shifter."

"I see." Violet looked at me from under the brim of her hat, her eyes strikingly chartreuse. "Why did you help him?" she asked.

"Why? Well, because I know what it's like to feel inadequate. And because he needed someone to help him through it."

"Mm." Violet tossed a yellow squash into the basket. "You're not pack, though. You shouldn't have felt obligated to help him."

I paused. *I'm not pack?* The statement confused me even as it hit me right in the chest. It felt wrong. And mean. How could she say something like that to me?

My hands clenched, and I met Violet's gaze. "I know I'm human, Violet, but I wasn't trying to step on anyone's toes. I never felt obligated to help him. I just did what I felt was right."

Violet stared at me a few moments more, and then a smile replaced her frown. The shift in her expressions confused me. *Was she testing me? Does her smile mean that I passed?*

"You know, with your fierceness and your kind heart, you remind me of someone I know."

"Who?"

"My son."

I snorted, waving that thought away. Violet was obviously just teasing me; there was no way that I was anything like that brooding, often infuriating Alpha.

"Oof," Violet said, standing up, pressing her palms to her lower back. "My back. I might be getting too old for this kind of work. I'm going to go and get some rest. And in the meantime, Bryn?"

"Hm?"

"Keep your mind open. You never know when the earth will speak to you."

"Oh. Uh, sure." Mom said things like that all the time when we worked the land, so I figured Violet was just waxing poetic about the garden. As I got back to work, still struggling with the idea that I was anything like Night, I heard a rustling from the tree line about fifty yards from where I stood.

At first, I saw nothing, just darkness and bushes. I almost went back to my work, but something told me to keep looking. I scanned the tree line again until my eyes landed on a russet-brown wolf standing among the trees. It gazed at me with white-silver eyes. I froze. I didn't recognize the wolf, but it didn't seem threatening.

I remained motionless as the wolf slowly began to approach. My heart was beating hard and fast, but I wasn't afraid, only curious. When the wolf was within fifteen feet of me, I saw that it had a small cut on its left ear. I stood slowly, watching and waiting. I couldn't say why, but I felt some sort of connection to this wolf, even though it was a stranger to me.

Suddenly, as if in a trance, I slid the work gloves from my hands, dropping them on the ground by the vegetables I hadn't yet picked. I began to walk slowly toward the wolf. When I was close enough that I could almost reach out and touch its thick fur, it turned and headed back into the tree line, where it looked back at me.

I have to follow it. Heedless of the remaining restrictions that Night had placed on me, forgetting about the work I had yet to do, I followed it into the woods, pushing my way through branches and bushes as I kept the wolf's gorgeous pelt within sight.

As I moved, I realized how easy it would be for me to escape. It was still light out, and no one was coming after me despite Night, Dom, and Violet's warnings that there were sentries always keeping an eye on me. It was a beautiful day, and I could run for miles without anyone knowing I was gone. My pace slowed as I thought about leaving the Wargs' compound behind. It didn't sit well with me to leave everyone I'd come to know.

Ahead of me, the wolf looked back my way, seemingly asking me to hurry up.

I'll just see what this wolf wants, I reasoned. *Then maybe I can think clearly about this.*

With my mind temporarily settled, I increased my speed and continued following the wolf deeper into the woods. Before long, the dense trees parted to reveal the craggy maw of a small cave. The wolf sat beside it. It looked at the cave's dark entrance, at me, and then back again. *It wants me to go inside, but why?*

"Why did you bring me here?" I asked it. I hoped it would shift or give some other indication of an answer, but it remained silent. It looked between me and the cave again. Anxiety took hold of my legs, and I hesitated. I had never liked tight spaces or dark caves, but my instincts were telling me that I needed to trust this wolf and venture inside. I just had to be brave.

"Alright, fine," I grumbled, zipping up my jacket. "I see you're not too eager to go in yourself, wolf."

Of course, the wolf said nothing. It just watched as I entered the cave. Inside the cave was dark, wet, and extremely cold. I thrust my hands out as I navigated through the darkness. I gasped when I stumbled over a stalagmite, my shoulder crashing into the cave wall. I squeaked as pain shot through my arm. With the pain came a moment of clarity. *What am I doing?*

It was so, so stupid to try and navigate my way through some random cave, by myself, in literal pitch-black darkness. I had half a mind to head back out, strange wolf be damned. But at the same time, I felt a tug at my senses—the same feeling that had urged me to keep looking when I hadn't immediately seen the brown wolf.

No, I shouldn't be overthinking or second-guessing. I needed to trust my instincts. I took a few deep breaths, resolve filling me, and began to trust the feeling that was urging me onward.

I kept a hand on the cool rock wall. I moved slowly, but each step was confidently placed in front of the other. I wasn't worried about tripping over another stalagmite or walking into a group of bats. I just needed to stay steady and sure.

Eventually, I rounded a turn in the tunnel, and the ceiling suddenly dropped so low that I had to crawl on my hands and knees. I was freezing, the cold growing more and more unforgiving as I inched forward. Adrenaline pushed me forward, and the strong sense that I needed to keep going distracted me. Finally, thankfully, the tunnel opened into a much larger space. A few rays of sunlight shone in from a large hole above, and I sucked in a sharp breath.

On the ground lay a wounded, dark-brown wolf, struggling to breathe. I immediately rushed to its side.

Its eyes snapped open, and its snarl brought me up short. My movements had startled it. At least now I was close enough to see what the problem was—its left hind leg was bloody and bent at an odd angle. I glanced up to stare at the hole. It was large enough for the wolf to have fallen through it. Judging by the large amount of moss, leaves, and branches scattered around on the ground, it likely hadn't seen the opening until it was too late.

The wolf tried to move, but it fell back down with a whimper. I stepped a bit closer, trying to assess any other injuries. There didn't appear to be any aside from its sharp, rasping breaths. It likely weighed at least 150 pounds—a full-grown wolf. If I was a shifter, I might have been strong enough to help it out of here. But I knew I'd never be able to get it back to the tunnel.

"C-can you shift?" I asked. "In your human form, I can help you out of here. As you are, you're too heavy for me."

The wolf glared at me, its bright blue eyes full of mistrust and confusion. *Damn it.* I looked around and spied the plant matter on the ground. Could I fashion a gurney and drag it out? No, the moss and vines wouldn't be strong enough to take its weight. The best I could do was make the wolf a bit more comfortable.

But that was better than nothing.

I piled the vegetation into a bed and moved toward the wolf. It snapped and snarled and scratched at me as I tried to heave it onto the bed, but I knew that it wasn't because it wanted to hurt me. It was like I could sense the wolf's fear. It was likely in shock, unable to think or behave the way it would normally. I'd learned in school that when shifters experienced trauma or great emotions, their logical human minds receded, leaving the animal brain to react on instinct.

A few bruises and scratches later, I managed to haul the wolf onto the bed. I made sure to pad the spot where the injured leg rested. I heaved a sigh and stepped back. The wolf's eyes were already starting to droop with exhaustion, and before long, it was snoring.

I ran both hands through my hair as I looked from the wolf to the opening of the tunnel. I was losing daylight. How the hell would I get the wolf out of here?

You could leave. The thought hit me suddenly. *You've done all you can here. You could take off and go see Mom. You know she must be freaking out about you.*

I decided that now was as good a time as any to sort out my thoughts on escaping, on heading home. I missed Mom so badly that my stomach ached, but I couldn't see myself going back there. Not willingly, anyway. The way Troy treated me and his threats—which I knew he intended to make good on—were too frightening. The Wargs pack had made me feel welcome and had given me a place I felt with increasing certainty was my home.

I dropped the idea of trying to find my way back to my mom. I knew I would be miserable leaving behind all the relationships I'd formed with the Wargs, especially with Pax, Jasper, Tavi, Dom, Violet…and even Night.

I'd made my decision to stay, but now I needed to figure out what to do about the large problem snoozing at my feet. It was getting dark, and soon there wouldn't be enough light for me to find my way back. My only options were to leave the wolf behind and get help or to stay and get stuck here overnight. *I can't do this on my own. I need another shifter to help me—*

A low growl sounded from deep in the cave, sending chills down my spine. I turned toward the entrance of the tunnel as the scuffling, snuffling sounds of enclosing predators came closer. I backed against the wall of the cave, standing next to the sleeping wolf. I knew that the wolves that were drawing near were not friendly. Their growls were foreign and wild.

I searched for a possible weapon and found a stick near the hole that the wolf had fallen through. I grabbed it with both hands and crouched next to the injured wolf. I held my breath, hoping against hope that they would move on.

I heard their claws scratching against the cave floor as the wolves crawled toward us. Their eyes peered out from the darkness of the tunnel, followed quickly by sharp, gleaming teeth that dripped with saliva.

That was when I knew that I was about to die.

Chapter 26 - Night

I was looking through the reports from the sentries on my dining table. They still hadn't found Vince, and as the hours went on, I became less and less sure that they would find him alive—if they found him at all. As I sat there worrying, pressing a hand to my throbbing temple, I heard quick footsteps rushing toward my front door. I was already standing by the time Mom burst inside, her face the white of a corpse.

I was at her side in a flash. "What's wrong?"

"Bryn is gone."

The words sounded like a foreign language. "What did you say?"

"I—" She paused and took a few deep breaths. When she spoke again, her voice was calmer but laced with worry. "Bryn and I were in the gardens when I went back inside to rest. I wasn't gone for more than half an hour, but…but something felt *off*. I went to check on her, and she was gone!"

"What do you mean she's gone? Did she run away?" Part of me knew that Bryn would never be dumb enough to venture out into the woods to attempt the four-day trek to the Kings, no matter how badly she missed her home. But a larger part of me was immediately pissed off at the thought that she might try.

After all that had happened, with only ten days until the next full moon, would she really try and head back to the Kings? After all the connections she'd made and after the gentle conversations that Bryn and I had shared, would she willingly return to Troy's clutches?

"Night, focus!" Mom took my face and made me look at her. "She *didn't* run away. I *know* she didn't."

She couldn't know that. She hadn't seen how hard Bryn had tried to run home the days following my kidnapping her. But now wasn't the time to argue about this. I needed to figure out where Bryn was. Now.

"How do you know she's not somewhere on the compound?" I asked. "Maybe she's in the library."

"You don't understand. When I got out there, she hadn't finished harvesting the vegetables. She'd left her gloves on the ground, even though she always makes sure to put them back in the crate. She's the tidiest creature I know—she would never leave a job half-finished. She would never leave a mess."

Now that my rage had started to fade, the dread began to creep in. I already had a wolf missing—what if I lost Bryn too?

What if Troy had sent someone for her?

I raced out of my cabin, calling for my mom to stay put. In my mind, I called for Dom as I rushed toward the garden. I found the gloves where Mom had said, lying by themselves in the dirt with the unharvested plants. I inhaled deeply, catching the remnants of Bryn's scent on the air, but she'd obviously been gone for a while.

Dom ran up seconds later, followed by Tavi and *Jasper,* of all people. My wolf was clawing at me, desperate to get me to shift so he could search for Bryn. But he was too manic, too desperate; I didn't think I could trust him to make any real progress.

"What's going on?" Tavi demanded.

"Bryn is missing," I said through sharpening teeth. "I don't know how, but she's fucking gone."

Tavi gasped, covering her mouth as tears shone in her eyes. Jasper snarled, and Dom released a growl. The three of us shifted into our wolf forms while Tavi remained as a human. Jasper started moving toward the tree line, and my wolf snarled at him, a challenging growl. Thankfully, Dom's wolf bumped mine, pulling my mind away from Jasper and onto Bryn. Now wasn't the time to cede control to my wolf, who seemed eager to challenge Jasper—Bryn could be in trouble.

I put my nose to the ground. The moment I picked up her scent on the soil, I launched into the forest, eager to follow it before it dissipated.

"I'll go find the other trackers," Tavi called after us, which was good. I was far too focused to try and reach them myself.

The deeper into the woods we went, the more I had to fight the feeling that Bryn might really have run off— that she'd played all of us this entire time. This path would have taken her to the river, and after she crossed it, she would be in Kings' territory again.

Damn. This was why I didn't trust anyone. Why would I ever open up my heart when I had been burned countless times before? I was stupid to think that I could let her in, to believe that she might be my mate like Dom had said.

Dom pushed his way into my mind. "*The rain is getting worse and worse by the mile,*" he said. "*Something might have happened to Bryn. How would she know to take these paths? It's possible that she's been taken or lured away somehow…though, I can't smell any other scents mixed with hers.*"

I wasn't sure what the hell was going on either, but it wasn't looking good for Bryn and her supposed sense of loyalty.

I wasn't guarding my thoughts, so Dom caught the tail end of my thinking and groaned. *"Stop thinking the worst of every person you know. Bryn didn't leave on her own. There's something more at play here."*

I heard his words, but I was afraid to hope. Instead of responding, I closed my mind to him and kept running.

Finally, we came upon a cool, dark cave. The setting sun had disappeared behind stormy clouds. Steady rain was pouring from a smoke-gray sky. I knew without a doubt that Bryn was inside. Worry surged inside me, followed swiftly by an awful, inky dread. *What the hell is she doing in the cave? She could get hurt in there!*

I sniffed at the cave and then snarled. There were male wolves in there…and the scent of blood. I howled, and Jasper and Dom's wolves joined in. They had caught the foreign scents too, and all three of us knew that the wolves weren't Wargs. With that thought, my wolf shoved me to the background and took full control.

He sprinted inside, vengeance already on his mind. But I was in agreement. Neither of us gave a shit if we were running into an ambush of a whole pack of feral wolves. *Nothing* would stop me from getting to Bryn.

When I reached the entrance to a small tunnel, Bryn's scent was so strong that my wolf nearly bit Dom's head off for bumping next to me. My wolf was on high alert because Bryn was in that tunnel with at least three other wolves. They smelled wild, not of any pack.

I knew I needed to take a second to plan before I rushed in. If I rushed inside, I could be leading Jasper and Dom into a really dangerous situation, but when I heard Bryn scream, my wolf took over. He forced me into the tunnel, shoving my large wolf frame into the tight space so I could get there faster. Behind me, I heard Dom and Jasper crawling in after.

Finally, I emerged on the other side of the tunnel to a terrifying scene. Bryn was cornered by three large male shifters. She cowered over something she was guarding with her body, and my nose picked up a fourth wolf. It was Vince. I recognized him immediately. Bryn had thrown herself over his body, and she seemed to be protecting him with her life, even as three feral wolves snarled at her.

I understood all of this the second I emerged from the tunnel. In the following seconds, the three wolves whipped around, finally taking in my presence. Behind them, Bryn's frightened gaze darted from the three foreign wolves to Dom and Jasper. She pressed more tightly to the injured wolf's side...until her gaze fell on me. She visibly relaxed when she saw me there.

She recognized my wolf? She trusted him? Emotion pulsed through me, but I didn't have time to pick apart what I was feeling. Bryn was trembling, likely from a combination of fear and adrenaline. I needed to get her the hell out of here before she suffered anymore.

First, I had three shifters to take care of.

Two of the wolves moved forward, the third backing toward Bryn and Vince. I saw red, lunging toward the wolf closest to Bryn, my teeth gnashing. The other two wolves tried to catch me between them, but I was too quick. I reached the wolf closest to Bryn and, without hesitation, sank my fangs into his throat. Hot, salty blood rushed into my mouth and dripped from my teeth.

I would have tightened my grip on his throat, but I dropped him when another wolf hopped onto my back, biting into my shoulder. I grunted in pain and tried to shake the wolf off. Fortunately, Dom was there in an instant. He bit into the feral's leg, bones snapping in his powerful jaws. The wolf whimpered in pain, and Dom jerked him down off me. Behind them, the remaining wolf sprinted for Bryn and Vince, its teeth flashing in the light that shone down from the hole above.

Bryn closed her eyes, bracing for impact. But before the wolf reached her, Jasper tackled it, wrestling it to the ground. I had to fight my wolf's need to be the one to protect Bryn, to save her from every threat in that cave. Winning the fight was way more important than who took down each wolf.

The wolf had managed to sink his jaws into Jasper's flank. I bounded over to Jasper's side and bit the wolf by the scruff of its neck. As it snarled in pain, I tossed it across the small space and into the cave wall. Its body made a meaty thump against the wall before crumpling to the ground.

"Night, look out!" Bryn called.

My wolf looked at her instead of looking where she pointed. He, like me, was eager to make sure she was alright, but this left me wide open. The first wolf that I had taken down, the one I thought I'd killed, barreled into me, still dripping blood from its wounded neck. It slammed me into the wall, breaking ribs. I wheezed out in pain, landing hard on the ground.

The bleeding feral turned toward Bryn, growling. She again threw her body over Vince's. *Why don't you run?* I thought desperately. *Get out of here, Bryn!*

The wolf neared her, eager to taste her blood, Vince's wolf tried to snarl, but he was too weak to effectively protect her. She screamed, kicking the wolf's snout as it got too close. It bared its teeth at her, and I knew it was about to strike.

With a surge of wrathful energy, I hauled myself to my feet. Pushing through the pain in my ribs, I shot across the distance that separated me from Bryn. I tackled the wolf to the ground, ignoring its snapping fangs. I bit into the wolf's neck again, and this time, I ripped its throat out. Blood sprayed across the cave wall in an arch. His carotid artery spurt, spurt, spurt until its stream of blood became a trickle.

The fight was over. Dom and Jasper dispatched the two other wolves themselves, and neither of them seemed terribly injured. I looked at Bryn, who was staring back at me. Pride flushed across her beautiful face even as tears of relief dripped from her chin and onto Vince's fur.

My wolf was eager to get close to Bryn—to rub on her and make sure that she really was okay. But I held it back. For one, it would be inappropriate and disrespectful for me to dote on her in front of Dom and Jasper, who had risked their lives for us both. For another, I didn't trust that I'd be able to keep myself upright, not with my ribs aching like they were.

Instead, I turned to Dom and spoke to him through our link. *"We need to get them out of here, but one of us has to carry Vince."*

"I'm game," he said. *"I've just got a small cut on my front paw."* It would be nothing more than a scratch on his hand when he shifted.

Jasper's wolf walked over to Bryn, sniffing at her. But she paid him no mind. She only had eyes for me. I stilled, meeting her gaze. It reminded me of a dream that I'd had with her—I had approached her in this form, and she had reached out to touch my fur.

She searched my eyes for several long seconds. And when she found what she was looking for, she sighed. Because she was only human, whatever strength or adrenaline had been keeping her alert faded before my eyes. She slumped forward onto Vince, unconscious.

Chapter 27 - Bryn

I emerged from the unconscious void slowly. As I did, the words, "strange wolf," were soft on my tongue. The first thing I noticed was the smell of green grass, earth, and the freshness of the woods. I buried my head deeper into the scent, the hard, smooth surface beneath me barely giving way to my snuggling. I could have stayed burrowed in its warmth forever and never opened my eyes again.

As I became more aware of my surroundings, I realized that the hardness beneath me wasn't an object but a body. I knew that it was Night's chest that I was pressed against, just like I'd known in the cave that the midnight black wolf with the blazing green eyes was him. He had come for me and saved me from certain doom. For the second time.

I could make out voices around me, but the heat emanating from Night's body made me want to curl up and go back to sleep. The moment the fight ended, the adrenaline and fear that had kept me going evaporated. When I'd looked into Night's eyes, I knew I was safe again, and I'd blacked out. Now that I was recalling more about what had happened, I realized that the blond, almost-white wolf was likely Dom. I couldn't be sure who the wolf with the brassy, coppery coat was, but he had to be pack too.

Dom, Night, and the third wolf must have brought me and the injured wolf out of the cave somehow. It couldn't have been an easy process given how tight that tunnel was. Worry twanged at the back of my mind. Night had been injured in the fray. I remembered that he had been slammed into the cave wall and that it had taken a lot for him to pick himself up and save me. But now, he was able to hold me, and my nuzzling into his chest didn't seem to be hurting him at all.

My worry began to subside, but fresh concern filled its place. What about the injured wolf? Had it survived all of that?

Concern for the wolf forced me out of my warm, sleepy cocoon. I opened my eyes, but I was still surrounded by darkness. I must have been under the covers, nestled deep in the crook of his arm. I shifted to try and prop myself up in Night's arms. Only, his arm refused to budge an inch as if it was made of iron. He wasn't going to let me go.

"Night, Bryn's awake." It was Violet's voice.

Night said nothing and refused to move, his arm still strapping me against his side.

"You big brute," Tavi said. "Let her go so I can hug my best friend."

Night gave a warning growl in response.

I sighed quietly. I needed to get out of this on my own. I didn't want to leave the warmth of his bare, sculpted chest, but there was no way I could stay here when I knew that the others were waiting to talk to me.

I tried to wiggle out from under Night's arm. "I'm up," I said, my voice muffled by his muscle. "I'm okay. You can let me go now."

Night still refused to release me. I wiggled a bit more, and the movement started to make things too warm. Finally, I popped my head out of the covers and turned to take in my surroundings. We were in Night's cabin, in his living room. Night and I were on the couch. I lay across his lap, and my face had been buried between his side and the crook of his arm.

Violet, Tavi, Dom, and Jasper stood around the couch. They had their arms up, and though their expressions were calm, concern was evident in their stiff postures. They looked like they were trying to convince a lion to set down a baby. Like they were dealing with a wild animal.

I looked up and found Night's lips pulled back in a snarl, his teeth still sharp and wolf-like despite being in his human form. His pupils were dilated to the point that I couldn't see the green of his irises. They twitched from person to person like he expected them to take me from him.

I wasn't sure what had happened to put Night in such a state, but I wasn't afraid of him even though I was literally inches away from those sharp teeth. Listening to the same instinct, which had encouraged me to go into the cave, I freed one of my arms and reached up to touch the side of his face.

The moment my hand touched his cheek, he relaxed, and his hold on me softened. He still held me against him, but less desperately. Slowly, his wolf receded—his teeth returned to normal, and his pupils slowly contracted until they revealed the beautiful green of his eyes.

Those eyes scanned my body, likely looking for injuries, even as he pressed his cheek into my hand, worry written all over his face.

I felt like that look was chipping away at what remained of the walls I'd built to protect my heart. The way he looked at me, like he cared, like I was someone that mattered, made me want to melt against him. I knew I shouldn't feel that way. He and I weren't even friends—he was my captor, and I was his prisoner. But I didn't believe that was all we were anymore. I knew that something had changed between us, something important.

Suddenly, Night's gaze slid away, and his face closed off, returning to the stoic mask he always wore. His grip on me loosened further, and I climbed off the couch. The moment I was free of him, he got to his feet and stalked toward the kitchen. He probably wanted to get himself something to drink.

Tavi rushed to me and hugged me almost as tightly as Night had. She was crying, her tears moistening my sweater like they had the night of the bonfire.

"I thought you were dead," she sobbed. "I thought someone had taken you. I thought you had been injured. I—I thought you were never coming back." She sniffled, holding me even more tightly. "Why did my best friend have to be human? If you were a wolf, I wouldn't have to worry so much about you."

I forced a laugh and patted Tavi on the back. I'd thought the same thing in the cave. If only I were stronger, if only I were a wolf—I would have been able to protect the injured wolf better. I might have even been able to bring him home by myself.

Violet came to my rescue. She pulled Tavi off me so she could fold me into a much softer embrace.

"You did so well," she whispered. "I'm proud of you, Bryn."

"I did?" I didn't understand what she could mean.

Violet pulled back and winked. "You've made connections and promises that you're not even aware of. Yet. But these things will become clearer to you with time."

"Oh. Uh. Sure." I gave a confused look to Dom and Jasper over Violet's shoulder, but they shrugged back. They didn't understand her words either.

Jasper cleared his throat. "I'm glad to see that you're okay, Bryn," he said, pink coloring his cheeks. "I was so worried about you when I saw you in that cave."

"Oh! You were the third wolf!" I said. "Thanks, Jasper, and thank you, Dom, for saving me."

Dom grinned back. "You can get lost anytime you want, Bryn. I haven't had that much fun in a long time."

Laughter bubbled through the room, an expression of relief and joy. I was so happy to be back among friends that I almost felt light-headed. But Night's low growl from the kitchen silenced all of us. He stormed back into the living room, his eyes burning as he made a beeline for me.

"I want everyone out," he said. "Now."

The room cleared within seconds. I didn't move. I knew that he wanted me to stay.

"How *dare* you wander off?" he raged. His voice was louder than normal, but it wasn't quite a yell. A man with a voice as deep and as full as Night's didn't need to yell to make it clear that he was upset.

"How dare you try to leave, to run from me? From us? It was so stupid of me to give you even an inch of breathing room. The minute I take my eyes off you, you're deep in the forest in some random cave, making me think you'd run back to the Kings or that you'd been abducted."

My fists clenched at my sides. I opened my mouth, a retort hot on my tongue, but something about Night's behavior gave me pause. I realized that his anger wasn't truly anger. It came from a place of fear. He had been scared for me. He had *worried* about me.

Alright. I'd let him get it all out before I made any response. I knew this came from his concern for me, but I wouldn't let him walk over me.

"It was so fucking reckless," he went on. He jabbed a finger toward the door, back in the direction of the cave.

"What kind of idiot, what kind of human idiot would try to protect a wolf when she can't even protect herself? You should have run away, but you didn't. You were *this close* to losing your life right in front of me, and you...you didn't even care."

He stopped, breathing hard. I could almost hear the thunderous pace of his heartbeat.

"I wasn't wandering off or running away," I snapped back. "I thought about trying to leave, but I didn't, and do you know why?" I didn't wait for a response. "Because I have *nowhere* to go, even if I could run away. I was *led* to the injured wolf, and I was brave for staying, not reckless. You're such an asshole, Night. You piss me off no end!" I glared up at him, stepping closer. "You think I wasn't scared? I was fucking terrified in that cave, Night. I thought my life was over, and that I'd never see anyone again. But you," I jabbed her finger at him, "you have saved me twice now, and I am so *grateful*."

Tears pushed behind my eyes, but I forced them back. I wasn't done with him yet. "I knew I was safe the minute I saw your wolf. I knew I couldn't leave when you were fighting for my life because what if something happened to you? What would I have done then? *You're* the idiot, Night." I jabbed my finger in his chest again, and he actually stepped back. "An idiot Alpha who can't even see what's going on when it's in front of his face. I would never leave you behind. I would never leave this pack behind. This place is my home now, even though it shouldn't be, and it's all because of *you*."

In the wake of our explosive argument, I was breathing hard. I glared into Night's eyes, and he gazed back, his face full of shock, confusion, and something like wonder.

Eventually, I closed my eyes and calmed my breathing before I finally turned away from Night. I headed outside, where the others were waiting for our argument to end. I made my way to Dom, who stood leaning against the outside of Night's cabin.

"I just want to know, did that wolf survive?" I asked. "The injured one in the cave?"

"Oh, Vince? He's fine."

"Vince?" He was the one who'd told Tavi's story. "I met him at the bonfire a few nights ago. But I had no idea that was him." I'd had no clue if the wolf was pack or not, but I was happy to find out things had turned out this way.

Dom nodded. "He's one of our trackers, actually. He went missing a couple of days ago, but I guess now we know where he was all this time."

I'd heard about the missing wolf, but I hadn't known that it was Vince who was missing. I wasn't able to figure it out in the cave when I was so alone and so panicked; all I'd been able to think about was how I could get back to Violet's cabin.

"He's recovering at home, and he'll probably be better tomorrow now that his leg has been set properly."

I smiled. I was glad that everyone was safe and sound and that none of the injuries suffered were severe. "If you see him before I do, tell him I'm glad we both made it out safe."

Dom winked.

I looked from his face, to Jasper's, Tavi's, and Violet's. They all stood nearby, waiting for me. I realized I was surrounded by people who cared about me, and my heart couldn't have been fuller. But I was exhausted, and staying at Night's cabin when there was so much tension between us was not an option. So I started walking home.

"Where—" Night's voice was tight as he called after me. "Where are you going?"

I glanced back over my shoulder. He stood in the doorway, looking after me with bright, emerald eyes. "Home," I replied. "I'm fucking exhausted, and I need some sleep."

Chapter 28 - Night

Bryn walked away, with Tavi and Jasper following to make sure she made it back to Mom's cabin safely. My wolf began to howl as she moved further away from me. He ached in her absence and pawed for control to make me follow after her. I reeled him in.

I would have loved to have Bryn in my arms again, but I knew that some space would do us both a lot of good. I wasn't sure about her, but my emotions were still too high. I still felt so tender.

I turned to Dom, who stood near the front door. The sight of his stupid smirk irked me. I didn't have to reach into his mind to know exactly what he was thinking. I couldn't say that there was nothing going on between Bryn and I, not at this point. I couldn't deny that my wolf and I were extremely protective of her. And I couldn't deny the way my heart stirred in my chest whenever she was nearby.

But I didn't know anything about human/shifter mating. I didn't even know where to start.

I turned and headed back inside my cabin, with Dom following me.

"So, what do you plan to do now, Night?" he asked.

I sighed. "I honestly don't know."

"I guess you've got some time to think about it." Dom's smile told me that he wasn't going to tease me more about it. For now. I supposed that was as good as I was going to get from my beta.

Dom and I stood in the living room. I had walked into the room without thinking, unconsciously following the lingering fragrance of Bryn's scent. Dom probably would have teased me about that too, but when he spoke again, his voice had grown serious.

"Those wolves," he began, "how did they get so close to our territory without our sentries seeing them?"

"I've been thinking about that," I said. "Iggy mentioned that she'd scented them around our borders. I asked her to keep an eye on it."

Dom cursed under his breath. Iggy's death was not only a tragedy and a massive loss for the pack, it had also created a loose end—one that had come to bite us in the ass.

I sighed and crossed my arms. "We need to verify that these were the same wolves she was talking about. They didn't smell like pack, but maybe they were from a group that was just wandering through town."

"I'll send some men into Colville. You could be right about the wandering packs, but I think they were hungry ferals. They looked scrawny enough to be."

I thought back to the fight and nodded. I hadn't even noticed how gaunt those wolves looked at the time. My wolf and I had been so focused on keeping Bryn safe that the other wolves were little more than shadowy dangers that were in my way. Now that she was safe, I reflected more about the incident. If those wolves were desperate and hungry ferals, then it made sense that they would keep going after Bryn even after we started killing their companions.

"We should speak to the other wolves who were with Iggy when she scented the ferals. We'll all go together to the cave and verify that the scents match."

"If I could interject," Mom said, speaking for the first time since Bryn left. She stood in the doorway to the kitchen, leaning against the wall. I hadn't even heard her come in. "I think Dom should go alone so you and I can have a talk, Night."

I frowned. "Mom, this is important."

"I know. I know. I'm just saying it doesn't take two to get it done. Besides, I know that you're really just looking for something to do so you don't think about our Bryn while she's gone."

I stared at her, my cheeks filling with hot blood, while Dom tried to hold back startled laughter.

"You can't hide anything from me, love." She patted my cheek and walked further into the living room.

Dom looked at me, still trying (and failing) to hide his snickering. "If they were the same ferals, it won't take me an hour to confirm."

I avoided looking back at him. I didn't want him to have the satisfaction of seeing me blush. "I know. Keep me posted."

As he left to do the investigation, I turned to my mom. She gestured for me to sit on the couch, and I did so. Bryn's scent was still on the fabric, and my wolf whined. I wished she was sitting with me again—that I had more than just her scent to keep me company.

Mom took a deep breath and closed her eyes. When she opened them again, she wasn't looking at me but off into the distance at something I couldn't see. I could tell that she was about to tell me a story about the old times.

"Many centuries ago," she said, her voice easing into the gentle monotone of the story, "when the first pack mothers started the original packs, no one was sure what to think of them. They had all been human women who had been ignorant of the paranormal forces of the world until they were chosen by the greatest spirit, fate herself, to give birth to the first generation of shifters and to become shifters themselves." She clasped her hands in front of her, gazing reverently into that middle distance.

"Over the years, the shifter communities grew, and no new pack mothers were created by fate. Instead, the communities populated on their own, and the pack mothers faded away. Or at least, that's what some choose to believe. Those of us who know, who understand that the old ways never die, know that their power has been passed down through the generations. The wounds caused by the murder of pack mothers have produced a ripple effect, one that still wounds us shifters to this day."

I sat quietly. I knew the story, but I wasn't sure where she was going with it. I had never heard that the pack mothers were human first, but everyone knew that their familial lines ended with their deaths. The last pack mother had died only a few decades ago, after hiding for years with the Wargs until she was killed by the Kings. Her death was a huge blow, and it allowed the Kings to take control of the Kaniksu National Forest from us.

Mom stared at me expectantly, but I wasn't sure what to say. "It was a tragedy," I said hesitantly. "I think, despite that, wolves have managed pretty well."

"Night!" Her voice cracked like a whip, and for a moment, I was seven years old again, scolded for uprooting the sprouts when I went into the garden to play. "How can you be so blind and closed off from the magic of the land?"

She raised her hand to smack me, and I winced, bracing for impact. After a pause, instead of hitting me, she rested her hand on my head. "I suppose you're not ready to understand what I mean. I know you've got a lot on your plate, baby." She stroked my hair, and then she kissed my forehead. "I'm going to go check on Bryn. I'll see you tomorrow, Night."

And just like that, I was thinking about Bryn again. I was pretty sure Mom had mentioned her name on purpose—a bit of a punishment for missing the point of her story.

Fortunately, I wasn't left alone with my thoughts for long. In a few minutes, Dom had returned with confirmation that the ferals were indeed the same ones Iggy had scented at the border.

"That could have been really, really bad," Dom said. "If we were even a minute later, Bryn might have—"

I cut him off with a snarl. The thought of how close Bryn had come to death made my blood boil. "She can't be allowed to be alone again," I raged. It sounded ridiculous even to me, like I was trying to imprison her all over again. "I don't care what I have to do to make sure she never leaves my sight."

Dom waited until I finished my tirade, and then he asked, totally deadpan, "So, why do you think that is?"

I paused. The question was so far out of left field that it actually gave me pause. "What the fuck, Dom?"

"I'm just saying," the smirk was back on his face, "that you're doing this thing again. You only get this way about Bryn. It almost makes me wonder if you and her might be—"

I pointed at him. "Don't you dare fucking say—"

"—mates." Dom finished with a grin that was a mile wide.

I groaned and shook my head. But the more I heard the word, the more I thought about it, the more right it felt. I couldn't deny the way I reacted when I thought Bryn was at risk, and I certainly couldn't ignore how recklessly *I* had behaved when she was threatened right in front of me.

My wolf had completely taken over, something he had never done before. I couldn't let that happen again. My immediate response was to assure everyone that I would keep myself in check, but a promise without taking action would mean nothing.

I knew what I needed to do, if I was being honest. I'd been ignoring my wolf and quieting him every time he yearned for Bryn. By stifling him, I'd basically forced him to take control of my body.

"I don't think she'll accept me," I said finally. "Not after all that I've done and said, not after how badly I've treated her."

Dom chuckled and bumped me with his shoulder. "You need to get your shit together and treat that woman the way she deserves. If you're gentle with her, I think you'll be really surprised by Bryn's response."

I wanted to believe he was right. Somehow, the universe chose this human to be my mate, and she would be. I just needed to figure out how to convince her to give me a chance.

Part of me didn't think she would give me the time of day, but a greater part of me no longer cared about my doubts. I was sick of my own bullshit. Sick of my hesitations. Because of my fears, I had neglected my wolf's needs, and it was past time for me to listen to my other half.

Chapter 29 - Bryn

I slept for nearly forty-eight hours after the ordeal, waking just long enough to use the bathroom, drink some water, and nibble on some crackers. On the brief occasions when I was awake, I remembered Violet telling me that I'd had visitors—Dom, Tavi, and even little Pax—but she'd sent them away with the assurance that I would be alright.

Out of my mind with exhaustion, I had nodded in response to Violet's reports. I apologized for not finishing my gardening work before I'd left for the cave and then returned to bed.

Finally, when I had rested long enough, I got up to take a shower. I felt sweaty and sticky with sleep, and I stayed under the water for a long time to make sure I was clean. When I emerged in a cloud of steam, my hair wet, my face washed, dressed in comfy leggings and an oversized sweater, I went down the stairs to find Violet waiting for me with warm food.

The moment I saw the assortment of meatloaf, mashed potatoes, and gravy, I threw myself into the chair and inhaled my food. It was delicious, I knew, but I ate so quickly I was only aware of a consistent state of tastiness on my tongue. Violet calmly drank her coffee, watching me with kind eyes.

Finally, after finishing two and a half helpings, I reached for a glass of water to wash it all down. When I was finished, Violet moved to clear the table, but I stopped her, placing a hand on her arm.

"No, no let me," I said with a smile. "It's the least I can do after you took care of me."

Violet eased back into her chair, and I quickly washed the dishes and wiped down the table. When I returned to where Violet had been sitting, I found that she had moved into the living room.

"Grab us some tea or coffee, girlie," she said, "and then come sit with me."

Tea sounded divine. I brewed two cups of lavender chamomile, each with a dollop of honey before I sat by Violet on her tiny love seat. We sat beside each other in companionable silence and enjoyed our drinks.

As the tea warmed my belly, I thought back to everything that had happened in the cave. I remembered how terrified I had been of the wolves and how close I'd come to death. I remembered the way Night had emerged from the tunnel, all teeth and righteous fury, and I remembered feeling safe in his arms.

Then I replayed the events leading up to the cave, how I'd spotted the russet-brown wolf between the trees, how it had come to me and led me to the cave. Now that I looked back on it, I was beyond confused. Who was that wolf?

"Violet, are there any packs near the Wargs compound?" I asked. "I know Colville National Forest is on the other side of the mountain from us, but maybe a neighboring pack came through the area?"

Violet shook her head. "There isn't another pack within a hundred miles of us. The three wolves who attacked you were feral wanderers, likely banished from their own packs. But we'll likely never know where they came from. For all we can tell, their original pack might as well be across the country."

"Oh. Right…" I hadn't been asking about those wolves. I was thinking of the russet wolf with the silvery eyes. I was tempted to ask if Violet had ever seen such a wolf hanging around the woods, but I felt like a crazy person the more I thought about it. No one had mentioned seeing or smelling a fifth wolf; it might not have happened at all.

Violet surprised me when she patted the pack of my hand. "Bryn, honey, how much do you know about your past?"

I was caught off guard by the question. I thought I'd already told Violet about my origins, but I didn't mind telling her again.

"My mom, Glenda Hunter, found me in the woods. I was just a newborn and apparently abandoned by my birth parents. I still had the umbilical cord attached to me. None of the wolves in the Kings' pack had been pregnant, and no one knew where I had come from. At first, Mom was certain that I was a wolf, but when she took me home, she quickly realized that I was human. Gregor wanted her to get rid of me, but she chose to raise me anyway. Mom always said to me that the magic of the world had brought us together," I finished.

Violet smiled. "I think I'll like Glenda very much."

I gave a sad chuckle. Violet said that as if she was going to meet my mom sometime soon, but that was silly. Mom was a four-day trek away, and Troy stood between us. For now, I would have to settle for this. My heart ached for my mom, but I was so grateful for the speed at which the Wargs pack had become like my family. Twenty years with the Kings had only left me feeling like an outsider.

"Do you know much about the Wargs?" Violet asked next. "About the Alpha who ruled us two generations ago?"

I thought about it. I knew that before Night, there was a scrawny stand-in Alpha who squandered away what little was left in the wake of the Alpha before him and abandoned the pack in the prime of his youth. He was the son of the kind and benevolent Alpha, who had led the Wargs into prosperity.

I explained this to Violet, who nodded with a smile.

"I'm proud that you've kept up with our history. You're right. Before Night, there was Peter, who was an idiot, and before him was Gregor, and before him was his father, Alpha Craig Stone."

"Gregor? That Alpha has the same name as the Kings'…" I trailed off, realization slapping me in the face. "No, they're the same Gregor, aren't they? But I thought…"

Violet nodded. "Yes. Gregor Redwolf used to be Gregor Stone. He abandoned us to take over the Kings."

I gasped. Suddenly, it all came into sharp focus. I'd thought that Night's grudge against the Kings had seemed to run deeper than simple vengeance. If the Kings and Wargs had once shared the same Alpha, then Night would have every right to be upset at that betrayal, to want to pay Gregor back for what he'd left behind. And yet, unlike the selfish Gregor or his arrogant, hot-headed son, Night never resorted to cheap tactics to get what he wanted. He was open about his designs to take over the Kings, and he had the strength to do it.

Violet watched as I navigated through my thoughts. "It looks like you understand my son a bit better now, Bryn," she said gently, "but the story I want to tell isn't really about Gregor. It's about his father, Craig."

"Oh." I turned my focus back to Violet. I didn't know anything about that Alpha.

"You've heard that Craig was the loving and kind Alpha of the Wargs, but that wasn't originally true. Craig ruled the Wargs with an iron fist. He was an angry, bitter Alpha with a chip on his shoulder and a lot to prove. His father before him had also been angry, jealous, and mistrustful of everyone, including his pack and his mates. Though he would take many lovers, he doubted that any of his children were truly his. Many said that it was because he was crazy or driven so by his own paranoia. But it doesn't matter now. His children were abused by him and grew to loathe their father and themselves.

"Craig was the only one of his father's sons who wanted to take the role of Alpha, but when he did take over, he was shaping up to rule just the way his father had. He treated his pack like he hated and resented them for his misfortunes. Many Wargs left, fed up with his treatment, but Craig didn't care. The only person he trusted was his younger brother. When his brother was murdered, Craig snapped. With vengeance on his mind, he relentlessly pursued the man who had done it. But when Craig had stalked the man into a corner, and it was time to deal the final blow, the murderer's daughter, Dawna, came out of hiding and protected her father with her body. She begged Craig to spare her father's life in exchange for her own."

I gasped, enthralled by the story. I felt like I could see it happening in my mind's eye, all of it playing out in perfect clarity.

"Craig accepted the exchange, but for years afterward, he wouldn't understand why. He didn't abuse Dawna, even though he had treated his own pack like they would eventually abandon him. The woman, true to her word, stayed by his side even when he was emotionally closed off or said cruel things to her. Over time—over *years*—she coaxed him into trusting her bit by bit until finally he realized the error of his ways. He announced to his pack that he had turned a new leaf, that he would never mistrust them or hurt them again. He lived his life seeking repentance for being a poor Alpha, and under him, we flourished."

"But how did she change him?" I asked. "She was the daughter of the man who killed his brother. How did he learn to trust her?"

"It wouldn't have happened if she was an ordinary woman. To Craig, she was the world, the moon, and the sky. She was his soul mate."

"Soul mate," I repeated, tasting the word.

"Yes. Soul mates are chosen by the spirits, not by two wolves who have fallen in love. It's the rarest, most precious kind of love there is, and it produces some of the strongest loves the world has ever known."

Though I was enchanted by the story, it felt too much like a fairy tale. I looked at Violet with some suspicion. "Is that a true story?"

"It is! You can read our history books if you don't believe me. Though, to be honest, I wrote the most recent ones." She grinned.

"But if Gregor was born from the love between Craig and Dawna, why did he turn out so awful?"

"Ah." Violet's smile faded. "That I don't know, Bryn. All I can say is that sometimes, people change on their own, and there's nothing we can do to stop them." She turned away, but not before I saw her wipe away a stray tear.

I placed my hand on Violet's back and patted gently. She must have suffered greatly at the hands of the Kings. "Thank you so much for sharing that story with me. You told it beautifully."

Violet laughed. "You're a fantastic listener, Bryn. Much, much better than my hardheaded son."

I laughed and took our empty mugs to the kitchen to be washed. "Honestly, Violet, I'm not sure if that's a compliment." I turned on the tap to wash the cups when a knock sounded on the door. I jumped, almost dropping one of the mugs.

I started to walk to the door, but Violet was already most of the way there.

"Don't worry. I'll get it." She walked to the door and pulled it open.

"Hello, Violet." It was Jasper's voice. "Is Bryn awake?"

Violet must have answered in the affirmative because he bounced into the kitchen, a bright smile on his face.

"Hey, Jasper," I said, smiling back. "Long time no see."

"Yeah, no kidding. It's a huge relief to see you on your feet again."

I finished washing the mugs, and Jasper and I sat at the table to chat. It was the first time we'd had a conversation with just the two of us, but things weren't awkward or stilted between us. Jasper could talk and talk like Tavi, but his ramblings were more chilled. He had a smooth voice, and it was nice to listen to.

As he spoke to me, I tried to admire his lean, muscular frame, his soft, bronze hair, and his big, blue eyes. I knew I ought to be more attracted to him, but whenever I thought about getting closer to him or kissing him, my mind wandered instead to a pair of bright-green, soul-searching eyes, to black, silken hair, and to a kissable mouth. That mouth could scowl at me or smile at me—either way, he left me feeling breathless and excited.

"Bryn?"

I blinked, coming out of my daydream. "Sorry, what was that, Jasper?"

He smiled back at me, not at all upset by the fact that I'd missed what he'd said. "I was saying that there's a big get-together tonight, and I'd like you to come with me if you're interested."

I thought it over, wondering why Tavi hadn't invited me. But I shook my head, figuring she must have sent Jasper to do it. She might have been too busy helping prepare for…whatever the get-together was for.

"Sure," I said. Having a bit of fun might help the ache in my chest and the longing I felt for a certain someone. I wished I were sitting across from Night instead of Jasper.

He whooped in excitement and hopped to his feet. "I'll pick you up in a couple of hours, alright?"

"Sure," I said again with a smile. I watched him zip out the door, a moment of confusion settling over me. We were going together, but just as friends, right?

Chapter 30 - Bryn

I smoothed my hands over my dress as I looked at myself in the mirror. I wore a soft, cornflower-blue dress that stopped a few inches above my knees. It was shorter even than the sweater dress I'd worn to the bonfire, but I felt beautiful. The dress flared out at my hips, giving me more of an hourglass figure than I thought I had.

There was something about the scene that struck me as very familiar. I had admired herself in the mirror the night of Gregor's funeral as well. Mom and I had complimented each other's outfits. Unfortunately, that night had ended with my dress ruined with mud as Troy and the Terrible T's laughed at me.

Tonight, I knew, wouldn't end the same way. I had never felt more excited to get dressed up and spend time with the people I loved. Here, I had friends and a purpose. Violet, Mable, Frankie, and so many others had told me that my gardening abilities helped the pack tremendously. My chest filled with pride as I thought about how much I'd been able to help out and how rewarding it had been. I also loved working in the mess hall, chatting and laughing alongside the others. It was wonderful to feel part of something greater than myself.

My skills had always gone overlooked and underappreciated by the Kings, but that wasn't the case here.

I walked over to the small box where I kept the few makeup items that Violet and Tavi had given to me. I pulled out a red lipstick, the one that Tavi had dared me to wear.

"It'll make your eyes pop against your dark hair—especially if you wear it with that blue dress," she'd told me days ago. "You'll look like a goddess!"

I put it on and smacked my lips in the mirror. *Wow,* I thought, surprised at how flattering the vibrant red was on my mouth, *Tavi knows her shit.*

I ran a brush one last time through my wavy locks, my hair falling to my middle back. Violet let me know what Jasper had been too excited to tell me. The party would be in the mess hall, so I would be plenty warm in my short sleeves, even as the night grew cooler. Next, I stepped into a pair of tall, knee-high chocolate-brown boots. Violet had been responsible for these. Apparently, she had requested them from Colville. My legs looked amazing in the boots.

Finally, I was ready. When the knock came on the door, I rushed downstairs, swinging it open to find Night, not Jasper, standing on the porch. My breath caught as I looked up at him. He never knocked. It was his mother's cabin, so he usually just walked inside without a care.

And…there was something different about him. Something about the perfection of the tight, dark jeans that outlined his strong thighs and tapered waist perfectly, or maybe it was the black button-down shirt, the sleeves of which were rolled up to his elbows and which put his incredible forearms on display. It might also have been the way his shiny, silken black hair was pushed back out of his handsome face.

I wasn't the only one staring. Night took his time, letting his eyes drop down and then slowly back up my form. My body felt hot under his devouring gaze. His eyes widened at the way my dress clung to my torso. There was just enough cleavage on display to make me feel naughty but not slutty. Finally, his jade-green eyes met mine, and suddenly the mood shifted to one that was less hot and more awkward.

I should have asked him if he was going to the party too, but the words wouldn't come.

"Bryn!"

The sudden voice came from behind Night, and it startled us both. Jasper emerged from behind his Alpha. He wore a pair of dark gray slacks that looked tailor-made for his lithe form and a light blue button-down shirt. The top few buttons were undone to show a few inches of his tan chest. He looked hot, for sure, but he didn't make me *feel* hot. He didn't make moisture pool in my panties the way Night had with one look.

Jasper took in my dress, cursing gently under his breath. "Amazing," he said to me.

He looked at Night to address him formally, but Night was already growling. Before I could react, he grabbed Jasper by the collar of his shirt and threw him off the porch. I gasped as Jasper caught himself on the ground like a cat. He stood up straight, sending a bewildered look from Night to me before bowing his head. Night stomped off the deck and stood over Jasper. His erect posture and broad shoulders made him look so damned commanding.

Jasper stole another glance at me, his eyes filled with longing and sadness. But another growl from Night— who stood over him, fists tight at his sides—made him bow his head lower. Jasper nodded, his eyes no longer coming up from the ground to meet mine, and then he rose, turned away, and walked off without another glance in my direction.

I didn't know what the fuck that was, but I understood that Night had just ruined an opportunity for me to hang out with one of my friends. I stomped off the deck, ready to tear into Night, to rip him a new asshole for scaring off Jasper like that, but then he looked at me, and I froze where I stood.

There was something so incredibly *arousing* about the possessive way he looked at me. Like he was claiming me with his gaze. His eyes roved over me, his pupils dilating with need. A few strands of his black hair had fallen over his forehead and into his eyes.

I struggled to take in a breath. My thighs began to rub together, unable to chase off the need for friction in my core. He watched me, inhaling deeply. I knew that he could smell my arousal, and that knowledge only heightened my own need.

My breathing increased to an almost-pant. *What the fuck is happening?* The thought ran through my mind over and over again, as if the more I asked it, the better my chances were of finding an answer. But there were no explanations for what was going on between me and Night.

For some reason, I felt like punching him in the face one moment, only to be drawn to him like crazy the next. I shouldn't want the man who had kidnapped me, but as I looked at him now, I no longer saw him as my kidnapper. Instead, I saw a big, strong Alpha who loved his pack and adored his mother, who had taken care of the quirky, chatty Tavi like a little sister after she lost her family, and who made my heart race uncontrollably with only a look. I knew I felt something for him that I had never felt for another man. He had saved my life twice. And right now, I needed him. Desperately.

I continued stepping off the deck, and his eyes watched every move I made. I liked the way his eyes followed me—it made me feel brave and confident and desirable. The final step off the deck propelled me forward. I ran toward him, crossing the few feet of distance between us in just a few steps. I felt like the wind that played around my thighs and the hem of my dress had given me the ability to fly.

Now only inches away from Night, I moved even closer, closing the space between us. My hand pressed to his chest, and his heart beat hard against my fingers. He rumbled, his eyes closing briefly at my touch. When his eyes opened again, those green orbs glowed with all the hunger I felt rising inside my own body.

Before I could second-guess myself, I let my other hand slide up his chest to the back of his neck, pulling him down for a kiss.

Night

She's kissing me.

I had come to my mom's cabin in the hope that Bryn would finally be awake. I had planned to talk to her. To try and explain what I thought was going on between us. I wanted to tell her that she could be my mate. But when she opened the door in that little dress, her hair soft around her shoulders, those bright blue eyes staring up at me, everything I'd planned to say died in my throat. I couldn't think or talk, but I knew she was perfection—and what's more, I knew that she was mine.

Bryn is kissing me.

Unfortunately, before I could get my shit together and pull some kind of coherent sentence out of the jumble of thoughts and feelings that my mind had melted into, Jasper had showed up. I had snapped at the boy before I could think better of it. My wolf had growled for control, and I threw Jasper bodily off the porch. I surged into his mind and forbade him right then from pursuing Bryn any further.

I hated to use that power—the Alpha command. It was an intrusion of rights, meant only for emergencies. But Bryn—*kissing me, touching me,* with *me. Mine*—was worth it. She was my mate, and I would be damned if I let any wolf take what I knew was mine. I'd ordered the boy not to look at Bryn if he couldn't do it without desire. He had bowed low because he was unable to gaze at Bryn without wanting her.

If I hadn't wanted to slaughter Jasper for his thoughts, for the arousal wafting off him at the sight of Bryn, I would have told the kid that I understood why he wanted her.

I had thought she would put up a fight—that she would yell at me for scaring Jasper off. I expected her to call me an asshole, the way she always did. I was ready to let her rip into me and get it all out of her system before I looked her in the eye and told her that she was mine, that she was always meant to be mine, and that I wanted her to stay with me. But I should have expected her to surprise me.

She had come to me, her skirt lifting slightly in the cool breeze, making me harder than I'd ever known I could be in my jeans. She drew close to me, smelling delicious and warm and so, so perfect, and brought me down for a kiss.

And the kiss was *everything*. The minute her lips touched mine, the breath left my lungs, my heart pounding loudly against the palm that she pressed there. Each beat was a single word—*Mate.* It echoed over and over in my head, through my blood, carried in every cell of my body. I pulled her against me, unwilling to let either of us breathe without the other.

She moaned into my mouth, a soft little mewl that drove me fucking insane. I reached around, cupping the ass that I had literally dreamt about, and lifted her up until her feet were off the ground. She wrapped her legs around my waist—the movement causing her to grind against my straining cock. I growled loudly into her mouth, eager to take her right then.

But no—this wasn't for anyone else's eyes; *she* wasn't for anyone's eyes but mine. I took her back inside my mom's cabin. I set her down begrudgingly, and she stepped away from me. She stared up at me, wanting, needing. Her lips were slightly parted and swollen from my devouring kisses.

I bit my lip, wanting to taste her again, knowing exactly what she needed because *fuck,* I needed it too.

"Grab whatever you need for the night," I said.

She blinked at me.

I growled, impatient. "Bryn, you can either get your stuff and come back to my cabin on your own, or I can throw you over my shoulder and take you there myself."

She gasped, eyes widening as she understood what I was saying. She rushed upstairs to her room, and I tried to adjust myself in my pants. My thoughts were a mess. *What the hell am I doing?* I had no clue. I wasn't sure of anything except that Bryn was my mate and I needed her. I had smelled the sweet spice of her arousal on her, but now it was on me too. It was intoxicating, just like everything else about her.

She came back downstairs, a small bag of toiletries and a pillow I swore had once been in my cabin in her arms. I couldn't wait any longer. I took her hand, yanking her against me so I could kiss her again. I caught another one of her delicious moans in my mouth, my free hand running through the soft strands of her hair. She pulled my bottom lip in between her teeth, which was a dangerous move. If I were a lesser man, I would have shredded her dress right there in my mom's foyer.

Instead, I forced myself to pull away from her, glaring at her with a mix of reproach and lust. She giggled as I pulled her behind me toward my cabin. The sound of that laugh went straight to my cock, and I picked up the pace. If I wasn't inside her soon, I might actually explode.

Mate.

Chapter 31 - Bryn

I was so overwhelmed and so turned on that I was afraid I was going to start dripping down my leg. Night pulled me into his cabin, slamming the door behind us. He pushed me up against it, claiming my mouth with his again. I was helpless under the wonderful pressure of him, the tantalizing heat of him, but I loved surrendering the control. I never imagined it would be like this—all chemistry, all intensity. I had no idea what made him decide he wanted me, why he chose me, but I wanted him so badly I couldn't think straight.

He pressed against me, and I felt his hardness against my leg. I gasped, almost a squeak of anxiety. The sheer *length* of him.

Are we about to have sex right now? I asked myself in a sudden rush. *Do I want to have sex right now?*

The answer swelled up within me, a complete and resounding *Yes!* I had fallen helplessly and totally in love with this man, and I knew that I was already his in every way possible. But would he fit inside me? He was so massive...

Eventually, Night pulled me away from the wall. We stumbled through his cabin, breaking a vase and knocking over books on the way. Neither of us cared about the damage we'd done. We were pressed to each other, hands everywhere, exploring everything. I laughed, an almost manic sound, as his hand tickled across my thigh.

Finally, with only a few feet between us and his bedroom, he lifted me and carried me inside. He threw me onto his bed and kicked the door shut. His eyes were like a predator's as he took me in with a hunger that matched my own.

I removed my tall boots, tossing them to the side, and then got onto my knees on the bed. He prowled around, that low rumble emanating from his chest. I bit my lip as I watched him pace. My brain tried to work through the haze of desire clouding it. There needed to be some sort of conversation before we went any further. I knew it, but I was so hot right then that I could barely speak.

He started to approach me, to pull me against him, and I put my hand out. Stopping him seemed to cause us both physical pain. He looked at me, confusion replacing the lust in his eyes. I still hadn't found my voice. I tried to plead with only my eyes. *I just need a second.*

He backed off and resumed his pacing as if he couldn't stand still while I collected myself to the point that I could speak.

"I—I've never done this before, Night," I blurted gently. "I'm still a virgin."

Night stopped, his eyes widening. He was probably remembering that he'd found me tied up and about to have everything stolen from me just a month before. Had it really only been a month? It felt like a lifetime to me.

Night closed his eyes and took a few deep breaths. His hands opened and closed as he regained control of himself. When he opened his eyes again, there was an apology in their depths.

"I understand," he said, his voice still so deep, so growly. "I'm sorry I didn't take that into account." He released a tight breath and ran a hand through his hair. "I won't—"

"No." I cut him off, shaking my head. "I didn't tell you that so you'd stop, Night. I just wanted to make sure that…" I hesitated, my face hot. "That I could take all of you."

Night paused for a few seconds, and then he laughed. When he looked at me again, his eyes had softened, and I gulped. I knew for sure that I was in love with him—that this was right even though it shouldn't be.

He slowly approached the side of the bed, standing in front of me. With the bed boosting me up a few inches, we were almost the same height as I got up to my knees. His hand came up to caress my cheek, just the way mine had done when he was lost and holding my unconscious body so tightly after he rescued me from the cave. I sighed, leaning into his touch. I'd never felt so safe, so secure.

"Are you sure you want this? That you want me?" he asked gently. "Do you understand what a night together means?"

"I know exactly what it means," I whispered, staring deep into his eyes. "But I don't think a human losing her virginity is the same as with wolves."

I knew that mating used to be a much more serious event in a wolf's life. These days, there were many female wolves who had sex with whoever they wanted, racking up a tally just as freely as human women could if they wanted to. But more traditional wolves knew that a female had one chance to choose her forever partner. It was something that should be honored and respected.

"Are you sure?" he asked, his eyes searching mine.

When he asked me that, I knew he was talking about tradition. He didn't view me as just a human girl, someone who was less valuable than a female shifter. He saw me as an equal.

Night was asking me if I could promise to be his and know that I would never be anyone else's. That question sealed it for me.

Night might have taken me from my home, but he'd given me the opportunity to find a new one that was full of love and possibility and warmth. Even though I was human, even though I wasn't technically "pack," I loved the land, loved the Wargs, and most importantly, I loved the man who had taken my heart.

I leaned forward and kissed his chin, his jaw, his neck. My hands slipped under his shirt, eager to feel his hot skin under my palms. I let my hands explore every bend and curve of his muscles before sinking lower to his belt. Every touch, every caress was an enthusiastic yes, and I felt him melt beneath my touch.

"Bryn." My name was a moan on his lips as I undid his belt and then the buttons and zipper that kept his jeans closed. "Bryn, I promise I will worship you. I will make it so good for you."

I moaned, licking his throat.

"I'll take things slowly," he murmured. "I'll let you feel everything."

"I know," I whispered. He shivered as my breath brushed over the spot I'd just licked. "I trust you, Night."

His answering growl was so loud, I worried that someone might come running to check on us. But that worry disappeared when Night pushed me down onto the bed, easing me flat against the mattress. He sank to his knees at the side of the bed. I expected him to climb on top of me and take me then, but he didn't. Instead, he took my hips and pulled me close until my knees were off the side of the bed, and my core was inches from his face.

If I was hot before, I was torrid then. Was he going to do *that* to me? That special thing I'd believed only happened to women in novels? I was almost scared to hope.

"Wh-what are you doing?" I asked breathlessly.

He shushed me, running his hands up and down my thighs. "Trust me," he murmured, "I just want to make you feel good."

How could I refuse him? I relaxed my tense thighs. I trusted him implicitly, but I'd never had anyone so close to such an intimate part of me before.

He pressed kisses up my inner thigh. I wiggled and gave a small, whimpering moan as his lips moved closer and closer to where I was aching for his touch. His hands slipped up my skirt, his fingertips tickling across the waistband of my panties. I shivered as he slowly pulled them down my legs and over my feet.

With them gone, he pulled me even closer to the edge of the bed until my ass was nearly hanging off the side. I gasped when I felt his hair tickle against my inner thighs, a gasp that became a moan as his lips finally touched me *there*. He kissed me, letting out a low groan at the first taste of me. Then he went in for more, lapping at my dripping slit.

I moaned louder, my hands clutching at the sheets. His tongue plunged deep inside me and then came out to taste that most sensitive nub, the one that was so eager for his attention, it throbbed.

"Night," I cried, my thighs pressing against the sides of his head. I reached down to bury my fingers in his hair. My body had come alive with pleasure and electricity. Each movement of his wicked tongue took me to new heights of ecstasy.

I called his name again, and his answering groan was a muffled vibration against my core. My heartbeat had grown so loud, so powerful, and it beat at a galloping pace. I felt the pulse of it in every inch of my body; that persistent beat and my own gasping moans were the only sounds I could hear.

I writhed beneath the heated insistence of his tongue. I felt like I might die from the pressure that continued to mount inside me long before I felt the release. How was he so good. How did he know exactly what to do to make me feel even more deeply, more intensely?

Finally, when I thought I couldn't take anymore, my pulse filling my ears over the sound of my panting breaths, the pressure spilled over. I clenched my legs tight around his head, my toes curling, back arching off the bed. Pleasure gushed from my core, and I screamed. The delicious, crackling climax crashed over me. Wave after wave of hot, wonderful bliss rippled across my body, leaving me tense, immobile, and covered in sweat.

As I came down from that impossible high, my body relaxed into the bed. Weak from my orgasm, I propped myself up on shaking elbows to look down at Night. I found him watching me. His tongue ran slowly across his bottom lip, and his eyes were the bright green of hot flames.

"I—I didn't know I could do that," I stammered. "I'm sorry, I would've warned you if—"

"No." His voice silenced me, gentle but firm. "I never want to hear you apologize. Not for that."

The way he was looking at me right now, the way he turned his head to lick the inside of my knee, caused desire to flare within me again. Though I'd just had my first and an unbelievably intense orgasm, though I could have fallen asleep feeling more satisfied than I had ever felt before, I was eager for more.

"Are you ready for more?" he asked like he could read my thoughts.

I nodded, but he would have been able to see the affirmative in my eyes. He got to his feet, removing his shirt and kicking his pants and shoes away. He pitched an incredible tent.

"I want you out of that dress," he said, his voice almost impossible to decipher over the rumbling in his chest. "I want you naked. Now."

I went along with his command without question. I sat up slowly, reaching around to undo my bra. I removed it first, pulling it over my head and tossing it to the floor. Night watched me hungrily. He pushed down his boxers, his cock finally free to stand proudly erect.

I gasped at the sight of it. I'd known he was large, had felt him against my leg. But seeing it now—uncut and twitching with lust, the tip moistened with beads of precum—the worry I'd had about it not fitting was replaced with desperate excitement. I wanted him to rip me in half.

"Bryn." Night's voice was half commanding, half pleading. "The dress, please."

My eyes snapped up to his, and a slow smile spread over my face. "I don't think I've ever heard you say please," I said. The bravery I'd felt earlier returned as I slowly eased the dress up my body, watching the way his eyes followed my movements. "I think I ought to reward you."

"Bryn." His tone was a warning, but there was excitement under it too. He liked the way I spoke to him.

I pulled the dress over my head and threw it over my shoulder. I was exposed now, every bit as naked as Night himself. The women in my romance novels often felt self-conscious the first time they were nude for their lovers, but I didn't want to hide my body from Night. I saw the awe—the reverence in his eyes. I saw the way his Adam's apple bobbed when he swallowed. I basked in his attention, loving the way his eyes coveted every inch of my body. I felt powerful and lovely and desirable beneath his gaze. Why would I hide when all I wanted was for him to have me, to love me?

"Come here, Night. I want to taste you too."

Night bit his lip, but this time he obeyed my command. He stepped closer to the bed until he was within arm's length. I reached for him, my hands smoothing gently up and down his hard length. He twitched, his breath easing between his teeth. Taking that as encouragement, I moved closer. I took a tentative lick, just at the tip of his cock, and Night just about jumped out of his skin. I giggled and then licked at him again, this time following the length of him down to the base, which was covered in curly, dark hair.

"Ah," he breathed, smoothing his hands through my hair. "Bryn, you…how are you so g—"

He cut off with a grunt as I slowly took him into my mouth. I tasted the salt of his precum on my tongue and hummed with pleasure, working my way down another couple of inches. I began to bob back and forth over his cock, mindful of my teeth, and of the way I pressed my tongue against him. I loved the way he filled my mouth, the slightly sweet taste of his skin. I wanted to give him the best blowjob of his life, but I wasn't confident enough to take more than the first few inches of him. Thankfully, Night didn't seem to mind.

"Fuuckkkk," he shuddered, even as he watched me, his eyes bleary and tender with pleasure. "Bryn, I…"

I increased my speed, steadying myself with my hands on his hips. I wanted to pay him back for the pleasure he had given me, to make sure he knew that I wanted to make him feel as good as he had made me feel.

"Bryn." His growling, stern voice made me pause.

Worried that I'd lost control and scraped him with my teeth, I released him from my mouth, the hollow *pop* sounding through the room.

"Are you okay?" I asked, wiping saliva from my chin with the back of my hand. "Did I hurt you?"

His answering, breathless chuckle eased my fears. He took my chin in his hand, bending to kiss me gently on the lips. "You could never hurt me," he murmured. "It was *too* good. It was getting too hard to hold back."

I was confused at first, but my face heated again as I understood. I smiled, pushing my hair behind my ear. "Well then, I'm ready if you are?"

He answered me with another kiss. This time, I could taste myself on his tongue, and I moaned into his mouth. He growled back, pushing me against the bed. He kissed down my neck and over my breast, where he sucked my nipple into his mouth. I moaned again, louder this time.

Excitement was a sweet ache deep within my core, an ache that only he could soothe. I *needed* him.

He covered me with his hard, warm body. I slowly pushed my hands up his chest and over his shoulders before wrapping my arms around his neck. My legs opened for him a second time, and he fit his hips between them. The tip of his cock caressed my opening, prodding me gently. I shivered, trying to open myself wider for him. Night reached between us to steady himself, and then he guided the first inches of his cock inside.

I broke our kiss with a sharp, surprised gasp.

Night gazed down at me, his eyes a warm, forest green. "You okay?" he asked.

I didn't answer right away. It was the strangest sensation to have something inside me in a place nothing had ever been before. But soon, my body adjusted, and the slight, throbbing ache subsided. I kissed his chin. "Keep going."

He went more slowly the next few inches. His moan told me how difficult it was for him to take his time, and I loved him even more for being so patient with me, so gentle. I felt his stomach press flush against mine when he was all the way in. I shivered, surprised but so pleased that I'd been able to take all of him.

And then Night began to move. True to his word, I felt every inch with each slow, purposeful thrust. Though awkward at first, my body was quick to warm up to the sensation, and what had started out as a slight ache soon became hot, deep ecstasy.

Night pressed down into me, hiding his face in my neck as he increased his pace. My nails dug into his back. My nipples, hardened and sensitive from all that he'd done and was doing to me, grazed against his chest, sending electricity through my body. His name became a breathless pant on my lips, and I begged him to give me more, to go harder, faster.

His hands gripped the sheets at either side of my head. My breasts heaved and bounced, my body rocking with the motion of his needy thrusts. Tears filled my eyes and spilled over. I was close to another release. I could sense it just at the edge…

"Cum for me, Bryn," he growled into my neck. "*Now.*"

It was all I'd needed to push me there. I couldn't even scream with the force of my orgasm. It tore through my body, and I trembled in the wake of it. As I clenched around him, his low, rumbling growl reverberating from his chest and into mine, I felt his mouth, full of wolf's fangs, on my shoulder. I thought with bated breath that he was going to sink his teeth into me. At that moment, I'd never wanted anything more than for him to do it.

But he stopped short of biting me. Instead, he came, filling me with his hot seed. I ran my nails down his back as the aftershock of such intense satisfaction flowed through my body. After a moment, Night slowly pulled out of me. Both of us shivered when our connection was severed, but he quickly gathered me into his arms.

I felt so good, so safe.

We had mated, and even though I was human, I had promised myself to him. He didn't claim me, and that somewhat tempered the happiness I felt after what we'd done. But I pushed that thought away. I wasn't sure that a claiming bite would work on me anyway, and it didn't matter. I didn't need it to know that I was bound to him in ways that I would never be bound to another. I cuddled against his side, my eyes slipping closed. Night murmured something under his breath, something I didn't quite catch, and then exhaustion carried me to sleep.

Chapter 32 - Night

I stood on my porch and sipped a cup of coffee. The morning air was crisp and cool, and the sky was painted the warm, hazy orange of the incoming dawn. My chest was full, my body sated, and I hadn't stopped smiling since I woke up with Bryn still nestled in my arms.

Last night with her had been more than anything I could have imagined. I wasn't a stranger to sex—whenever I went to Colville, there were human women who wanted me, and I'd been with female wolves who had either lost mates or who didn't believe in the mating tradition. But with Bryn, with my *mate*, the night was full of nothing but firsts.

She had been so wild but innocent, eager, and cautious all at once. It was adorable how concerned she'd been that she'd hurt me while tasting my cock. She held nothing back; she was so open, trusting in me completely.

I lowered my coffee, my smile fading.

That was why I couldn't claim her. Not yet. When Bryn and I had made love, it was more than perfection. Being with her made me feel invincible. It was like the world had suddenly come into sharp focus, and I could see everything with total clarity. But when it came time to bite her, to officially claim her as my mate, I couldn't do it.

I hadn't told her that she was my mate yet. It didn't feel right to bite her without that communication. Though I loved her, though I needed her, I wanted to give her the opportunity to deny our bond rather than taking away her choice. I owed her that much.

My wolf, who had been purring and sighing contentedly since last night, suddenly jumped at the thought that she would reject us. I didn't like the thought any more than he did, but I needed to consider the facts. The moment I bit her, our souls would be bound for eternity. At least, that was the way it worked with wolves. Now, because Bryn was human, I wasn't sure the same rules applied. I would need to check with the Elders and ask for guidance.

Until I was sure she understood what a claiming bite meant, I wouldn't do it. It wouldn't be right for me to do something like that when she still didn't know the truth about me. She had no idea that I shared blood with the Redwolf monster who wanted to abuse her. How would she react when she found out that I was the son of the Alpha who had let her live in misery and half-brother to the wolf who tried to rape her and keep her as a slave after years of tormenting her?

I knew it was selfish to keep that truth from her, but I was terrified that she would turn away from me the moment she found out the truth.

My wolf howled, panting with fear that I was going to deny his feelings for Bryn again. I tried to soothe him. *I'm going to tell her today, I promise,* I told him. *I'm feeling scared that she'll leave when she finds out who I really am, but I don't actually think that she will.*

My wolf, not fully convinced, growled in my mind. He worried that someone else would take our mate before we could claim her. But I shook my head. No one could have Bryn, not unless she wanted that. And she wouldn't. I knew she felt as deeply for me as I did for her. I had to believe that it would all be okay after I explained everything to her. And then we could officially be mated.

My hand tightened around my mug. I just hoped I wasn't lying to myself and my wolf.

I tried to ignore the doubts so I could return to enjoying my coffee, to feeling whole for just one more moment. But then a terrifying shriek came from my bedroom. I dropped my mug, the pottery shattering against the porch. I sprinted back inside, taking the steps three at a time, bursting into my bedroom to be at my mate's side.

But she wasn't in the room anymore. In her place, where I'd left her snoozing on my pillow, her hair resting gently across her cheek, I found a struggling mass. I caught sight of a tail, a paw, and finally a snout as the wolf fought to get free of the blankets. When she landed on the floor, her paws slid awkwardly over the smooth wood.

As she gained her balance, she sat carefully at the foot of my bed and stared up at me. The wolf had a rich, chestnut-brown coat, and though she was a bit smaller than most other female wolves, her body was lithe and strong. She was stunning in the sunlight peeking in through the blinds. I knew immediately that she was Bryn, but all I could do was stare with my jaw on the fucking floor.

Bryn actually growled at me, which came as both a shock and a delight. I tried not to laugh as I met her steel-blue gaze, which glowed even in the morning light. When I left my mate that morning, she had been a human, but somehow she sat in front of me in shifted wolf form, and she was still the most beautiful, enchanting creature I had ever laid eyes on. My wolf echoed the sentiment, panting and running around in tight, excited circles.

Bryn got to her feet again, apparently eager to try walking again. I stayed in front of the door in case she tried to bolt. She seemed calm, but I couldn't be sure; every wolf was different the first time they shifted.

She shook out her fur and almost lost her balance again. I bent, wanting to help her, but maintained my distance so I didn't spook her.

"Hey, it's okay," I said, keeping my hands low, trying to make myself look as nonthreatening as possible. "You're okay. I'm here with you, Bryn."

She gazed at me and then began to step cautiously toward me. As she neared, I knelt slowly so we were at eye level. I wanted to talk to her, but I wouldn't be able to do that if she didn't feel safe enough to shift back. Her wolf would protect her no matter what.

"It's okay," I said again, keeping my voice low, gentle. "You are glorious, the most beautiful wolf I've ever seen. You can shift back whenever you're ready."

Bryn's wolf sat in front of me, her tongue lolling out of the side of her mouth. She didn't seem scared, but she showed no signs of intending to shift back. My wolf howled more insistently and pawed again for control. He wanted to be with Bryn's wolf, to run and play with her.

That would be innocent enough, if not for the fact that my wolf also wanted to claim her.

"Bryn, your coat is lovely," I said. "And you have such long, graceful legs. I can't believe how beautiful you are both as a human and as a wolf."

Compliments were known to work for pups who weren't sure how to shift back into their human forms or for wolves who were stuck. But it didn't seem to have much of an effect.

"Are you waiting to meet my wolf?" I asked. "Is that why you're determined to stay?"

Her tail shifted from side to side against the floor. I took that as an adorable yes.

"I'm sorry, but I'm not going to let him come out right now. It's not time. For now, I want you to shift back, alright?"

Bryn's wolf stared back at me. I couldn't see any sign of the human woman I loved, and I began to get anxious for her to return. I hated doing this to her, but if being gentle and pampering her with compliments didn't work, my only option was to make it happen. After all, I could be wrong about her waiting for my wolf. Maybe she was stuck and didn't know it.

I locked eyes with her, pushing into her mind with the force of an Alpha. *"Shift,"* I commanded. *"Now."*

Her body began to tremble as the fur left her body. Bryn gasped, once again in her naked, human form, and I let out a relieved breath. I reached out for her, and she reached back. She let me pull her into my arms, where she was safe. Where she belonged.

We sat together in the silence of my room, both of us reeling from what had just happened. *How the fuck had Bryn become a shifter? And what do we do now?*

Chapter 33 - Bryn

I'm a wolf. I kept repeating that simple fact over and over in my head, occasionally mumbling it out loud while Night continued to hold me. Shortly after I'd shifted back under his command, I began to cry hard from the shock of both my first shift and the way his voice had forced its way into my brain.

Night held me so gently and kissed the top of my head. He apologized for commanding me like that, said that he hoped I wasn't scared of him. But how could I be afraid of him? I trusted him when he said that he hadn't known what else to do. It was my first shift, and I had no idea what caused it, let alone how to return to my human form.

I'd since calmed down. I let myself melt into his arms as I told myself over and over again that I was a shifter—a wolf! And I realized that I sensed another presence in my mind. It wasn't the lingering effect of Night's Alpha command—it was something that paced back and forth and scratched and panted within me. It was my wolf. But the only thing I understood from her was a single word—*Mate.*

I wanted to ask Night why my wolf, who I had just met, kept repeating the word like it was the only thing she could convey. But before I could speak, Night kissed me softly.

"We need to get dressed," he told me, tenderly wiping the remainder of a tear from my cheek. "You have to see my mother and the Elders."

I had never met the Elders before, and the thought of doing so made me nervous. "Do you think they'll be able to tell us why this happened?"

"I don't know," he replied. The answer made me even more nervous, but I appreciated his honesty. "But they might be able to give us some clue."

"Okay."

He pressed his lips to my forehead, and I felt some of my anxiety disappear. He was so gentle with me, so careful, as though I would break to pieces the second he let me go. But I held myself together. I was nervous about the elders, but Violet and Night would be there. I knew I didn't really have anything to worry about as long as they were with me, but my concerns lingered.

Eventually, we separated long enough to get dressed. I put on one of his large t-shirts and a pair of leggings I'd grabbed from Violet's cabin the night before. I quickly washed the remainder of the makeup off my face, brushed my teeth, and pulled my hair up into a messy bun.

When I emerged, Night took my hand, holding it gently in his.

We headed for Violet's cabin and walked in without knocking, finding Violet waiting for us at the kitchen table. She beamed at us both and quickly hopped from her chair. She pulled me in to give me a tight hug, much tighter than any she'd given me before. I noticed that Violet's herby scent had grown deeper now that I had sharper senses. It was something I would always be able to pick out of a crowd.

When she stepped back, she tapped her nose and let out a quick breath as if to say I smelled potent. My face burned bright red while Night rolled his eyes.

"Mom, stop that."

"Fine, fine. But you can't blame an old woman for having her fun." She gave me one last, lingering smile and then turned back to the kitchen. "I made enough coffee for you two. Come sit with me at the table."

Night and I sat together at the small table while Violet served coffee. We were both quiet as Violet sat across from us; neither of us were sure how to broach the subject. Violet, for her part, just set her chin in her hands and kept smiling at me, and I couldn't help but smile back.

"So, Bryn," Violet said, "how was your first shift?"

The question shocked both Night and me. We exchanged a quick look, but neither of us had expected Violet to ask such a thing.

"How did you know? Did you…" My eyes widened as I recalled some of the cryptic language Violet had used around me. "Did you know this would happen the whole time?"

Violet shook her head and sipped her coffee. "I suspected, but I didn't know for sure. Actually, Bryn, I tried to tell Night, but like I told you before, he's not as good a listener as you are."

I giggled, and Night, to my surprise, actually turned a bit red. He sat back in his chair, his hands in the pockets of his jeans. "Great, you two are going to gang up on me all the time."

The comment just made me and Violet laugh harder. When we calmed down, I heard footsteps outside the front door. I tilted my head. It was more than one person, but I couldn't determine the exact number of visitors.

"Don't worry," Violet said, giving me a knowing smile. "It's just the Elders."

I ducked my head, a bit embarrassed that I had been so distracted by the noise. "Oh. Gotcha."

Soon, two older gentlemen and one elderly woman walked inside without pausing to knock. The first man was bald. An old, brown scar ripped across the top of his head. I knew better than to stare, but I was curious about how he'd received what could have been a mortal wound. The second man had tufts of gray hair starting at his temples, which wrapped around to meet at the back of his head. The woman had a full head of gorgeous hair that was almost as white as Violet's. She kept it short and curly—it looked like a cotton ball on top of her head.

They began to seat themselves at the table but needed another chair. I started to grab a chair from the living room, but Night caught my wrist. He pulled me to his side and sat me in his lap. It was an unorthodox way of providing an extra chair, but I wasn't upset; I was just as eager to stay close to him. I leaned back into his chest, and he immediately wrapped his arms around me.

The Elders smiled at us, not at all perturbed by our public Display of Affection. "It's a pleasure to meet you, Bryn Hunter," the woman said. "And Alpha Night, it is, of course, always a pleasure when we get to see you."

Night nodded in acknowledgment of the greeting while I stuttered out, "It's nice to meet you all too."

"I am Elder Patrice Woods," she said.

"I am Elder Neil Thread," the bald man said.

"And I am Elder Jacob Westley," the final man said. "We three are the Elders of the Wargs pack."

I nodded reverently. I felt meeting them was an honor even though I was sitting casually in my mate's lap. The three seemed nice enough, but their dark eyes were filled with eons of knowledge and wisdom. I shifted in Night's lap, uneasy that their attention would soon be on me.

After the Elders had taken their seats, Night cleared his throat and began the conversation. "Bryn shifted unexpectedly this morning," he said. He didn't mention that we'd had sex or that he'd taken my virginity, but if Violet's reaction to our hug were any indication, the Elders would likely already know that from our scent alone. I tried not to sink into myself with embarrassment.

"Is this something that can happen between a shifter and a human?" Night asked. "I've never heard of anything liked this before."

Violet spoke up. "We have records dating back decades that detail something like this happening," she said. "But the records are vague. Whoever was taking notes was clearly as stumped as we are, Night."

I had a vague memory of hearing a story about a human and a wolf mating before, but I couldn't remember when. It might have been a story my mom had told me once at bedtime, or it could have been something I'd overheard.

When the Elders remained silent, I couldn't take the suspense.

"So, why did this happen to me?" I asked. "Why did I shift, and why hasn't it ever happened to me before?"

Instead of answering immediately, the Elders and Violet exchanged looks with each other. They had a full conversation with only their eyes, never speaking a word as they came to a decision.

"Bryn," Patrice said, "we believe that you are a direct descendant of the original pack mothers."

Night and I stiffened at the same time. "I…I'm *what*?"

Violet reached across the table to pat my hand.

"Do you know anything about the pack mothers, Bryn?" Patrice asked.

"Yes." My mother had told me about them when I was younger, and I reached into the depths of my memories to try and pull the information out. "They gave birth to the first wolf packs. They were blessed with magic, were connected to each other, and they lived longer than any other creature that we've seen since."

"You're exactly right," Violet said, smiling at me.

Night's arms tightened around my waist. He adjusted in his seat so he could lean forward and rub his nose along the back of my neck and behind my ear. He was breathing me in, which made me feel giddy and a little light-headed. It was hard to believe that we'd gone from denying any and all attraction to each other to being totally addicted to each other's touch. It was a surprise, but I wouldn't have it any other way.

Neil cleared his throat, snapping me out of my thoughts. "By the way," he said, "has anything strange happened recently, Bryn? Anything that stood out to you or that could help us verify that you are a descendant of the pack mothers?"

When I hesitated, Night told them about the way I'd disappeared, how I'd wound up in a cave on a path I wasn't familiar with, to find our missing tracker. The Elders nodded, but it was clear that they were already familiar with that story. Their eyes were on me, on what they knew I hadn't revealed.

After a few moments more of deliberation, I decided it was better to tell them. "The truth is that I was led to that cave and to Vince," I said. "I saw a wolf standing at the tree line, and I followed after it."

Night stiffened. "Another wolf?" He shook his head. "We tracked you down, Bryn. There weren't any scents other than yours that led us to you."

I touched his arm, soothing him with smooth, back and forth motions. "I don't know how I can explain it better," I said, "But I know that I was led there by another wolf."

"Why didn't you tell me?" he asked, stroking my cheek with his thumb.

"I don't know," I said. "There was something really strange and mystical about it. I wasn't sure if it had really happened or if I had just dreamed it. And then we had that fight, and then I slept for two days, and then we..." I didn't need to finish. The memory of last night's passion came quickly to both our minds.

"Bryn." This time it was Violet's voice pulling me back. "Could you describe the wolf for us?" Violet asked.

I nodded. Now that I was sure it hadn't just been in my mind, I was able to give a detailed description of the wolf's russet-brown coat, the slice in its left ear, and the piercing white eyes that were like melted silver and snow.

Violet pressed a hand to her mouth, and the Elder's mumbling grew more intense. I turned, sending a worried look at Night, but his handsome face and steady gaze calmed me.

Finally, Violet held up her hands for silence. The Elders immediately went quiet. My wolf whined within me, pacing back and forth. It was such a bizarre feeling to feel another consciousness within me, but it was so amazing at the same time.

Violet looked into each of the Elder's faces, and they all nodded. She took a deep breath and returned her attention to me. "You mentioned something about seeing a wolf when Night returned with you."

"I did?"

Violet nodded. "The Elders and I talked about what this could mean, but hearing you describe it confirms it. The wolf you saw was the spirit of one of the original pack mothers."

My eyes widened.

"This is something very, very few shifters have ever experienced, and it means that you were chosen by fate for a great cause."

I found it difficult to breathe. "What cause?" I whispered.

Violet shook her head. "It's not clear. Not yet."

"Oh…" I lowered my gaze to the table. I felt light-headed all over again. The words *fate*, *great cause*, *pack mother*, and *spirit* echoed in my mind. They smacked into me over and over again, so hard I felt I would fall over if Night hadn't been holding me. I wasn't sure how to feel after everything I'd learned. After twenty years of feeling like I would never belong anywhere, I had just found out not only that I belonged with the Wargs at Night's side but also that I had been chosen for something even greater.

Chapter 34 - Bryn

When we arrived back at Night's cabin, I was almost as exhausted as I'd been the night that the wolf spirit had led me to the cave. But as tired as I felt, as eager as I was to crawl into bed with Night and go to sleep, I was also terribly hungry. I opened my mouth to tell him, but my stomach beat me to it.

"I'll get us some food from the mess hall," he said with a laugh. "Why don't you get comfy in the meantime?"

I nodded. "Just hurry back, okay?"

He laughed again and gave me a kiss. And then another. And one more before he headed out. While he was gone, I trudged up the steps and headed for the bathroom to take a much-needed shower. I took off my clothes and stepped under the warm stream. As the water seeped into my hair and dripped down my body, I tried to process my thoughts.

Now that I knew the truth about who I was, a fresh wave of horror poured over me when I remembered what Troy had almost done. In taking my right to choose a mate away from me, he might have also forced me to shift. I trembled at the thought of being alone with Troy in such a vulnerable moment. Night had been so tender with me when he'd found that I'd shifted, but I knew Troy would be nothing like that. I didn't even want to imagine what he would have done to me then.

I felt I ought to thank Night again for saving me that night, for taking me far away from an awful, painful fate. After all that had happened, I didn't care that our relationship had started with a kidnapping. He had acted so indifferently at first, but now I'd seen into his heart. I knew him to be every bit the wonderful Alpha that the Wargs all respected and rallied behind.

My life with the Wargs had resulted in so many good things—friends, freedom, family, and even love. These were all things I never would have experienced with the Kings, and I was sure that I wouldn't have found them if I had somehow escaped into human cities nearby. Here, I felt so safe and content and *wanted.*

I bit my lip, remembering the evening before when I'd given everything to Night. I had been so desperate for him, and now under the warm water, I wanted him all over again. *How long has it been since he left?* I wondered. My wolf gave a similar whine. Though I still didn't understand her, the two of us were in agreement about missing Night. When I closed my eyes, I could still feel him pressing against me, his mouth on my neck, his cool breath across my skin.

He couldn't have been gone for more than a few minutes, but that didn't matter; to me, it felt like he had been gone for hours. I longed for him with every beat of my heart—I craved him. My wolf howled for him, both of us needing his presence. I felt so close to him, but something was missing. Night was in the mess hall, obviously, but it wasn't just him that I was missing. There was something else, something that gnawed and gnawed at me, but I couldn't figure out what. Then again, it was probably just me not understanding my wolf.

My wolf. I allowed myself a brief, tiny squeal in the shower. Holy shit, not only was I a wolf, I was also a descendant of the pack mothers. It was so amazing, so incredible, but it still didn't feel quite real. So many things had changed in such quick succession that I felt a bit like I was floating above the news. There was so much to think about, to consider, but I didn't know where to begin.

I wished I could confide all this to my mom. She always knew what to say when I felt lost or overwhelmed, and maybe she had more information about the day she found me—information that might help me make sense of my new reality.

I pictured Mom's smile and the scent of lavender that seemed to cling to her hair no matter which herbs or vegetables she picked. I thought of her voice, her hugs, and her warmth. I wondered what she would think about me being a shifter.

I missed her terribly. Perhaps I would see her again when Night confronted Troy, but who knew when that would happen? It could be weeks or even months from now. I could probably ask Night about his plans, but I didn't want to dwell on that right now.

I closed my eyes and let the hot water slide down my skin and calm my feverish thoughts. I reached for the soap and began to scrub up. Suddenly, I paused, feeling a tug in my chest. I smelled Night as if he was right here with me. I pulled the curtain, eager to see him, but he wasn't in the bathroom with me. If I concentrated a bit harder, I could hear his footsteps coming up to the porch. I smiled, pleased that he would be with me again soon. My senses had sharpened since I shifted, but it seemed they were even sharper where Night was concerned.

I closed the curtain and tried to rush through the rest of my shower. I was eager to see him again, and now the shower I had been so eager to take was getting in the way. But there was no need to rush after all.

Within seconds, the shower curtain was pulled open again. Night stood there, taking me in. His eyes roamed my wet, naked body, which burned with need.

"I missed you like crazy," he said, his eyes on my breasts, my stomach, my thighs, my core.

I laughed even as I soaked up his ravenous gaze. "You were gone for just a few minutes."

"Ten," he told me. "But who's counting?"

I grinned, moving my hands over my body. I wanted to finish my shower so I could press against him again. "I missed you too," I said.

Night watched my hands, and that rumble filled his chest. I slowed down, taking my time with the suds and the water. Night kept his eyes on me, his gaze burning me from inside.

"Do you remember when you first showered in my cabin?" he asked.

"Mmhm…as memory serves, you were rushing me to get done." I moved my hands over my nipples.

"It was because I scented your arousal," he said. "I knew you were touching yourself in here. And I wanted you then."

"Oh?" I let one of my hands cup my breast while the other slipped down my stomach and lower. When I reached between my legs to stroke the ache that pulsed there, his hand caught mine.

"I am the only one who is allowed to bring you pleasure," he growled, pulling me close and taking my chin in his other hand. "Do you understand?"

"Oh, yes…" I purred. "But only if you get those damn clothes off and get in here to finish what you started."

Night let out a growly chuckle. In seconds, he had ripped off his clothes, leaving them in tatters across the ground. Then, finally, he crowded into the shower with me and captured my lips with his.

I moaned, pressing my wet body flush with his. He growled into my mouth and pushed my back against the wall. He lifted my leg with one hand, and with the other, he took his cock and stroked it against my opening. Sparks of heated pleasure ignited within me with each stroke. I gripped his shoulders and cried out with need.

"Fuck, Bryn," he panted and pushed himself inside. There was no need to wait for my body to adjust this time. I'd had a taste of him last night, and now I craved more. As he filled me, his hand grabbed my other thigh and lifted me up. I automatically wrapped my legs around his waist, and he pressed me harder against the wall, pushing in even deeper.

We groaned and shuddered together. The hot water continued to warm us as he pumped inside me. His movements were quick, but not hurried—eager, but not uncontrolled. I wrapped my arms around his neck and pressed my forehead to his. The sound of wet skin smacking against wet skin joined our grunts and moans.

"Yes, yes, yes," I whispered. "Night…"

He pressed even closer until there was no space between us for the water to get through. I was trapped between his hard, hot chest and the cool shower wall, and there was nowhere else I wanted to be. Night covered my neck with kisses and licks and love bites that would surely leave purple marks later. I dug my fingers through his hair and tugged.

"Bryn," he growled, and his nips and love bites became more intense.

The flashes of sweet pain were lovely, heightening the pleasure even further. But I wished he'd *really* bite me. I longed to feel his teeth deep in my skin and to know that it was my blood that filled his mouth and coated his tongue. Night didn't bite me, but his rhythm increased. I cried out, my legs tightening around him.

"Your screams drive me wild," he murmured against my skin. "How did I fucking survive without you?"

I moaned louder. I didn't know how *I'd* survived without *him*, but after this, I knew I wouldn't be able to live without him again.

I wanted to tell him that I loved him, that he meant everything to me, that he was the only man on my mind, but my thoughts were a jumbled mess. My voice could do nothing but scream and gasp and moan. My body shuddered against his—it was nothing but a vessel for the white-hot ecstasy that he thrust into me over and over and over again…

After two rounds in the shower, I was deliciously sore. My legs trembled with each step, so Night lifted me in his arms like I was a princess and carried me into his bedroom. I needed the rest more than ever, but I wanted to spend a bit more time with him, and I wanted to finally have something to eat.

We sat next to each other at his dining table to enjoy the assorted dishes he had retrieved from the mess hall. There had been some extra sausage links and pancakes from breakfast, but the cooks on duty had also begun to prepare chicken potpie. Though it was technically against the rules for them to serve lunch so early, everyone was all smiles and eager to please us, according to Night.

"Why's that?" I asked around a mouthful of pancake. "Did you exert your Alpha privileges?"

He smiled and brushed a stray crumb from my cheek, sending goosebumps down my back. His touch had been so heated in the shower, but now it was feather-light. Almost not there at all. "No," he replied. "It's because they know you and I are together."

"Oh, I see." Now that I possessed the heightened senses of a shifter, it should have been obvious to me that they would be able to tell just from being near him. It made me feel so wonderful to know that the others accepted our relationship. That I belonged.

Amusement shone in his eyes as he gazed at me, watching me eat. "Dom gave me shit the minute he saw me."

"What did he say?"

"Damn, Night, I could smell you coming a mile away." Night's impression of his beta was surprisingly spot on; he managed to match not only the easy cadence in which Dom spoke but also the way his voice rose and fell when he was teasing someone or being sarcastic. I laughed.

Night chuckled too. "Tavi was there, of course, and she was practically in tears, she was so happy."

"Can you do an impression of her too?"

Night gave me a look. "I don't know if anyone could do an impression of that girl. She talks way too fast."

"Let me see…" I drank some water and cleared my throat. I tried to replicate the smooth, almost melodic way that Tavi's voice sounded when she was really deep into a story as I said, "Night gave me so much shit when we were kids about being a late shifter—"

I stopped when Night leaned back in his seat and laughed, his hand on his chest. It was wonderful to hear him laugh so hard. The sound of it filled my heart and made my wolf's tail wag from side to side.

"Did I pull it off?" I asked, grinning.

"It was pretty good," Night said, still chuckling as he ran a hand through his hair. "But I'm more surprised that she told you about that at all."

"It was because I told her about Pax's problem," I said. "Though, I guess if anyone's a late shifter, it's me."

"Oh, that's true, isn't it?" He reached for my chair and pulled me closer to him so he could press his nose into my hair, still damp from the shower. "I know that the Elders and my mom put a lot on you this morning," he said. "I don't want you to be scared about magic or pack mothers or fate right now. That's not our priority."

I shivered at his closeness and pressed closer to him. "Then what is?"

"You." He kissed my temple. "Us." My cheek. "And your wolf." My jaw. "I want to help you get more comfortable shifting and more in touch with your wolf."

"Okay," I breathed, my heart quickening. "I think I can focus on those things for now…as long as I've got you to help me."

"You've got me for as long as you want me." He kissed my jaw again, nibbling at my skin and making me giggle.

I pulled away so I could look into his eyes.

He smiled at me, and my heart sang. "What is it, beautiful?"

"I want you forever," I said and sealed those words with a kiss.

Two days passed, and I hardly left Night's cabin. Part of it was because of the mind-blowing, delicious sex and the fact that I couldn't stand the idea of him being more than a few feet away from me. The other part of it was that I still hadn't mastered how to shift at will.

"I'm sorry," Night told me, "I don't want you to think I'm trying to lock you up again. I just don't think it's safe to walk around before we're sure that you could shift or stop a shift at will."

I nodded. This was nothing like when he'd first brought me here as his prisoner. Unlike before, I wasn't bound to just a single room in his cabin; I could walk from room to room, and I could go to Violet's cabin and help in the garden when Night was called away. I knew that he wasn't doing it to punish me; when I had more control, I could go back to my normal schedule.

I just needed to get the hang of this shifter thing and my wolf. When I shifted the first time, I had been having a strange, terrible dream. All I could remember of it was that I had been overcome with fear of…something, and then the shift just sort of happened to me. I had no idea how to do it again intentionally.

Night and I were in his room, and I was sitting cross-legged on the bed. It was late, almost eleven o'clock, but I wasn't feeling sleepy. Night stood over me and rubbed a puzzled hand over the stubble that had grown along his jaw. He hadn't shaved that morning, not that I minded. It added an extra element of roughness and texture to our lovemaking.

"You're not in sync with your wolf," he explained. "I think that might be the problem."

"Oh?" The slight purr in my voice caused his eyes to flash to mine. A smirk played on his soft lips, and my heartbeat quickened in my chest.

"Not now, Bryn. We need to focus, remember?"

"Sorry, sorry. You were saying—I need to get in touch with my wolf?"

"Yeah, you can think of it that way. You mentioned that it was difficult for you to know what she's thinking or what she wants."

Except when it comes to you, I thought. *We're in agreement about how badly we want you.*

"I want you to close your eyes, breathe deeply, and reach out to her," he said. "When you find her, don't be afraid to let her in and to make her an equal in your mind. You have to let her know that you trust her. Don't be scared. I'll be here with you the entire time."

I nodded and closed my eyes. I tried to push out my noisy thoughts—especially the horny ones about Night— and reach out for my wolf. It didn't take long to find her; she rushed up to me, panting hard, as though she were just as eager to get to know me. It was a bit startling at first, how quickly my wolf responded, but I tried not to flinch or turn away.

I took a few deep breaths to relax, and then I opened myself up to my wolf. She purred in response, and I smiled. She was like the presence of a dear friend in my mind, like a warm memory. Though the process was a bit intimidating at first, I found I liked leaving myself open to my wolf, who already felt so familiar to me even though I'd only known her for a short time.

Violet came by a little while after that because she had a bit more information about my sudden shift. She'd been convening with the Elders and reaching out to the spirits every day.

"The Elders believe that your wolf was trapped deep inside of you, Bryn," Violet said. The three of us sat on Night's couch. He sat on the armrest next to me while Violet and I sat on the cushions beside each other. "The spirits tell me that your birth mother, the pack mother, was murdered the day you were born, and you were ripped from her womb. The murderer abandoned you to die, but then your wolf mother, Glenda, found you."

I let the news wash over me. I had never wondered if my birth mother was still alive. I think some part of me had always known that she wasn't around anymore. But to hear it confirmed, to know that there was no chance that I would ever see her again, brought a small lump to my throat.

"After such a terrible trauma, your wolf tried to protect you from the pain, shielding you from it so efficiently that she was lost deep in your mind, unable to surface until your heart had healed from the damage it suffered."

I hadn't even known my heart was so badly hurt. I turned to look at Night. His eyes were intent on me, concern in the slight frown on his lips. He touched my cheek, his calloused fingers gentle across my skin. I leaned into his touch, my heart fluttering in my chest. I knew that choosing to trust him and give myself to him completely was exactly what my wolf needed to find her way back from the recesses of my mind.

"I'm sorry that there wasn't a better way to tell you all of that, Bryn," Violet said. "I know you must have so much on your mind."

"I do," I said. "It's a little intimidating to hear all of this, to know that my birth mother was actually the last pack mother. But I think I'll be okay." I looked again at Night and smiled. The slight frown on his lips disappeared, and he smiled back at me.

Violet smiled too and pushed herself away from the table. "I think it's best if I give you some time to digest all of this. If you have any questions, Bryn, you know where to find me when you need me."

"Yes. Thank you so much, Violet. It means everything that you're working on this for me."

She gave me a tight hug and then left.

"Your wolf was so strong to keep you safe for so long," Night said.

I nodded. My wolf purred low in appreciation of his praise. "I think I want to talk to her about all this. My wolf, I mean. I had no idea she was with me all this time."

"I understand." He kissed the top of my head. "I'll make you some tea."

"That sounds wonderful."

I walked outside to sit in the grass. I was in jeans and a light t-shirt, but thanks to my newfound shifter warmth, I barely registered the cool midnight air. I tried to focus my energy inward. I wanted to try talking to my wolf again to bridge the gap that prevented us from becoming whole.

Hey, I tried to call. *Are you there?*

It was a silly question, and my wolf's answering snuffle told me as much. I smiled. It was already getting easier to understand her, though there was still some distance between us.

I wanted to thank you for what you did for me, I said to her. *I had no idea you had been protecting me this whole time—that you loved me even when the person who killed our mother left us to die.*

She whined softly.

Night tells me that you're beautiful and powerful and strong, I told her. *And I know now that you helped me survive all the stress and angst that we suffered over the last month. You helped me to be brave.*

My wolf did nothing, just waited with her head cocked to hear the rest of what I had to say.

I think that's why I feel connected to you, because you've been with me all this time. And I know that because I have you, we'll be able to face whatever fate has in store for us. Tears pushed at the back of my eyes as I added, *I'm so grateful to have you—to be a shifter. But I know there's a lot that I need to learn about treating you properly and being comfortable in my skin. After everything you've done for me, I can only hope that I make a good partner to you…*

She howled and ran to join with me. I gasped out loud as we became one, and my body began to change. In the few seconds it took for me to shift, I realized that there was another reason my wolf and I had been out of sync. As awkward as I was about shifting, my wolf had been scared that I would hate her. She believed it was her fault that I had suffered so much in the Kings' pack, that in shielding my mind, she had also cut me off from the strength I needed to protect myself from Troy and the Terrible T's.

That's so silly, I thought as the shift completed. *How could I hate the wolf that sacrificed so much to keep me safe?*

My wolf tapped her front paws in the grass and turned in a circle, a kind of happy dance that made me laugh.

Behind me, I heard Night suck in a deep breath. He looked different through the eyes of my wolf. He was still gorgeous, perfect, and *mine*, but there was something else too. He was surrounded by warm light, a halo that brought him into glorious, wonderful focus.

Mate. My wolf's voice was clear as a bell to me. She said it again, louder, and I wondered if it was true. If he was my true mate, then it made sense that even when we had tried to hate each other, it was impossible for us to stay away from each other—impossible not to feel something when in each other's presence. And it explained how desperately we needed to touch and to be close.

It made so much sense, and yet not all the pieces fit into place. If we were mates, why hadn't he claimed me? Why wasn't he shifting to be with me now? He could have bitten me that first night, or any of the other times we had made love. My wolf whined, shaking her head. She was thinking the same thing. Why hadn't Night claimed us officially? Was it because he didn't want us forever?

My wolf sat as Night set down the tea and approached me. My wolf and I watched him kneel in front of me, our chest filled with equal parts sorrow and love. Night smiled at me, running his hands over our body. It felt like magic the way his fingers parted our fur and scratched behind our ears.

"You're the most beautiful thing I've ever seen," he murmured, continuing to stroke me. "How did I get so lucky to have someone like you at my side? Hm?"

His compliments were sweet, and his praise was even sweeter, but they fell on sad, doleful ears. He didn't say he loved me, and he didn't shift to be with me. He didn't call me his mate. I felt so confused as the hurt settled in. Had I misunderstood my wolf? But no. The ache in my wolf's chest mirrored mine.

Night tilted his head, sensing something. "You okay, Bryn?" he asked, scratching under my chin.

We couldn't respond. Had I jumped into things too fast? Had we given ourselves to him too quickly? What had I done wrong? I ached deep inside as my sadness and my wolf's combined.

Night Shepherd had rejected the mate claim every time he'd had the chance to complete it. That meant that he didn't love me the way I loved him.

Chapter 35 - Bryn

Two more days passed. Night and I were still inseparable. After the first time I'd intentionally shifted, Night had me practicing connecting with my wolf so my interacting with her would be second nature. And when he wasn't coaching me or offering advice, the two of us were having sex, which I didn't mind at all.

I floated on cloud nine for the most part, but after the realization that Night didn't want to claim me, I sometimes teetered on the edge of total despair. Self-doubt, combined with my wolf's unmet need for Night to claim me, had almost overwhelmed me. I tried to convince myself that I was just missing some crucial aspect of mating and claiming traditions. I had, after all, lived as a human for twenty years; maybe there was something I didn't understand, or maybe my wolf and I still had a few kinks to work out about our bond.

It was all so confusing.

I knew that part of the problem was that I couldn't think straight. Being close to Night, inundated with his scent and his touch and his kisses, was too distracting. I needed some time to talk through my insecurities with

Violet and Tavi. They would be able to tell me if I was missing something.

Night and I lay next to each other in bed. We'd had sex in almost every room of Night's house—especially the shower. We were sated, content, and enjoying each other's closeness. Eventually, I turned on my side toward him.

"Night, can we talk?" I asked.

He turned to face me and pulled me close. "Of course. You can talk to me about anything."

I hesitated for a few seconds, uncertain how to start. "I...I think I'd like some to have some girl time with Violet and Tavi."

"You want to leave?" I wouldn't have thought that the powerful Alpha, who could scare the pants off anyone with just one look, could pull off puppy eyes. His frown tugged at my heartstrings, but I needed to stay firm.

"Not for long," I rushed to assure him. "Just for a few hours. I...I miss them, and I want to talk to them."

Night continued to frown. I thought for a second that he might say no, and if he did, would I have the strength to ask him again? I didn't want to leave his side either, but my unanswered questions were tearing me up inside. I didn't want to be stuck in a constant state of uncertainty about Night or the way he felt about me. It was far, far too painful.

Eventually, Night sighed, and I heard the yes in that sigh before he spoke the word. We got dressed, and Night walked me to Violet's cabin.

"I'll be with Dom," he said. It was only the fifth or sixth time he'd assured me of that. "If you need anything, I'll be a short distance away."

I chuckled and touched his cheek. "I know, don't worry. Time will pass by so quickly, you won't even notice I'm gone."

"Ha. Not a chance of that." He kissed me once, briefly, and then again more deeply. When he pulled away, my eyes felt heavy, and desire began to kindle deep inside me. He licked his lips, his eyes glowing. "Are you sure you want this?"

Oh, but it was so tempting to say no so he could carry me back to bed. I forced myself to nod and gave him a smile. "I'll see you soon, Night." I hopped up to kiss his cheek, and then I quickly went inside, avoiding those large, warm hands before he could kiss me again or otherwise tempt me away from my goal.

Tavi and Violet were waiting for me at the dining table. I had seen Violet a few times since Night and I had mated, but I hadn't seen Tavi since the day Night rescued me from those ferals. So when Tavi hopped onto her feet, almost knocking over her chair, I rushed to meet her. We embraced tightly, and Tavi was already emotional.

"I missed you so much!" she cried. "I thought Night was going to keep you all for himself like the selfish prick he is."

I giggled. I had never noticed what Tavi smelled like before, but she had a really fresh, sweet scent. It was like maple syrup with a hint of pink peppercorn. I committed the scent to memory and then pulled back. It was amazing what my new power could do for me—how I felt like I now knew Tavi and Violet and Night even more than I had thought was possible.

"I want to know everything!" Tavi said, pulling me to the table.

I glanced at Violet, who wore her trademark, knowing smile. There was no way I could tell Tavi *everything*, not with Night's mom only inches away. But I did share the things I felt comfortable telling.

"I've never felt so good in my life," I said. "Night is amazing. He's so wonderful to me, and he makes me feel like I'm meant to be with him. It's kinda crazy to think that just a few weeks ago, he and I could barely stand each other." The woman I had been before felt like a past life, a shadow of the person I had become thanks to Night and my wolf. I had never believed that love was in my future, but I had been so, *so* wrong.

Tavi sighed, pressing her hands to her chest. "I'm living vicariously through you, Bryn until I find a guy of my own."

I laughed. "You'll find him," I told her, thinking of Dom.

"So, what about your wolf? How has that been?"

I paused. Now that she'd brought up my wolf, the real reason I decided to leave Night's side came to the forefront of my mind. I took too long to respond, and my silence worried Tavi and Violet.

"Bryn?" Violet asked. "Is everything going okay with your wolf?"

"Oh, yes, I'm sorry." I shook my head, forcing myself back to the present. "Actually, she and I are bonding beautifully. I'm finally getting used to shifting and listening to her and letting her in."

"That's great news!" Tavi exclaimed. "I told you it would be cooler if you were a wolf." She winked.

I scoffed and crossed my arms. "You can't take credit for my wolf, Tavi. She's been with me all along."

She grinned. It was clear that she had missed our conversations just as much as I had. "Well, I just think it's funny that only a couple of days after I said what I said, you suddenly find your wolf. I don't think it's entirely a coincidence, Bryn."

I started to respond, but Violet interrupted.

"You mentioned that your wolf has been with you all along," she said. "Talk more about that."

I uncrossed my arms as I shifted from teasing to serious again. "I know that my wolf was lost in my mind after my mother was murdered," I said. "But I don't think she was ever completely gone. I can think back to moments when I felt pulled in a certain direction or protected in some way. There are times when I swore I heard a whine in my mind when something was about to go really badly."

Violet and Tavi glanced at each other and smiled. "That sounds familiar," Tavi said.

"Yes. That's what your wolf is supposed to do, Bryn. She's aware of things that your human mind isn't. If she's got a bad feeling or if she's pushing you to do something you don't understand, listen to her. Trust her."

I nodded. "I'm getting better at that, but there's something that's been holding me back."

"Oh?" Violet set down her tea. "What do you mean?"

"Well, it happened when we were m-mating. Or—I mean, it didn't happen." I stopped, getting flustered. "Night didn't claim me." Each word felt like a mouthful. "Okay, this is really, *really* embarrassing to talk about, but I have to know because it's eating me up inside, and my wolf is so upset about it."

"Bryn, tell us," Tavi said.

I took a deep breath. "She's worried that Night might not actually want us to be his mate, and it's hard for me not to think that too."

Violet and Tavi went quiet for a few seconds. I shivered, shame burning from my face down my neck, my heart beating quickly. I didn't like having to admit that I was ignorant about something that was so fundamental to wolf culture, but I *hated* telling them that some part of me doubted Night's feelings for me. It felt like I was betraying him by doing so.

Still, my wolf and I couldn't stand not knowing.

"Bryn," Violet's soft voice encouraged me to lower my hands from my face. She and Tavi were looking at me with empathetic smiles. "You're not missing some vital part of mating. Remember what I said about your wolf? If she has doubts, you should trust her."

"But…" My lower lip wobbled. Large, sorrowful tears that I hadn't noticed building up slipped down my cheeks. "But doesn't that mean that Night is—"

But Violet was shaking her head. "Neither of us can answer that for you. It wouldn't be our place."

Tavi stood up to grab a few tissues and brought them back for me. "Anyone can see that Night would break his own legs if it meant he could do something for you, Bryn," Tavi added. "But, I mean, I think you have to ask him yourself. That's how relationships work."

Oh. It sounded so simple when they put it so plainly. I had been in my head, so worried that *I* had done something wrong that I hadn't even considered that I might be able to talk to Night about this. Another tear slipped down my face, but I caught it with my tissue. I wiped my face while Violet stood to get some more tea.

Tavi leaned in while Violet rummaged around in the kitchen. "So, Bryn," she whispered, "how *was* it? I mean, like, was it as amazing as those books you've been reading?"

My eyes widened.

She giggled. "I borrowed one or two from your room while you were with him. No wonder you were so *focused* on reading."

My face warmed, but I pressed my hand over my mouth when it filled with giggles. "I can't believe you looked through them when I wasn't here!"

"I looked through them too," Violet called from the kitchen.

Tavi and I gasped that she'd overheard us.

"Don't even think about trying to give any more detail than you've already given, Bryn," she called. "There are some things a mother isn't meant to know."

We cracked up, leaning against each other as the laughter bubbled free. It felt good to relax, to let off some steam.

"I'm gonna freshen up a little," I said, wiping away another stray tear, though it was caused by laughter this time, not sadness. "I'll be right back."

As I mounted the staircase, I felt my wolf stiffen. I paused on the steps, confused at the shift in her mood. Downstairs, someone knocked on Violet's door, and the sound of it caused my wolf to howl, scratching for me to let her out.

Night

I paced back and forth in my kitchen. Dom sat at the table, watching me lose my shit with a smirk on his face. I had dropped Bryn off minutes ago, but I was going crazy not having her at my side. Was this how everyone felt with they found their mate? How did men not just lose their minds completely? There ought to be so much in-fighting that being part of a pack was impossible.

"Night," Dom said. "Did you hear me?"

I stopped and looked at him. "Of course I did," I grumbled. "You were talking about the trade."

"Uh-huh…" Dom grinned, leaning forward with his chin in his hands. "It's only three days away from the next full moon, which means you'll have to hand her over—"

I snarled at Dom with all the righteous fury of a wolf hopelessly in love. Now that Dom understood why I'd been having so many violent outbursts, he wasn't alarmed by them anymore. In fact, he seemed concerningly delighted by my momentary lapses in control. I almost wished Dom didn't know. It made dealing with him so much more of an annoyance.

"Obviously," I said, my eyebrow twitching as he snickered, "that trade is not happening."

"I figured as much." Dom straightened as he became more serious. "How are you going to deal with the fallout?"

I had taken Bryn's virginity, which meant that the conditions Troy had set were broken. But Bryn's wolf made the situation even more complicated. She wasn't human, so the exchange, the deal—all of that no longer mattered. Now, I just needed to figure out how to keep her safe.

"Maybe we could get one of our wolves to trade places with Bryn," I said, rubbing my chin. "We would dress her up in Bryn's clothes to confuse them. They probably won't notice it's not her until the challenge ceremony is underway." I still didn't like the idea of putting any of my people in the clutches of the Kings, but at least the decoy would know how to defend herself.

As I started pacing again, Dom snuck in one last tease. "By the way, it was my idea to take Bryn off the table."

I glared at him, a deep growl in my chest. I didn't mean anything by it, and Dom knew that.

"Still so testy even after you've met your mate," Dom tsked. "What's got you all worked up?"

I turned pale. "Right. Mate." I stopped pacing. Dom raised a brow, curiosity in his gaze. But slowly, that curiosity turned to horror as he realized what I was implying.

"You claimed her, didn't you, Night?" he asked. "You bit her the first time you had sex, right?"

"Ah…No, not yet."

Dom leapt from the chair and shoved me hard against the wall. The entire cabin seemed to shake from the force of it. I stepped away from the wall, brushing bits of sawdust from my shoulder. I had every right to snap at Dom and put him in his place, but I knew that I needed to listen to what he had to say.

"You dumbass," Dom seethed. Standing before me wasn't the man who had teased me about Bryn or who could charm any person with his smile. This was the wrathful Dom, the one that I took with me into battle. "If you have any sense, you'll go and claim Bryn right this second," he growled. "An unfulfilled, unclaimed true mate bond is dangerous as hell, Night."

"What do you mean?"

Dom narrowed his eyes. "Haven't you paid *any* attention to the stories your mother tells us? I guess not if you're this ignorant about it." He sighed and turned away from me. "When true mates consummate their relationship, if the claiming isn't done, it can actually kill the wolves."

My body went still and cold. "What?"

"If the mates go too long without claiming, it will be as if they were rejected. Their hearts will break, they'll never recover, and terrible, mystical shit will happen to them. I don't remember all of the specifics, but I know that what you're doing is fucked up."

I rubbed my chest where Dom had shoved me, my thoughts spiraling down and down into the depths of my fears. "Bryn hadn't shifted yet," I found myself saying. "Not on that first night. I wanted to explain to her that she was my mate and what that meant for us, but I didn't get the chance before we ended up in bed together."

"And then?" Dom asked. "We both know the two of you have had sex after, so why not bite her during one of those times?"

I hesitated. "I just...it didn't feel like the right time. I was intent on getting her to shift and teaching her about her wolf. Bryn only recently learned that she's descended from the pack mothers. I thought claiming her would be putting too much on her plate."

Dom growled again. "That's not the whole truth," he said. "Tell me all of it, Night."

"Alright, alright." I ran both hands through my hair. My wolf keened inside me, urging me to speak my worries to my beta. "I was afraid," I admitted finally. "I couldn't shake the feeling that she would reject me somehow and abandon me like Gregor abandoned all of us. I haven't told Bryn anything about my relation to Gregor or to Troy. She doesn't even know that we had a plan to give her back to the Kings. And now, with this claiming thing, I can't imagine what she and her wolf are going through." I looked at my beta. "Dom, if Bryn doesn't want me after she learns the truth about all this, I don't know if I will survive it."

Dom's hard gaze softened now that I had come clean. "Ah," he sighed. "You idiot. You've been keeping all of this inside, but that's not fair to you, your wolf, or to Bryn—especially not now that she has a wolf of her own. The Night I know would never run from a challenge, so why are you doing that now?"

Damn it. He's right. For all that I had coached Bryn to let her wolf in and be open with her, I had once again closed off my own wolf and denied him what he needed. It had been a mistake not to claim her when I had the chance, but it wasn't too late for me to fix it.

I needed to show Bryn that I wanted her completely, not just her body. I needed to open up to her and trust her, just like she'd trusted me that night. She wouldn't reject me; I ought to have known like my wolf knew, that rejection would be the last thing on her mind even if she did get angry with me. Bryn and I were mates. Forever. It was time I proved that to her.

I grabbed the beer I'd abandoned off the table and downed the rest of it. Dom slapped me on the back, smiling again, back to his usual, friendly state. "Go, get your girl, Night."

Yes. I was ready. I headed for the door, but before my hand touched the knob, I heard a tiny, frantic fist knocking hard against the wood. I threw it open and found Pax, of all people, panting at my door. His face was red from exertion, and the shoulder of his shirt was torn. There was a bruise on the exposed skin.

"Hey, hey." I pulled him inside and crouched down to look the poor boy in the face. "What's wrong, pup?" Behind me, Dom emerged from the kitchen.

"A-Alpha Night, I—" his tiny voice stammered. His body was shaking like he'd seen his own ghost. "I'm so sorry." He dissolved into tears. "I w-wasn't strong enough or big enough, and I *failed!*"

I started to calm him down, to parse out what the boy could mean, but a wave of dread washed over me, unlike any I had felt before. It clutched me by the heart, squeezing and squeezing like it wanted to stop my heart from beating altogether.

Dom took the boy when I stilled. He wiped the tears from Pax's face with a tissue. "Tell me what's going on, Pax. What's got you so hurt?"

But I already knew. Somehow, I knew.

"I went to give Bryn a picture I drew for her in school," he said. It was hard to understand him between his sobs, but with a bit of focus, Dom and I heard him clearly. "But there were wolves running around and around the cabin. They weren't pack. They smelled weird. Bad. I knew Bryn was in danger, so I shifted, but they pushed me back and held me down. I was so scared. I heard screaming in the cabin, but they wouldn't let me go until they'd already done it." He paused to fill his lungs with a deep, shuddering breath. "I wasn't strong enough. I couldn't stop them. They took Bryn and Tavi from the house, and they ran off with them into the woods."

I flew from the house, my feet covering the distance to Mom's cabin in seconds. The door was already open, hanging from its hinges. The first scent that hit my nose was the stench of the Kings' pack and of blood. My mom was on the floor in a pool of red, her throat a ruined mess. I dropped to my knees beside her still body, soaking my jeans in her blood. Dom burst into the house right after me, cursing and spitting at the scene.

Bryn and Tavi were gone, I could sense as much, but now that I was in the house, there was one scent that overpowered the others. I knew exactly who had done this.

He and I were supposed to have an arrangement. I still had two days left before it was time, but the fucker came onto my land, violated my turf, and hurt the three women I loved most.

Troy Redfield had come for my mate and my family. And he was going to fucking pay.

Printed in Great Britain
by Amazon

37962346R00274